W

Pr

D0479411

'Evocative, original world-building and a wonderfully feisty heroine: top marks to Lucy Hounsom' KAREN MILLER

'A brave heroine, a perilous destiny, and an intriguing world full of myth and mystery make for an enthralling read'

GAIL Z. MARTIN

'I thought it was great, reminding me of Trudi Canavan; it had me turning pages way into the night . . . What a mix: immersive world-building, secret societies, a flawed and hugely likeable protagonist, and awesome magic. There's a lot to like here, but be warned, this book will seriously damage your sleep'

JOHN GWYNNE

'Has all the elements to become a modern classic of the genre. It's essentially a coming-of-age story that breaks out into a wide-screen fantasy extravaganza with huge stakes'

Independent on Sunday

'For those readers with a yearning for a novel with a Trudi Canavan/David Eddings-type vibe, but with a contemporary twist, *Starborn* may be just the ticket' *SFFWorld*

'An exciting new high fantasy story . . . the story moves along at a brisk pace' *SFBook*

'A genuinely impressive debut, and Lucy Hounsom is definitely one to watch' *TheBookBag*

'Highly imaginative, complex and original'

FantasyBookReview

BY LUCY HOUNSOM

The Worldmaker Trilogy
Starborn
Heartland
Firestorm

Firestorm

Lucy Hounsom works for Waterstones and has a BA in English and Creative Writing from Royal Holloway. She went on to complete an MA in Creative Writing under Andrew Motion in 2010. Her first novel in the Worldmaker trilogy, *Starborn*, was shortlisted for the Gemmell Morningstar Award for Best Debut.

lucyhounsom.co.uk

Lucy Hounsom

FIRESTORM

The Worldmaker Trilogy:
Book Three

✳

PAN BOOKS

First published 2017 by Pan Books
an imprint of Pan Macmillan
20 New Wharf Road, London N1 9RR
Associated companies throughout the world
www.panmacmillan.com

ISBN 978-1-5098-4051-9

1 3 5 7 9 8 6 4 2

A CIP catalogue record for this book is available from the British Library.

Map artwork © Hemesh Alles

Typeset by Ellipsis, Glasgow
Printed and bound by CPI Group (UK) Ltd, Croydon, CR0 4YY

For Paul
Now it's your turn

ACKNOWLEDGEMENTS

I can't quite believe I've reached the acknowledgements for the final book in the trilogy. I began this journey at the same age Kyndra began hers – seventeen – when I'm sure I was just as naive and twice as stubborn. We've been on and off the road together ever since; it will be strange and a little bit sad to watch our paths finally diverge.

Between my head and these lovely printed pages are a fair few people, who worked hard to make the books the best they could be. I've been lucky to work with two brilliant editors, Bella Pagan and Julie Crisp, whose guidance and insight have, I feel, made me a better writer. Bella, thank you for your belief in this series and for always championing my corner. Julie, thank you for untangling my confusing nest of paradoxes. I promise I won't do time travel ever again . . .

Thanks to Phoebe, Saba, Natalie, Alice and the teams at Pan Macmillan for their help with all the trappings – copy-editing, cover design, publicity – you're all superb and I owe you cake. To my agent, Veronique Baxter: this trilogy wouldn't have happened without you. Thank you for taking a chance on me and for your continued support. I'm excited to see where we go next.

To my colleagues at Waterstones Exeter who are such fine

folk to work with: thank you for being as excited about my books as I am, for your immense hand-selling skills, your beautiful artwork and superior table arrangement. You are all champions – especially those baristas who give me free coffee – and I am lucky to know you.

Before Megan invited me to co-host *Breaking the Glass Slipper*, I'd never worked on a podcast before. We're now at the end of our second season and I've learned such a lot. We've had some high-profile authors on the show, recorded a dozen diverting interviews and generally had a good time dissecting tricky topics. Thank you Megan and Charlotte; long may the Slipper reign.

To James Southwood, Josi Palm, Reda Haq and Kimberley Croft for being top friends who put up with my rants about the world with remarkable grace. I don't see you often enough, but when I do, we always have the best time.

Thank you to fellow writer-sister, Laura, for her unerring ability to help straighten the kinks in any plot or character arc and also for just being an excellent sister. Read her books, they're good. Thanks to my aunt and uncle for letting me descend on their home without warning whenever I need to go to London. And thank you Mum and Dad for your obviously biased yet unswerving belief in me and this all too ethereal purpose to which I've put my life. I can't express how much your love and support means to me.

Finally and perhaps the biggest thank you to everyone who has stuck with Kyndra until the very end. You are the reason I can do what I love and be who I am.

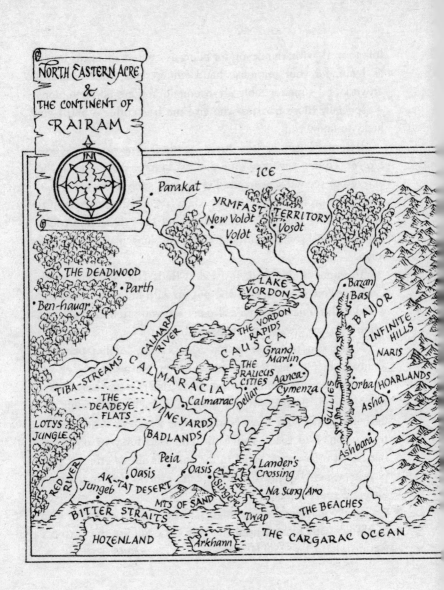

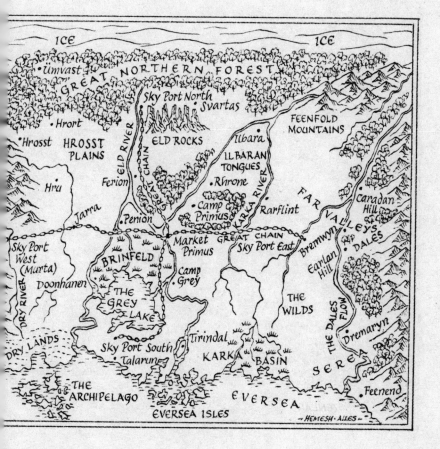

'Nothing is so painful to the human mind as a great and sudden change'   *Frankenstein*, Mary Shelley

'In dreams begins responsibility'   W. B. Yeats

The Last Days of Sartya

To understand the Starborn's role in the downfall of Sartya, it is necessary to understand how she came to find herself in Acre. Raised in rural Rairam, she was, for many years, unaware of her heritage. Taken to the fallen citadel of Naris by Brégenne and Nediah – names now well known to many – she came into contact with the last Starborn, Kierik, who died shortly afterwards. Interested parties may seek out the text, *Starborn*, the only account she has given of this period.

After restoring Rairam to Acre – an act equal to her father Kierik's in magnitude – the Starborn gathered a fellowship around her and crossed the border. Much of what happened next is uncertain – the Starborn has not given any official account – but sources describe her journey through Acre as tumultuous. Her slaughter of five hundred Sartyan soldiers did not endear her to the military, and though many see this act as the catalyst of the empire's fall, cracks had already started to appear in its façade.

The rise of the Defiant, for example, whose consistent sorties chipped away at imperial control. They were too well funded, too well connected; it became clear that their ragtag operation was merely a front for the greater organization

1

known as the Republic, whose network of influence had strengthened invisibly, hidden from imperial spies. When Khronostian assassins began to remove the most prominent nobles in court, Sartya was undermined on all sides. In such turbulent times, defections were inevitable.

Arguably the greatest defection – some have called it betrayal – of all was General James Hagdon's. It is still unclear how long the commander-in-chief of the Sartyan Fist had held sympathies with the Republic, but with such a powerful man on its side, the clandestine group could finally leave the shadows and declare itself the official opposition to the Fist.

With Hagdon went Relator Realdon Shune, now recognized as a High Wielder of Solinaris. Despite his advanced years, Shune publicly abetted the erstwhile general in his murder of the emperor. The death of imperial rule might have been quick and clean were it not for another key player in the struggle for power: Iresonté, Captain of Sartya's stealth force. Ignoring the Khronostian threat, she rallied the army around her, promising the conquest long denied Sartya: an invasion of Rairam.

The Starborn's primary concern, however, was Khronosta and its threat to undo history with the aid of Medavle, one of the Starborn's companions, and the last living Yadin – that ageless race created by the Wielders of Solinaris. Did the Starborn experience guilt for her role in bringing him to Acre? Or was the danger so great that it transcended all personal sense of obligation? Whatever the case, the Starborn prepared to battle Khronosta, while the Republic confronted Iresonté.

Turbulent historical periods have one overwhelming thing in common: the role of the individual. The Starborn was not the only major player in the downfall of Sartya; indeed, her companions carved out their own paths. What of the former slaver, Char Lesko, revealed as one of the dragon people? What of his guardian, Ma, who turned her back on Khronosta? And what of those who accompanied the Starborn into Acre: the Wielders, Nediah, Kait and Irilin, Brégenne and the man known as Kul'Gareth, about whom such fanciful stories are told? The following chapters will examine each in detail in an attempt to illuminate this tempestuous era.

PART ONE

I

Kyndra

She was a being of light.

Stars in her skin, power in her veins, her mind full of their names. She had but to call, to focus her will, and they would hearken to her. She clenched fists of molten fire and smiled, armoured in *Tyr*, shielded behind a field of force that clung to her flesh.

She was a being of darkness too.

There were no roads between the stars, only the void, lightless, unchanging. The chill emptiness, numbing her to any feeling, dwelt in the paths of her heart, and she could no more brighten them than she could the void itself. *The curse of the Starborn*, she thought. *The price I paid for my power.*

The air rushed past her face; it was much colder up here amongst the clouds. Birds swooped and soared a safe distance away and the ground was a hazy blur.

'Is this as fast as you go, Boy?'

Kyndra glanced over her shoulder at the woman called Ma. Dark-skinned, dark-eyed, dressed unfamiliarly in fleece-lined clothes to combat the chill, she was looking forward, past

Kyndra, towards the horned head of the dragon on which they flew. 'The eldest will not waste any time.'

In answer, the dragon tipped sharply into a roll and Kyndra's hands contracted on the black scales. Her stomach swooping, she watched the ground become the sky and then right itself. Ma was swearing. 'Do you want to kill us?' she shouted. 'Fly straight, fool.'

Kyndra half smiled. She leaned forward and scratched the dragon's huge pointed ear. The scales were thinner there and warm, and she remembered a time when he'd stood close beside her, the rush of a stream in their ears, grass underfoot. He'd been human then.

Not human, Kyndra corrected herself. She felt a faint ache at the memory, a distant regret. But what mattered was that Char – *Orkaan* – was now his true self, that he could carry them to Magtharda, riding the rising winds of an Acrean winter.

'I am *not* a cat.'

Char's voice was soft thunder; Kyndra felt it rumble through his body. She stopped her scratching.

After a moment the dragon said, 'Did I ask you to stop?'

'He's very bossy now,' she commented to Ma and the woman snorted.

'He always was.' She slapped the dragon's flank, though Char probably couldn't feel it.

'If you've finished discussing me, it's getting dark,' he said. 'We should look for somewhere to land.'

'Go ahead, Boy, your eyes are better than ours.'

They flew for another five minutes or so, while the colour of the sky deepened to purple. And then, without warning, Char tipped into a steep dive. Kyndra heard Ma shriek a curse; the woman had her eyes closed and was desperately clinging to the dragon's back. The ground was rushing to meet them and it looked sharp. Splinters of rock poked up from the earth like the stony spines of an enormous beast. Char banked again and – not for the first time – Kyndra wondered whether he really had got the hang of flying.

There was a surprised bleat, so loud and close that it made her jump. Char's muscles bunched; he snatched at something, his sleek head darting out with the speed of a striking serpent. Then they were off, the dragon's powerful wings sweeping them up and away from the rocks. Ma let out another stream of curses.

Char's reply was muffled. He briefly turned his head to look at them and Kyndra saw something woolly between his jaws, a goat. They landed on a high plateau, partially sheltered by wind-bent pines. The dragon crouched, letting Kyndra and Ma slide stiffly from his back. A second unfortunate goat was clutched in his front claws. He dropped it and, without further ado, began to crunch up the one in his mouth. Ma winced.

'That's yours,' Char said graciously when he'd swallowed, nudging the bony creature towards them. Then he spat out a slimy, sodden bundle. 'I *hate* the wool.'

Ma eyed their evening meal unenthusiastically.

'I'll prepare it,' Kyndra said. 'We kept them in Brenwym.'

The name of her home might once have stirred in her a surge of longing, but not any more. She'd been to Brenwym, seen the town being rebuilt . . . watched her mother sobbing into her stepfather's shoulder. Reena missed her. She wanted desperately to know whether her daughter was alive and well. Alive, yes, Kyndra thought, but *well* . . .

She shook her head, dispelling the image of home. She was better now than she'd ever been. It was a relief not to struggle with her feelings, to rid herself of all that foolishness. She was able to think clearly, to see what must be done.

'That man – Hagdon,' Ma said once the goat was spitted over the fire, 'he is keeping our Wielder safe, I hope.'

'One of Hagdon's companions – Amon Taske – is looking after him,' Kyndra said, picturing the fragile old man. She still had Kierik's memories of him – when Shune's hair was brown, his cheeks unlined, facing down a Starborn before the other high Wielders on the eve of Solinaris's fall. He had somehow defied the passage of time, using the Solar to extend his years.

Prompted by that thought she said, 'Can you really send me back in time to challenge the eldest?' The whole idea still sounded outlandish.

'I can,' Ma said shortly. Fat dripped into the fire; the flames hissed and spat. 'But first I need the power the Khronostians used to construct the dragons' prison.'

'Why? Will it make a difference?'

'Yes.' Ma leaned forward and poked a stray piece of kindling into the fire. 'That power is drawn from a Khronostian's own timeline. Once freed from the prison, I believe it can be . . . repurposed.' She pressed her lips together; for a moment her face darkened with memory. 'The *du-alakat* paid a high price for locking the dragons away. Some were disfigured so severely that they could no longer function. I saw enough before I fled.'

Kyndra glanced at Char. The dragon was stretched out across the ground, his head tilted, as if listening closely. It was such a Char pose that she almost smiled. 'What do you mean a Khronostian's own timeline?' she asked Ma.

'It is my fault,' the woman whispered, staring into the flames. 'As the founder of their order, I taught them how to feel their own time streams, to become aware of the river in which we all stand. With enough practice, enough discipline, it is possible to venture a little way in either direction. But if exercised incorrectly or greedily, as the eldest has done, the power to move through time exacts a price on the body.' She paused. 'Eventually, it exacts a price on the mind as well.'

'Should I call you by another name?' Kyndra asked.

Ma shook her head. 'Khronos is long gone. This is no world for a man of peace. He taught through meditation, not violence.' She retrieved a kali stick from her belt, ran a hand along its length. The smooth wood gleamed in the firelight. 'I am Ma of the Beaches now,' she whispered.

'I don't understand,' Char said in his dragon's rumble. 'Khronosta was searching for the Kala. You spent twelve years with them – they raised you. Why didn't they realize who you were?'

'For those twelve years, I was only Mariana. Unusually gifted, but otherwise unremarkable. I had no memories of my previous life. I grew into them later.' Ma switched her gaze to Kyndra. 'Much like you and your memories, Starborn?'

'Yes,' Kyndra said. She no longer felt any hostility at the use of the title, remembering the stifling mix of shock, anger and despair it had once caused her. 'It was around the time I came of age.'

'But even if you had no memories,' Char pressed, 'surely the eldest, or someone else in Khronosta, could have recognized you.'

Ma looked briefly sad. 'By the time of my rebirth, it was already too late. The eldest had grown unstable. He had founded the *du-alakat*, given Khronosta a new warlike purpose. Nothing remains of the people they once were.' She gave a rueful shrug. 'And I doubt they were looking for a girl-child.

11

Their memories of me are so warped – they had only the story they told themselves and the promise I had made them to return. The eldest played his part in eroding everything I was until all that was left was the image of a man who retired to a stone beneath the ancient sky in sight of water and learned to master time.'

The description had the ring of rote and Kyndra wondered whether it was recited by the children of Khronosta just as the Relic devotion had been recited at the Inheritance Ceremony in Brenwym.

'How long ago did you live?' Char asked almost timidly. 'As Khronos, I mean.'

'Before the Sartyan Empire when the world was at peace.' Ma looked at him and then away. 'For all my mastery, it took me a long time to return. Too long.'

Kyndra was aware of *Ansu* listening intently, alongside a star she hadn't spoken with before: *Era*. The latter shared a constellation with *Pyrth* and concerned itself with cycles – of life, death, rebirth. It was the star that ensured a Starborn would always walk the lands of Acre. How many had it witnessed come and go in its span?

Many, it answered, *but it is not my place to remember them*.

Kyndra had a sudden sense of dislocation, as if she were looking back down the ages from a time yet to come. Would her name be noted beside Kierik's in the pages of Acrean history? Or would she stand always in his shadow? The daughter of the Worldmaker.

'I don't know you at all.' Char raised himself, shaking out the spines of his mane. 'Everything you told me about yourself was a lie.'

'And what would you have had me tell you?' Ma replied,

unexpectedly fierce. 'That I was Khronostian? That I had once lived another life? That I had betrayed my people and fled my home because I could not let them murder an infant?' She got to her feet and advanced on Char, as if he were still a young man she could slap for his impertinence. 'That the infant I rescued was not *human*?'

Perhaps Char momentarily forgot his new shape, for he drew back, cringing slightly in anticipation of a blow. But Ma put her palms on either side of his long, narrow face and looked into his eyes. Her human form appeared fragile against his scales. 'I am sorry for any pain I caused you, Boy,' she said softly. 'I pledge to undo the wrong your people have suffered at the hands of mine.'

They stared at each other a second longer before Ma's expression clouded and she turned away. 'I do not know what we will find in Magtharda,' she said. 'The Lleu-yelin have been trapped for twenty years.'

Char resettled himself on the bare rock, his spines sleek against his neck once more. 'Do you think we will find my parents?' he asked.

Ma avoided his eyes. 'I do not know.'

'I wouldn't know how to speak to them anyway. What would I say?'

Kyndra had kept quiet throughout, only part of her listening to the exchange. The greater part busied itself laying plans for when they reached the dragons' city. Khronosta *had* to know that they would seek to release the Lleu-yelin. Now that she'd set herself up as his enemy, the eldest wouldn't allow Ma to gather the power to oppose him. No, it was almost certain that they would meet resistance. Smiling, Kyndra flexed her fingers. Repelling it would be her job.

'What are you smiling about?'

She'd been staring into the night. The valley below them was utterly dark; the only light coming from their fire and the stars that shone crisp and clear above. She felt them in her blood. Sometimes she longed to join them, wrapping herself in isolation, removing herself from the world.

'Kyndra?'

She looked back at the dragon. Char's yellow eyes met hers unflinchingly and she felt some warmth return. Maybe it was hearing that name – the name her mother had given her, the one she had worn through childhood. Or maybe it was realizing that she couldn't – and shouldn't – solve Acre's problems alone.

'I think the goat is done,' she said.

The black dreams began that night.

She stands upon a precipice, a glittering spire. Solinaris, the fortress of the sun, just as it looked before the first ever Breaking – in the days before Kierik's mind shattered the world. She is not alone. Medavle is there, feet planted on the treacherous glass, his ageless face impossibly aged. And at his back, a figure, one claw-like hand grasping at the last Yadin. When the eldest sees her, a rasping, choking sound escapes his lips. It takes her a moment to realize it is laughter.

Kyndra woke, that laughter in her ears. For once, the stars and the night were equally silent and the hairs on the back of her neck stood up in an echo of fear. She hadn't seen Medavle since he'd fled their battle, but his parting words were seared into her memory.

'The last five hundred years were a mistake. They should never have been.'

Now, with Khronostian help, Medavle had the power to erase those years. Kyndra suspected his reason for doing so was very different to the eldest's.

'You don't care about the world.' Her own response echoed back to her. *'You're doing this for the woman you loved. For Isla.'*

'What would a Starborn know of love?'

Kyndra turned her face away from their dying fire. Reasons didn't matter. All that mattered was stopping Medavle before he and the eldest ruined them all.

As they flew further north, the air became colder. The pattern of foliage below them shifted gradually from orange to brown to bare, skeletal branches. Low cloud hid them most of the time, but occasionally they'd emerge into clear blue, where the clouds were wispy and scudding high over narrow valleys. Mountain goat became a staple, though Char once managed to flush out a deer. Despite his huge wingspan, he was getting better at navigating the rocky gorges.

Every evening, Kyndra would ignite solid stone with a touch and they would sit around the flames, discussing what they might encounter when they reached Magtharda. That the eldest would send *du-alakat* to stop them was a given, but they could only guess at their numbers. Then there was the time prison itself; Kyndra envisioned it as a vast bubble, its walls invisible to the naked eye.

She caught her first glimpse with the first snow. They'd been flying steadily north-west until the land had pushed itself into peaks around them. Now, wherever Kyndra looked, she saw mountains. Steel-clad, white-capped, they were a line of silent priests, oddly menacing in their stillness. The sky was flat, reducing their world to a palette of greys – they'd left the colourful autumn valleys behind. Char was the only one who looked at home here; his dusky scales could have been sculpted out of the mountains' hide. Kyndra's hair was an alien streak of fire on the wind.

Magtharda appeared between one blink and the next. At first, Kyndra thought its towers were merely spires of rock thrusting free of the mountains, but, looking closer, she saw windows cut into them; dark, eye-shaped portals that marched around the outside of each soaring barbican. There were half a dozen, guarding the buildings beyond.

Char made a strange sound in his throat; perhaps he'd attempted to whistle.

They flew beneath a great arch, a portal carved from solid rock. No gate or portcullis hung from its frame; it was unnecessary, Kyndra thought, when only those with wings could reach it. The ground was lost to view.

Magtharda lay on the other side. A tiered city, vast courtyards open to the sky, it rose in levels, keeping pace with the mountains that cradled it. Everything was built of the same greyish rock, left rough to echo the landscape. Waterfalls spilled over stone, falling hundreds of feet into deep channels that bisected the streets. The water was the only thing that moved.

With two quick beats of his wings, Char landed on one of the wider thoroughfares and lowered his head to drink.

'Stop,' Ma said sharply. Both she and Kyndra slid off the dragon's back, scanning the empty streets. 'Can you tell if it's safe?' the mercenary asked Kyndra. She was frowning at the water, rushing opaque under the dull sky.

Kyndra bent down and scooped up a handful, calling on

Lagus. Clean, the star told her. 'If there *was* poison in the water, there's no trace of it now,' she said.

Char gave a huff of relief and plunged most of his head in.

Ma's profile was rigid. She watched the streets, as if expecting an ambush, but nothing leapt out to break the city's stillness. Kyndra, too, stood tensed; *something* was out of place here, out of step.

'You feel it,' Ma said. Her eyes travelled over the high buildings, the large, graceful arches, searching. 'They are here, the Lleu-yelin, all around us.'

'What?' Char shook out his mane, showering them. He scanned the courtyard too. 'Then where are they?'

'Frozen,' Ma said. 'They are being held.' She briefly closed her eyes. 'I can feel the strands of it linking them together.'

'The strands of what?' Kyndra asked.

'A focus.'

Char's brow bunched. 'What does it look like?'

'It might not be an *it*, but a *who*,' Ma said, a touch evasively.

Char took a few clawed steps towards the centre of the city. 'You mean a Khronostian?'

Ma shook her head. 'I don't know. We need to go further in.'

It was an eerie walk, as they crossed Magtharda, their footsteps ringing on grey stone. The wind blew and the water tumbled and still they saw no sign of life. The windows of the buildings they passed stared down at them unblinking, the stone doors closed. With the sky above and the city below, it was a colourless world, save for the hues they brought with them.

Great flagstones paraded up the thoroughfare, bisected by a straight dark line that branched off at ninety-degree angles into smaller lines. These ran to unlit lamps and then onwards into the smaller streets. 'What are those for?' Kyndra wondered aloud.

To her surprise, it was Char who answered. 'Ambertrix.'

She frowned. 'How do you know?'

'I feel it,' the dragon said, swinging his head around to look at her. Grounded, he wasn't nearly so graceful. 'There's none here now, but—' He broke off and lowered his muzzle to the nearest line. Kyndra watched his belly swell, ribs expanding as he drew in a breath. It emerged again as a thin blue stream, slowly, with none of the force he'd used during their earlier battle with the Sartyans.

'You've been practising,' she said, pleased.

The stream of ambertrix touched the line and Kyndra heard Ma gasp as the tributary flamed into life, blazing blue. The light spread towards the lamp, igniting it and moving on. Wherever it flowed, more lamps blazed. It touched the doorstep of a house and from inside came a series of clicks and clacks as if some long-dead contraption were groaning to life. Char looked proudly at his handiwork. But then the blue light faded and darkness travelled up the line, dousing lamps, stilling the house until all was silent once more.

Char gave a huff of annoyance and drew in another breath, but Kyndra laid a hand on his flank. 'There's no point,' she said and knelt, tracing the dark line with a finger. 'The Lleu-yelin must have had another way to keep them alight. Whatever you do will just be temporary.'

'I wish I knew what this place looked like before the Khro-nostians came,' Char rumbled. He turned away. 'Let's find this focus.'

The city changed gradually as they moved further in. The buildings became more elaborate, the carvings above their lintels painting a picture of Lleu-yelin life. One house with a wide veranda carried some faintly disturbing images of serpentine creatures intertwined with humans – humanoid, Kyndra corrected herself. Their limbs were too long, their faces too pointed for ordinary people.

The main thoroughfare ended at a triangular archway set into the largest structure they'd seen yet. Several Chars could fit comfortably through with room to spare. Kyndra felt dwarfed as she passed into its shadow and shared a look with Ma. The woman's face was drawn, as if something she dreaded waited around the next corner. Kyndra summoned a sphere of starlight, which she sent up to hover over their heads.

Under its chill glow, they saw a vestibule. A pair of doors confronted them, their carvings showing a dragon with a figure upon its back. Ribbons streamed from the rider's wrists, as they held them out to either side, head tipped back in the ecstasy of flight. The dragon's slitted eyes were rubies, scales picked out in the same topaz as the rider's shining hair. Kyndra and the others stopped, transfixed by the image. Then Ma stepped forward and laid her ouroboros palm on the door.

'In here,' she said.

Without being asked, Char reared onto his hind legs and pressed his front claws against the carving. The doors swung open.

Red suffused the chamber beyond. A vast mandala had been burned into the floor. White sand traced its curving lines, so intricate that it made Kyndra dizzy. They ebbed and flowed around each other, beautiful, deadly, rather like the *du-alakat* themselves. But they all led, inevitably, to the centre.

'No,' Ma whispered in horror.

An ancient dragon towered at the mandala's heart, blood

seeping from dozens of wounds. It ran unerringly into the white sand, turning it black before being absorbed. Little flashes of blue flickered over the dragon's flesh; its wings were spread wide, cords in its neck straining in evident agony. The chamber was bitter with the stink of blood. Char let out a snarl.

'Monstrous,' Ma said, still in a whisper. 'They have trapped it in the moment they attacked. It will bleed forever, but never die.'

'*Him*,' Char growled. 'They have trapped *him*.'

'How does the prison work?' Kyndra asked, studying the dragon with interest. A part of her felt queasy upon seeing the injured creature, but *Era*'s fascination was stronger. *They have interrupted the cycle of time*, the star said in its echoing way, *used the blood to bind the rest of his kin.*

'Then where are they?' Kyndra asked aloud.

'We cannot see them,' Ma answered, as if she had heard the exchange. 'This one is the focus, so it is visible in the present, but the others are imprisoned in the moment the creature was captured, bound by the mandala and the power of their shared blood. Abhorrent.' She shook her head. 'And unbearably clever.'

'We are glad you think so,' said a voice.

2

Gareth

The man who was and was not Gareth Ilda-Son craned his neck to watch the airship pass overhead. Torn leaves leapt like sea spray before the keel and whirled down around him – brown leaves, dead leaves. He stood on the fringes of the Deadwood, aptly named, for where the trees had not been reduced to kindling, they loomed around him in seared rows and the sound of leaf against dry leaf was a death rattle.

It was a sound he knew intimately.

Gareth forced the dark smile from his lips. Apart from waking up on the deck of the airship with a heart that no longer beat, he remembered little of preceding events. What he did recall was too unpleasant to dwell upon. The sailors' whispering on board the *Eastern Set* had followed in his wake, whispers that spoke of bad luck, of fear, of a dead man walking. *They are right to fear me*, he thought, and then wondered whether it was *his* thought.

Gareth looked at the trees surrounding them and flexed his fingers. They opened stiffly, reluctantly. He had to fight the rigor mortis that had set in since that night a week ago . . . the night he'd died. He shuddered and found himself touching his chest again. The flesh was cold and still beneath his hand.

'Gareth?' came a voice and, grateful for any distraction, he turned to Brégenne. She regarded him with wary eyes, the plait of her white-blond hair pulled over her shoulder.

'Yes, it's me,' he said.

She seemed relieved. 'Are you ready? Do you need to rest?'

Gareth glanced at the gauntlet on his arm. He didn't need to rest, not since awakening to this death-in-life existence. He shook his head.

'We should wait until dawn,' Kul'Das said. The woman from Ümvast's — his mother's — court carried her usual air of arrogance. 'My staff does not function at night.'

Brégenne huffed. Gareth knew she'd been trying to convince the shaman that the staff was just an inanimate length of wood, but Kul'Das remained adamant. 'No,' Brégenne answered irritably. 'Until you're ready to be honest and admit you're a Wielder, we travel at night.'

Gareth didn't protest. Although he, too, was a Wielder, the Solar power seemed different now; he hadn't touched it in a week. Suspecting the gauntlet's influence, he studied the ebony metal enclosing his right wrist. It left his fingers bare but reached halfway to his elbow, fully part of him now. If only he'd known the danger when he'd stolen it from Naris's archives . . .

The memory made him think of Shika and Irilin and he wondered where his friends were. Perhaps he should be glad that they couldn't see what he'd become. *Serjo.* The thought, not his own, came right atop the other. *Once we were friends, Brother.*

'Ben-haugr is west,' Brégenne said, her voice muffled by the surrounding trees. She gave Gareth a narrow glance. 'Are you sure you can find it? We might come out too far to the north or south – Kyndra only gave me a rough idea of its location.'

'I can find it.' As soon as his feet had touched Acrean soil, Gareth had felt a nagging pull to the west, an itch no amount of scratching could relieve. When he closed his eyes, an image came to him of twisting stone, sunken pathways, a labyrinth leading to a vaulted chamber, an occupied throne . . .

Gareth quickly blinked it away. That pull *had* to be the other gauntlet – once he united the pair, he'd be free of this curse. But he knew it must lie deep inside Ben-haugr, in the tomb of Kingswold, built atop the ruins of an ancient city. The thought of what else he might find there turned him cold.

'I don't like this place,' Kul'Das said. The sun had already fled the sky and the Deadwood lay before them, wreathed in shadows. A cry came and the three of them started. Halfway between owl and wolf, it would have raised the hairs on Gareth's neck if they still responded to feeling.

'I don't like it,' Kul'Das repeated. Her fingers tightened around the staff, knuckles bone-pale in the fickle moonlight. 'This forest is wrong.' She cast Gareth a reproachful look. 'I still say we should have kept the warriors.'

They'd left the handful of warriors who'd accompanied them from Ümvast aboard the airship. Gareth knew they were there on his mother's orders; if he'd been himself, he wouldn't have had the authority to send them away. But he wasn't himself. They'd seen what he'd done to the bandits who'd attacked the airship. They'd watched living flesh rot before their eyes with a single touch from his hand. They'd witnessed Gareth die and wake again. So when he'd asked them to stay behind, they had stayed and nothing Kul'Das had said could force them to return to their duty.

'It's too dangerous,' Gareth told her now. 'The warriors will be safer with Argat.'

'I notice it's not too dangerous for *us*, though,' Kul'Das said with a touch of indignation, but she looked oddly satisfied all the same.

'Let's go.' It came out harsher than he'd intended. Silently, Brégenne took his lead and started out, her eyes glowing silver in the gloom.

Gareth's senses seemed heightened as he walked. They, at least, still functioned. He could smell charred earth, though whatever fire had swept through here was long extinguished. The rattlesnake leaves blew fitful in the breeze and his footfalls stirred up little puffs of ash. Some trees had weathered the flames, scarred but whole, while others were bent and broken, branches littering the forest floor. Gareth found himself thinking of Vorgarde, the lightless land; warriors of Ümvast believed they would forever roam those dim battlefields after death.

That was how the night passed, with Gareth's every sense taut, primed for trouble. It was almost a shock to see the sky lighten above them, dawn painting the trunks red. Gareth felt the Solar power wake, a shining golden thread he could follow to the heart of the sun. Except that his connection to it felt strained somehow. The thought of reaching for it wearied him, but he'd put this off long enough.

Wan gold, streaked with shadow, formed in his hands and Brégenne turned sharply to face him. He was aware too of Kul'Das watching. Neither woman totally trusted him. He didn't trust himself.

Gareth opened his mouth to speak, but the golden light in his hands grew hotter and began to burn. It took him a moment to recognize the feeling as pain – the first pain he had felt since his *death*. How many times had he held the Solar, feeling that warmth, that life, like the beating heart of the world? Now, weak as it was, it scorched him. He released it with a yelp.

'Gareth,' Brégenne said, advancing a step towards him. 'What is it?'

'The Solar,' he mumbled. 'It hurts to hold it.'

For a moment she seemed speechless. Her eyes moved from his face to the gauntlet and he knew what she was thinking; he was thinking it too. *The Solar is life . . . and I am dead*. He had to crush his surge of revulsion. Brégenne made to lay a hand on his shoulder, but perhaps she thought better of it, for she drew back.

'We may as well rest here,' she said, inspecting their surroundings. There was little shelter – or camouflage – to be had in the Deadwood, Gareth realized. They wouldn't do much better than the slight hollow they currently stood in; its curving sides offered scanty protection from prying eyes.

'I will take first watch,' Kul'Das said, though she sounded weary and leaned heavily on her staff.

'No.' Gareth's voice was quiet. 'Let me watch. I don't need to rest.'

Their answering looks said it all. He tried to tell himself he didn't care whether they trusted him or not, but . . . He glanced at Brégenne. After the months they'd spent travelling together, it hurt to see the doubt in her eyes. He saw himself reflected in them: skeletally thin, waxen, mottle-skinned, his eyes like flat black pools. Gareth looked down at himself. He'd been large all his life, big boned like the rest of his people. Now those bones stood out starkly, the flesh lying slack over his shrunken chest. He felt another wave of disgust; he barely looked human any more. Ghoul-like, the gauntlet had fed on him, stripping away his life, layer by layer, until even his heart stopped beating.

And still it wasn't finished with him.

As the women slept, or pretended to sleep – he was sure one of them kept an eye on him – Gareth watched the sun slide between the black trunks. Even his friend Shika, who always found something to laugh about, wouldn't laugh this time. *He won't recognize me.*

The day passed as uneventfully as the night. Once or twice Gareth thought he heard a twig snap and he rose to his feet, listening. But nothing disturbed the stillness of the burned-out forest. By the time the moon climbed again, Gareth's caution was somewhat blunted. 'So where are these "unsavoury types" Kyndra warned us about?' he asked Brégenne, as the Wielder swung a cloak around her shoulders. 'I thought she said people lived in the Deadwood.'

'Are you so keen to meet them?'

Gareth looked away. 'No.'

'Perhaps we're out of their range.' Brégenne briefly laid a hand on his arm. 'Are you sure you don't need to sleep?'

He nodded, uncomfortable in her presence. Brégenne might have trusted the old Gareth, but she didn't trust *him*. He missed the easy friendship they'd struck up along the road to Market Primus. Together they'd escaped the Wielders sent to subdue them. They'd fought back to back against the wyverns attacking Ümvast's fortress, he with the Solar, she with the Lunar. When he'd . . . when he'd killed those men, she had risked her life to bring him back to himself. Yet now there was a wall between them and he didn't know how to breach it.

White raises, black fells.

He clenched his hands, the gauntlet a fist of darkness. His

other hand looked vulnerable, white knuckled and bare. He wasn't whole, merely a shadow self. How had this happened? Could Serjo have lied? *'Ljúga, Serjo,'* his voice sounded strange in his ears, *'heit vinna einhendr einn.'*

Silence brought Gareth back to himself, the strange words tasting like a cold blade on his tongue. Brégenne and Kul'Das were staring at him, the latter with the twist of a frown. 'What was that?' she asked.

'I . . . don't know.' Gareth uncurled his fists, finding it difficult to focus. He was afraid of losing himself again, but the echo of the phrase remained, as if a door he'd never seen before had opened and been left ajar. He wasn't sure what would happen if he went through it.

'He said it would work on its own,' he whispered.

'What would?'

'The gauntlet.' Gareth looked at Brégenne. 'Serjo told him it was safe to wear.'

'Told *who*?' she asked, her silvery eyes sharp on his face.

'Kingswold.' Was it his imagination or did the gauntlet contract at the name? 'Serjo was his brother.'

'How do you know this?' Kul'Das demanded.

Gareth knew he was right, in his very bones, he knew it. But that didn't mean he wanted to voice it aloud. Both women stared at him, their breath steaming gently in the cooling night. He shook his head and started out again.

Brégenne moved to walk at his side. 'Have you considered that it wasn't just coincidence that led you to take the gauntlet from the archives?'

Gareth stumbled, grabbed at a tree trunk for balance. When he let go, his left palm was as charcoal-black as his right and he brushed it hurriedly down on his cloak. Brégenne was silent, awaiting his response. 'What do you mean?' he asked uneasily, looking around at her.

'As you no doubt saw,' the Wielder said, her tone a little wry, 'there are hundreds of artefacts stored on the seventh level. And yet you found and took the gauntlet.'

'It . . . called to me.' Gareth shook his head. 'But Shika was with me. Later, when the Nerian attacked, he could just as easily have put it on.'

For some reason, Brégenne looked pained, but it vanished a moment later. 'He didn't, though,' she said. '*You* did. And when we learned from Ümvast that Kingswold was of northern blood, I started thinking that *your* finding the gauntlet wasn't an accident.'

'Because I'm a northerner too,' Gareth said softly.

'Blood calls to blood. Perhaps it still seeks its master.'

'Preposterous,' Kul'Das interrupted. She'd been lagging slightly behind, placing her feet with care on the crunchy layer of twigs. 'Kingswold has been dead these five hundred years. Nothing of him remains in the world.'

'Do you exist to refute everything I say?' Brégenne snapped over her shoulder. 'I tell you, some part of Kingswold lives on in the gauntlet.'

Kul'Das gave Brégenne a look of deep dislike, but didn't deny the statement. If Gareth's heart still beat, it would have been racing. *Kingswold.* To hear Brégenne voice the name aloud gave it credence and suddenly he remembered how Kyndra described hearing Kierik's thoughts as her own. At the time, Gareth had struggled to visualize the idea, but was his situation so very different?

They walked by the faint light of a Lunar flame and Gareth gazed into it, silent. Not only because he feared Brégenne was right, but because he might find himself speaking in the unknown language again. He'd already lost his body and health to the gauntlet; he wouldn't lose his mind.

The ambush came without warning, just before dawn.

Perhaps Brégenne's senses were dulled by the long, uneventful hours of walking, for she barely threw herself aside in time to avoid an arrow as it streaked through the gloom and *thunked* into a tree behind her. A warning shot. Kul'Das crouched instinctively and Gareth leapt in front of Brégenne as the Wielder struggled to regain her feet. 'Stand close to me,' she said and a shimmering Lunar shield expanded to surround the three of them.

More arrows came, repelled by the shield, but it turned them into an unmissable target. 'Move,' Brégenne snapped and Gareth heard the strain in her voice. She jerked her chin. 'This way.'

'It's nearly morning,' he said, looking at the sky.

Brégenne didn't reply; the barrier was taking all her concentration. Gareth knew that maintaining a shield while moving was much harder – they'd practised it as novices a few times – and Brégenne was shielding three people.

Dark figures began to circle the barrier. As the sky lightened, he could just about discern them through the translucent walls. Kul'Das had seen them too; white-faced, she clutched her staff tightly to her chest, almost tripping on Brégenne's heels. They couldn't go on like this. Gareth squinted at their attackers, feeling the gauntlet grow cold on his arm. *No,* he thought at it – at himself. He remembered the horror he'd unleashed before, the boiling tendrils of rot that corrupted living flesh. He would not call on that power again.

Something blue and crackling shot inches past his nose. Gareth had only a moment to feel thankful that the projectile hadn't hit any of them before the Lunar shield shattered into a thousand bright shards.

Brégenne's eyes widened. She looked at her hands, still glowing with weak moonlight, and then up at the figures surrounding them. Gareth followed her gaze and saw a woman holding a device that resembled a crossbow. Blue energy flickered around two small metal discs fixed to the frame and its holder smiled as she fitted another bolt into place.

A new shield sprang up around them, Brégenne's fists clenched inside her leather half-gloves with the effort. But the archer fired and, once again, the shield crumbled.

Gareth could feel the chains that bound the Solar power falling away, as the sky rapidly lightened. He studied their attackers; there were about fifteen, clothed in the shades of the Deadwood. They were all women. Each bore two horizontal stripes across her left cheek.

'Who are you?' he demanded of them. 'What do you want?'

The woman with the crossbow gestured it at Brégenne. 'Take the aberration alive,' she said in a guttural accent that almost buried her words. 'The Sartyans pay well for them.'

Kul'Das stepped in front of Gareth, holding her staff at the ready. He was almost knocked back by the blast of heat as fire erupted along its length. 'You think to stop *us*?' she said with a valiant attempt at her usual disdain.

Her display had the opposite effect. Grins spread among the watching women and their leader looked delighted. 'Someone's smiling on us, Takendo,' she said to a hooded woman standing at her shoulder. 'Two aberrations . . .' she looked hopefully at Gareth – 'perhaps three?'

Automatically, he shook his head, but the woman didn't seem disheartened. 'That one shouldn't be a danger,' she said with a dismissive nod to Brégenne, as if she were speaking of an animal recently subdued. 'But that one—' She broke off in a gasp as Kul'Das swung the staff and a sheet of fire blasted across the short distance between them.

Gareth used the distraction to tug Brégenne away from the fighting, pushing her in front of him. 'Go,' he said, keeping an eye on their scattered attackers. Kul'Das sent out another wave of fire before turning and fleeing with them. Perhaps, like Gareth, she was wary of the glowing crossbow and what it could do.

They managed about ten yards before a dreadful shriek brought them stumbling to a halt. Kul'Das was on her knees. A bolt pierced the hand holding her staff, pinning her flesh to the wood. Kul'Das wasn't looking at her hand, however; her eyes were fixed on the staff, on the vertical crack running up and down its length. As Gareth watched, the top piece sheared away, sending the shrivelled raven heads tumbling to the ground.

Kul'Das stared at them. Fingers trembling, she reached out and picked one up. Blood dripped from her other hand onto the feathered head. The remainder of the staff split around the bolt and fell in two pieces, leaving the metal buried in her palm.

Gareth eyed the approaching women. A couple limped along; the leather of their clothes smoking where Kul'Das's flames had caught them. Others bore scratches on their faces and arms. But most were unhurt, including their leader with the crossbow and the hooded woman at her side.

'Kul'Das—'

Before he could finish his warning, Kul'Das regained her

feet and whirled to face their attackers. Tears glinted on her cheeks – of grief or outrage, Gareth didn't know. With a snarl, she threw out her hands, the right dripping blood, and a wave of force hit the nearest women, knocking them off their feet.

Kul'Das seemed in shock as she gazed at her own hands. Her eyes travelled from the broken staff back to her palms and she fired a look over her shoulder at Brégenne.

It was the distraction the hooded woman needed. Faster than Gareth thought possible, she darted at Kul'Das, something small clutched in her fist. It was thin and blunt and Gareth couldn't understand why Kul'Das screamed at its touch, tottering on suddenly unsteady feet. The hooded woman thrust the object at her again and the shaman's body contorted, knocking her to her knees. The woman raised the device a third time. It was pronged like a fork, blue energy crackling between its metal points. Before she could strike, Gareth leapt in front of Kul'Das and caught the blow on his shoulder.

Expecting pain, he tensed, but nothing happened. The woman looked equally surprised. She raised the device and struck him again. When he didn't react, her smile slipped and she stumbled back. Gareth didn't hesitate – he scooped up Kul'Das and turned to run.

He'd gone only a few paces when something heavy struck his back, staggering him. A feathered shaft protruded from his shoulder blade. He spared one glance behind to see another woman, armed with an ordinary bow. Already she'd nocked a second arrow. It took him in the calf.

He ignored it.

Another struck his back, a fourth his thigh, a fifth his arm. He pulled Kul'Das in closer and kept on, feeling the thuds as the arrows hit, but no pain. He glanced over his shoulder again.

The archer's disbelief was swiftly turning to fear. When the hooded woman shouted something, she lowered her bow.

Brégenne's running feet stirred up the ash. It choked the air; in his arms, Kul'Das began to cough. Despite the arrows, Gareth could have kept up his staggering run until his legs rotted beneath him. But Brégenne, clearly exhausted by a night of walking and shielding them, eventually slowed. There were no signs of pursuit. For now.

'Kul'Gareth,' the woman in his arms said faintly. 'I think you can put me down.'

Gareth did as she asked, steadying her when she seemed about to fall over. Her face was pale; she still clutched a shard of her staff.

Brégenne gasped when she turned and saw him. He would have found it funny once, stuck like a human pincushion, but he couldn't laugh, not when the reality was so terrible. He wasn't even human enough to bleed.

'I'm fine,' he said shortly. 'Can you get them out, Brégenne?'

He noticed that she trembled slightly as she approached him, her gaze moving from one arrow to the next. But when she touched his back, her hands were firm. 'You won't hurt me,' he assured her when she hesitated.

'I don't want to do more damage,' she answered. 'Until you're back to normal –' her voice wavered a little – 'I can't heal these wounds.'

'Just work them out carefully, then,' Gareth said tonelessly. 'Don't you think it would look suspicious if somebody saw me?' He paused. 'I'm probably the reason those women didn't come after us.'

Brégenne hesitated a moment longer before sighing. 'Sit down,' she said. 'Kul'Das, come and help me.'

Her blue eyes rather glassy, Kul'Das wandered over and crouched beside Gareth. She followed Brégenne's instructions in uncharacteristic silence as they removed, with some difficulty, over half a dozen arrows from Gareth's flesh. No blood dripped from the arrowheads. When he looked at the open wound on his calf, it was surprisingly clean; the blood dry and clotted, his flesh unyielding.

When the last arrow came free with an unpleasant *pop*, Kul'Das stood up very quickly, her hand over her mouth. 'I'm sorry,' she said, taking several large strides away. Even Brégenne was looking rather green.

'Thank you,' Gareth murmured. He knew his body reeked, the decomposition arrested halfway through its gruesome work by his continued mobility. He wasn't sure what was keeping him sane when he began each day wondering how much mutilation his body could take before it released him from this nightmare.

'I think we might be nearing the edge of the Deadwood,' Brégenne said and Gareth climbed to his feet, trying to shed his dark thoughts. The trees did seem thinner, more widely spaced. Beyond their black trunks, Ben-haugr waited. He was close, so very close. Something stirred behind his eyes at the thought, like a sleeper at the bottom of a well.

I am come home.

3

Char

The chamber was full of figures, limbs wrapped in grey bandages. '*Du-alakat*,' Char heard Kyndra hiss.

'Where is the eldest?' Ma's command echoed in the hollow chamber.

The warrior who'd spoken was unmasked. She stepped forward, shadowed by her brethren. 'He prepares. He has sent me, my brothers and sisters, in his stead.'

'A mistake.' Ma stepped forward too. But not a surprise. He lacks the power to stand against me.'

'Why do you do this, Mariana?' One of the Khronostians reached up and unwound their bandages, revealing a woman. Like all *du-alakat*, time had warped her features. It was impossible to guess her age, but she had the same dark skin as Ma.

'Jin?' Ma's fierce stare wavered.

The woman moved closer. 'You would fight us? Fight *me*? We were family once.'

'You give me no option.' Ma shook her head sadly. 'Cousin, the eldest has lost his mind. What he plans to do is an abomination. If he is not stopped, he will tear the fabric of time.'

'You lied to me, Mariana,' Jin said, taking another step.

Ma raised a hand. 'No closer.'

'I could have helped.'

'I don't want to hurt you, Jin.'

'If you'd been honest with me, told me who you really were, none of this would have happened.'

Ma's expression grew cold. 'The only thing my honesty would have earned me is a cage.'

There was a moment as the two women locked eyes. Then they sprang into motion so swiftly that Char couldn't tell who had moved first. Ma's ironwood kali sticks met Jin's and the hollow clack of wood on wood filled the chamber. A flash caught his eye; Kyndra was gone in a swirl of her cloak. She reappeared behind the *du-alakat* leader, who swept out her own weapons to intercept her strike. Kyndra's skin was clad in a familiar dark silver – the star *Tyr* shielding her better than any armour. Kali sticks wouldn't fell her. As he watched, more *du-alakat* closed in, hiding her from view.

Others made for him, their strides determined, and Char backed away, trying to keep them all in sight. He was clumsy on the ground, still unused to this new body. Once, he'd have raised his own kali sticks in defence, balanced on the balls of his feet. He'd have sought the calm centre, as Ma had taught him, struggling against the rage that had threatened to tear his soul apart.

And he'd have died. He couldn't have taken on this many *du-alakat*.

Now he drew a breath, felt heat in his belly, and let it out as blue-veined force. It knocked a warrior off their feet, but the others avoided it easily. They continued to stalk him and he backed away further. The captured dragon hung above them all, a gruesome totem frozen with wings spread wide, and Char felt a fresh surge of fury.

Hunkering down, he took another breath. It roiled in his belly, desperate to be free, but he was used to that feeling – he'd spent three years resisting it. So he checked it, focused on finding the blue heart of it.

A blow landed behind his ear where the scales were thinner. He gritted his teeth against the pain, screwing his eyes shut. More blows came, more pain. They were clearly familiar with all the most vulnerable parts of his body. He concentrated on the blue force, feeling it tumbling over and over, remembering the effort it had once cost him to control it. The Sartyans called it ambertrix. They'd tamed the energy, forced it to power their crude devices. But in its pure form, it was raw and unbridled; it was wild.

Blood slid down his scales; they'd prised off several sections, revealing the dark flesh beneath. Char snarled. He wouldn't end up like the dragon that hung, twisted and tormented above. Refocusing on the energy, he *changed* it. Now the force in his belly was spitting, crackling like lightning. Acting on instinct, he released it upwards and outwards through his scales; it caught those *du-alakat* whose weapons were in contact with his body, surged into them, and they screamed, burning from the inside out. When he looked around, only one had escaped, staggering and singed. Char's head darted out, caught the dazed warrior in his jaws and bit down. Hot blood filled his mouth, the Khronostian screamed once and then Char's teeth sheared him in half.

The moment he paused to take stock, his pain seemed to double. His exposed skin stung and he couldn't hold back a growl. Although Ma was fighting half a dozen Khronostians, she turned at the sound. On seeing him, she bared her teeth and flung her sticks to the ground. Crooking her fingers, she raked the air in front of her face, the ouroboros on her palms blazing white.

The air solidified around the six warriors. Their movements became slower and slower and consternation showed on every face. 'What have you done?' Jin demanded. The question reached Char word by word, each syllable distorted. Ma turned away, dismissing them, and started towards him. Beads of sweat glinted on her brow.

Jin jerked suddenly, as if she'd tried to move and was pulled up short. She grimaced, her body suffused with a whitish light. Stumbling forward, she raised a kali stick, aiming at Ma's unprotected back.

Before Char could shout a warning, Ma spun. She brought her hands together and then snapped them apart with a strange twisting motion. Jin screamed. The bottom half of her body seemed to shrink, her legs shortening, while the top half sank in upon itself, muscle and flesh mottling, withering as she watched. It was the work of years done in seconds. Jin lay on the floor, the tiny feet of an infant poking out of grey bandages, while the heart of a hundred-year-old woman faltered and died in her chest. Her clouded eyes, when she turned them on Ma, were disbelieving and full of horror.

The remaining warriors looked from Ma to Jin's crumpled form. They stared at Char, at the bodies of their comrades that lay in a bloodied circle around him. 'Throw down your weapons,' Ma told them, breathing hard. Char thought she deliberately avoided glancing at Jin.

The *du-alakat* looked to their leader, who stood outside the battle surrounding Kyndra. The woman's eyes were fixed on the Starborn as she turned some object over in her hands. Half a dozen warriors were down, some little more than smoking piles, others literally frozen solid, or bleeding from missing limbs. But Kyndra couldn't fight forever. Those *du-alakat* still on their feet were wearing her down second by second, fast enough to avoid many of her attacks, which were growing clumsier. She might have the power of the stars, Char thought, but Kyndra was no warrior. He'd seen that plainly enough when he'd tried to teach her the sticks. And he'd heard the story – Kyndra had told him herself – of the time she lost control, obliterating half a thousand men, rending up the very earth. In such a confined space as this, perhaps she feared to call on *Sigel* lest she hurt him and Ma.

Instead of throwing down their weapons as Ma had demanded, the *du-alakat* surrounding them disappeared, rematerializing in the throng around Kyndra. They were fighting on the edge of the mandala. Although their feet touched the pattern of sand, it did not scuff, as if the dragon's blood somehow fused it to the stone.

Jin's death had stolen the hard mask from Ma's face, but now it returned. 'They have chosen their course,' she murmured. She looked at Char. 'We take out as many as we can. Every death weakens the eldest.'

He nodded, and they moved towards the fray. A gap opened up and Char saw Kyndra, her face a grimace of concentration. In her left hand she held ice; in her right, wind, which caught up the nearest Khronostian, hurling him over the heads of his comrades to smash into the chamber wall. Their eyes met in that instant, blue to yellow, and Char knew what was about to happen before it did. He opened his mouth to roar a warning, but the Khronostian leader was already there.

Swift, steady, the woman's hand flashed out . . . and clamped something on Kyndra's wrist. Kyndra spared it only a glance before she plunged her own hand into the woman's chest.

Everything stopped. The battle halted. The Khronostian glanced down at the arm embedded in her flesh and up at Kyndra, who snarled and pulled her hand back, clutching the woman's heart. Although blood gushed from the wound, the Khronostian's eyes strayed to Kyndra's left wrist and she smiled as she toppled backwards.

As if her death were a signal, the *du-alakat* sheathed their weapons, joined hands and were gone in a wisp of whitish light.

The sudden silence was disorientating. The sharp stink of blood and spilled human offal mingled with the older scent of dragon until Char's sensitive nostrils could barely stand it. He breathed through his mouth instead, tasting the same blood upon his tongue. Unlike animal blood, it made him feel sick.

Kyndra looked at her wrist where the Khronostian had clamped an ugly iron bracelet. 'Kyndra,' Ma said sharply, 'don't touch—'

Kyndra gestured; the bracelet glowed yellow-white as if returned to the forge and melted, dripping harmlessly off her *Tyr*-covered skin.

'. . . that,' Ma finished too late. Because there was a pattern hidden in the tarnished metal, a pattern that ominously resembled a Khronostian mandala. It pulsed once before sinking into Kyndra's wrist.

The effect was immediate. One by one, Kyndra's fingers began to wrinkle, the skin sagging, the knucklebones standing stark. She gazed at her hand, first perplexed then horrified, suddenly no more than a teenage girl. Ma seized Kyndra's hand, pressing one of her ouroboros-patterned palms against the Starborn's. Kyndra gasped, squeezing her eyes shut, while Ma muttered under her breath. When Ma took her palm away, Kyndra's fingers were still wrinkled and crooked, but the deterioration seemed to have stopped.

'That was foolish, girl,' Ma snapped. She looked exhausted. 'Why don't you think before you act?'

Kyndra's cheeks were ashen as she stared at her changed hand. 'What . . . was that?'

'They needed you to destroy the bracelet – it was the only way to activate the mandala.' Ma shook her head, chiding. 'I should have known the eldest would try to compromise you.'

'And what has it done to me?'

'It's based on the same mandala that binds the Lleu-yelin,' Ma said with a glance at the dragon behind them. 'A time trap powered by your own life force.'

'But you've stopped it, haven't you?' It was the most emotion Kyndra had shown in weeks, Char thought.

'Only slowed its progress. It will kill you . . . eventually.'

Kyndra's dark eyes widened before turning introspective; she must be speaking to the stars. Abruptly her body dissolved into shadow and light, as it had done on the day they'd fought the Khronostians. Even without her flesh, the mandala remained as a serpentine coil, circling her formless wrist. Char and Ma watched silently until she reappeared as herself, the determination fading from her face. She closed her eyes once and opened them slowly. 'They don't know what to do,' she whispered. 'They do not know this magic.' She glanced at Ma. 'It's as you say – the power is tied to my life. Only death can end it.'

'Not quite true,' Ma said grimly. Her eyes strayed to the grey-bandaged bodies that made a bloody battlefield of the chamber.

'If you can kill the person who created the mandala, it will stop the corruption.'

'The eldest,' Kyndra said softly.

Ma nodded. 'If you needed another reason to oppose him, to follow him into the past, you have it.'

Kyndra turned her palm up, frowning at the crooked fingers of her left hand. 'How long do I have?' she asked matter-of-factly.

'Weeks,' Ma said. 'Perhaps a month or two – it depends how potent the binding is.'

Kyndra took the news with equal serenity, but Char saw her swallow as she clenched her fist and lowered it to her side.

'Are you all right?'

'Yes,' she said with a hint of her old defiance, a defiance he was glad to see. It was a foolish thought, but Char missed the other Kyndra, the Kyndra who was unsure of herself, but did what had to be done. The Kyndra who, like him, had struggled vainly against her fate. The Kyndra he had kissed by the little stream, who had told him, fiercely, that he wasn't a coward.

But that Kyndra was gone. That Char was gone. They were both changed and there was no going back.

'I don't feel as if we've won much of a victory here,' Kyndra said, looking around the chamber. Her eyes came to rest on the tortured form of the dragon. '*Can* we free the Lleu-yelin?'

'If that was the best the eldest could throw at us,' Ma replied, 'I fear *you* were his true target. The return of the dragons isn't something he would want to see, but if his plan succeeds, this future won't even exist.'

'Nevertheless, we *are* freeing them,' Char said, unable to keep the growl out of his voice. His wounds itched as they began, slowly, to heal. It would take only a few days for the scales to grow back, but that wasn't swift enough for him. He rolled his bleeding shoulder at Kyndra. 'Can you do something about this?'

To his consternation, she shook her head. 'I'm not Nediah,' she said. 'You don't just need power to heal, you need knowledge. I don't know the first thing about the body, be it human or dragon.'

'But surely the stars do.'

'They aren't mortal. They have no flesh, no blood, or beating heart.'

'How do you shift your form back and forth, then?'

Kyndra shrugged. 'That's different. It's a pattern. *My* pattern. I can always find it. I don't know anyone else's though.' She paused. 'It's also why I can't get rid of the mandala.' She hefted her wrist. 'I can't change my pattern.'

'So it's not entirely true about Starborn being all-powerful,' Char said. 'The tales people told of Kierik . . .'

Kyndra smiled somewhat bitterly. 'I don't know all the tales,' she said, 'but I know what Kierik could do. It was far more than I can.'

'You just need practice, girl,' Ma said absently. She was kneeling down, fingers stroking the concentric lines of blood and sand.

'Will you free him now?' Char asked her.

Forehead wrinkled, Ma moved her gaze to the frozen, spread-winged dragon that filled the chamber and sighed deeply. 'It is the only way,' she said after a moment.

'What is?' Char recognized her expression; it was the one Ma had worn most often over the years they'd lived and worked as slavers: reluctance, resignation. 'What's wrong?'

Ma stood. 'He is the focus, Boy. It is his blood, his *life*, which sustains the prison.' She glanced back at him. 'The link must be broken.'

'You're going to kill him.' Char felt that familiar rage uncoiling in his belly; little sparks shivered over his scales. 'I can feel his suffering, and you're going to kill him.'

'It is the only way,' Ma said again; almost a snap. 'As long as his blood feeds the mandala, the Lleu-yelin will never be free.'

Char turned his back on her, moved to stand before the dragon. His talons left scratches in the stone, but did not disturb the mandala atop it. The trapped Lleu-yelin was larger than he and far older. The mane that lay sleek and full against Char's neck was a handful of bristles on the ancient dragon. His blue scales had faded, in places, to dun, and blood glistened between the cracks in his skin. The eyes, though, deep and dark, alight with anger kindled in the moment of attack. The mandala was killing him regardless; a slow death, a withering. It was not a death those eyes deserved.

The rumble that left Char's throat was somewhere between rage at what had been and grief at what had to be. 'End it, then,' he heard himself say. 'End it and be done.'

4

Brégenne

That was *not* an experience she wanted to repeat.

The shock of the Lunar being torn from her grasp stayed with Brégenne, mocking the control she'd worked hard to hone. She'd never heard of a weapon that could counter a Wielder's power. They had to find out more about it and fast.

She rubbed a weary hand over her face. Her legs ached and her eyes were sandy from lack of sleep. Ash coated her clothes; her hair felt full of the fine dust. Brégenne found herself fervently wishing for a bath.

When she looked round, Kul'Das still stood silently, gripping her broken staff.

'Are you all right?' Brégenne asked her.

Kul'Das raised her head, fresh tears on her cheeks. 'My staff,' she whispered, turning the shattered piece over in her hands. 'He told me it was powerful, that it had magic.' She swallowed and her voice hardened. 'He *lied*.'

'Your mentor?' Brégenne asked carefully. She'd tried to get this information out of Kul'Das before to no avail.

The blue-eyed woman jerked her chin. She threw down the

remains of the staff, its pale wood ill-at-home against the charred earth. Her hand was no longer bleeding, Brégenne noticed. The bolt was gone, but the flesh around the wound was puckered and still seeped red. Kul'Das had clearly tried to heal it herself.

'I'll look at your hand later,' Brégenne promised. 'As soon as the moon's up.'

Kul'Das ignored her, staring transfixed at her injured hand. Slowly, as if they were climbing out of her skin, golden flames curled up and filled her palm. A smile split the woman's usually sour face, a fierce, joyful smile that set Brégenne's teeth on edge. That was all they needed – an overzealous, untrained Wielder.

'Those women,' Gareth said suddenly, 'who do you think they were?'

'I'm more interested in their weapons,' Brégenne replied. The day was growing warmer; she shrugged out of her cloak, rolled it up and secured it to the pack at her feet. Beneath it she wore scuffed leathers over a shirt and knee-high boots. Still angry at the thought of that strange blue energy, she brushed herself down and then vigorously unbraided and rebraided her hair.

'As am I,' Kul'Das said, seeming to break from her reverie. 'That forked dagger – she didn't stab me, just rested it against my skin. The pain . . .' Her eyes clouded. 'I could not move.'

'And the same power managed to dispel my shield twice.' Brégenne frowned, struck by a thought. 'Could this be the energy Kyndra described – the one the Sartyans use?'

'But those weren't Sartyans,' Gareth said. 'That's who they wanted to sell you to.'

'It did not work on you, Kul'Gareth,' Kul'Das said abruptly.

Gareth looked uncomfortable and Brégenne remembered the feel of the arrows as they came free of his dead flesh. 'I didn't feel anything,' he said.

'If it weren't for you, they'd have captured us.' Brégenne's attempt at a reassuring smile did not feel at home on her lips.

'I ran away,' Gareth said. His eyes grew unfocused, as if he saw something she and Kul'Das could not. 'There was little courage in it,' he added softly.

'Until we know more about those weapons, it was the right thing to do,' Brégenne said, suddenly keen to change the subject. Whenever that distance entered Gareth's eyes, he seemed less . . . himself.

'I would like to put a little more space between myself and those women.' Despite the words, Kul'Das looked weary at the thought of more walking and Brégenne didn't blame her. 'I'll not sleep soundly until we're out of this infernal wood.'

Kul'Das got her wish: by sunset, they'd left the Deadwood and its dangers behind. The trees had continued to thin, eventually petering out into rocky moorland. They'd had only a brief view of the landscape; now it was utterly dark, the moon obscured by dense cloud. No lights flecked the horizon. The only thing moving was the grass, agitated by the wind that swept down from distant hills to the north.

Brégenne had walked a little away from their camp on the pretext of setting wards, but truthfully she wanted some time alone to practise. Now a curving slice of moonlight hung in the air before her. Brégenne frowned at it. *I know it's possible.* This would be so much easier if she had Solinaris's resources, but all the useful texts had long been destroyed.

She sighed, gestured, and the shining curve contracted into

a flat disc. It was similar to the supports she'd made to assist with the reconstruction of Naris's bridge. When the disc measured roughly three feet across, Brégenne stepped onto it. So far so good.

She was three metres off the ground before an audible gasp reached her from somewhere below. Brégenne looked down. Eyesight sharpened by the Lunar, she quickly picked out the shape of Gareth, hiding among some rocks. Feeling a faint flush in her cheeks, she dropped lightly back to earth and the disc vanished.

Gareth climbed sheepishly from his hiding place. 'Sorry. I didn't mean to pry, but I've never seen . . .' He shook his head. 'Was that levitation? I thought the ability was lost with Solinaris.'

Brégenne folded her arms. 'It's not perfect yet.'

'It seemed pretty good to me.'

In the light of the Lunar, Gareth's skin looked even more corpse-pale than usual and, though it wasn't fair to him, Brégenne experienced a fervent desire to be elsewhere. 'I need to finish the wards,' she said.

He frowned. 'I thought you just did them.'

'A few more won't hurt.' She swept off into the darkness, leaving him standing there, perplexed. She rounded a cluster of rocks and sank down on one, biting her knuckle. Gareth's intrusion had cut short her nightly practice. Practice which served to distract her from a thought that grew stronger with every step she took on Acrean soil.

Nediah was here – somewhere.

She'd worked hard to put him from her mind. She'd had plenty to keep her busy, after all – what with the Trade Assembly, Ümvast and Gareth's gauntlet. But now, with the end of their journey in sight, Brégenne's thoughts turned to the future. She and Nediah had parted in such strained circumstances. He'd told her he loved her and *she'd* told him to leave, while she stayed behind. Brégenne bit harder at her knuckle. She'd stayed and Kait had gone – Kait, who had once been Nediah's lover. They'd travelled together for months now. Who knew what might have happened between them?

Why should I care? Brégenne threw at the image of Kait's pleased little smile. *It doesn't make any difference to me.*

She stood up and strode angrily back to camp before her own voice could tell her she was a liar.

They had their first sight of Ben-haugr the following morning.

Gareth had led them, his steps unswerving, across the moorland. A herd of wild ponies frisked to the south, legs obscured by the long grasses. The day was as grey as the great stone tors that thrust up from the earth around them.

'We're close now,' Gareth said tensely, clutching the gauntlet. Brégenne noticed little wisps of cold rising from its frozen surface and the strange sigils began to thrum audibly like a low note on a lyre. They climbed a small rise and there, on the other side, lay the overgrown necropolis of Ben-haugr. It was a vast network of grassy mounds, linked by shattered stone. Some of the mounds had shed their green caps, showing bare roofs that curved down beneath the soil. Brégenne was silent. They all were, smothered by the pall of *loneliness* that hung over it all.

'It's huge,' Kul'Das whispered finally. 'How many are buried here?'

'According to Kyndra, Ben-haugr was built on the remains of a city called Kalast.' Brégenne clasped her elbows, hugging them close to her body. She fancied the cold wasn't just in the air. It seemed to flow from the very earth. 'There was a great battle here. The city fell.'

Gareth abruptly began to cough, his left hand raised to cover his mouth.

Alarmed, Brégenne steadied him. 'Gareth, what's wrong?'

'Smoke,' he said faintly and then he shook her off. 'I mean . . . I'm fine, Brégenne. It's this place, the memories. I can see them, smell them.'

Brégenne exchanged a look with Kul'Das. She suspected they shared the same thought: whatever corrupting power was in the gauntlet had grown stronger. They needed to find the other one and free Gareth before it was too late.

'I'm not mad,' he said angrily. 'There's something here, something keeping the land from forgetting.'

Before Brégenne could reply, he started down the hill. She and Kul'Das followed hastily, slipping on the silky grass. As they lost height, the mounds gained it, until they loomed like slumped giants, mossy chests stilled in death. Brégenne spotted a hint of road here and there, but most of Kalast had been swallowed by the earth, its buildings long since fallen. The silence was extreme; they'd left the wind behind on the hilltop.

'Can you feel that?' Kul'Das whispered. 'There's something here. Suffocating. I cannot describe it.'

Brégenne couldn't either. 'Hard to breathe,' she agreed, pulling at her collar.

Gareth glanced around. 'It's not safe for you,' he said. 'Go back.'

'We've come this far together.' Brégenne tried to ignore how tight her throat felt. 'I won't abandon you now.'

'You don't understand.' Gareth held her gaze. 'This is not a place for the living.'

'You're no safer than we,' Kul'Das said.

He shook his head and a bitter smile pulled at his lips. 'But I am, Kul'Das. I am.'

'We're fine,' Brégenne said more firmly than she felt. 'Let's just keep going.'

Gareth immediately turned westward, crossing over uneven ground that could conceal any number of horrors. The earth-works of the dead towered over them and it was all too easy to imagine their fragile top layer shearing away at the pressure of the bodies packed inside.

Then, without warning, Gareth's right arm lifted and he broke into a stumbling run. Brégenne heard his hiss of shock and she reached for him, but he was already several metres ahead, his gauntleted arm rigid before him, as if some unseen force had hold of it.

'Gareth!'

It was becoming harder to breathe. The suffocating pres-ence in the mounds pressed against her chest and Brégenne drew in great gulps of air. 'Gareth, stop!' she gasped.

'I can't!' She heard the panic in his voice and willed herself to go faster.

Up ahead, Brégenne caught sight of a much larger mound; long instead of circular, its shallow ends rising to a peak in the middle. She gave a shout of frustration. 'Do something,' she shot at Kul'Das.

'I . . . I don't know –' The woman beside her was in no better state. Kul'Das's brow creased, her hands beginning to glow, but Brégenne could see it in her eyes – she hadn't the first clue how to wield the Solar.

The walls of the mound loomed larger than ever. Mosses sheathed the stone, their slimy green blanket oddly menacing.

Gareth cried out, dug in his heels and slowed just enough for Brégenne and Kul'Das to grab hold of his waist. His arm was scant inches from the wall. Brégenne gritted her teeth, but the gauntlet's strength was incredible. Her fingers began to slip.

'No,' she gasped. 'Gareth!'

He managed a strangled scream before the gauntlet pulled him headfirst into the solid stone.

5

Hagdon

They say that when a wind sweeps through the blackened heart of the Deadwood, it brings with it the scent of fire. At least that's what James Hagdon had heard. He tilted his head back, sniffed the air, and, indeed, caught the acrid tang of charcoal.

He'd had little cause to visit the wood during his years in the army. A ravaged place, home to bandits and cutthroats, it had no strategic or economic importance. And as the Fist's general, he'd always had more pressing battles to fight. Hagdon shrugged deeper into his cloak. Every day, he strove to put that time behind him. Every day, it was a challenge.

'Is this the only way to Ben-haugr?'

Irilin rode beside him. The young Wielder's hair lay tangled in the feathers of her cloak; wind had left a dusting of ash on her temple and Hagdon felt a passing urge to brush it away. Instead he said, 'No, but it's the swiftest.'

The edge of the Deadwood loomed ahead of them; despite the distance they still had to cross, Hagdon could clearly see the line where scrubland met blackened earth. Irilin gave it a dark glance. 'I don't much like the look of it.'

'I thought you wanted to reach this Gareth as quickly as possible,' Hagdon replied mildly.

Out of the corner of his eye, he saw Irilin stiffen. 'Why are you doing this?' she asked with a hint of defiance. 'Why are you helping us find him?'

'I told you. It'll be good to have another Wielder on our side. Plus,' Hagdon added, squarely meeting her gaze, 'he's your friend.'

Irilin looked away, a faint flush in her cheeks.

Behind him, Hagdon could hear the tumbling tramp of many hooves. About fifty men and women accompanied him, all mantled in the black feathers of the Republic. Amon Taske, his old commandant – *and the man who offered me this job*, Hagdon thought wryly – led another group, aiming to gather intelligence on Iresonté. Hagdon's fist tightened on the reins. How long had she been planning this takeover? She'd not lifted a finger to help the emperor, but had calmly watched him bleed to death at Hagdon's feet. He fought back the memory. *It's over*, he told himself harshly. He led the Republic now, and that meant preventing Iresonté from marching the Fist into Rairam, the one land Sartya had never managed to conquer. If she dug in there, they'd never dislodge her.

Hagdon sighed. *I need more men.* The Republic might have contacts all over Acre, but using them to gather a force strong enough to challenge the Fist seemed impossible. Taske, however, was convinced of finding Sartyan soldiers still loyal to Hagdon, that once news of the emperor's death began to spread, they would come forward to join him.

Hagdon wasn't so sure. Having served in the Sartyan Fist for most of his life, he had been bred to obey, to respect the hierarchy, to stamp out any resistance.

Now he *was* the resistance.

'What are you thinking?' Irilin asked him.

'That Taske is wrong. We won't find many friends among the Fist.'

'Perhaps you are both wrong,' Irilin said, her eyes on the dark smudge of the Deadwood ahead of them. 'There *are* men loyal to you, but they won't come forward without a show of strength. The Republic is a fractured group with no base of operations, no visible presence.' She switched her gaze to him. 'If you were not already committed, would *you* side openly with us?'

Hagdon studied her. 'Taske claims the Republic has connections in all the major cities, including New Sartya.'

'Then use them.' She returned his gaze evenly. 'The time for secrecy is over. Someone has to come forward to lead.' Irilin raised an eyebrow. 'Do you want it to be Iresonté?'

She made a good point, Hagdon thought. They did need a solid, visible presence in Acre. If there *were* Sartyans sympathetic to the cause, they would not declare for the Republic without, as Irilin said, a show of strength. 'What do you propose?' he asked.

'Isn't there anywhere the Republic can call home?'

He shook his head. 'I don't believe so. While the emperor lived, it would have been too dangerous.'

'Well, then,' Irilin said, 'now that the emperor is dead, there is no reason not to establish the Republic as an official power. All you need is a base.' She paused. 'A fortress would be good.'

Hagdon chuckled. 'Spoken by someone who's spent most of her life in an impregnable mountain. If only there were a stray fortress just lying around.'

Irilin folded her arms, letting the reins rest in her lap. 'This is Acre. You're saying there isn't?'

'Of course there—' Hagdon reined in abruptly, held up a hand.

'What?'

'Horses ahead of us.'

Irilin tilted her head. 'Where? How do you know?'

'Hoof beats. Can't you hear?'

As if to confirm his words, Nediah and Kait cantered up beside them. 'People ahead.' Kait pointed vaguely to the north. There was ash in her hair too, grey upon brown.

'How many?' Hagdon snapped, feeling himself slide back into the habit of command.

'Twenty, perhaps more.' Nediah glanced at the sky; the sun had already slipped far down the horizon, weakening the Solar powers they both commanded.

'Don't worry,' Kait said, nudging the other Wielder. 'Nediah and I can deal with them.'

Nediah moved his horse away from her. 'You forget I'm not in the business of killing.'

His words deepened the spots of colour in Kait's cheeks. 'Fine,' she said, turning back to Hagdon. '*I'll* deal with them.'

Hagdon gave the signal to halt and the soldiers of the Republic formed up around him. They were only a league from the garrison at Artiba. It might be a normal patrol. Then again it might not – likely, Iresonté had some stealth force stationed in the old fort. One message from her could rouse fifty men against him.

The hoof beats were easily heard now, metal shoes ringing against dirt. Hagdon caught a glimpse of familiar red plate as the horsemen crested a rise in the land. The dying afternoon cast a bloody glow over their armour and Hagdon felt a strange pang that he no longer wore it. He counted swiftly; thirty, give or take a few. Could be better, could be worse. Much of the Republic was still untrained and those who were able to fight would struggle to match a soldier of the Fist. Better if it did not come to bloodshed. But that was a hope he couldn't afford to entertain.

Hagdon squinted at the group as they neared; of the uncovered faces, none were familiar. He felt the unease of those behind him in the shifting of their horses, in the creak of leather as hands curled around hilts.

The Sartyans reined in and there was silence as the two forces studied each other. One soldier raised the visor of their helm. Hagdon saw a woman with pale eyes under dark brows and, for a terrible, frozen moment, thought it was Iresonté herself. But this woman was older. Without a word, she reached down, untied a sack from her saddle straps and opened it. In one smooth motion, she drew out a head, still bloody at the neck and tossed it into the dirt at Hagdon's horse's feet. The face was obscured, but it made no difference: he'd recognize the mask of the stealth force anywhere.

'General,' the woman said and smacked a fist to her shoulder.

It took the relieved Hagdon several seconds to return the salute. 'Your name?' he asked, hearing his voice crack slightly.

'Mercia,' she said. 'Lieutenant of the Artiban Garrison.'

'Mercia.' Hagdon nodded. 'First, general is no longer my rank. Second, where is your captain?'

'Disinclined to break with tradition,' Mercia said in the crisp tones of the Vordon lakelanders. 'He will swear allegiance to Iresonté.' Her lip curled. 'Her agents were in and out faster than a gull on a fish. I don't know what this one offered him –' she nodded at the head – 'but I ensured she wouldn't make the same offer elsewhere.'

'The emperor is dead.' Hagdon felt a numbing chill in the pit of his stomach; it had been there ever since he'd driven his sword into his ruler's chest. 'You know this, I presume?'

For the first time, Mercia hesitated. 'Yes.'

'So you know that you'd be joining a traitor.' He paused. 'A murderer.'

Mercia swallowed. Other Sartyans exchanged glances. Hagdon was aware he'd confirmed the story Iresonté must have spread. Perhaps these soldiers had believed it to be just that, a tall tale of treason to discredit the ex-general, to discourage any desire to rally behind him.

They needed an explanation, but Hagdon wasn't sure what to give them. He had no wish to talk about his nephew, Tristan, dead at the emperor's hands, or his sister, the boy's mother, swinging from the tree in her little garden. He focused on those faces turned to him, trying to banish Tristan's.

'Change is coming. The emperor was a symbol of the old order, an order that has been falling apart for twenty years. Our strength, our success, was based on ambertrix, not good government. Our resources dwindle, outlying territories falling into poverty. Slavers once again thrive in the Beaches. Did the emperor address any of this? No. He was content to see Acre dissolve around us.'

Hagdon heard mutters; whether they were mutters of agreement, he couldn't tell.

'In the days following Rairam's return, we need new leadership, a body comprised not only of Heartlanders, but of people of every territory. I will not ask you to swear allegiance to *me*,' he added, meeting as many gazes as he could. 'If you join us, you will no longer be part of the Fist, but the new Republic.'

More muttering, and this time it was animated. *Too much too soon?* Hagdon wondered. He hurried on. 'Iresonté is waging the wrong war. We cannot afford to treat Rairam as an enemy when the true and greater threat is Khronosta.' He caught Irilin nodding out of the corner of his eye and, strangely heartened, added, 'They seek to change history, to alter what has been.'

Silence.

Hagdon almost let slip a wry smile. Once, he too would have found it hard to believe. He took a breath. 'The Starborn works to stop them in the past. I work to build Acre a future.'

He'd been prepared for it, known it was coming, but the hostility on every face still shocked him.

'You're allied with *her*?' Mercia said, disgust plain in her voice. 'She slaughtered five hundred of us.'

'An act my poor leadership forced her to commit,' Hagdon said firmly. 'The deaths of my men rest, as ever, on my shoulders.'

A volatile mix of unease and anger rippled back through the thirty or so Sartyans. Any hope of an alliance might have ended there, but for Irilin. She urged her horse past Hagdon's, stopping in front of Mercia. 'Kyndra is my friend,' she said bravely into the face of the other woman's anger. 'She may have made mistakes, mistakes for which she punished herself far more severely than you ever could, but she's also a young woman who shouldered the burden of leadership because no one else wanted it.' She paused, looked to the east. 'She reunited Rairam with Acre, she came for peace not war. And now she works to save the very people who captured her, cornered her and forced her to kill when all she wished was compromise. I know there is bad blood between you, and I'm sorry for the part I played in that.' She glanced over her shoulder at Hagdon, at his face, at the scratches long since faded from his cheek. 'But why make an enemy of her when there are enemies enough already?' She smiled then, albeit grimly. 'I watched her fight *du-alakat*. You'd much rather stand beside that power than against it.'

In the silence that followed her speech, it seemed Irilin abruptly became aware of where she was and what she was doing. Flushing, she glanced at Hagdon again and he rode up to join her. 'What do you say, Lieutenant Mercia?' he asked the pale-eyed soldier. 'Will we fight this day? Or will you and your men stay to hear the whole story?'

He could almost feel the Wielders tensing, ready to call down fire at a moment's notice. Beside him, Irilin trembled slightly, but she sat tall in her saddle. Without her Lunar power, she was defenceless and she knew it. Hagdon admired her courage.

Finally, Mercia sighed. 'You should get her to write your speeches, Hagdon.'

They told their story beneath the eaves of the Deadwood. The charred forest loomed on their left; they were camped at its fringes, waiting until they had light on their side.

'The Sisters have expanded their territory,' Mercia said, biting into a steaming haunch of venison. She wiped the juice from her chin. 'Their numbers too. We've been half expecting a raid.'

'The Sisters are thieves and smugglers,' Hagdon said, frowning. 'Why would they attack you?'

'We have a long-standing agreement that they bring us aberrations in exchange for coin.' Mercia gave a grunt of displeasure. 'But they grow increasingly bold in their demands.'

Across the fire, Irilin looked up sharply. 'My friends passed through there,' she said. 'Do you think they ran into these women?'

'More than likely.' Mercia gestured expansively with the haunch. 'The Sisters know the Deadwood, have turned it into a trap. You see, aberrations fleeing Sartyan patrols will take the forest road rather than pass too close to the garrison.' She shook her head. 'Caught between the two of us, poor fools.'

'You pity them?' The question was out before Hagdon could stop it; he felt the chill around the fire as the Wielders turned frosty gazes upon him.

'I do,' Mercia said, ignoring the tension and ripping off another mouthful of meat. She chewed slowly. 'Buying aberrations only to put them to work in Parakat – it's no better than slavery.'

Irilin closed her open mouth. She looked somewhat chastened as she stared at Mercia. 'Do more Sartyans share your opinion?' she asked.

'Good venison.' Mercia finished the haunch, licked her fingers. 'A few. Others believe the aberrations should be restrained for their own protection. The rest take the emperor's line and think to work them to death.'

Hagdon could have sworn Irilin flashed him a dark glance. For a moment he shifted uncomfortably before some of his old defiance returned. 'Years ago,' he said, 'when I was assigned to the prison wagons, we stopped at a village known to be sheltering aberrations. It was a family – the father and all three children born with the ability. When he saw us coming, he told his children to go inside and lock the doors.' Hagdon could hear it in his voice, the dispassion he'd cultivated over years of doing the emperor's work. He glanced at his listeners. Kait looked as fierce as she always did, Nediah simply sad. Irilin's eyes were narrowed; he couldn't read her expression at all.

'I won't repeat the details,' he said more harshly than he intended. 'The father set the house ablaze and then himself. His wife burned while trying to rescue their children. No matter what we tried, we couldn't put out the flames.' He paused. 'That's why aberrations go to Parakat. They are unstable, a threat to their communities, to themselves.'

'They wouldn't be if you just left them alone,' Kait said sharply. 'People don't like being imprisoned.' Her eyes were haunted, but not, Hagdon thought, by his story. 'You *forced* that man into a corner. The only choice you left him with was whether to take his children's lives before you could.'

'What will happen to Parakat now the emperor is gone?' Nediah asked. For a quiet man, his tone was unusually direct.

Hagdon rubbed his forehead. 'When Iresonté looks at an aberration, she sees potential instead of a problem. I don't know what she plans for them.'

'Tava worked for her,' Irilin said.

Hagdon remembered the boy, his amber eyes and hollow loyalty. 'Yes, but she miscalculated, didn't she? Tava was not as tame as he appeared.'

Irilin scowled. 'We're not animals.'

'A metaphor, sorry.'

Nediah had been listening closely, hands steepled beneath his chin. 'The aberrations in Parakat have no love for Iresonté,' he said, 'or the army. The only way they'd cooperate is under duress.' He dropped his hands, leaned forward. 'But we can offer them far more than she can.'

A slow smile crept over Kait's face. 'Freedom in exchange for their service.'

'We'll teach them, hone their skills.' Nediah's eyes were bright. 'How many in Parakat, Hagdon?'

Hagdon shook his head. 'I can't say.'

'Between fifty and a hundred, I think,' Mercia spoke up. 'Parakat is built to hold far more, but few survive a year there.'

'The lieutenant has a point,' Hagdon said. 'Many will be too young, too old or too ill to fight their way out.' Despite his words, his mind had begun to turn over the possibility. He'd seen Kait's and Nediah's power, had Irilin's turned against him. The aberrations were weaker, but only, perhaps, through lack of training. Although he couldn't deny that the Republic needed the numbers, the thought of letting them loose raised the hairs on the back of his neck.

'Then we will need a very good plan,' Kait said.

Hagdon studied the three Wielders in the firelight. 'You are seriously considering this?'

'Can we afford not to?' Nediah rejoined. 'You say you don't know what Iresonté plans, but she's seen our abilities and has a history of making use of them. If we don't go after the aberrations, she will. She'll use her new position to change the rules, offer them terms before we can. If conditions in Parakat are as bad as you say, few people would turn down such an offer, no matter who was making it.'

The cogs in Hagdon's mind ground faster. He didn't care for the idea, but if it gave them an opportunity to out-manoeuvre Iresonté . . . 'Let's say we set Parakat in our sights,' he began, 'we don't have the numbers to storm it by force.'

'Then we'll play Iresonté at her own game,' Irilin said.

Hagdon thought he could discern the shape of an idea in her face. 'We trick our way inside.'

He raised an eyebrow. 'You have a plan?'

'I do.' Irilin flashed him a crooked smile. 'But it requires Lieutenant Mercia and her men.'

'Breaking into Parakat?' Mercia shrugged. 'It's not like I had anything better to do.' And she ripped off another haunch of venison.

6

Kyndra

Ma stood in the centre of the mandala, booted feet planted on the seven-pointed junction where the dragon's blood pooled. Eyes closed, she muttered under her breath. It sounded more like cursing than arcane words. Kyndra wasn't sure the Khronostians even used words as part of their rituals. The scions of time were a mystery to the stars.

Ma extended her arms. Air distorted around her; she appeared to ripple. Char gave a grunt of alarm, but he didn't move from his place. The bloodstained sand turned white around Ma's boots, the cleansing spreading across the complex lines of the mandala, until it reached the wide circle that encompassed it. Here Ma seemed to pause. Sweat beaded her forehead; her breath came in gulps. She extended her arms further, turning her palms forward, and the dragon's blood smoked as it left the sand.

Kyndra found herself breathing shallowly. The chamber had grown close, as if a storm brewed between its walls. When she drew air into her lungs, it had a sour tang. She almost expected lightning to flash against the roof.

Char's hackles were raised now; a low growl issued from his throat. Above them, the great dragon began to stir as the blood disappeared from the mandala, leaving its sand pristine. Wind struck Kyndra, sent her stumbling back: the sweep of a huge wing. Ma gritted her teeth, her gaze fixed on the Lleu-yelin. There was a moment when they locked eyes, the dragon's glittering and dark, Ma's warm brown. Kyndra wasn't sure but something seemed to pass between them. The ancient creature turned his head to look at Char and spoke in his own language, a language Char had never learned. But Kyndra knew it, as *Ansu* knew it.

Vengeance, the dragon said in a howl of pain and rage. *May your teeth meet in flesh.*

If he wanted to ask Char's name, there was no time. With a tremendous crash, the dragon's emaciated body fell to earth, decaying, becoming bones before their eyes: twenty years of postponed time passing in an instant. Char gave a cry of his own, somewhere between horror and anguish.

Ma stood tall as the dragon's bones toppled around her. The pressure in the room grew until Kyndra felt a trickle of blood run from one ear. She crouched, wrapping herself in *Tyr*, but the star couldn't protect her against the sudden surge of time suppressed. Before it could catch her and Char up in its stream, Ma brought her hands down sharply and the storm seemed to reverse itself, spiralling back towards the woman who stood at its heart.

The ouroboros on Ma's palms flared to life. Veins of light spread from them up her bare arms, her neck and cheeks, turning her eyes white. For a moment, her whole form was ablaze, a pillar that connected her to the mandala, then the intricate pattern was gone, seared from the stone, and Ma fell to one knee, hand braced against the floor.

Char had covered his head with a wing. Now he rushed forward, nosing at Ma until she raised an arm, putting it over his long neck. With his help, she stumbled to her feet. Her eyes were still white, but she blinked the brown back into them. 'It's done,' she sighed.

'What did you do?' It was *Era*'s question, the star's interest keen on Kyndra's tongue.

Ma took a few moments to compose herself. 'I broke the link, absorbed the mandala's power.'

'Couldn't the eldest have tried the same?'

Ma shook her head, her expression grim. 'Besides freeing the Lleu-yelin, the act of absorbing it would have torn him apart. Instead, he will take what he needs from my people, no matter the cost to them.'

Char gave a grunt that sounded like reproach. 'You didn't say it was so dangerous.'

'I did not,' Ma agreed. Her smile was brief and sad. 'But you forget. I am Khronos, the first. I taught them *everything*.'

Kyndra gazed at the pile of scale and bone that moments ago had been a dragon and felt a flicker of melancholy. 'It is a shame it had to be this way,' she heard herself say.

Char swung his head to stare at her, yellow eyes aglow in the dusty air. It was a strange look, appraising, and Kyndra didn't understand it. Uncomfortable for some reason, she glanced aside.

'They are coming,' Char said suddenly. Ma let go of him and they all moved to stand before the rounded double doors of the chamber. When they opened, Kyndra could only stare, left breathless by the majesty of the Lleu-yelin.

There were around a dozen of them, all seven feet tall and humanoid in appearance – just as Char had looked after the first part of his change was complete. Long, wild hair swept from every head in shades ranging from midnight to dawn grey to fire. Ridged cheekbones, pointed ears, their only adornment sinewy ribbons looped about each wrist. Kyndra had to crane her neck to look up into their slitted eyes. She couldn't read their expressions and it occurred to her how this would appear: the three of them spattered with blood from the battle, standing among the bones of a dragon.

In moments, they were surrounded. The eyes of the Lleuyelin went straight to Char. He was hard to miss, after all. A crimson-scaled female came towards him, and Char, to Kyndra's surprise, dipped his head in obeisance.

'Who are you, risling?'

Char brought his head up. 'I don't understand.'

'She asked you who you were,' Kyndra supplied helpfully. Char gave her a look and she shrugged. 'Do you want me to translate, or not?'

'There is no need,' the female said with a slight frown, reverting to the common tongue. It sounded oddly sibilant in her mouth. 'I asked after your parentage.'

Before Char could answer, another female snapped, 'This will wait.' Golden-haired, tawny-scaled, she rounded on Kyndra and Ma. 'Who are you? Where are the Khronostians?'

'Gone,' Ma said calmly. 'The battle is long over.'

A ripple ran around the Lleu-yelin circle and Kyndra couldn't help noticing how long their talons were. Gazes strayed to the remains of the dragon, to the great skull that rested nearby. 'But we felt the Chimer's passing,' one said, plainly confused, 'only minutes ago.'

The tawny female peered over Ma's head at the heap of bones. 'We felt his pain and his thirst for vengeance.' The slitted eyes she turned back to them were full of suspicion. 'Why would he feel such?'

'You were imprisoned in a pocket of static time for twenty years,' Ma said casually, as if something so remarkable were commonplace. 'The Khronostian eldest used your Chimer's life-force to maintain the prison. He was the focus.' She bowed her head. 'I broke the link that kept him alive. It was the only way.'

'She speaks the truth,' Kyndra said to the tawny female. 'I know it must sound confusing, but we're not your enemies.'

Gleaming eyes traced the patterns on Kyndra's face. 'You are Starborn,' the female replied, seeming surprised. 'The Starborn do not choose their allies lightly.'

'No,' Kyndra agreed.

The female pointed at Ma. 'But *she* is Khronostian, no? I see the marks on her hands.'

'Ma left her people. It's down to her that you're free now.'

Silence. Most faces wore confusion. *And I don't blame them*, Kyndra thought. For the Lleu-yelin, no time had passed since the attack twenty years before.

'Kierik is dead, then,' a third Lleu-yelin spoke up, a male near the back of the group.

'I am his daughter.' Kyndra felt nothing now at the truth of it. 'I was forced to break his power, restore Rairam to Acre.'

For the first time, the tawny female seemed unsure. 'Rairam, the lost continent, has returned? When did this happen?'

'About four months ago.'

The female exchanged looks with the other Lleu-yelin before turning to the steps outside where a fully fledged dragon crouched, his scales the darkest blue. They locked gazes; silent words seeming to pass between them. Her mate, Kyndra guessed.

'Much has changed while you have lain unknowing,' Ma said.

'Normally, I would take you to the Chimer and let him decide.' The female's golden eyes returned to Kyndra. 'But we have always respected the Starborn. If *you* vouch for the Khronostian's story and agree to tell us it in full, we will let her live.'

'What do you remember?' Kyndra asked curiously.

A snarl grew on the female's lips. 'Fighting,' she said. 'Chaos. The attack came as a surprise. We were unprepared, had no time to shelter our young, but still we were winning.' Amidst growls of agreement, she added, 'And then I felt the Chimer die. It couldn't be – I swear the Khronostians hadn't passed beyond the outer circle.'

'Twenty years separated that attack and your Chimer's death,' Kyndra said.

The Lleu-yelin slowly shook her head. Others echoed her movement. 'I cannot believe it. Do the children of Khronos truly possess such power?'

Out of the corner of her eye, Kyndra saw Ma flinch. 'They do,' the mercenary said. 'And they only grow stronger.'

The female fixed her with a hostile gaze. 'And what of your part in this, Khronostian? Why have you come here now, professing friendship?'

'I was with the *du-alakat* that attacked Magtharda,' Ma said, ignoring the flexing of claws, the angry hiss that swept around the Lleu-yelin circle. 'I was a child. I could do nothing to stop them.' She gestured at Char. 'But I could do one thing. I could save an infant, separated from his mother in the chaos of battle.'

Everyone's attention returned to Char. He was silent, caught up in Ma's tale. Kyndra guessed that this was the first time he'd heard it told truthfully.

'I took him from here,' Ma said. 'I left my people and I raised him among humans.'

Sounds of disgust greeted her words. 'Humans would not have taken well to one of ours,' the tawny female said, folding her arms. 'How did you keep him safe from them?'

'By delaying his change.'

The Lleu-yelin's lip curled. 'Such a thing has never been done. It was shameful to force him to wear the human skin past his time.'

'It kept him alive and undetected by my people,' Ma snapped. Char was one of the only subjects over which she lost her composure. 'I knew they would come for me. And when they did, they would discover who I was protecting.'

'The change cannot be denied forever,' the female said after a moment. Her mouth twitched. 'I expect it was something to behold.'

'You could say that,' Kyndra agreed.

'Who gave him his name?'

'I did,' she said. 'But I didn't know it until I knew my own.'

The Lleu-yelin did not ask her what she meant. Instead the tawny female addressed Char. 'I am known as Sesh. What is your name, risling?'

The atmosphere in the chamber seemed to solidify. 'Orkaan,' Char told them.

'It is proof beyond all you have said,' Sesh murmured. 'When I saw you last, you were no larger than my forearm.' She glanced over her shoulder at her mate. 'Go. Bring Ekaar.'

The blue dragon swung his head in acknowledgement,

spread mottled wings and took off. When he was gone, Sesh turned back to Char. 'Your scales,' she said, half lifting a hand as if to touch them. 'You have her mark about you.'

'Who is Ekaar?' But Char's yellow eyes were widening; Kyndra could tell that he already knew.

'She is your mother,' Sesh said.

7

Gareth

The first thing Gareth knew was darkness.

It was deep, this darkness, and close. Instead of the heaviness of stone, the weight of earth pressed upon him, musty, dank. Being buried alive might feel like this, sound muted by dirt – he could hear Brégenne's calls as if through water, distorted by the smothering walls of the mound. But he wasn't alive, Gareth thought grimly. He belonged here in the silence of the tomb.

The gauntlet gave off a fitful eldritch light. Under its illumination, he saw a path curving away from him. Humps arrested its shallow descent at even intervals. Gareth didn't want to know what lay beneath them.

The ceiling was low. He reached up, running his hands along the packed dirt. If it weren't for the gauntlet, he could punch his way out with the Solar, but it was too painful to wield. *And the gauntlet would never let me leave so easily.*

Gareth turned back to the winding path. It rounded a corner a little way ahead, dropping out of sight. Staring at it, wondering whether it led to an exit, he realized that whatever force had dragged him through solid earth had gone, the compulsion ebbing away now that he was here.

It was strange to feel fear without *feeling* it. No sweaty palms or racing heart. No gooseflesh or hairs standing on end. Perhaps it was this which moved his feet – the fact that what was dead could not die. *There are worse things*, he thought, or the *other* did. The presence seemed stronger here inside the mound. Snippets of that strange, familiar language ran through his head. Part of him did not understand; another part did.

He turned the corner to find more passage. It reminded him of Naris and his journey through the archives. So far away now that it might as well have happened to someone else. *Shika*, he thought suddenly. *Shika would hate this*. Because worms burrowed through the walls, their bodies pale in the sickly light of the gauntlet. Gareth fixed his gaze ahead and kept on, gradually leaving the earth and its creatures behind.

Stone began to line the passageway. Carvings that looped and spiralled until they were lost in themselves. Gareth reached out, rested his cold fingertips against the colder wall. Again there was something familiar about the markings; he felt like a stranger in a foreign land instinctively recognizing words that ordered his death. He took his hand away.

He no longer needed the gauntlet's glow. Rusted candelabra stood here and there, flames tinged an unearthly blue. *Who lit them?* he wondered, *How long have they burned? What power rules here?* Gareth shook his head. He knew what power ruled here, he'd seen it in his dreams. These empty passages invited him to meet it.

Rounding the next corner, he saw a pillared room, lit with more candelabra. The passage he followed ran right round it and a rough balcony and steps led down to the sunken floor.

Gareth stopped, staring at the great table laid as if for a feast. Tarnished pitchers, once filled perhaps with wine, lay cobwebbed among silver plates. Bones rested there, the flesh of whatever animal they belonged to having long withered around them. Little bowls of salt were the only things to have survived the centuries. It was a feast for the dead and stone chairs circled the table.

Some were occupied.

Gareth took an automatic step back, scanning the chamber frantically before he realized they were just skeletons, their bony wrists propped upon the armrests. Several reclined, as if replete after a large meal, others sat straight. Rags hung from their shoulders, the remnants of once-fine clothes. Whoever had arranged them as corpses had a dubious sense of humour, Gareth thought, or, rather, no sense of humour at all. There was an air of utter seriousness about the tableau, as if this macabre gathering was meant to last for eternity. Studying the skeleton at the head of the table, he wondered who it had worn in life. It clutched a silver cup in its left hand, ivory digits curled around the metal, on the cusp of raising it to drink. A sword leaned against the chair.

Gareth's foot touched the top step. He hadn't meant to descend, but rather to follow the balcony round to the opposite side. But something about the scene called to him, as if a part of him wished to take a place at the table, to feast on dust and memory. Moving slowly, he walked down the wide stairs and across the floor. Close up, the table appeared larger, long enough to seat twenty men. Gareth peered into one of the pitchers; only a rusty patina remained to stain its sides.

A flutter of movement caught his eye and he froze. Slowly,

slowly, the skeletal warrior in the top chair turned to look at him.

Gareth watched with dreadful fascination as its fingers closed tighter around the silver cup. They squeezed the metal until it crumpled like paper. With the same slow grace, the warrior stood, easing out of the chair. It stooped to retrieve its sword, gave it a practice swing. The gesture was so human, so out of place that Gareth felt light-headed. *The dead don't walk.*

'*Not unless I ask them to.*'

The voice was both within and without. Gareth felt it resonate in his chest cavity; saw it shiver through the walls of the great tomb, as if to imbue the stone with life. Other figures rose, skeletal hands reaching for blades: the only things not rusted or tarnished, Gareth realized, stumbling back. He was ungainly in this decaying body, his movements stiff and stilted – unlike the fleshless warriors. They came for him with deliberate, unhurried steps.

One swing of that greatsword would sever limbs. It wouldn't kill him – at least Gareth didn't think so – but how would he walk or fight? So he drew his mother's sword, the Kul blade she'd hurled at him when he'd left home, and brought it up before his face.

He backed towards the staircase, but it was too wide, too open. He needed to find a bottleneck, somewhere they could only come at him one at a time. Turning his stumbling into a measured retreat, Gareth edged his way up the steps and along the corridor that formed the balcony, glancing over his shoulder to check the way was clear. The warriors followed with no sense of urgency; to them, Gareth guessed, time had lost all meaning.

The first lunged at him just as he reached the bend in the passage. He caught the blow on his sword, but it staggered him;

the warrior's strength was amazing. With a cry of effort, he forced the thing back, but it swung again, uncaring of the gap it left in its defences. Gareth thrust his sword between its ribs and tore downwards. He expected to feel the pelvis shatter; instead, his sword was wrenched out of his hand as the warrior stepped back, Gareth's blade stuck fast in its lower ribs.

For a moment, Gareth blinked, stunned, then he had to leap aside as the greatsword came again, slicing a shallow gash in his chest. He clamped a hand to the wound, but there was nothing, no blood, no pain, and he found himself smiling, a rictus grin. He tripped the warrior, planted a foot on its fallen femur and, with another shout, pulled his blade free.

The attacking warriors had no throats to cry out their challenge. Even in the midst of battle, Gareth wondered how long it would be until his own larynx decayed to the point where he could no longer speak. Was this the fate that awaited him? The dead came at him, each giving way to another as they failed to draw blood. But nothing Gareth did could harm them either. There was an archway on the far side of the balcony, leading deeper into the tombs. Another snatched glance revealed a kind of portcullis, its mechanism rusty but seemingly undamaged. If he could reach it . . .

Another blow parried, another warrior held at bay. Gareth began to inch along the balcony, rounding the corner, keeping his opponents always in sight. He was steps away from the portcullis door when the nearest warrior's hand shot out, catching him off guard. Gareth's sword skittered uselessly off its breastbone, severing the decaying straps of an ancient cuirass. The next moment, thin fingers closed around his throat.

The grip would have crushed the windpipe of a living man. Gareth found himself wondering whether, if the skeletal warrior had had a face, it would have worn consternation. He backed up, taking the thing with him, until he was underneath the gate. The mechanism was little more than a handle set into a metal plate. Gareth struck it with the hilt of his sword.

He leapt back, as the portcullis plummeted. Its downward spikes missed his nose by inches, but ripped the warrior away from him. Pinned to the stone floor, all semblance of life left the creature; it became a shapeless pile of bones and rotting cloth. With a grunt of disgust, Gareth plucked the dismembered hand from his throat. It fell to dust between his fingers.

When he looked up, the other warriors simply stood there, studying him. Even though the gate stood between them, the regard of the dead drove Gareth back until a bend in the corridor blocked them from view. He could still hear them, though; the grating jangle of ancient armour, the sheathing of swords as they left the gate. They would find another way through. The thought was a chill one. *They won't give up.*

His only option was to go on and hope he lost the warriors in this maze of chambers.

Before Gareth could take another step, wind roared through the corridor and knocked him off his feet. '*Hverr nálgask sjá stadr?*'

The voice came and went with the wind. This time, he felt no kinship with it. Gareth hauled himself up with the help of a torch bracket. 'Who are you?' His shout was more of a croak. He watched the straight corridor ahead for any sign of movement, but there was none and the voice did not answer.

He couldn't afford to waste time here. The warriors knew Ben-haugr; it wouldn't take them long to catch up with him. Holding tightly to his mother's blade, Gareth set off down the corridor. When he reached an intersection, he didn't hesitate but took the left passage, prompted silently by the gauntlet.

'*Hví ydarr ki svar?*'

Buffeted by the wind, Gareth straightened, struck out again.

'*Why do you not answer?*'

This time, he weathered the wind, braced himself against a spiral-carved wall.

'*You have the blood, but not the tongue.*' Gareth thought he detected faint disgust beneath the confusion. '*And you think to challenge me?*'

'I'm here for the gauntlet.' His voice wavered, partly with the effort it cost to force it through his throat.

'*You wear what is mine.*' Anger now. '*You are here to return it and to die.*'

'I am already dead,' Gareth whispered, but the voice heard him.

'*Your death is a gift from Hond'Myrkr. Few would consider it such.*' Amusement. '*Come to me and I will take it from you.*'

'Hond'Myrkr,' Gareth murmured and the gauntlet gave a dark pulse. 'So that is your name.'

'*A true son of Yrmfast would know this. You are unworthy.*'

'We'll see,' Gareth said. He tried to inject strength into his failing voice. 'When I come for you.'

'*Come, then,*' Kingswold whispered.

8

Hagdon

'Soon we'll have two more Wielders on our side when we go to Parakat,' Irilin said to Hagdon the next morning as they wove their way between the Deadwood's blackened trees.

'The Republic needs all the help it can get.' His horse's ear twitched irritably; Hagdon leaned forward and brushed off some ash. 'In theory, freeing the aberrations is a sound idea. In reality, potentially suicidal.'

Irilin laughed. 'Don't forget you have me.'

'I couldn't,' he murmured.

'Wait until you meet Brégenne,' she said rather quickly. 'She's a Lunar too, but much stronger.' There was no jealousy in her voice, only admiration. 'That's why I don't fear for Gareth's life. Brégenne will look after him.'

'Tell me more about your friend and this gauntlet of his,' Hagdon said.

Irilin had only given him a brief version of the story. The full tale, as she told it now, went right back to Naris and the night she, Shika, Gareth and Kyndra had sneaked into the archives. Hagdon had a vision of them all, out of bed like errant children, and felt uncomfortable. 'It's easy to forget how young you are,' he said, thinking of Kyndra. Eighteen years old and already she'd done so much. At her age, he'd only just received his first commission, a young officer, wet behind the ears and hungry for command. Foolish.

'I'll be twenty-two in a month,' Irilin said stiffly, snapping him back to the present. 'I'm not a child.' Chagrined, perhaps, at her own words, she flushed.

'I didn't mean to imply that you were,' he answered carefully. 'What happened next?'

'When the Nerian attacked, Gareth put on the gauntlet. He didn't know it wouldn't come off again. Now they believe it belonged to Kingswold, one of the cursed pair he wore into battle.'

'Kingswold . . .' Hagdon nodded to himself. 'Yes, I've heard the story. A master warrior, leader of the famous knights.' He sighed. 'Slaughtered by Sartya at Kalast. They came from the tribes of Yrmfast.'

'In Rairam, it's pronounced Ümvast. Gareth's home –' Irilin paused – 'that's interesting. Gareth finding it is almost like fate.'

'I don't believe in fate. It's too easy to shirk responsibility in its name.' Hagdon knew his tone was bitter, but he couldn't lighten it. 'We must be held accountable for our actions.'

'Including you?'

Her gaze was direct. 'Especially me,' Hagdon said. He did not look away.

They didn't talk much after that, though the silence wasn't an unpleasant one. Hagdon found himself remembering his manservant, Carn, not ragged and ripped as he had last seen him, but as he had been in the days they'd travelled together.

He remembered the banter they'd shared, Carn's laments over Hagdon's appearance, mocking words softened by a grin.

His eyes prickled. Shocked, he blinked rapidly, took several deep breaths. Irilin wasn't looking his way and he swiftly dragged a sleeve across his face. He couldn't remember the last time he'd wept. Even when he'd found his sister's body in the garden; Paasa – driven to suicide by her son's murder. His anger at the emperor had hardened any tears into ice. Only Carn and his easy friendship had ever been able to thaw it. Perhaps his brother might have too, but Hagdon hadn't seen Mikael for years. His own duties kept him busy in the far south.

'Wait.' Irilin held up a hand. She pulled on her horse's reins and slid out of the saddle almost before the animal stopped moving. Hagdon reined in too, watching the young woman as she bent down. 'There are tracks here,' she said.

Hagdon dismounted. Crouching beside her, he drew a finger through the ash. 'Recent,' he agreed.

'They lead north-west.' Irilin smiled. 'We're on the right path.'

He stood up, offering her a hand. After a moment's hesitation, she took it. Her fingers were small and warm.

'What is it?'

Hagdon quickly let go of Irilin's hand and stepped back to show Nediah their find. 'Tracks,' he said, 'and not a day old, I'm guessing.'

'It has to be Brégenne and Gareth,' Irilin added. She looked happier than she had in days.

The Wielder glanced at the scuffed footprints; when it came, his smile was a little strained. 'That's good,' he said finally. Kait neither dismounted nor bothered to hide her ill humour. She also ignored Nediah when he attempted to speak to her. Hagdon remounted, wondering what had upset the woman.

An hour's ride later, they found an arrow sunk firmly into blackened wood. It was about head height for someone standing; Hagdon leaned over and yanked it free.

'Let me see.' Mercia stroked a thumb over its grey fletching. 'The Sisters use arrows like these,' she said, her eyes sweeping their immediate area with a soldier's practised vigilance. 'I think your friends might indeed have met with them. Look there.'

Hagdon followed her gesture and saw blood, garish in the monochrome world of the Deadwood. It was concentrated in one patch; drops freckled the ashen ground around it, as if the wounded party had thrashed or grappled with an opponent.

Nediah's face was grim. 'They can't be far,' the healer said before dismounting to run a finger through the mix of blood and ash. 'Yes. It's only hours old.'

'I suggest we split up,' Mercia said. 'We may have a sizable force, but we're deep in the Sisters' territory and I don't know their numbers. Takendo always was careful to keep that information close.' She looked at Hagdon. 'We don't want them to flank us. We've men enough to fan out and flares enough to send up a warning.'

Hagdon regarded her through narrowed eyes. After the incident at Khronosta, when Iresonté had abandoned him to the mercy of the *du-alakat*, he'd sworn not to trust so easily again.

Mercia's smile was crooked. 'No, I'm not working with the Sisters and I don't intend to betray you.' She swept an arm at his followers. 'But feel free to send some of your people with me.'

'Forgive my caution, but I'll do that.' Hagdon nodded at the man and woman Taske had appointed his lieutenants. 'Hu, choose ten others and accompany Mercia north. Avery, you parallel us to the south. The Wielders and I will follow the trail.'

Avery frowned. 'That doesn't leave you with much backup, Commander.'

Hagdon waved away her concern. 'I have the Wielders, remember.' He smiled tightly at Kait and Nediah. 'They're more than enough on their own.'

Kait bared her teeth at him.

When the afternoon began to fail, however, evening filtering between the trunks, Hagdon had to admit that perhaps he'd miscalculated. They had ridden the day away, following the scuffed trail through the Deadwood, constantly alert. Now he could feel his concentration waning. If this was part of the Sisters' plan, it was a sound tactic, one employed by thieves and bandits, groups that relied not on military prowess but on surprise.

'Only minutes,' Nediah told him softly, 'then we'll have to rely on Irilin.'

'You say that like it's a bad thing,' the young woman complained.

Kait waved a hand. 'Blades are blades, whether they're made of metal or flame.' She raised an eyebrow at Hagdon. 'And our *commander* here isn't without ability.'

Hagdon tested the edge of the handaxe that hung from a loop on his belt. He felt the weight of the sword strapped across his back, a dagger at his waist, another hidden in his boot. Kait was right. They *should* be able to handle an attack.

When it became necessary for Irilin to light their way, the silver glow made Hagdon uncomfortable; he felt as if he stood under a spotlight. 'We need to stop,' he told the others. 'We're too vulnerable here. With a camp, we can at least stand sentry.'

He glanced at Irilin. 'If the Sisters see that light, they'll know it isn't natural. Mercia said they make a living hunting aberrations.'

'I wish you wouldn't use that word,' she muttered. 'Aberration implies that there's something wrong with us. We're Wielders.'

'Sorry,' Hagdon said absently. His senses were taut, primed for the slightest movement. They halted in the lee of a large boulder, part of a series scattered east to west across this part of the wood. With lack of movement came a greater stillness; the darkness seemed to conceal a myriad host; little sounds that could have been footfalls in ash, an exhaled breath, or merely wind. The sharp, burned tang of the forest filled Hagdon's nostrils, obscuring any possible scent of sweat, or old leather, such as a group of bandits might wear.

When the horses were lightly tethered, he said, 'Keep alert. I don't want—'

The widening of Nediah's eyes was his only warning. Sword in hand, Hagdon whirled around, his blade clashing against another wielded by a dark-eyed woman, two horizontal stripes crossing her left cheek. She swung her blade down and disengaged with a snarl. Now that she'd broken cover, others emerged from the shadows, swiftly surrounding them. Before he could tell her not to, Irilin blazed silver.

'I thought we saw a little aberration magic,' one of the women said. She held a crossbow levelled at Irilin, two points of blue glowing on its frame. 'If you come quietly, child, I won't have to use this.'

The pause she left was punctuated by the ring of steel. Kait stood ready, twin blades in hand, radiant with the thrill of anticipated violence. Hagdon scanned the darkness, trying to gauge their opponents' numbers.

Irilin answered with a wave of force, so that the woman with the crossbow fell to one knee. In the time that bought her, she raised her hand and traced a hasty shape in the air, light trailing from her fingertips. Irilin slapped a palm to its centre, the rune spun into the Sisters' midst and exploded, Lunar flames cart-wheeling in every direction. The woman with the crossbow threw herself aside, cradling the weapon to her chest. The sole of one boot smoked.

Others weren't so lucky. One woman clutched her face, screaming, and for a moment Irilin's fierce expression wavered. She lowered her hands.

Hagdon knew what was about to happen. He leapt forward, but his lunge was arrested by a hooded woman, both hands clamped around a stave as she forced him back. Her strength was incredible for one so slight, but then he noticed the tell-tale glow of ambertrix infusing the wood. The crossbow fired; from the corner of his eye, he saw Irilin throw up a shield, Lunar walls solid and bright.

He watched the bolt tear right through it.

The shot was a careful one, taking Irilin in the shoulder. The aim was to incapacitate rather than maim or kill. She fell with a mingled cry of surprise and pain and Hagdon was shocked at the intensity of the rage that thundered through him. He drew his handaxe, took a chance. The hooded woman parried one blow, but the other came up from beneath to shear the stave in half.

Or it should have done. Hagdon cursed. Who had supplied them with ambertrix weapons – weapons so scarce that only a handful of the emperor's elite owned one? Was it Iresonté? He saw Nediah hurry to Irilin's side, kneeling down despite the danger. Kait covered them both, balanced on the balls of her feet. One of her blades was already bloodied and the nearest women circled her warily.

Hagdon backed away, eyeing the stave. Behind him, Kait was fending off five opponents at once. When she screamed, he automatically glanced back and saw her hunched over, every limb shaking. One of the women held a blunt device against Kait's leg, which spat and crackled with blue.

Teeth gritted, Irilin threw a shield between them. Kait fell back, her body still trembling uncontrollably. Another two women tore Nediah away from Irilin, blades pressed to his throat. The Wielder's face was twisted with fury, perhaps at his own helplessness. Although the Lunar clothed Irilin, it couldn't withstand the *asatha*. Hagdon recognized the device now, having only seen it once before. A weapon of the stealth force, developed exclusively to use against aberrations.

Cursing, Hagdon took in the situation. It wasn't good. With Kait and Nediah down, only he stood between the Sisters and Irilin. His still-healing shoulder ached. Before they could stop him, he swiped the flare from his belt. Its crimson light lit the upturned faces of the Sisters as they watched it explode far above.

Hagdon retreated to stand in front of Irilin. 'Whoever you're signalling will come far too late,' the hooded woman said. She tipped her head on one side. 'I recognize that feathered mantle. You're a rebel, part of this new Republic.' She smiled as her comrades closed around him. 'Perhaps Sartya will pay for you too.'

'Or perhaps only his head, Takendo,' said a woman beside

her. She raised a dagger, ready to throw it, but the hooded woman's hand snapped out and caught her arm.

'Wait.'

Takendo took a step nearer Hagdon. 'Bring the light,' she said and another woman came forward from the rear of the group, holding a torch. In its fickle yellow glow, Takendo studied his face, moving from the scar across his cheek down to the shoulder he still favoured. Her eyes settled on the hilt of the Sartyan general's sword still strapped across his back. 'No,' she breathed. 'For the Wood to smile so warmly upon us . . .'

She turned to her Sisters. 'I believe we've found Sartya's disgraced general.'

In the hush that followed her statement, someone said, 'How much do you think Iresonté will pay for him?'

Takendo smiled beneath her hood. 'Enough to set us up for life, Sisters.' Her gaze moved past Hagdon to Nediah and Kait. 'And these must be his so-called allies, the Wielders from Rairam.' She shook her head, eyes lingering on Nediah. 'They don't live up to the stories.'

Nediah returned her gaze, eyes defiant, and Kait snarled. But her struggles were weak; one of the Sisters restrained her easily.

'How much of a fool must you be, Hagdon?' Takendo said. 'Straying willingly into the Deadwood?'

'And how long have you scraped and bowed to Iresonté?' he retorted. 'I thought the Sisters had no master.'

Takendo's lip curled. 'The Sisters answer to no one.'

'That sounds like a lie from where I'm standing.' Hagdon nodded to the *asatha*. 'Don't tell me you acquired ambertrix weapons on your own. Iresonté gave you your power. She can take it away.' He knew his expression was bitter. 'She's become quite proficient at it.'

'Iresonté has her uses,' Takendo said with a good attempt at carelessness, but Hagdon could tell he'd struck a nerve. 'And I grow tired of talking.' She gestured. 'Take them.'

It was in that moment, when Hagdon knew it was hopeless, that light like cold water drenched them. Squinting, he turned to look behind him.

A figure crouched on top of the sheer-sided boulder: a dark shadow amidst the light, which cast everything into relief, as winter under a full moon. Lunar power, but it was unlike anything Hagdon had seen Irilin produce. The figure straightened: slim, female. When she spoke, her voice sounded as clear and unfaltering as the light.

'These are my people,' she said. 'And they are under *my* protection.'

9

Brégenne

Brégenne hammered her fists against the stone. Then she kicked it. When nothing happened except for her toes smarting in pain, she stepped back and glared at the place where Gareth had vanished. 'Why did it have to be day?' she growled, only dimly aware of Kul'Das standing behind her. 'I could have stopped it from taking him.'

'I'm sorry,' Kul'Das said so contritely that Brégenne glanced round. The woman stood still, staring at her upturned palms. 'If I knew more magic, I could have helped.'

'It's not called magic.'

'The Solar, then.' Kul'Das continued to glare at her hands. 'I should have listened to you.'

Brégenne blinked and then, despite herself, she began to laugh. 'That's something I never thought to hear.'

The laugh shocked Kul'Das out of her daze. She looked up and some of her old pride returned to redden her cheeks. 'Don't expect to hear it again.'

'Maybe we can find an entrance,' Brégenne said, sobering.

'Gareth and I have come this far together. I can't leave him alone.'

Kul'Das tilted her head. 'Have you considered that this is something only *he* can do? That your part is over?'

Brégenne opened her mouth to deny it, but paused. What if Kul'Das was right? She'd done all she could for Gareth; she'd brought him this far. Perhaps he *was* supposed to face this last trial alone.

Stubbornly pushing the thought to one side, she said, 'There has to be a way in.'

They split up to circle the mound. Unlike the others, it was long, almost rectangular, and they each took a side, moving slowly down its length. Brégenne ran her hands over its grassy surface. Stone showed in places; in others bare earth. The further she walked into the necropolis, the stronger grew the uncomfortable feeling of being watched.

Brégenne squared her shoulders and moved on. When a dark shape turned the corner ahead of her, she leapt back with a gasp, but it was only Kul'Das. The other woman was pale. Clearly, she found Ben-haugr just as unnerving. 'Nothing,' she said.

'Nothing,' Brégenne agreed. She bit her lip, thinking of Gareth trapped in the earth with the dead as his only companions. *Perhaps he is safer than you are*, came a thought. *He's not alive, so he cannot die.*

Was that true? Brégenne wondered. What if death was the least thing Gareth had to fear? She vividly remembered the time she'd tried to free him from the gauntlet. It had assailed her with visions – a trampled banner, fallen knights, a city's ruined towers . . . But the image that haunted her was the figure on the throne, skeletal hands curled around its armrests waiting . . . waiting.

'We have to find a way in,' she said with renewed vigour. 'Even if we must make one ourselves.'

'Make one ourselves?' Kul'Das looked dubiously at the stone. 'You mean blow it apart.'

When Brégenne nodded, the other woman rapped her knuckles against the stone and winced. 'I don't know how to do that.' And then in a softer voice, she added, 'I'm not sure I'm strong enough.'

'But I am,' Brégenne said, 'and you will be with practice.' She glanced at the sky. 'For now, though, we'll have to wait until moonrise. I'd prefer not to spend the day here.'

'What about Kul'Gareth?'

Brégenne laid a hand on the mound before letting it fall heavily to her side. 'He will have to trust in himself.'

They had retreated to the edge of the Deadwood to wait out the day. Brégenne felt better away from Ben-haugr, no longer scrutinized by unseen watchers, no longer short of breath, and her confidence had grown as the day waned. Twilight, however, did not come alone. Dread followed on its dusky heels and suddenly the last thing Brégenne wanted to do was to return to the necropolis. The thought of breaching the walls of the mound in such a way, exposing the dead to the unquiet sky, was abhorrent.

Still, she owed it to Gareth to try.

'What's that?'

Brégenne looked up. Kul'Das was pointing not towards Ben-haugr, but back the way they'd come, into the Deadwood. A moment later, Brégenne saw it too: little flashes of silver light. She'd know the Lunar anywhere.

Her heart began to beat faster. 'Wielders,' she said, climbing to her feet.

'Or aberrations.'

'A battle,' Brégenne whispered. 'The women we encountered . . .'

'They've found other targets,' Kul'Das finished grimly. If Brégenne strained her ears, she could hear shouting, the clash of metal on metal. A moment later, silver split the gloom and Brégenne caught its after-image – a seven-sided rune. 'They're Wielders,' she heard herself say decisively. 'No aberration could use runic *substantiation* without training.'

And then she was moving, scooping up her pack, plunging into the ashen forest. 'Kul'Gareth?' she heard the other woman call, but Brégenne shook her head. 'We'll come back for him. I have to know, have to help . . .' Because, if Wielders were here, there was only one group it could be. The thump of her heart kept her company as she ducked and wove between the charred trees.

Red streaked the sky; some kind of signal. Perhaps there were others abroad in the forest tonight. A moment later, Brégenne realized that the sounds of fighting had stilled. The sudden silence alarmed her, spurred her faster. A familiar boulder loomed up, one they'd passed earlier. Voices came from the other side. A woman and the deeper, huskier tones of a man. They weren't friends, she could tell that much.

'Wait here,' she hissed to Kul'Das. 'Keep out of sight.'

The other woman gave a sharp nod and Brégenne was glad she didn't argue.

Using the technique she'd been practising, she created a disc of light and stepped onto it, carefully controlling her ascent. When she reached the top of the boulder, she let the disc fade, dropped to her belly and crawled forward until she could observe the scene.

Directly below lay the novice, Irilin, her shoulder bleeding freely. A man in a feathered mantle stood guard over her, weapons in hand. His stance proclaimed him a soldier. *Hagdon*, Brégenne assumed. Kyndra had told her about the general turned commander of the Republic. She looked to the left and her heart contracted.

Nediah crouched, restrained by two women. She could just make out the shadow of a bruise rising on one cheek. Kait was down, moving feebly despite no visible injuries. A powerful feeling hit Brégenne, a chaotic mix of anger, relief, doubt – she couldn't untangle it and she didn't have time. All that mattered was the danger.

The Deadwood fed on shadows; only a meagre torch lit the gloom and Brégenne noted that most of the women stood in front of it so as not to damage their night vision. She smiled, rose to a crouch. Drawing on the burning silver heart of the Lunar, she flung it into their midst, until the wood was as bright as day. Cries met her ears; nearly all the women fell back, save the hooded one. She looked unflinchingly into the light, straight at Brégenne.

Slowly Brégenne rose to her feet. That open defiance fuelled her anger. 'These are my people.' Her voice rang clear between the trees. 'And they are under *my* protection.'

'Watch out, Takendo,' the woman with the crossbow warned, but the hooded woman ignored her.

'You came back,' she said delightedly, without a trace of fear. 'What have you done with your companions?'

Brégenne didn't answer. She was too busy sizing up the situation. There was only a single blunt device, she noted, held by the woman standing over Kait. She flicked her eyes to one side, picked out the crossbow's blue glow; unless the women had any other tricks up their sleeves, those weapons were the only things Brégenne truly had to be wary of.

She took a deep breath and fixed her gaze on the crossbow. The woman fired it at the same moment that Brégenne struck her with a barrage of force. Knocked off-course, the bolt flew wide, taking another woman through the eye. In the shocked pause as she toppled backwards, Brégenne waved a hand and the frame of the crossbow glowed hot-white. The woman dropped it with a yelp, but it didn't burn as Brégenne had hoped. The ambertrix seemed to protect it from Lunar flames.

Common arrows flew at her. Shielding with one hand, Brégenne raised the other. Up here, she could feel wind on her cheeks, catching in the plait of her hair. She seized that breeze and bolstered it with Lunar power until a small tornado roared in her grasp. When she let go, it tore across the clearing, snatching up anything not tied down. Over the heads of those who'd thrown themselves protectively to the ground, she saw the crossbow whirl high into the air, enough to clear the stunted tops of the trees. So the ambertrix only protected it from pure Solar and Lunar, not from a natural force, and not from one strengthened by a Wielder.

Good to know.

Hagdon seized the distraction, taking the offensive, though he never strayed far from Irilin. Despite her wound, the young woman climbed to her feet. Teeth gritted, she drew another rune, slapped a palm to its middle and flung it into the face of a woman attempting to flank Hagdon. It exploded and the woman screamed, tearing at her skin as it smoked and blackened.

Brégenne created another disc, dropped to earth and joined the fray, laying about her with the same silver darts she'd used on the wyverns back at Stjórna. They were much more effective against humans. She found herself grinning with the euphoria of power, the Lunar supple and compliant in her hands. She shot two darts at the women holding Nediah and they fell with joint cries. Brégenne couldn't stay to meet his gaze. She was forced to leap aside as a blade came for her, raking the air with her darts as she went. Her attacker toppled backwards, silver piercing her neck.

Then, without warning, Brégenne's leg collapsed beneath her. Pain followed by numbness spread through her calf, climbed up to her thigh. Brégenne gritted her teeth, drew on the Lunar, but as long as the little blunt weapon touched her skin, it kept winking out. Cursing herself for overconfidence, she looked into the smiling face of the woman paralysing her.

Metal parted the woman's lips, freezing the smile, spraying Brégenne's skin with blood. Disgusted, Brégenne dragged a sleeve over her cheeks, spat on the ground, and looked up in time to see Kait pull the blade free. '*Bitch*.' The tall Wielder kicked the dead woman onto her front. She bent down, retrieved the stunning weapon from where it had fallen and tucked it through her own belt.

The thought of Kait holding the device was far from reassuring. Brégenne looked at the other woman, but Kait ignored her, swept up a sword from the charred earth and launched herself into the melee.

Their opponents were no novices to battle; the loss of their ambertrix weapons didn't appear to slow them. Hagdon fought three women, two wielding swords, another with a morningstar, which she swung with perilous force. Kait was a deadly whirlwind, blade in one hand, paralysing device in the other. Grinning fiercely, she sent each opponent to their knees before finishing them with the sword.

Ripples still ran up and down Brégenne's leg, threatening to collapse it again. She turned to see Nediah pick up a weapon. He held it awkwardly, perhaps hoping to protect Irilin if she fell. Their eyes met for a breathless second and then a scream rent the air.

Hagdon was staggering back, his arm hanging strangely. The woman with the morningstar hefted it again, preparing to swing. Feeling was returning to Brégenne's body too slowly, the Lunar like smooth glass in her grasp.

There came movement through the trees, accompanied by the heavy tread of armoured feet. At first, Brégenne thought they were more of the Deadwood women, but she blinked, looked closer, and a thrill of horror ran through her. She recognized the red plate from Kyndra's description: Sartyans. There had to be thirty of them, enough to tip the balance firmly out of their favour.

Takendo whipped around, raising a hand. Her expression cleared. 'Lieutenant Mercia.'

The dark-haired Sartyan came up to her, blade in hand and eyes narrowed as she assessed the scene. Her gaze alighted on the injured Hagdon, swept over Irilin and Nediah, Brégenne herself, and came back to rest on the hooded woman, who smiled and said, 'Your timing is fortunate.'

She kept on smiling even as Mercia calmly ran her through.

Takendo blinked. She glanced down at the blade buried in her chest, then up at Mercia, her expression faintly surprised. The lieutenant pulled her sword free in a gush of blood and the woman's knees folded. Mercia wiped her blade clean on

Takendo's cloak and turned to signal. Sartyans fanned out through the trees and cries of dismay met Brégenne's ears, metal parting flesh . . . the sounds of a slaughter. The women of the Deadwood struck using surprise — hit-and-run tactics designed for a swift victory. Against trained soldiers, they stood little chance. Blood flowed and Brégenne looked away.

Straight into Nediah's eyes.

He was nearly as pale as Irilin; killing always sickened him. The bruise on his cheek was swiftly purpling, but, otherwise, he seemed well. She tried to concentrate on those things, on her practical assessment of his health, but his face was so familiar. Despite the battle around her, she could not stop herself seeing, with fascinating detail, all the places where their bodies would fit together.

He studied her with the same intensity, his gaze travelling over her, as if he, too, checked for injuries. Finding none, his eyes returned to her face. She saw him swallow. 'Brégenne?'

'Nediah.' His name emerged as a whisper. Already beating hard from the battle, Brégenne's heart beat even harder. It would only take a few steps to close the distance between them . . .

'You're really here.' His smile was warm; she felt her face flush. Not just her face; heat rushed through the rest of her, making her palms tingle, burning in the soles of her feet. She took a step towards him, just as Nediah moved towards her, reaching out his hand.

'And you're here why exactly?'

Kait seized Nediah's outstretched hand, planting herself firmly at his side. The tall woman's stare was even more hostile than usual.

'I'm here saving your lives,' Brégenne said, though the sight of Kait holding Nediah's hand made her hackles rise. Exactly *what* had happened between them during their months in Acre? Her imagination tormented her with possibilities.

'We didn't need your help.' Kait's hold tightened on Nediah and he glanced down at his hand, frowning. 'We were fine without your interference.'

Nediah shrugged out of Kait's grip and though Brégenne knew it was petty, she felt a surge of satisfaction.

'Are you well, Hagdon?'

The Sartyan's question broke their standoff. Brégenne looked around to see Lieutenant Mercia standing at the ex-general's side. Her blade dripped blood.

Hagdon's teeth were gritted. 'It might be fractured.'

'I can mend it,' Nediah said at once, 'if you can hold on for a few hours.' He paused then, looked at Brégenne. 'But I forget – I'm not the only one who can heal.'

She shook her head, feeling a tightness in her throat. 'You will make a neater job of it. Your skill is second to none.'

'Brégenne?'

Irilin was staring at her, eyes round. She managed one step before her knees buckled. Though it must have caused him pain, Hagdon caught her with his good arm and lowered her gently to the ground. Brégenne hurried over. 'Let me see,' she said, placing her hands on the young woman's injured shoulder. The crossbow bolt was buried deep.

Despite the pain that whitened her face, Irilin smiled wryly up at Hagdon. 'Our positions seem to be reversed.'

For a moment, the soldier's expression remained inscrutable. When Brégenne's palms began to glow, however, he returned Irilin's smile. 'If only *I'd* had a Wielder on hand.'

'Be careful,' Brégenne told Irilin when the healing was

done. The bolt lay on the ground beside her. 'I'm no expert and you've lost a lot of blood. You too,' she added to Hagdon, taking his arm. 'I can mend the fracture, but Nediah should look at it in the morning.'

Hagdon seemed nervous at the sudden easing of pain. *He doesn't trust us*, Brégenne realized. *He's spent his life hunting us down.*

'Thank you,' Hagdon said with an obvious attempt at casualness. His gaze did not stray from her face. 'I believe there are introductions to be made.'

'I almost forgot. Kul'Das, it's safe now.' With her Lunar-enhanced sight, Brégenne picked out the woman crouched in the shadow of the boulder. When she beckoned, Kul'Das came over, her blue eyes wary. 'Kul'Das is my –' *friend* seemed too strong a word – 'companion,' Brégenne finished. 'She serves in the court of Ümvast.'

Hagdon tilted his head. 'A pleasure. And yourself?' he asked, turning to Brégenne. 'Your arrival was rather . . . timely.'

'My name is Brégenne. I'm a Wielder of Naris,' she said. Of course he'd be suspicious. Without her intervention, this could have ended very differently.

'Not just a Wielder,' Nediah spoke up. 'She's a council-woman. One of our leaders.'

Kait gave an undisguised grunt of disgust and, despite her best efforts, Brégenne felt her cheeks colour. She was grateful for the gloom. 'I doubt I'm that any longer,' she said to both men. 'I left Naris against the wishes of my fellow Council members.' A brief smile touched her lips as she remembered the day she'd escaped with Gareth aboard the *Eastern Set*. She'd seen their pursuers reduced to impotent specks as the airship gained height. 'They sent a party of Wielders to track me down.'

She could feel Kait's eyes burning into her cheek. Brégenne shrugged uncomfortably. 'It did not go well for them.'

'It seems we're all rebels here, then,' Hagdon said somewhat ruefully. Hand on heart, he added, 'I am James Hagdon, who currently finds himself commander of the Republic of Acre. This is Lieutenant Mercia . . . whose arrival was almost as timely as yours.' The dark-haired Sartyan grinned. 'Though,' Hagdon added, 'she won't be considered lieutenant for very much longer.'

'Long enough for us to reach Parakat, I hope,' Mercia murmured.

The Sartyans were regrouping, wiping their blades on the garb of those they'd killed. Watching them, Brégenne felt a flutter of disquiet. They were so calm, so controlled. It was easy to see how the soldiers of the Fist had upheld the empire's rule for centuries. Few, it seemed, could stand against them. And this was only a single unit. Brégenne eyed Hagdon warily, wondering at the things he'd witnessed in service to such a force, at the orders he'd carried out, at those he'd issued. Here was a man half her age, who'd risen to command the greatest army the world had ever known. What did that do to you? Having that power at your fingertips? She knew what power was; she'd wielded it since the age of thirteen. The ex-general might not command the Solar or Lunar, but his power was just as potent. She sensed it came with just as high a price. In his scarred soldier's face, Hagdon's eyes were those of a haunted man.

'What are you doing here?' Hagdon asked, snapping Brégenne out of her reverie. 'We were under the impression you'd already reached Ben-haugr.'

Before Brégenne could reply, Irilin said, 'Where's Gareth?'

Moving stiffly, she climbed to her feet, gripping a charred trunk for support. 'Where's Gareth, Brégenne?'

'He's inside Ben-haugr.'

'You *left* him?' Irilin's pale cheeks flushed. 'You said you were looking after him.'

The words stung because they were true. 'I know.' Brégenne looked down. 'It was the gauntlet. Somehow it pulled him through the wall of the mound.' She forced herself to meet Irilin's gaze. 'It happened this morning. I couldn't stop it from taking him.'

'We were to return tonight,' Kul'Das chimed in. 'Then Brégenne saw your battle from afar.'

'I don't want Gareth to be alone. We came to help him too.' Irilin took a wavering step towards Brégenne. Hagdon made a small movement, as if he intended to steady her, but thought better of it.

'Brégenne,' Irilin lowered her voice. 'How was Gareth . . . when you told him about Shika?'

Brégenne hesitated. 'He doesn't know.'

'You didn't tell him?' Irilin's small fists balled at her sides. 'You kept it secret?'

'You haven't seen him,' Brégenne said quickly. 'He's changed, Irilin. I watched him die and return to—' *not life* – 'return to us. I made the decision not to tell him. He's so frail. I didn't know what the news would do to him.'

'He deserves to know,' Irilin said in a low voice. 'Shika was his best friend.'

Brégenne closed her eyes briefly. 'I'm sorry, Irilin. Maybe I was wrong. I had to watch the gauntlet strip him down to bones.' She paused. 'You won't recognize him.'

'We'll see,' Irilin said, though she looked a little less sure.

'You say this gauntlet pulled him *through* the wall?' Hagdon asked.

Brégenne sighed. 'Don't ask me how. No power can turn a body incorporeal.'

'Except a Starborn's,' Irilin said. 'Like when Kyndra fought the Khronostians.'

Brégenne felt a strange pang. Was it protectiveness or pride? 'How is Kyndra?' she asked quietly.

'Different,' Irilin said.

She didn't have to say more; Brégenne knew what she meant. Kyndra: the girl she'd rescued from a burning town, whom she'd brought to Naris, the young woman who had ended the Breaking and the Madness, who'd saved the citadel . . . gone.

Power always came with a price.

10

Char

Mother.

As he waited on the steps of the Chime – the chamber where Ma had broken the mandala's hold – Char's insides roiled. He found himself looking at Ma, but she wouldn't return his gaze. Her face was carefully blank; he knew the expression well. Whatever she felt, Ma was determined to hide it. She was good at hiding.

Char tried to catch hold of his feelings, to separate them, but they were a jumble he could not unpick. The Lleu-yelin waited impassively. Their aloofness reminded him of Kyndra – the new Kyndra – and the way she stood, gaze introverted, completely unaware that she wasn't alone. If the Lleu-yelin were a feeling people, they kept it as well hidden as Ma.

Perhaps it was his years as a human that made him this way. Char was only just beginning to grasp the edges of what it meant to be Lleu-yelin, to witness centuries come and go, to be so *removed* from the world. It was the opposite of everything he had experienced in Genge's caravan, living each day on a razor's edge. Every slave they'd captured and sold reinforced life's transitory nature. *Nothing lasts forever.*

But here, amidst this grey city dug out of the mountain's heart, was the sense that some things *did* last forever. The world's problems were far away.

Then why had the Lleu-yelin given ambertrix to Sartya?

Char knew he was using these thoughts to avoid the more personal and pressing one. *Ekaar.* His mother's name. She was here, only moments away. Once he'd dreamed of finding his parents, of asking them why they'd abandoned him. But that was a lie Ma had told to hide his heritage. Over the years, his yearning for them had turned to anger and then slowly to indifference. Ma was the only parent and friend he needed. He glanced at her again and this time caught her whipping her gaze away.

Ekaar. What would she look like? What would he say? She was a stranger who—

Wingbeats put an end to his fevered musing. Char looked up to see two dragons approaching. One was Sesh's mate; the other was black and carried a rider.

Char's throat tightened. The black dragon's scales were the same teardrop shape as his own, the same dusky hue. Her eyes were violet. She landed and her rider, a male, slipped gracefully off her back. He was tall, scaled skin somewhere between orange and black and his eyes –

Yellow. Yellow like mine.

Ekaar took a clawed, tentative step. 'Orkaan?'

He found he couldn't move. His gaze swept over her: she was larger than he, her ruff finer, talons golden – painted? – he wasn't sure. Her horns were the same shape as his: sweeping up and back.

'Is it *you*?'

Still he couldn't move. The male rider stood silently beside Ekaar, his gaze equally intense. His claws were yellow-tipped, like the flickering tongues of fire.

'Go to her, Boy.'

Ma's words were quiet; only for him. She stood with one hand on his hide, but lifted it when Ekaar's eyes swept over her. Char had felt it tremble. Slowly, he descended the wide steps. Pausing on the last, he looked back at Ma. She nodded encouragement, but her eyes were a portal to her thoughts. Pain and pride, a flash of jealousy, bitterness, resignation – all of it disappeared between blinks. Char wanted to go to her, to throw his arms about her neck. His arms, however, were spiked and talon-tipped; they would harm her now. Unable to look any longer, he turned back to Ekaar and her mate.

Ekaar seemed to understand something of what had passed between them. Her violet eyes had narrowed to slits, but widened when he came to stand before her. She lowered her head as if to scent him. 'It is you,' she said, her voice the softest thunder.

Perhaps he sensed something Char did not, for the yellow-eyed male placed a comforting hand on Ekaar's hide. 'I do not understand,' she said. 'It seems I held you only moments ago, yet here you are, a risling.'

'The Khronostians trapped you,' Char said awkwardly, uncomfortable under the general scrutiny, 'for twenty years.' He hesitated, head swinging round to point at Ma. 'Ma rescued me. She raised me.'

'A human dared to take you from me?'

'We were separated in the attack,' Char said quickly. 'Ma knew the *du-alakat* would kill a helpless infant.'

His words only seemed to inflame Ekaar. She took a threatening step towards Ma, a growing rumble coming from her throat. 'Lies. She acted out of avarice, as all her kind do. She saw an opportunity and she *stole* you.'

When she took another step towards Ma, violence in her violet eyes, Char found his wings spreading, surprised to hear a dreadful hissing coming from his throat.

Ekaar froze at the sound, staring at him. He sensed her shock, as if he'd thrown a terrible insult. '*Orkaan.*'

Char did not back down. 'If she wished me harm, do you really think I'd be standing here today?'

They glared at each other for a few fierce moments before Ekaar's spiked ruff flattened against her neck. 'I do not know you,' she said, 'you are a stranger to me.' And she took off in an angry gust.

Char lowered his wings. Guilt wanted to overwhelm him, but he stopped it. She had threatened Ma.

'Apologies,' said the rider she'd left behind. 'She's always been like that. Quick to anger, quick to forgive. But stubborn.'

'Sounds familiar,' Ma murmured.

The rider heard her. 'Indeed?' He was the very opposite of Ekaar, relaxed and smiling. 'I am Arvaka,' he said to Char, 'your sire.'

It was so casual Char almost failed to grasp the fact that he'd just met his father. 'There will be time for talk,' Arvaka said with a glance over his shoulder, 'but now you should go to her.'

Char looked at him uncertainly. 'I don't think she wants to see me.'

'She expects it. You must understand. Offspring are born to us so rarely and she has missed watching you grow.' His smile turned sad. 'We both have.'

'Then I will go.' Char glanced around until he found Kyndra. The Starborn was standing off to one side, seemingly only half her attention on the scene. She met his gaze and nodded, knowing what he asked. Ma could certainly look out for herself, but Char wasn't taking any chances.

'I will be quick,' he said.

'I'd make no promises,' Arvaka warned.

Char hoped his running leap didn't look as clumsy to the watching Lleu-yelin as it felt. He followed Ekaar's retreating scent; her smell reminded him of the desert evening, of the air after a burning day. She wasn't flying very fast – perhaps Arvaka was right and she did want to talk. Char found her atop one of the rugged walls, where she perched like a great eagle. He landed with difficulty beside her.

'You chose to take after me. I am glad.'

It took Char a moment to understand what she meant. 'Yes,' he said, remembering with a shudder the change that had overtaken him during the battle on the steps of Khronosta. 'I suppose I did.'

'It is fitting,' she replied.

'I'm sorry we don't know each other,' Char began awkwardly when she said no more. 'I'm sorry that I wasn't here.' He hesitated, went on. 'But Ma is a good person. She did the best she could.' He wasn't about to go into their life with Genge; there were some things Ekaar was better off not knowing. 'If not for Khronosta, none of this would have happened.'

'You say twenty years have passed,' she said, gazing out at the grey expanse, 'but when I look at you, I see the infant I held only hours ago, at least so it seems.'

Char's throat tightened. He didn't know what to say.

'I do not understand.' She swung her head to look at him. 'Why would Khronosta punish us so?'

'To cripple Sartya,' Char answered.

'Ah,' Ekaar breathed. 'The Ambertrix Concord.'

'I think I can guess what that is.' He shook his head, ruffling his mane. 'Why ally with Sartya?'

'Why not?'

Char blinked. 'Some friends of mine would say the empire is oppressive and cruel. That it imprisons or slaughters any who oppose it.'

Ekaar's claws left gouges in the rock. 'When have humans ever done any different?'

'All right,' Char conceded, remembering Genge. 'But Sartya only maintained its power with Lleu-yelin help. What did you get out of such a deal?'

'The Concord was agreed with Sartya's emperors by the Chimer, not I,' Ekaar said a touch defensively. 'But you ask what we received in exchange. The answer is knowledge.'

Char snorted, a coil of bluish steam drifting from his nostrils. 'Knowledge? You're dragons.'

'We,' Ekaar corrected him. 'You have worn the human skin too long.'

'What could you possibly learn from Sartya?'

'You would know this had you grown up under my wings.' She refolded them fussily. 'Who do you think designed Magthar-da's streets, the amberstrazatrix mechanisms that facilitate the luxuries we enjoy?'

'Amberstrazatrix?'

'Sartya calls it ambertrix.'

'I can see why they shortened it.' Then the impact of her

words hit him and Char felt his eyes widen. '*Humans* did that? But they would have had to have come here.'

'We brought them. We shared our power, they their power of invention. Both of us benefited.'

'Yes, while the rest of the world was enslaved.'

The accusatory statement didn't seem to rile Ekaar. 'We have little interest in human politics.'

'It won't perturb you to know that the emperor is dead, then.'

She stilled. 'When did this occur?'

'Mere weeks ago.' Char paused, remembering a conversation he'd had with Ma. 'But it was bound to happen sooner or later – that was Khronosta's plan. They weren't prepared to face you in combat. They knew their losses would be too heavy. So they came up with the time prison instead. All to deprive Sartya of ambertrix. You were never the true target.'

Ekaar was silent. 'If Sartya is your enemy,' she said finallly, 'why is Khronosta not your friend?'

'Because of a man called the eldest. He seeks to travel back before the sundering of Rairam from Acre, as far back as he can, in order to destabilize the empire before it consolidates power.'

She snorted. 'Impossible.'

'No.' Char shook his head. 'Kyndra's companion is helping them. He is one of the Yadin.'

'The Servants of Solinaris,' Ekaar mused, memory in her violet eyes. 'I thought they'd perished.'

'Most of them did. But Medavle – that's the Yadin's name – survived. He says he was the one who defeated Kierik.'

'He *defeated* a Starborn?'

'So he claims.'

'And this happened in Rairam? That is why we did not know?'

'Yes. Kyndra told me.'

'The new Starborn, I see. She came from Rairam?'

Char sighed. 'Would you like to hear the story?'

She nodded, so he told it, careful to omit the parts about Genge, focusing instead on being hunted by the *du-alakat*, who'd mistaken him for their Kala. His meeting with Kyndra, discovering the truth about Rairam, learning that she and her companions had come to broker peace. He told of their journey to Khronosta, alliance with the new Republic, led by none other than Sartya's own general. He related their defeat at the hands of Khronosta, the emperor's death.

'Few of her decisions sound like those of a Starborn,' Ekaar said suddenly.

'She . . .' Char hesitated, struck by his memories of Kyndra as she had been. 'She wasn't like that at first. She was different.' At that moment, he was glad he could no longer blush.

But it seemed he'd already given something of his thoughts away, for Ekaar said, quite flatly, 'I hope you did not mate with her.'

'I . . . gods, I can't believe you just –' He looked away. 'It doesn't matter now anyway. I am what I am and she . . . she is what she is.'

'Good.' Ekaar seemed satisfied. 'All know that such unions are cursed.'

'Can we talk about something else?'

'We should return,' his mother said, shaking out her spines. 'I wish to speak with the Starborn.'

Somehow Char did not have a good feeling about this.

11

Gareth

The dead feasted.

He'd passed a dozen chambers, each with a long laden table as its centrepiece. Once or twice, the chairs were empty, some pushed back as if abandoned in haste. Gareth didn't want to know where the occupants had gone. More often, warriors like those he'd escaped ground to life when Gareth's foot touched the stone balcony. But the portcullis doors were many. It had become a simple matter to hurry around the balcony's edge, hitting the release mechanism to ensure each door came crashing down behind him. He knew this respite was temporary; the dead would find another way around. And when they did, he'd have hundreds to face, a skeletal army.

Unless he reached Kingswold and the gauntlet.

Gareth had no plan and only twenty years to his name, unlike the restless knight. But Hond'Myrkr drove him on. The dark gauntlet both yearned for and resented its partner. The man who united them would be the one to command the hosts of Benhaugr. Something inside Gareth shuddered at the thought. Because no mere human could wield the power of life and death.

He found himself thinking of Shika again and what would have happened if he'd never found the gauntlet. Destiny, Brégenne had said, but Gareth didn't believe in destiny. A series of decisions had led him to this moment, blind chance, luck, the influence of others. They'd never have gone to the archives if not for Kyndra. Remove her from the equation and everything – *everything* – would be different.

I can't blame her, he chided himself, crossing into a circular room. After all, he'd been the one to steal the gauntlet.

Lost in his thoughts, he only just saw the slight floor depression in time. There was a *click* and Gareth leapt clumsily aside, grasping at the wall to keep his feet. Most of the stone slid back, revealing the real floor below, studded with spikes.

A living person would have breathed slowly out, their heart thudding relief. Gareth merely pushed himself off the wall, stepped around the hole and continued, following the winding passage through an archway and down a shallow slope.

Time was beginning to fray around him. He couldn't work out how long he'd been inside Ben-haugr, caught in its labyrinthine embrace. Were it not for the gauntlet, he'd have been lost. But Hond'Myrkr knew its way; its tugging grew stronger with each step he took.

Gareth tried to roll the stiffness out of his shoulders. He gritted his teeth, wondering how he must look to the creatures of Ben-haugr. Nearly one of them, he supposed; the only difference being that he still had free will. He glanced at the gauntlet. *If you could call it that.*

Gareth halted at a small sound, listening. When he heard nothing more, he edged forward again, peering around the next corner.

A narrow chamber, ringed by a balcony, each wall broken by

a portcullis door. A fifth was set into the floor, like the gate to a feeding pit. Gareth eyed it closely, but couldn't see any depressions that indicated traps. Still, the feeling that pervaded him would have raised hairs all over his body. He was being watched.

Sarcophagi dotted the chamber. All had carven lids, mostly battle scenes, but four were engraved with Kingswold's emblem: two crossed fists. They were larger than the others; each stood vertically against a wall facing into the crypt's centre.

There was a tug from the gauntlet. His path lay across this room, through the wide archway on the other side. He was close now, so close, and he lifted a foot, preparing to set it down onto the patterned floor.

Without warning, wind rushed into the chamber, carrying Kingswold's voice with it. *'Awake, arise, ek kalla. I summon you out of sleep.'*

Crack.

He'd been half expecting it, but the whiplash noise was so loud, so terrible, that Gareth jumped. His raised foot touched the floor.

Crack. Crack. Crack.

Lids fell forward, ancient stone shattering on impact. Figures stepped from the sarcophagi. Rooted to the ground, Gareth could only stare. They weren't like the skeletal warriors he'd already encountered, for flesh still covered their bones. It was leathery and brown, sagging in places, stretched in others. Lank hair hung from mottled scalps, brown teeth set in the grinning rictus of skulls. They wore sets of plate armour, but incomplete. One lacked gauntlets, another greaves. Only two had helms, horned and silver. The nearest bore a shining breastplate, its surface buffed to a mirror finish. Down here, amongst the tarnished relics of a buried age, it looked out of place.

At first their movements were as slow and stilted as Gareth's, but once hands closed upon weapons, rigidity left them. Gareth found his fist wrapped around the hilt of his mother's sword. He didn't remember drawing it. Holding it up before him, he took a step back into the corridor, so that they couldn't encircle him.

The undead knight with the breastplate reached him first. Unlike the lesser warriors he'd already encountered, this one didn't attack in a blind flurry. He regarded Gareth as one opponent sizes up another, horned head slightly tilted. In the breastplate's mirrored surface, Gareth saw himself; a ragged figure not unlike the dead that stalked him. His clothes hung off his wasted frame. Waxen-skinned, his face stared back at him, eyes like sunken wells. Ironically, the gauntlet was the only thing that had substance. If he met another human here, they would think him part of Kingswold's forbidding host.

Disgust warred with fear inside him. No matter his appearance, under the knight's gaze, Gareth felt *very* human. He wished Brégenne was here beside him. He wished he was not alone.

The moment his sword clashed with the knight's, Gareth knew who the better fighter was. It was all he could do to defend, parrying an upper cut, a lower, a reverse thrust to the ribs. The other knights pressed in, forcing him back. Gareth's parries were fierce and inaccurate; he could hear mocking laughter in the air, in the swishing wake of each knight's swing.

The dead could never tire, but his opponent drew back, lending the fight to a comrade. The eyes had long ago shrivelled; pinpricks of light gazed out at Gareth from empty sockets. The second knight had no cuirass, just greaves and pauldrons, but it fought as well as the first. In his normal state and without the Solar, Gareth knew he would be exhausted by now, covered with bleeding lacerations where he'd not been swift enough to counter. But the lacerations didn't slow him; neither did they bleed.

The knight's foot came down on an uneven patch and Gareth saw an opening, thrusting his sword into the creature's chest, blade shearing through leathery flesh.

The warrior stumbled and Gareth found himself grinning. Then, feeling resistance, he glanced down. Just as his blade was buried in the knight, so was the knight's buried in him. Bound together, they stared at each other. The knight twisted his sword; Gareth felt nothing. He was still standing, so the blow had missed his spine. Instinctively, he copied the knight's movement, turning his blade inside the creature's chest.

He thought he sensed a faint confusion from his opponent, the vestige of emotion, before the knight tore his blade free. Gareth did the same and both of them stumbled. He took another step back, wracking his mind for a plan, any plan. Why had he let himself be backed into this corridor? He couldn't retreat, knowing what pursued him. Caught between the two forces, he would be hacked to pieces.

The gauntlet pulsed again; he heard that spectral laughter. This battle was being watched. The third knight shouldered his way forward, a two-handed greatsword held ready. They would fight until they brought him down – it was Kingswold's will driving them on.

Kingswold who wielded the light gauntlet.

White raises, black fells.

Gareth glanced at Hond'Myrkr. *He* was its master, despite Kingswold's claims. Hadn't it done his bidding before? *But I wasn't myself*, he found himself thinking. *Whenever I used it, I felt him working through me.*

He fended off a swing from the greatsword, but the strength behind it staggered him and the edge cut deep into the meat of his left arm.

There was no pain, but the arm flopped in response when he tried to lift it, now truly a dead weight. Gareth crushed a fresh surge of fear and sheathed his sword.

The suicidal action must have taken the knights aback, for they halted. Gareth could smell them; sweet rot like fermenting fruit. He glanced at the gauntlet, tried to swallow, but death had turned his mouth dust-dry.

Crouching, he thrust his fist into the stone.

Or tried to; the gauntlet simply rebounded. Wide-eyed, Gareth tilted his head to look up at the nearest knight who stood over him, blade raised to strike. With a strangled yell, he launched himself at the warrior's legs, brought him crashing down. The moment the gauntlet touched that dead flesh, Gareth felt it, saw it in his head – a connection like a thin blue thread that tethered the knights to Kingswold's will. It ran throughout their bodies, lending them life.

Black fells. Gareth tightened his hold.

The same dark tendrils that rotted men's flesh spread over the knight's form, latching on to the blue threads. As the two forces fought, Gareth thought he heard a wordless melody, a siren song, bright but terrible, and instinctively he knew that it was Hond'Lif, the light gauntlet, its name springing into his mind with its cry.

As the blue threads dimmed in one knight, they strengthened in another and Gareth had to throw himself aside again, or lose his head. The knight in the silver breastplate swung; Gareth steeled himself and caught the blade on the edge of Hond-Myrkr. Immediately, its dark tendrils flowed up the sword, into the hand that held it, extinguishing the bright threads. The knight's fist opened; sword clattered to stone.

Gareth didn't hesitate. He forced a charge, thrusting the falling knight into his comrades, bringing them all to the floor. He struck again with Hond'Myrkr – the power that had trapped him in this decaying form – and that same power ripped the life from the dead as easily as it did the living.

There was a roar of fury, or was it more laughter? Gareth stood up, stepped over the now-inanimate bodies of the knights and returned to the chamber.

It was filled with shambling figures.

There must have been twenty, cracked skin stretched tightly over bone. Some held swords, others bows of yellowed ivory. The nearest opened its mouth wider than it could have done in life and screamed at him. It wasn't quite wordless. Gareth caught expressions of anger, of mockery, as if directed at an enemy about to be engaged.

This was Kalast, he recalled. A great battle was fought here, perhaps on the very ground he stood upon. The Kingswold Knights against the Sartyan Fist. If Kingswold hadn't given in to desperation and donned Hond'Lif, might the outcome have been different? Gareth grimaced at the irony – in another time and place, these warriors might have been his allies, both of them united against Sartya.

There was no more time to reflect. When Gareth dropped into a crouch, an arrow whistled through the space his head had occupied but a moment before. Without hesitation, Gareth plunged Hond'Myrkr into the floor.

This time the gauntlet sank through stone, halfway to his elbow. Gareth gritted his teeth, forced the tendrils to spider out, climbing up the legs of each warrior, stripping Hond'Lif's power from them. Those struck toppled silently and Gareth found a reserve of anger, which he channelled into the gauntlet. *Kingswold,* he cried silently, *enough of this. Come out and face me yourself.*

There was no reply. Except, a moment later, those warriors still standing dropped like cut puppets to join their inert comrades. Gareth could see Hond'Lif's power withdrawing from them, curling out of dried pores. A challenge accepted. He stood and walked towards the archway.

Hond'Myrkr continued to take from him; when Gareth looked at his arm, the flesh had blackened to his elbow. He felt a sick horror at the sight, at the knowledge that the gauntlet could speed his body's decay. He needed that body to fight Kingswold. Even if he managed to win, if he wrested Hond'Lif from the ancient knight, would there be anything left of him to wear it?

He entered a wide corridor, walking slowly, eyeing the sarcophagi that lined the walls. But no more dead rose against him. Piles of dusty gold sat in tribute between each tomb. Emeralds peeked out from ornate cups. Rubies gleamed. A drinking horn, chased with silver, balanced atop like a ship on a swell. Gareth wondered whether it even had value any more; according to Kyndra, Acre had abandoned gold as a currency. Back home, though, just one small heap would make him a rich man.

Gareth left it behind.

Reliefs adorned the walls. They reminded him of the one in Stjórna, his mother's hall, of the battle scene on the throne-room doors. In these, warriors with streaming hair clashed against giants and nameless beasts of claw and snout. Here was a body pierced by a curving talon, agony etched forever on the warrior's stone face. And there was a man with an improbable sword as long as he was tall, felling, in one swing, two vast opponents. The engraver had picked out the giants with surpassing detail, from their bandolier trophies of skulls to the crinkled leather of their great sandals.

Gareth realized his feet had slowed. Everyone knew giants were a myth to frighten children, but then why had the unknown engraver chosen to depict them?

Only one thing was certain: Ben-haugr wasn't a tomb for the Kingswold Knights. It must have existed long before they were buried here. Perhaps it had lain under Kalast for centuries, pre-Sartya, when Acre wasn't even Acre but a wild place that had never known the hand of civilization. And yet the artistry in these carvings was the finest he'd seen.

A door blocked the way ahead. Semi-circular, it bore two concentric rings, one white, the other black. Without hesitating, Gareth pressed the gauntlet against the dark ring. For a moment, nothing happened, but then the circle turned counter clockwise and the whole door rose with a grating of stone on stone, showering his boots with dust.

Gareth stepped inside.

The chamber was the largest he'd yet seen, vaulted ceiling disappearing into the gloom. Bluish torches illumined the area, burning with the light of Hond'Lif. He stood at the head of a bridge, but a bridge over what? Darkness reigned to either side of it, concealing air or water or stone, he couldn't tell. Only that he did not care to lose his footing. The bridge, guarded by two great carven beasts, led to a small dais. And on the dais . . .

It was the vision he'd seen so often in his waking mind, in his dreams. A throne, hewn out of the rock. And on the throne a man, who would have been broad shouldered in life, but who was now little more than bones. Upon his lowered head sat a horned helm, and by his side a sword, its ivory grip browning with age. Armour hid what wasted flesh remained to him. His hands curled around the armrests, one bound in iron, the other –

Hond'Lif shone like white gold. In the dim crypt, its light was almost blinding. Sigils clustered; graceful, faintly sinister at second glance, as if they had changed their shape in the blink of an eye. Gareth felt the same allure as in the archives, when he'd first seen Hond'Myrkr resting in its niche. The same urge to slip it on, to clench his fist and watch the metal mould itself to his skin. The things he could do with both, the power he would wield . . .

The figure on the throne raised his head. Eyes flared in empty sockets, blue-white fires drawn from Hond'Lif. Just as the dark gauntlet kept Gareth from death, so did the light keep Kingswold. They were both doomed, bound to the will of the gauntlets. Once again, Gareth felt an unwelcome kinship with the man.

Kingswold knew it too. And he knew, like Gareth, that only one of them could unite the pair. Only one of them could use that power to return to the world outside. The other would lie in Ben-haugr forever.

12

Kyndra

With its ambertrix renewed, Magtharda was a sight to behold. Its rugged towers and waterfalls had already impressed her, but now that power flowed through the streets once more, the city was unlike anything she had seen. Magtharda made Market Primus and Cymenza – the only other major settlements she'd visited – seem like farmsteads in comparison. It was the future, Kyndra thought, as she listened to the low-level hissing of the ambertrix. This power could be used by everyone if the dragons deigned to share it with the world. *But look how that turned out*, she reminded herself, picturing Sartya's war machines, its marching legions, the cities burned, the people slaughtered. Perhaps humanity could not be trusted with such a power.

'You have heard the Starborn's tale.'

Sesh stood before the gathered Lleu-yelin, her tawny scales glowing under the weak sunlight. They were only fifty or so in number. *A small people*, Kyndra thought, wondering how rarely offspring were born. Throat dry from her story, she stood awaiting their verdict. She'd described her role in reuniting Rairam with Acre, contending with the political chaos, meeting Char, being hunted by Khronostian assassins.

Medavle's betrayal.

Kyndra rubbed her withered hand. *Could I have stopped him?* It wasn't the first time she'd asked herself. The dark-eyed Yadin had once saved her life. He'd helped navigate Acre; freely offered counsel when she'd sought it. And day by day, he'd grown distant. In the rare times he slept, she'd heard the moans of someone enmeshed in a nightmare. But it wasn't a nightmare – it was the past. Medavle had tried and failed to save his love, Isla, and he had never forgiven himself.

Or Kierik.

'Now,' Sesh continued, speaking the common tongue presumably for Ma's benefit, 'there are things we must discuss.' Her eyes passed over them, beyond them, to the grey haze that hid the lowlands, many leagues to the south-east. 'We must speak of our future, of the Lleu-yelin and Magtharda.'

The sound of wings, like tanned leather snapping in a breeze, announced Ekaar's return. Char landed behind her, not quite as gracefully – he had to take two stumbling steps to find his balance on land. Ekaar looked at Ma; they exchanged civil, if not friendly, nods. *Good*, Kyndra thought. *We can't afford to be divided.*

'We "woke" to find ourselves in stranger circumstances than we could ever have imagined,' Sesh continued. 'The Chimer gone, his corpse little more than ash, as if his passing occurred many years ago. Our city devoid of amberstrazatrix.' She gestured at Char. 'And our youngest a risling of twenty cycles when by all rights he should be an infant. The world has left us behind.'

A rumble swept through the gathered Lleu-yelin like the first stirrings of a storm.

'Those responsible,' Sesh concluded darkly, 'walk free.'

This time the rumble was a roar. Before it grew out of hand, Ma stepped forward, seeking permission to speak. When Sesh nodded, she moved to stand beside the tawny female, holding out her arms for quiet.

'Not only do the *du-alakat* walk free,' Ma said in a ringing voice, 'but their leader plans to travel back in time, to change our very history. He will destabilize the empire before it grows strong, unravel the fabric of the last five centuries.' She paused, meeting individual gazes. 'For good or ill, you made a pact with Sartya. Thabarat technicians built Magtharda as you know it. Without them, all this –' she swept a hand at the city – 'would be undone.'

'Many of us regret the Concord,' one of the fully fledged dragons said. A male, Kyndra thought, from the tone of his voice, with scales as grey as the stone of Magtharda. 'Humans are undeserving of our power.'

Ma took a breath, exasperation in the crease of her brow. 'Be that as it may, a change of this magnitude – the disestablishment of Sartya – would have consequences for the whole world that even I cannot see.'

'And who are you, human?' the male asked, fixing her with an iron-grey eye, 'except a traitor to the very people you warn us against?'

Ma's face tightened. 'Be thankful that I *am* a traitor,' she said quietly. 'Or the world would be doomed already.'

'Listen to her,' Char called out. He worked his way clumsily through the gathering until he stood next to the grey-scaled male. 'She's telling the truth about Khronosta. She's here to help.'

'Silence, risling,' the other dragon snapped. Spines like steel swords flexed along the length of his spine. 'You go too far. But for this woman, you would understand the hierarchy of speech.'

'But for this woman,' Char retorted, 'I'd be dead.'

'I will not permit—'

'Oh do shut up, Vaachane,' Ekaar said from the back of the crowd. 'Let my son speak. I am your elder. He can have my voice.'

The grey dragon glowered, but, caught in his own trap, he backed down. Char glanced at his mother, grateful, Kyndra thought, for her help.

'I may be of you,' he continued, 'but I grew up human. It wasn't an easy life. I saw and did things I'd rather forget. I exploited others for personal gain. I put a price on compassion, showed kindness only if there was profit in it. I lived amongst those who cared nothing for the world, for politics or people. They looked no deeper than the lining of their pockets.' Char hesitated. 'You could say that I have seen the worst of humanity.' His voice dropped lower. 'You could say I *was* the worst of humanity.'

Kyndra noticed Ma gazing at him, her eyes wide and dark. The watching Lleu-yelin remained utterly silent. Wind hissed over the paving stones; clouds raced across the sun.

'Any knowledge of right and wrong, I learned from Ma.' He looked at her. 'Her life has been hard – harder than the one she gave me – and she has done things that the honourable would condemn.'

Kyndra, her ears sharpened by *Ansu*, was the only one to hear Ma murmur, 'Don't overdo it, Boy.'

'But she's saved my life more times than I can count. She's been –' Char glanced hesitantly at Ekaar – 'as a mother to me. Betraying her people was the price I cost her. And if you knew what she is to them, what they are to her, you would think it far too high.'

His voice died. In the silence that lingered, Kyndra detected a mixture of interest, of doubt, of plain confusion. Fleetingly, she wondered why Ma didn't tell the Lleu-yelin who she really was. It might make things easier. *Her secrets are not mine to divulge*, she thought. And Ma had made it clear that her time as Khronos was over.

'The eldest of Khronosta', Ma said, 'needs an anchor to enter the past – someone who was alive during the time of Sartya's ascendancy. He has the Yadin.' Her hand settled on the kali sticks tucked behind her belt. 'But we, too, have an anchor. A Wielder born in Solinaris itself. He has agreed to help us.'

'And you, Starborn?' Sesh asked, folding her scaled arms, 'What is *your* part in this?'

'Ma will send me back in time,' Kyndra said, feeling her heart quicken at the words. *Am I ready? There's still so much I don't know.* 'I will stop the eldest . . . or die trying.' She kept her gaze averted from her withered hand, unwilling to think about the confrontation that awaited her. There would be none to aid her but the stars. Automatically, she reached out to them, but again they were oddly silent, just like the time she'd woken from the dream of Medavle.

Sesh tapped one bronze-tipped claw against her folded arm. 'What is it you want from us?'

'The emperor is dead,' Kyndra told them. 'Acre is in chaos. This is our chance to break Sartya's hold, to end military rule. The Fist's ex-general leads the Republic, a force which seeks to dissolve the empire, to restore the traditional rights of its territories. I've agreed to support them.' A gust blew hair into her eyes and she brushed it back impatiently. 'But there's a problem. The woman who deposed Hagdon has taken command of the Fist. Instead of realizing the threat Khronosta poses, she intends to split our energies, to attack Rairam.' Her eyes drifted to the east, as if she could penetrate the leagues that separated her from the place of her birth. 'My country is undefended,' she said, turning back to the Lleu-yelin. 'The only resistance Iresonté will meet are the Wielders of Naris and they are too few to stop the Fist.'

The dragons were silent. With her sharpened hearing, Kyndra could just detect the hiss of ambertrix as it rushed through the channels beneath her feet, carrying power to every dwelling.

'I want your allegiance,' she said.

'We do *not* involve ourselves in human conflicts,' Sesh replied amidst nods and murmurs of agreement. 'Such is the way it's always been.'

'This is not just a *human* conflict. If Khronosta succeeds, you may find yourselves wiped from the pages of history.' Kyndra was surprised to feel the flush of vehemence in her cheeks. 'With Ma's help, I will deal with Khronosta. But I do not wish to return to this time to find my homeland subjugated and Iresonté installed as empress. We must free Acre together.'

'We have allied with Sartya in the past.' It was Sesh's mate who spoke this time. He spread a wing as if to encompass the whole of Magtharda. 'Look at what that alliance built.'

Kyndra shook her head, but before she could answer, Char spoke up.

'Did Sartya come to your aid when Khronosta attacked?' He squared himself off against the larger dragon. 'No. It was us who freed you. And we didn't do it so you could turn your back on the world.'

'The emperor's death marks the end of Sartyan rule,' Kyndra added before the dragon could voice his protest. 'The next weeks, months and years will decide what replaces it.' She held out her hands. 'Would you forfeit the right to a say in our future?'

'The future must look to itself,' Sesh answered, 'but the Lleu-yelin do not deny the service you and your companions have rendered us. And' – she looked around, as if for support – 'we owe Khronosta blood-vengeance. If you oppose them, we are blood-bound to aid you.'

Under the Lleu-yelin's rumbling agreement, Kyndra breathed a sigh. *Thank you*, she used *Ansu* to project at Char, smiling a little when he jumped at hearing her voice in his head. *I don't think they'd have agreed without your help.*

You did the hard bit, he thought back tentatively and she nodded to show she'd heard him.

'We have no Chimer,' Sesh said matter-of-factly. 'As eldest among us, I will seal our pact.'

About to hold out her hand, Kyndra swiftly retracted it, offering the other. Sesh's keen eyes didn't miss the movement. 'What happened?' she asked.

'The eldest,' Kyndra said, trying not to betray how much the sight of her own withered fingers unsettled her. Weeks, Ma had said, perhaps a month. *It has to be enough. I need time to prepare.* 'Ma's contained it for now, but my life depends on defeating him.'

Sesh held out her hand and they clasped wrists, pale skin against bronze scales. 'Then, Starborn, I wish you good hunting.'

13

Gareth

Kingswold rose with a rattle of armour. It hung off him, ill-fitting his bones. Without speaking, he descended the steps, leaving his sword behind. Gareth too kept his sheathed. This battle wouldn't be fought with swords.

Standing, the knight was tall, well over six feet, and Gareth found himself looking up slightly in order to meet his gaze. They were only steps apart when Kingswold stopped. Hond'Lif encased his fist in liquid light. 'What are you called?' His voice rasped; a knife dragged across ancient strings.

Once Gareth would have answered: *Gareth*. Perhaps he'd have included his second name, the one he had taken when his mother cast him out. But that was before the gauntlet, before it had doomed him to this waking death. So he said, 'Kul'Gareth.'

'A title of blood, if I am not mistaken,' Kingswold replied. 'I am known as—'

'I know who you are.' Gareth nodded at Hond'Lif. 'I know what you guard. What guards you,' he added softly.

His horned half-helm concealed much of Kingswold's face. Gareth was glad; the rasping voice was terrible enough. 'Then you are a fool to have come here,' the knight said, 'but a fool who has rendered me a service. Five centuries have I spent, unable to stray beyond the bounds of Ben-haugr. My brother and his Wielder ally saw to that.' Silently, he indicated the runes carved into his throne.

If Gareth's heart was capable of beating, it would have quickened. Perhaps Kingswold hadn't sensed his connection to the Solar. 'A Wielder did that?'

'Yes.' The word was a hiss. 'Meddlers, locked in their glass towers, too arrogant to see the threat that Sartya posed.'

'Solinaris fell,' Gareth said, though he didn't know why. A part of it was fear; if he kept Kingswold talking, it would postpone their battle just a little longer. 'When Kierik the Starborn sealed Rairam away.'

'So his plan succeeded.' Kingswold sounded pleased. 'A great warrior, a great man. With my knights, I aided him against Sartya when Solinaris refused to ally.' A smile touched the withered lips, little more than flaps of skin over bone. 'Truly he was worthy of the title he took: Worldmaker.'

'The new Starborn is his daughter.' Gareth paused. 'A friend.'

'Starborn have none.'

'Kyndra is—'

'I see you,' Kingswold tilted his head, 'a boy desperate to escape his fate. While I long for news of Acre, there is a swifter way to win it.'

His empty fist lifted, fingers spread, and Gareth found himself flying backwards until he crashed into the wall of the crypt. Something shattered within him. He glanced down and recoiled – bone protruded from his chest, a broken rib. He was riddled with fatal wounds; flesh punctured by arrows, body torn by the blade of a greatsword. If life was somehow restored to him, would he defeat Kingswold only to die?

These thoughts flashed through his head in the time it took Kingswold to advance across the bridge, each footfall the last gasp of a dying man. Gareth struggled to rise, feeling the sick grating of bone on bone, but Kingswold lashed out with the fist clad in normal armour and sent him sprawling back to the cold stone. Gareth rolled, instinctively shielding his head, and Kingswold laughed. He didn't need a sword, not when he could throw so swift and strong a punch. And he wasn't even using Hond'Lif. Gareth tried to dodge the next one, but his rotting body was too slow. The force of it slammed him back against the wall.

'I expected more,' Kingswold said. It wasn't a taunt, merely a statement. 'I thought Hond'Myrkr would choose a worthier bearer.'

He'd always been slow to anger. Rage had to be stoked, built like a careful fire to last the night. Ever since donning the gauntlet, all Gareth had felt was fear and uncertainty. If anger was there, he'd had no one to direct it at except himself. But it *was* there, he realized, smouldering somewhere out of sight. Now, ears ringing with Kingswold's insult, ribs shattered by the undead knight's fist, that slow burn finally flared to life. 'The gauntlet didn't choose anything,' Gareth said, raising it before his face. 'I did.'

He caught the knight's next swing; Hond'Myrkr closed about Hond'Lif and images like foaming water cascaded into Gareth's mind.

'Exquisite.' Serald lifts a finger to stroke the gleaming metal.

He catches it, brings it to his lips instead. 'No, Serald.' He kisses the finger, the knucklebone, the back of the bronzed hand. 'Don't touch them. They are dangerous.'

The squire laughs, perhaps with delight at his gesture, or to lessen the threat of his warning. The gauntlets lie on a table beside their bed, light, dark – perfect mirrors. Serald is the only one for whom he ever removes them. He runs his hand down the young man's leg, from naked thigh to knee. Serald leans into his touch. His skin is as burnished as the metal of the gauntlets.

Idly, he tells him so.

'Are they all you think about?' Serald frees himself, wraps the sheet irritably around his waist. 'You have compared my skin to them and my hair, even my eyes. Your true desires are clear.'

'Serald . . .' It is a feeble protest and they both know it. He would trade away every last one of their embraces if he had to. As long as the gauntlets, Hond'Myrkr and Hond'Lif, remain his.

Bedchamber became tomb. Kingswold disengaged with a snarl and Gareth stumbled back. *Did he see it too?* The memory of Serald lingered behind Gareth's eyes and its intimacy made him feel a voyeur. Abashed, he looked away.

It was a mistake. Kingswold lunged and this time it was the white gauntlet that seized the dark and pain – the first real pain he'd felt other than grasping the Solar – scythed through Gareth. He cried out . . .

. . . as he falls, small hands grazing the earth of the training circle, his wooden stave thumps down beside him and rolls out of reach.

'Pathetic,' says his mother. She stoops to collect his fallen weapon; with the other hand she hauls him up as a bitch would a pup, placing him back on his feet. 'Again.'

'Ilda, don't you think that's enough?'

Yaralf walks into the circle, fur mantle across his shoulders. 'The boy is tired. Six years is young to start training.'

'I began at five,' his mother says. The stave, sized for a child, barely reaches her thigh. 'I do not expect less from my son.'

Kingswold's grip loosened, just for a moment, but it was long enough for Gareth to wrench himself free. Both of them retreated, haunted by the forest, the training circle, Ilda's cold words.

'Your mother,' Kingswold said, 'she still lives?'

'Yes.' Gareth thought of the last time he saw her – the mantle of Ümvast heavy on her shoulders, grey in her hair. The pact they'd made, the pact that promised her the gauntlets.

He kept a healthy distance, determined not to be distracted. He had no desire to relive Kingswold's memories and even less desire to reveal his own. Because Kingswold didn't know that Gareth was a Wielder – not unless Hond'Lif pulled the knowledge out of his head. It might be the one thing that could tip the scales in his favour.

But I can't use the Solar.

He had no more time to muse. Kingswold's armoured boot flashed out, trying to trip him; he lurched drunkenly to avoid it, hearing the knight's laughter. 'Why do you resist? *Hrafnasueltir*, shamed one, you have nothing to prove, at least not to me.'

It was either seize or be seized and Gareth couldn't afford to let Hond'Lif into his mind again. He twisted his shoulder, knocked the knight's other arm aside and grabbed the white gauntlet, which shone like a star in the gloom of the crypt.

Hond'Lif is weightless in his hand. Silver-white, the brightest thing on this drear afternoon when blood is about to be spilled. He remembers its manic song tempered by the slow elegy of Hond'Myrkr. What will happen without that dark refrain? But Serjo claims it will be safe to wear alone.

Serjo . . .

He curses. His brother promised to be here and now there is no time. The Sartyan general himself stands upon the rise, protected by his soldiers and his ambertrix. His arm lifts; despite the distance between them, it's as if they lock gazes in a silent acknowledgement of what cannot be put off.

The general's arm falls.

He thrusts his fist into the gauntlet.

Hond'Lif's madrigal is chaos. Screeching and soaring, multi-stranded, it sweeps up everything in its path, including him. There is nothing to hold on to, no slow song to counter the rippling melody. But in the heart of chaos is beauty. Such beauty as to wring one dry of tears.

The last thing he sees is Serjo. His brother stands upon the walls of Kalast, already under siege from Sartyan artillery, watching him. Watching as maniacal laughter spills from his mouth, watching as tears course down his cheeks. Watching as the knights try to reason with him. Watching as Hond'Lif forces him to slaughter every last one.

'No!'

The word was lost in the scream ripped from Kingswold's throat. For a moment, he seemed to forget Gareth was there, for he crouched, covering his face with both hands.

Where is Serjo? Where is my brother?

The question came back to Gareth, the one he'd asked on the deck of the airship, when first reawakening to the world. 'He told you it was safe,' he heard himself say. 'He lied.' His eyes strayed to the throne, to the runes burned into its arms. 'It was he who bound you here.'

Kingswold raised his head, eyes flaring blue-white. 'He will answer for my death.'

'How can he? That was five hundred years ago.'

'He lives still, I know it. I can feel it.' The knight regained his feet in one swift movement and Gareth took a step back at the hatred emanating from him. Kingswold held out his hand, skeletal beneath the gauntlet. 'I tire of our struggle. Give me *Hond'Myrkr.*'

A strange feeling crept over Gareth. The crypt took on the unreal contours of a dream; nothing existed outside of it, no Acre, no Brégenne or Kul'Das, no Naris. It was as if everything he'd ever known had leaked away. 'I have come too far to surrender it,' he heard himself say.

Kingswold regarded him. 'I would think less of you if you did. But it changes nothing. I will have what is mine.' Before Gareth could muster any sort of defence, the knight was upon him, wrestling him to the ground. He kicked out, but Kingswold ignored it. There was nothing he could do, no pain he could inflict when they were both creatures of death.

Kingswold seized Hond'Myrkr with both hands and Hond'Lif's song carried Gareth into the past.

His mother's nostrils flare like a hunting wolf's. 'You would betray me for this magic-man and his tricks?'

'They are not "tricks", Madam,' the Wielder says. 'Your son has a gift.'

Ilda grows pale; Gareth has never seen her so angry. 'Please, Mother,' he tries. 'You don't know what it feels like. The things Master Hanser says I'll be able to do—'

'Tricks,' she spits, 'to compensate for a weak body, a weak heart.' She turns her glare on Hanser; the man visibly flinches. 'If he goes with you, he is no longer a Kul. He forfeits his blood.' She looks Gareth straight in the eyes. 'He will be my son no longer.'

The words hurt. He swallows the stone in his throat, closes his eyes. In the darkness behind them is gold, a thread that curls through his veins. It burns hot as the sun – it is the sun. He can't turn his back on it, not when it's inside him.

He lifts his head, looks at his mother. For the first time, underneath the fury that's turned her face pallid as the snow, he sees tears. But they are not enough to drown the sun. 'Then I am no longer a Kul.' The words sound absurd in his child's voice. 'I am no longer your son.'

For a moment, she only looks at him, her mouth a little 'o' of shock. Then she snatches the sword, the Kul blade, from the scabbard at her waist and hurls it at him. He dodges; it falls into the churned snow. 'Rot, then, you ungrateful bastard.' Ilda's voice is as muddied as the ground they stand upon. 'If I see you again, I'll kill you.'

Kingswold's grip loosened; he recoiled from Gareth as if from a striking snake. 'You are a *Wielder*.'

Gareth seized the opportunity to scramble gracelessly to his feet. 'Hond'Myrkr was kept in Naris, our city. I found it in the Wielders' archives, half a year ago.'

'Half a year?' For the first time, Kingswold looked uncertain. 'And you have worn it since? It should not have been possible.'

Gareth glanced at the gauntlet. Hond'Lif had left an imprint of white on the dark metal; but Hond'Myrkr's mark was also on the light gauntlet, curling fingers of smoke staining its alabaster hue. 'Perhaps the Solar shielded me,' he said.

'Yet you do not use it.'

'I am not alive.'

A dark smile grew on the knight's lips. 'Thus does Hond'Myrkr ensure you are no threat to me.' The smile widened; withered skin cracked. 'Even when worn by another, the gauntlet recognizes its master.'

Gareth had no reply. In all likelihood, Kingswold was right.

In silence, they faced each other. It was fast approaching, the moment when neither of them would hold back. Gareth had hoarded his secret, concealed it from Kingswold in the hope that he could somehow use it against the knight.

What hope, he now asked himself bitterly. The Solar was denied him as long as the gauntlet remained on his wrist. Only Kingswold had the power to remove it and Gareth would die when he did. He could see no way out. One of them had to defeat the other.

They circled, their paces perfectly matched. Kingswold stalked him, flaring eyes never leaving Gareth's face. Perhaps it was an effect of the knight's presence, but all remaining sensation began to fade from Gareth's body. It grew heavier, incarcerating; his consciousness felt like a trespasser. All he had to do was let go, to release his hold on his decaying flesh. He would be free. Lighter than light.

He stared at Hond'Lif, recognizing its siren song. Closing his eyes, he sank down, deep inside himself, calling on the counter-melody that had stripped him of life. When next he looked, vines like the tendrils of some dark creature twined about his wrist. Hond'Myrkr smothered its sibling's song with its own: iron bells tolling in an empty hall, a wind that whistled between standing stones, grey skies that came without relief. Ashes, darkness, ending.

Hond'Lif's spell broke. With a battle cry that had become an unearthly scream, Kingswold came at him. He attacked with the desperation born of centuries of limbo, with the promise of a second chance. Gareth met his charge with his own and they locked fists, white against black, life against death.

Images flooded him, memories of a world he'd never seen. Fields of the dead and dying; orders given that would take hundreds of lives; Sartyan swords, blades dipped in ambertrix, spitting as they met his own blade.

Serald's face, the shocking sweetness of his touch.

More images flooded him, *his* memories. Wrapped in fur, warmth, comfort: an early memory of his mother, before her smile turned bitter and her heart cold; snow covering trees like a white shroud; stink of the tanner's tent.

Shika laughing, as they lounged in the dormitory, trading jokes.

Power in his veins, on his fists; he could raise legions, slay legions, if only he was strong enough. He *would* grow strong enough. Serjo's piercing eyes that had always seen too much. His smile, his promises, his lies.

Power in his veins, drawn from the heart of the sun; day of the test: first pain then ecstasy, knowing he had passed. Years of lessons, needing to grow strong; he *would* grow strong. Kyndra, the chill in her eyes. Her face, so knowing, so uncertain.

Wild laughter, wild force, weeping as he slaughtered his men. Hond'Lif's mad song, beautiful, untempered, untamed. A chaos of light and screams; blood on the metal, in his mouth. Then darkness, a throne, a binding. Watching his body decay while he still wore it.

Finally: hope.

Fist plunged in solid earth. Tendrils seeking flesh, withering, exposing bone. Men's screams; his own body little more than a wraith's. Waking to death on the rocking deck of a ship; Brégenne's face, her poorly concealed horror. Journey to Ben-haugr, arrows pulled from his back, walking these halls, alone save for the dead.

Finally: hope.

He fought and the fight went on forever. There was nothing

but the struggle; death was not the end he'd thought it; life was not the days he'd lived. It was all one.

The balance shifted. He had a self again. He had a body. Metal sheathed his fists, white and black. A shuddering, as life coursed into his veins, carrying with it a beating heart, flesh whole and undamaged. He straightened. The crypt was full of eldritch light.

His name – his name was . . .

'Gareth,' he whispered.

14

Hagdon

No one wanted to remain in that den of carnage, its ashy ground churned up by blood and fighting. But Hagdon wouldn't leave until they'd gathered the bodies of the slain Sisters and built a pyre.

'A waste,' he murmured, watching as the sorcerous flames consumed clothes and flesh with ease. Unnatural, but they had no other fuel, not in a wood already charred black.

He sensed a presence – Irilin had come to stand at his side. She did not look at him, just gazed into the flames. A woman's open eyes stared back, the skin on her face just beginning to blister and curl in the heat. Without a word, Irilin gestured; the fire sprang up, hotter and brighter than before, and the corpse was lost to view.

'Sorry you had to see this,' Hagdon said without knowing why.

Irilin's face hardened. 'How do you know I have not seen worse?'

He didn't look away. 'Have you?'

She sighed. 'No.'

There was a pause. 'The battle with Khronosta was bad,' Irilin said, 'but I couldn't do anything then. This time was different. I am responsible for some of these deaths.'

'It doesn't get easier,' Hagdon said, turning again to stare into the hungry fire. 'It shouldn't.'

'You would know.'

'Commander,' Avery called before Hagdon could form a reply. She and Hu had come behind Mercia's unit, ensuring the downed Sisters stayed down. 'We're moving out?'

Somewhat relieved, he nodded at Irilin and left the pyre. Kait, he saw, was fussing over Nediah in a way quite unlike her usual self. 'I'm sorry, Ned,' Hagdon heard her say. 'If that weapon hadn't paralysed me . . .' She gently touched his bruised cheek. 'Does it hurt?'

Nediah caught her hand. 'I'm fine, Kait,' he murmured, flushing. It made the bruise stand out all the more starkly. He glanced at Brégenne. 'It's nothing.'

Brégenne stood stiffly, eyeing the Wielders' joined hands. Then she looked pointedly away.

'Do you have a plan for when we get to Ben'haugr?' Hagdon asked her.

'Find Gareth,' she snapped.

'Those burial mounds are vast, connected by numerous passages filled with traps.' Hagdon adjusted his vambraces, hoping to hide his scepticism. Wielder or not, the young man was probably dead by now. No one survived that place, especially on their own. 'He'll be hard to locate.'

'I have to try,' she said in a tone that brooked no argument. 'We've come this far together.' With another stolen glance at Nediah, she added, 'I won't abandon him.'

'Very well. Let's get out of here.' Shrugging back into his

feathered cloak, Hagdon led them from the clearing. Behind him the pyre sputtered, fading to embers, and the Deadwood claimed the Sisters' ashes.

They reached Ben'haugr just as morning lightened the sky. A man awaited them.

Although Hagdon drew his sword on reflex, stepping in front of Irilin, she immediately pushed him aside. 'Irilin,' Nediah cautioned, but the young woman didn't look round. Dawn turned the man into a stark silhouette: above average height, broad-shouldered, longish hair stirred by the breeze. The shadow of a sword was sheathed at his hip. Hagdon narrowed his eyes – a star shone on the man's left hand. Moments later, he realized it was pale metal, reflecting the sky: a gauntlet. A strange gloom gathered about the other fist, but Hagdon could just make out the shape of a second gauntlet. Instead of reflecting, it absorbed light.

The man began to walk towards them, ragged cloak billowing in his wake. He stopped just yards away, framed by the grim cairns of Ben'haugr. 'Gareth?' Irilin murmured, far too quietly for the newcomer to hear.

But he heard her and raised his head. Although he had the face of a young man, he stood with the bearing of someone older, authority in the set of his shoulders, the tilt of his chin. Hagdon had the impression that he was looking on a fellow commander, a leader of men. Beneath the cloak, the man's frame was thin, almost skeletal. His cheekbones were sharp ridges in pallid skin. And his eyes –

Warm brown, perfectly ordinary. Hagdon realized he was still holding his sword, blade angled towards the man who had climbed from the barrows of the dead. 'Who are you?' he called. 'State your name.'

'My name . . .' The stranger's voice was deep, deeper than his young face suggested. His brow creased, as if Hagdon had asked after the meaning of life rather than something as simple as a name. 'It's Gareth. Kul'Gareth.'

Irilin drew a shuddering breath. 'Gareth?' she said again. 'Is it you?'

'Irilin?' The man smiled. 'It's good to see you.'

'Are you . . . well?'

A shadow touched his face, but quickly passed. 'I am well.'

Despite the exchange, neither of them moved to embrace or otherwise. 'You look different,' Irilin said a little tremulously, her gaze ranging over his spare form. 'What happened to you?'

'Much,' Gareth said. He rolled his shoulders, as if easing an ache. 'I don't think you'd care to hear the full story.' His eyes moved to his left wrist, enclosed by the pale gauntlet, and he held it up to the dawn, murmuring, 'Beautiful.'

Hagdon could not pretend he wasn't thoroughly disturbed. Perhaps Irilin felt some of his unease, for she glanced at Bré-genne, who came forward to stand beside her. 'So you found it,' the Wielder said.

Gareth's eyes were still on the gauntlet. 'I won it.'

'From Kingswold?'

He swallowed. 'Yes.' The inflection in the word almost made it a question.

'And you're . . . better now, I see.'

Finally tearing his eyes away, Gareth smiled briefly; the smile contained little warmth. 'You mean my body. Yes, Hond'Lif saw to that.' The gauntlet gleamed in the newly risen sun. With-out warning, he clenched it.

A shockwave, like the peal of silent thunder, staggered Hagdon and the others. Gareth was the epicentre, standing calm and tall, his expression turned inward. Irilin and Brégenne backed away and a golden aura surrounded Kait and Nediah.

There was movement. Hagdon gripped the hilt of his sword and watched in horror as the barrows split open under the weight of the dead climbing from their graves. Their movements were stilted at first, a bluish-white glow splintering through their forms in a parody of veins. Some were little more than skeletons, others still had flesh, mottled strips revealed under rags and rusted armour. All held the weapons with which they'd been buried. Hagdon took a step back despite himself.

'Peace.' Gareth held up his hand. 'They won't harm you.'

The dead stood among the mounds, a grim and silent host. Every head turned towards Gareth, as if awaiting his command.

'Gareth,' Irilin said, in little more than a whisper. 'There's no one to fight.'

'I had to know,' was all he said. He opened his fist. As one, the dead returned to the earth, disappearing among the barrows.

Hagdon slowly eased his grip on the sword.

Between one breath and the next, Gareth's demeanour changed. 'Iri!' he exclaimed, as if he'd only just noticed her. Hagdon watched narrowly as he gave her a swift hug. Irilin flinched a little, but Gareth didn't react. He was smiling, his grin suddenly resembling a young man's.

'Brégenne,' he said, clearly delighted, and he went to embrace her too. Her answering smile was rather forced.

'I'm sorry,' she said when he stepped back. 'I wanted to come after you.'

Gareth dismissed her apology with a wave. 'Nediah.' He

turned to acknowledge the Wielder. They shook hands – with some reserve on Nediah's part, Hagdon noticed. He found his gaze straying to Irilin; she was frowning, eyes sharp on her friend's face.

'Greetings, Kul'Das,' Gareth said. 'I'm afraid you'll have to tell my mother that plans have changed.'

'What do you mean?' the blond woman asked suspiciously.

'I promised her the gauntlets.' Gareth paused. 'That's not a promise I can keep.'

He was still smiling and it raised the hairs on Hagdon's neck. Perhaps Kul'Das felt the same, for she took a tiny step back. 'I'm sure we can come to an arrangement.'

'Hond'Myrkr and Hond'Lif are mine.' His tone forbade argument.

'Gareth,' Irilin said into the uncomfortable silence. 'Don't you – don't you want to know why Shika isn't with us?'

He blinked at her. 'Where is Shika?' he asked obediently.

'He . . .' Irilin swallowed. 'He's gone. Killed by wraiths in the red valley.'

Gareth's face went perfectly blank. 'I see,' he said. The brown eyes were flat, but Hagdon saw something move beneath them, something vast and dark. 'How did it happen?'

'Quickly,' Irilin said, her voice breaking. 'He wouldn't have felt it, wouldn't have suffered. The wraiths stole Solar energy from Shika, Kait and Nediah and used it against us. When it hit him, he just disappeared. We couldn't . . . we couldn't even bury him.'

A tear rolled down Irilin's cheek and Brégenne put an arm around her.

'And Kyndra,' Gareth said with a frown. 'These wraiths were too strong for her?'

'Not exactly.' Irilin stepped out of Brégenne's hug. 'She defeated them in the end. But she was frightened. Frightened of using her power. When Shika – well, she was so angry. She fought them and we escaped. The rest of us would have died if not for her.'

'I see.' Gareth's gaunt face showed not a whisker of emotion. Then 'Shika's scarf,' he said, looking at the silken wrap Irilin wore about her neck.

'Yes,' she said, touching it. 'Would you like it?'

Wordlessly, Gareth held out a gauntleted hand and Irilin passed him the scarf. He wound the mauve silk around his forearm, knotting it just below his elbow. No one spoke. When he looked up, the dark creature in his eyes had submerged itself once more.

Someone had to break the tension, so Hagdon stepped forward. 'James Hagdon.' He raised a hand, but turned the movement into adjusting his cloak. He had no wish to touch those gauntlets. But it seemed Gareth could read his thoughts, for he said, 'They won't harm you, not so long as I wear them.'

'I'm glad we're on the same side, then.'

'Indeed,' Gareth replied. After a moment he added, 'You're the Sartyan general.'

Hagdon did not like his tone. '*Was*,' he corrected.

'Ah yes, I remember. You lead this Republic now.'

'Such is my lot,' Hagdon said, forcing on a smile like a too-tight tunic. Who could muster anything as human as a smile when confronted with that chill visage? 'These are my adjutants, Avery and Hu. And this is Lieutenant Mercia of the Sartyan Fist.'

Mercia seemed to be the only one of them not cowed by

Gareth's presence. When she gave him a brisk nod, some of the coldness left his face.

'An eclectic crew,' he said. 'What do you intend to do with them?'

'Defeat the Fist, dissolve the empire and restore sovereign rule to Acre's territories,' Hagdon said. 'Nothing much.'

To his surprise, Gareth barked a laugh. 'You don't think small, General.'

'Just Hagdon, please. I'm done with the army.'

Gareth tilted his head, fixing him with a stare that went all the way to Hagdon's bones. 'Once a general, always a general. We cannot escape our fates.'

The pronouncement sparked defiance. 'I mean to make my own fate,' Hagdon said, as much to himself as to Gareth.

Irilin was staring at him, her pale eyes large on his face. This time he did not look away. She did, flushing slightly. 'Will you come with us, Gareth?'

'What are you planning?'

'We're going to free the aberrations in Parakat and persuade them to join our cause.'

She made it sound so simple, Hagdon thought ruefully. He'd only visited Parakat once, but the sheer size of it, grim walls rimed with ice, had haunted him ever since. He couldn't forget the feeble cries of those who lacked the strength to work, who couldn't protect themselves from the whip that flogged them into unconsciousness; parents watching their children fade before their eyes; the bodies thrown into the chasm on whose lip Parakat perched. Hagdon had seen it all and had turned away.

There was a horror in him at the thought of going back.

'I cannot,' Gareth said, breaking Hagdon's grim trance. 'I promised my mother I would return.'

'Oh,' Irilin said in a small voice. 'We could have used your help.'

Hagdon wasn't so sure. He had a vision of Gareth standing above the chasm, calling up the shattered bodies of the dead, who would climb the sheer walls like pallid spiders, returning to a world that had brought them nothing but misery. He shuddered.

'I'm sorry, Iri,' Gareth said, suddenly sounding much more human. 'But I must fulfil my duty to my homeland.'

'This could work in our favour,' Brégenne said. The wind had teased out a few strands from her plait, blowing them across her face. She brushed them back with a careless, impatient hand and looked at Hagdon. 'You believe Iresonté plans to invade Rairam?'

He nodded. 'We already know she doesn't take the Republic seriously, and in its current state, she's right – we present little threat. You say Rairam has no standing army to defend it except the Wielders of Naris. She'll take your country with absurd ease and return to consolidate her hold on the Heartland.' He paused. 'She must be stopped.'

'Who is this woman?' Gareth asked.

The captain of the stealth force,' Hagdon said darkly. 'The one to whom I owe my current circumstances.'

'You say she has control of the army.'

'Yes, the greater part. However, my comrade believes there are pockets of soldiers loyal to me if only we could reach them.'

'And ambertrix?' Gareth asked. 'Has she access to artillery? Those machines could be Rairam's undoing. We have nothing of comparative power.'

He spoke of it with a familiarity he couldn't possibly possess. Hagdon frowned. The question was one he himself might ask; he wouldn't expect to hear it from a friend of Irilin's. He glanced at the young woman only to see his consternation mirrored on her face.

He'd let the silence grow too long. 'Very possible. She certainly has a stock of ambertrix cloaks when we'd long thought our supply exhausted.'

'My mother will fight,' Gareth said after a moment. 'She leads the North.'

'How many does she command?'

'We can call on five thousand,' Kul'Das said. 'Fewer, if they've lost more to the wyverns.'

Hagdon tried to hide his dismay. Iresonté had at least thirty thousand under her direct command and more would answer her call to battle, especially against Sartya's ancient bane, Rairam. 'How many Wielders?' he asked Brégenne.

'One hundred masters, just over a hundred novices,' she said. 'We lost many in the Nerian uprising.' She shot a dagger-filled glance at Kait, who returned it with contempt. Perhaps the doubt showed on Hagdon's face, for Brégenne added, 'Don't underestimate us, Commander. We may have little experience of battle, but we are not without ability. Many of us have trained for years.'

'I will return with Kul'Das,' Gareth said, 'and coordinate Rairam's defence.'

The frown Irilin had worn since the start of the conversation became sceptical. She crossed her arms. 'And what do you know about "coordinating Rairam's defence?" About commanding an army? You've never commanded anything in your life.'

'Haven't I?' They eyed each other for several seconds before

Gareth broke the contact. His smile was sheepish. 'I suppose you're right. But that doesn't mean I won't try.'

Irilin's frown eased a little, but did not go away. Perhaps that smile hadn't fooled her, Hagdon thought.

'And what about the Wielders?' Mercia said. The lieutenant had stripped off her gloves and tucked them behind her belt. Now she was laboriously cracking each finger joint. 'What are their plans?'

'I hadn't thought further than helping Gareth find the other gauntlet,' Brégenne admitted. She glanced at Nediah, he glanced at her and both looked quickly away.

'These aberrations are being held against their will,' Kait murmured. Her face seemed webbed with memory. It was strange to Hagdon, who hadn't seen her show much emotion apart from anger. 'I lived in the dark long enough to understand its terror.' She nodded at him. 'I will join you.'

Brégenne bit her lip. 'I should return to Naris,' she said, seeming less than happy about it. 'I'll be needed there.'

Nediah opened his mouth to speak but Gareth beat him to it. 'They'll arrest you,' he said. 'The moment you walk through the gates. The Wielders must have reported back by now – the other Council members will know we fought them and what happened.' He gestured with Hond'Myrkr, the hint of a dark smile on his lips. Hagdon wondered whether he even knew it was there.

'Come with us, Brégenne,' Irilin said, oblivious to the glare Kait gave her. 'We could use your help.'

'*You* shouldn't be going at all,' Brégenne replied. 'It'll be dangerous.'

'You think I don't know that?' the young woman flared. 'I've been in danger ever since I walked into Acre at Kyndra's side.

150

Now I'm here, I intend to do some good, not go running back to Naris to wait for Iresonté.' She looked at Hagdon as she said it and he felt a flutter in his belly that both worried him and made his palms sweat.

'Brégenne is right,' he heard himself say. 'It will be dangerous. We do not have the numbers to storm the fortress, which means we'll have to bluff our way inside. Success depends entirely on how long we can remain undetected.' The memory of the bolt hurling Irilin to the ground was fresh in his mind. 'They'll have ambertrix weapons, like those we encountered in the Deadwood.'

'I'm not afraid,' Irilin said predictably.

Brégenne sighed. 'My skills are yours. Besides, if these aberrations can be saved, they can be trained.' She shot an accusatory look at Kait. 'Naris needs new Wielders.'

'And you think you're the one to recruit them?' With some alarm, Hagdon saw a faint golden glow surround Kait. She stood with fists clenched. 'Maybe the Council will take you back if you bring enough? You haven't changed a bit.'

'Neither have you, it seems,' Brégenne said coldly. 'It's your fault Naris is weakened. How many did the Nerian kill in the Long Night? How many did *you* kill, Kait? People who'd never wronged you –'

'*Never wronged me?*' Kait trembled. 'You think the Nerian lived in the Deep because they liked it? The Council and its faithful brought this on themselves. They didn't have to imprison us, to subjugate us. I still bear the marks of their cruelty.' Ignoring her audience, Kait pulled aside the collar of her shirt and Hagdon saw the tail of a scar on her shoulder, disappearing down her back. He could guess what had left it; he'd ordered the same punishment a dozen times.

151

'That's enough,' Nediah said sharply. 'We already have enemies without creating enemies of each other.' Despite the dark glances he gave both women, his hands were gentle when they tugged Kait's shirt back into place. Brégenne watched every movement, her cheeks flushed. Kait's golden aura faded; she smiled at Brégenne over Nediah's shoulder.

'Gareth,' Brégenne said, turning away, 'send an envoi to Argat. You'll travel much more swiftly by airship. You know how to send an envoi?' She looked him over. 'Can you use the Solar now?'

Gareth conjured a fistful of golden fire in answer. 'It's a relief to have it back. And yes, I think so. I watched you do it enough times to get an idea.'

'We can travel together a little ways,' Hagdon said. 'It'll give us a chance to finalize plans. Then the road splits, north to the mountains, east to Causca and Rairam.'

Nods were exchanged in the awkward silence left by Brégenne and Kait's argument. 'We're moving out,' Hagdon called, his voice echoing unpleasantly between the barrows. 'We head north.'

The others swung into their saddles without delay, all keen to put the necropolis behind them. Forced to adjust his stirrup, Hagdon was the last to mount, so he thought he was the only one to see the ecstatic smile that spread across Gareth's features as they left Ben-haugr behind.

15

Kyndra

She climbs the tower. Stairs wind round and round; every turn promises to be the last. Her heart pounds, as it used to do when she was just Kyndra. As it used to do when Jarand set her a test, or when Jhren took her hand in his once as they were walking back to town, or when she stood in line, waiting for the Relic to show her the future.

She smiles now, at the memory of it breaking. That little bowl knew more than any of them could have comprehended. She'd destroyed it with a paradox. Darkness floods in at the thought; the crystal walls become onyx. She cannot see her feet. She cannot see at all. But she climbs, knowing who awaits her at the top. Knowing she will have to fight him, knowing she will have to win. Or the world will be lost.

Kyndra opened her eyes. For a moment, the black dream lingered on in shadows at the corners of her vision. Then it dissipated, a cloud revealing sun, and she saw dawn. It came in through the high, cold windows of the chamber in Magtharda. Char's mother was watching her, great violet eyes unblinking.

Kyndra sat up, somewhat unsettled, and the dragon drew back. They were alone. The room was large enough for several full-grown Lleu-yelin, cunningly heated by ambertrix channels hidden under the floor. Kyndra was grateful for their warmth. Mountain wind wailed beyond the door; now and again, chill draughts found their way inside. Whenever they did, Ekaar's scales shivered disagreeably.

'You dream,' the dragon said.

'How long have you been watching me?'

'Long enough, Starborn. Do not ignore them.'

Kyndra rubbed her eyes, blinked the sleep away. 'The dreams?'

'They are sendings,' Ekaar said.

'From whom?'

'The self.' She refolded her wings. 'Surely you know this.'

The wind rose up to fill the short silence; cold air gusted under the door and Ekaar shifted position, putting the chamber's central pillar between her and the wind. 'Winter is here.'

'Not a good time to start a war,' Kyndra murmured. 'Let's hope Iresonté waits until spring.' She glanced at her hand to find the curse had worsened overnight. In the chamber's ambertrix glow, her flesh seemed to shrivel before her eyes. 'I don't have that luxury.'

'There is nothing to be done?'

'Nothing except kill the eldest before his curse kills me.'

'It is easy to forget that Starborn are not invulnerable,' Ekaar said, regarding her closely.

'Everyone has a weakness,' Kyndra replied. 'I am the first to admit mine.'

There was approval in Ekaar's nod. 'I can see why my son chose to travel in your company.'

'He didn't have much choice,' Kyndra said, blinking at the abrupt change in subject. 'Khronosta hunted him. He couldn't evade the *du-alakat* on his own.'

'Just as you cannot hope to win this war on your own.'

Kyndra frowned. 'What do you mean?'

'What I say.' Ekaar curled her spiked tail around her legs, looking like an alarmingly large cat. Her violet eyes narrowed on Kyndra's face. 'You have gathered allies, Starborn. Do not ignore them. Do not believe you must make your stand alone.'

'I don't,' she said. 'I wouldn't have come here otherwise. I wouldn't have sought to free you.'

Ekaar tilted her scaled head. 'Your tame Khronostian needed our prison's power to challenge the eldest, true?'

Kyndra stood. The blankets she'd slept in tangled around her feet and she kicked them impatiently aside. 'How do you know that?'

'I spoke with my son.'

Damn it, Char. 'I didn't realize he'd told you,' Kyndra said, hoping to sound as if it hadn't come as a surprise. 'Yes. Ma's powerful, but she's alone. I won't pretend freeing you was our sole reason in coming here.' She folded her arms. 'And weren't we talking about allies?'

'We were.' Ekaar rose up too, an action that was far more impressive than Kyndra's. Her spiked mane was as ash-grey as her son's. 'You did not come here to find allies, Starborn. You came for the power in the prison. *You*, specifically.'

'Only Ma can use that power.'

'But where you go, she cannot follow. She must stay to maintain whatever portal she opens. And that is how you want it.'

Before Kyndra could answer, a stronger gust of wind signalled newcomers. The doors swung wide. Beyond them, Kyndra saw an iron sky, clouds hammered flat.

'Didn't I say you'd find her here?' Arvaka said as he entered with Char. 'Mithering the Starborn.'

'You did.' Kyndra thought she detected a certain nervousness in the way Char swung his head to eye the two of them.

'Arvaka,' Ekaar growled, 'were you born on a glacier? Shut that door.'

'Not yet,' Char said. 'The old Wielder's just arrived.' Sesh's mate had agreed to collect Shune two days ago.

Kyndra gave a sigh of relief. 'Good. Let's go greet him.'

Realdon Shune looked to be in a very poor mood. 'Starborn,' he called over the raw wail of the wind, knuckling his back with gnarled hands, 'I'm an old man. Tell me why I agreed to this.'

Kyndra raised an eyebrow. 'To save the world?'

'Oh.' Shune's expression soured further. 'That.' He hobbled out of the blue dragon's shadow, raising an arm against the wind. 'Magtharda. I'd forgotten how impressive it is.'

Ekaar regarded him approvingly. 'The elder has manners.' She nodded her head at Kyndra and Ma, who'd just joined them. 'I did not hear such courtesy from you.'

'We freed you from the mandala,' Kyndra said. 'I should think that shows courtesy enough.'

'Do you wish me to freeze to death?' Realdon Shune snapped. 'I thought you'd brought me here to help you.'

'This way.' Kyndra led them across the courtyard and through the huge doors of the chamber they'd made their quarters.

'Ah, the famous heated floor.' Shune settled on a pile of cushions, leaned forward and pressed both veined hands against the stone with a sigh. 'Got anything to drink?'

Kyndra handed him a flask. The old Wielder sipped it and made a face. 'Water? I'm old, not infirm.'

Arvaka moved to one corner, poured a viscous liquid from a pot. 'You might want to dilute it,' he suggested, passing it to Shune. 'It's not made for humans.'

Shune gave him a withering look. He tossed the drink back, scrawny throat bobbing with each swallow before coughing once and wiping his mouth. 'Better.'

While Arvaka looked faintly impressed, Kyndra seated herself beside the old man. 'What's been going on, Shune? Have you heard from Hagdon?'

'Not since they arrived at the Deadwood,' the Wielder said. 'But he should be pleased. Amon's singlehandedly resupplying the Republic. Plenty of men still loyal to the old general. Just need to find them.'

Ma dropped down on Shune's other side. 'News can wait,' she said sharply. 'We need your help to determine when the eldest might strike. I have to know how far back the Yadin's timeline goes. When did he come into being?'

Realdon Shune's eyes took on the distance of memory, carrying Kyndra with him. Again she saw him as Kierik had seen him: young, arrogant, dark haired. A shadow of that arrogance remained in his face. He'd defied Kierik, claiming the empire was Acre's future. She wondered what had made him so sure. And when he had changed his mind.

'It was a mistake, I see it now,' Shune said, 'bound to have repercussions impossible to predict. But Solinaris was at the height of her power. We had run out of challenges, yearned to create a legacy . . . such was the environment which bred the idea of the Yadin.'

'But *when*?' Ma pressed.

'I was getting to that,' the old Wielder said testily. '478 — during the early rise of the empire.'

Ma's face fell. 'That covers a broad range of years,' she murmured. 'So many possibilities.'

'*Can* the eldest undermine Sartya?' Char asked. 'What would he have to do?'

'Davaratch was the keystone of the empire,' Shune said, his head tilted thoughtfully. 'The first emperor. The man who built Sartya. By the time he died, it was an established power, already bringing multiple territories under its banner.' He paused. 'I think one can say, with some certainty, that without Davaratch, it's quite probable the empire wouldn't exist.'

'Sartya has shaped Acre,' Ma said, nodding. 'And the history of Acre. It is such an integral part of this world and its people that stripping it out could have consequences even the eldest cannot foresee.' Her expression hardened. 'It could warp the flow of time, create inescapable paradoxes. He *must* be stopped.'

'So targeting Davaratch himself seems the obvious choice,' Kyndra concluded. 'But as emperor, he'd be well-protected. We'd have to find out when he was most vulnerable.'

Shune gave her a considering look. 'Have you thought about asking the stars?'

She blinked at him. 'What?'

'Are they not eternal? Did they not witness Sartya's rise to power?'

'I . . .' Kyndra's mouth dried. *Era, are you listening?*

No answer. Kyndra frowned to herself. *Any of you,* she thought at them.

Still no answer. She was aware of the others watching her curiously. *I command you to speak to me!* She threw the words into the void with all the force she could muster.

Have a care, Starborn, Era's hollow voice replied, *there are things we are not permitted to say.*

Kyndra felt a flicker of affront. *Am I not your avatar? Aren't you supposed to obey me?*

We obey, Era replied frustratingly. *We obey* your *command.*

My? Kyndra stopped, struck by an impossible thought. *When did I give you this command?*

She sensed Era's evasiveness. *Before.*

Before what?

Before now.

Kyndra shook her head. *I don't understand. If I gave you a command, why can't I remember giving it?*

Because you have not given it yet.

She drew in a deep breath to swallow her annoyance. A paradox. *All right, you can't answer. But if I've already travelled in time, you must have told me where to go. Or how would I have known to go there?*

They were silent for a long time. At least so it seemed; in reality it could have been mere moments. *Ask the Wielder,* Era said tentatively, as if the star were afraid of revealing too much, or of breaking her own command. *Ask the Wielder about the failed assassination attempt.*

On whom? Kyndra pressed, but Era's presence faded. She sighed and opened her eyes to find the others watching closely. Shune looked especially fascinated. 'They're being evasive,' Kyndra said to him. 'They told me to ask you about a failed assassination.'

Shune's brow furrowed. For a few seconds, he stared into space before his eyes abruptly regained their focus and he slapped his knee. 'Of course!' he exclaimed and then waved his cup at Arvaka. 'More, dragon.' The Lleu-yelin muttered something under his breath before doing as the old man asked. 'I should have remembered before,' Shune said once his mug had been refilled. 'But five hundred years do tend to blur the memory.'

'Remembered *what*?' Ma said. She shifted impatiently on her cushion.

'That Davaratch was nearly killed.' Shune drank; this time he didn't cough. 'It wasn't the first attempt,' he continued. 'Wasn't the last, either, but it was the only time the assassin nearly succeeded.' He grimaced, burped, and Ekaar wrinkled her nose distastefully.

Ma leaned forward. 'Who was the assassin?'

'No idea. Perhaps they were in the pay of a rival house. In those days, the Heartland was an arena, a place of power struggles and poison. House Sartya had no other scions. If Davaratch had died, Sartya would never have maintained its grip on the capital . . .' Shune trailed off, his eyes on Ma's paling face. A chill premonition seized Kyndra.

'That is where the eldest will go,' Ma said, standing. 'That is what he will do.'

'Or what he's already *tried* to do,' Kyndra whispered, thinking of *Era*.

We obey your command.

Did the star mean this had already happened? Had that assassin actually been the eldest? Kyndra felt a headache coming on. *Do not think about it,* Era cautioned her. *What has been has been. What will be will be. But only if the conditions are right.*

'You're making it worse,' Kyndra snapped before realizing she'd spoken aloud. 'Not you,' she added with a vague, dismissive wave. 'I just can't get my head around the idea of time and time travel.'

'It took me my whole life,' Ma said and Kyndra was surprised to hear wry amusement in her voice. When she next spoke, it had faded, and Ma's expression was again sober. 'We must close the loop,' she said to Kyndra. 'Ensure the past remains unchanged. The eldest cannot be allowed to succeed where once he failed.'

'If we don't, what will happen?'

Ma spread her gloved hands. 'We will be sailing in unknown waters. Davaratch will die before he can stabilize the empire. Everything we know from that point on will be different. Will any of us even exist?'

The chamber stilled. Everyone sat frozen, staring aghast at Ma.

'Time is one of the stiches that holds together the fabric of existence.' In that moment, Ma's voice seemed to echo with an ancient timbre. 'If it is unpicked, unhooked from history . . .' she trailed off. 'It is difficult to explain in layman's terms. But the threat is greater than any of you know.'

For a while no one spoke, each attempting to process Ma's words in their own way, Kyndra thought. She felt a throb in her weakened hand and it jolted her from her own contemplation. They needed to act now. 'What must I do?' she asked in a near whisper.

'What you have already done,' Ma answered cryptically. 'Foil the assassination.'

'And you can send me?'

Ma nodded. 'With the Wielder's help.'

Shune, Kyndra noticed, looked less than enthused. She steeled herself. 'How long do you need to prepare?'

'Not long.' Without another word, Ma strode hurriedly from the chamber.

'Do you recall the year of this assassination attempt?' Arvaka asked Shune.

The old Wielder scowled. 'My memory isn't *that* formidable. Possibly somewhere between 485 and 495.'

'I will check our records.' The Lleu-yelin rose gracefully and followed in Ma's wake.

'Tell me,' Realdon Shune said into the space they'd left behind, 'why the Yadin is a willing accomplice in this plan.'

Kyndra sighed. 'Medavle helped me in Naris, rescued me from the test, told me the truth about Kierik. I trusted him. But when we came to Acre, everything changed. He grew distant, began having nightmares—'

Shune leaned forward. 'Nightmares?'

'About Isla. She was a Yadin too, killed by Kierik with the rest of her kind. The eldest promised to go back and save her.' Kyndra shook her head. 'I don't understand why Medavle would risk so much for this.'

Char turned to regard her. 'Because he loved Isla.'

'So? It was years ago.'

'Some loves don't fade with time. The eldest gave Medavle a way to save her – he couldn't have offered anything more potent.'

Kyndra frowned at him. 'I thought Medavle was stronger than that. The world is too important to risk for the sake of a woman long dead.'

'Clearly Isla *was* Medavle's world.' She thought she detected sadness in Char's yellow eyes as they studied her. 'You don't understand.'

'You're right – I don't,' she said with a bite of irritation.

What was there to understand? Medavle's actions were wholly irrational, especially for a man who'd lived centuries.

'I tend to agree with the Starborn,' Shune said crisply. 'This Yadin is obviously unbalanced. A flaw in the race's nature, I'm afraid. I argued against giving them the ability to love.' He snapped his fingers. 'Unswerving obedience is easier to achieve through punishment and reward.'

Char grunted disgust, deep in his throat. 'Medavle's no animal.'

'Unfortunately not.' Shune shrugged. Kyndra noticed Ekaar's hackles rising as well and wondered whether the Wielder realized how frosty the atmosphere had become. Luckily, Ma re-entered at that moment, stripping off her gloves as she came. The ouroboros on her palms glittered in the bluish ambertrix light.

'Wait,' Shune said on seeing her face. 'You want to do this *now*? You wouldn't give an old man time to rest from his journey?'

'If the stars are right, then Kyndra *must* be in place before the eldest.'

'What does my role require, then?' Shune asked somewhat nervously.

'We will link hands and minds. I must have access to your memories.'

'Out of the question,' he snapped. 'I carry secrets I swore never to divulge.'

Ma shook her head irritably. 'I do not plan to steal your secrets, old man. What use would I have for them?'

'That is scant comfort.'

'I cannot work without a link. I need to see your time-stream.'

'Shune,' Kyndra said when the Wielder opened his mouth to argue further, 'that's why we brought you here.' She narrowed her eyes. 'You *will* do as Ma says.'

Shune glared at her. 'Would you threaten an old man?'

'If I was threatening you, you'd know about it,' Kyndra replied evenly.

The Wielder muttered something inaudible, but dropped his protest.

She hadn't expected nerves, Kyndra realized, listening to her own speeding heart. Her palms tingled; thoughts chased each other across the surface of her mind. It was the enormity of the task, she thought. The enormity and the impossibility, for who would believe that the past could be revisited, let alone changed?

We're not trying to change it, she reminded herself, *we're trying to preserve it.* The deep irony of her task did not escape her. What would Kierik say if he knew she fought to protect Davaratch – a man who would go on to murder countless thousands? Kierik had thought Sartya unnatural and Kyndra finally understood why. No power was meant to grow so vast that it subjugated all others. That was what Starborn guarded against; they were protectors of the balance. And in order to guard humanity, they must stand outside it. Once upon a time, the revelation might have saddened her; now Kyndra felt nothing except the purity of understanding.

A cry interrupted her thoughts. She looked up in time to see a shining bird swoop straight through the stone wall. She held out her good wrist and the envoi landed. Each careful feather crackled with both Solar and Lunar energy. The detail was familiar: Brégenne's work, Nediah's signature in the Solar. So they'd met up at last.

She frowned as she read. Gareth was alive, but changed. He'd taken the news of Shika's death surprisingly well. *Shika.* She'd almost forgotten – no, not forgotten – but so much had happened since that day in the red valley to push the novice out of her mind. Kyndra read on.

Gareth has returned to Rairam, Brégenne reported, her neat hand spidering across Kyndra's palm. *Iresonté plans to bring the Fist across the border and the people of Rairam have only Ümvast and Naris to defend them.* Kyndra sighed. If she didn't have problems enough . . . *I promised Hagdon I would help him take Parakat,* Brégenne continued, *the fortress built to house aberrations. The Republic needs their support. And their imprisonment is monstrous. A Sartyan lieutenant loyal to Hagdon has joined us and she believes other garrisons will come when they see that the Republic's standard flies on the walls of Parakat.*

'They plan to do *what?*' Char said when Kyndra had passed along the news. 'Parakat's a fortress surrounded by a bottomless chasm. Sartya could defend it with a handful of raw recruits. What does Hagdon think he's doing?'

'Aren't you forgetting Brégenne, Nediah, Kait and Irilin?' Kyndra replied, though privately she shared some of Char's doubt. 'And Hagdon's a sound tactician. They'll have a plan.'

The black dragon sat back. 'It sounds like suicide.'

'Brégenne wouldn't agree to it if she thought they hadn't a chance.' Kyndra formed a reply in her head, telling Brégenne about the Lleu-yelin and the eldest's plan. *Raad,* she commanded when finished, *take my reply to Brégenne.* The wolf shape wasn't necessary, she thought, as she watched *Raad* assume it, but Brégenne wouldn't be able to see the star otherwise.

'481,' Arvaka said as he re-entered, holding a thin piece of metal. Words in the Lleu-yelin language glowed softly, ambertrix-blue. He gestured with it. 'The attempt was all the more extra-ordinary because it happened in the middle of the winter celebration, deep in the Sartyan stronghold – supposedly the safest place Davaratch could be.'

Char looked at his father. 'That's not good. How is Kyndra going to get in there?'

'Like this.' Kyndra clothed herself in *Fas*, vanishing from sight.

Char still seemed discomfited. 'I wish you weren't going alone. What if the eldest has *du-alakat* with him?'

'She is Starborn,' Ma said firmly. She'd been conferring with Shune. Now the Wielder's face was set, if a little pale. 'And the fewer who go, the less of a wound it will make in time.' She turned her palms up; the ouroboros swam in endless circles over her flesh. 'The eldest must use a mandala and it will not hold indefinitely, meaning he has a limited window in which to act. Your role is solely to thwart him, not to make changes of your own.'

Kyndra nodded. 'I understand.'

Ma's eyes narrowed on her face. 'Remember. Your own life depends on your success. And most likely the lives of everyone here.'

Kyndra noted the tense expressions of her companions. Arvaka, still clutching the metal tablet, stood beside his mate, a hand on her dusky scales. Char lashed his tail, his eyes never leaving Kyndra's face. She could feel the moment fast approach-ing. It was foolish to put it off now that they knew what they had to do.

'I won't fail.' Kyndra looked around the chamber. 'Don't you need a mandala too?'

'No,' Ma answered. 'Khronostians dance in order to align themselves with the timestream in which they intend to travel.' She lifted her chin. 'I do not need to align myself. I stand like a rock in the river – time flows to either side of me. I am constantly immersed.' She paused thoughtfully. 'To some extent, I am also the river. But subject to it.'

'Did you understand any of that?' Char said. His claws left scratches on the surface of the stone. Nobody answered.

'How do I come back?' Kyndra asked quietly. Her heart was beating harder now; so strange to feel even this small emotion. *Isn't it what you wanted?* she told herself. *To be left alone to do things your way?*

'Reach out to me,' Ma said. 'I will be listening.'

At least she had the stars, Kyndra concluded. As long as she had them, there was nothing she couldn't deal with. 'How much time will pass while I'm gone?'

'Time is a river full of shifting currents,' Ma said. 'Some flow swiftly, others slow and sluggish. You are travelling so far back that a day for you will be an hour for me. But I would advise you to hurry – even I cannot keep the connection open indefinitely.'

'Be careful.' Char nudged her with his nose. 'Don't take risks.'

Ma gestured for Shune's hand. It trembled as the old man gave it. 'Stand there,' she ordered Kyndra tightly. 'And stay still. I have not done this before.'

What little colour remained in Shune's face drained away. '*Now* you tell us,' he muttered.

The twin ouroboros on Ma's palms flared, light flowing under her skin, filling her eyes. At the same instant, Shune gasped. His own eyes flew wide.

An intricate cage grew around Kyndra. It reminded her of

the one Brégenne had conjured that night in Naris, the one that had saved her life. And then that thought was shattered by a bell, tolling and tolling, until her head rang with the awful sound. Remembering Ma's command, she stayed still, fighting the desire to cover her ears. It wouldn't do any good, she sensed; the bell was inside as well as outside. The longer she listened, the closer her internal note grew to the one beyond her until they harmonized in a sweeping, soaring chord. There was a rush, as though of water, which caught and whirled her through a roaring channel. She raised her eyes to Ma's face only to see white. The world had turned to snow.

She was kneeling in it, on hands and knees, ungloved fingers already going blue. Flakes drifted down around her, alighting on her face, her shoulders, and on the gleaming breastplate of the soldier who stood over her, drawn sword levelled at her heart. Automatically, she reached for *Tyr*.

And encountered nothing. Kyndra hurled herself at the void, but there *was* no void and no countless stars to fill it. The soldier's helmeted head stared down at her; she saw herself reflected in the shining metal. Her eyes were round with fear, set in a face that was pale and unmarked. As the chill reality dawned, panic took her: panic which convinced her more than the silent sky.

The stars had betrayed her. She was just Kyndra again, and she was alone.

PART TWO

16

Brégenne

'Something's not right about Gareth,' Brégenne said after they'd made camp for the night. She stood with Hagdon, Irilin and Kul'Das, firelight licking over their faces – they all wore the same uneasy expression.

'I know,' Irilin said. 'He's changed. Different. What was he like before he went into Ben-haugr, Brégenne?'

'Not his normal self,' she answered, double-checking that the subject of their discussion wasn't in earshot. 'Sometimes he spoke in a strange language and mentioned a man called Serjo. But more often he was just Gareth.'

'Did you see his face when I told him about Shika?' Irilin bit her lip. 'It looked like – like he didn't care.'

No one knew how to answer her, Brégenne included. 'I thought uniting the gauntlets would make him better,' she said eventually. 'They've restored him to life, but not to the Gareth we know.' She briefly closed her eyes. 'This is my fault. I let him go in there alone.'

'Don't be silly,' Irilin said, her tone surprisingly harsh. 'It's the fault of the gauntlet. You said it pulled him through the wall, led him to whatever he found inside Ben-haugr.'

'Kul'Das,' Brégenne said suddenly, taking the blond woman's arm. 'You will be all right, won't you? Travelling alone with Gareth?'

'Concern? For me?' Kul'Das smiled as she reclaimed her arm. 'I do not believe Kul'Gareth will harm me.'

'Even so, he's not himself.' Brégenne shot another cautious look over her shoulder. 'I don't think he ever will be again.'

'I'm going to speak to him,' Irilin said, 'while I still have a chance.' She marched off into the darkness and though her steps were sure, she hunched her shoulders, as if talking to Gareth was actually the last thing she wanted to do. Hagdon watched her go, his dark troubled eyes on her back. He excused himself, citing needing a word with Mercia, but Brégenne noticed he veered off in the same direction Irilin had taken.

'I had better repack if Kul'Gareth and I are to depart in the morning,' Kul'Das said and she left Brégenne alone.

They were camped at the foot of a shallow escarpment, studded with rounded boulders. Perhaps the sea had bellowed here once upon a distant time, nature's sculptor smoothing sharp edges from the rock. With the recent addition of Mercia's men, their group now numbered eighty – not, Brégenne reflected, much of a force to be reckoned with. *They will need my help.* The thought wasn't driven by pride, but pragmatism. Storming a fortress was the job of armies, not motley groups of rebels. At Hagdon's request, she'd sent an envoi to Taske, his second in command, asking for support. She'd rather have asked Kyndra, but the Starborn had her own, more perilous task.

A tent flap lifted and Nediah emerged, followed by Kait. The buttons of his shirt were half undone; he was swiftly fastening them. Brégenne's breath caught, a sick feeling uncurling in her chest.

'Not now,' she heard Nediah say. 'We've talked about this.'

Kait spotted Brégenne; the colour in her cheeks grew brighter. 'Ned.' She caught his arm and he turned. Kait leaned in to whisper something, her lips brushing his ear. She drew back with a secret smile and flicked her eyes in Brégenne's direction.

Nediah followed her gaze and saw Brégenne watching. His own eyes widened.

She turned away, her insides churning with hurt. All she could see was Kait and her smile, her lips on Nediah's skin. She felt tears prick her eyes. She *would not* cry.

'Brégenne!'

She walked faster, but he caught her arm, pulled her to a stop. 'Wait,' he said. For a moment Brégenne just stood there, gazing into the dark, feeling the warmth of his fingers curled around her wrist. Then she turned, yanking her arm free.

'What do you want?'

Nediah ran a hand through his hair; for a moment the familiar gesture made her want to reach up and push it out of his eyes. Brégenne swallowed the urge, holding fast to her anger.

'I . . . we . . .' Nediah stuttered to a halt, a flush spreading across his cheeks. 'We haven't had a chance to talk.'

When she didn't reply, his hands sought the pockets of his coat and the silence stretched, stinging her with the memory of how easy they'd once been in each other's company. Brégenne yearned for that casualness just as she yearned for something more. The something that had woken her in the middle of the night, heart aching with loneliness.

He'd said he loved her. Now *this*.

'Brégenne,' he began.

'No,' she said sharply. 'I don't want to hear it.'

Nediah frowned. 'Hear what? I was—'

'I said no.' Because now another image had risen in Brégenne's mind: Nediah gently covering up the scars on Kait's back; the memory of that gesture and the other woman's pleased smile made her blood boil.

Nediah stared at her. 'I was going to say I missed you.'

'You could have fooled me.' She glanced over his shoulder to see Kait watching them. Brégenne wasn't sure whether they were out of earshot and suddenly she didn't care. All that time she'd spent missing *him* . . . She felt herself stiffen. 'It didn't take you long.'

'What didn't?'

She clenched her fists. 'Stop pretending. I've seen you both together.'

Nediah glanced back too. 'So this *is* about Kait.'

Brégenne's heart pounded sickly. She turned away, but Nediah caught her arm again. 'Why are you so upset?'

She twisted out of his grip. 'How can you ask me that? You've been here with her—'

'No, Brégenne.' He lowered his voice, made to touch her cheek. 'It's not like that. You have it all wrong.'

'Do I?' she almost hissed. 'I know what she was to you. Didn't I spend months picking up the pieces when she left for the Deep? Well, now she's back and you've got what you wanted.'

The flush had begun to fade from Nediah's cheeks. 'That's unfair, Brégenne. You're not listening.'

Tears pricked her eyes. She wouldn't let him see. 'You're quite welcome to each other,' she snarled before whirling round and stalking off into the night. Brégenne bit her lip, trying to swallow the hurt and the shame. She'd carried around the fear of those words for months, never truly imagining that she'd have to speak them.

'Brégenne!'

She kept on walking. *If he cares,* she thought stubbornly, *he'll come after me.* Despite herself, she slowed just a little, but no footsteps followed her. Then it was too much and Brégenne found herself fleeing into the darkness. She made it another ten steps before she sank down behind a boulder, out of sight of the camp, and buried her face in her hands.

She must have fallen asleep because she dreamed of *them*, as she hadn't done in years.

Waking up under the bold Acrean moon, Brégenne lay very still, shocked at her pounding heart, at her aching heels which felt as if they really had just drummed upon the ground, her legs pinned down by her cousins all those decades ago. Her aunt had held her arms, the scent of her rose perfume heavy in Brégenne's nostrils. She'd always hated the cloying scent of rose.

Her mind wouldn't stop showing her pictures: her uncle pushing her head to the sweet summer earth. His chiding voice: *It'll be over soon, Genne, don't fight us,* as if he were not about to burn out her eyes, attempting to stem the powers she'd demonstrated as a child. His rough fingers as they'd all but ripped open her eyelids. Her desperate screams, and then the first scalding agony, her vision blurring, hiding their faces, their pity. Hiding colour, hiding sunlight, until Nediah came and gave it all back to her.

Brégenne whimpered. She realized she was curled into a ball, her eyes tightly closed.

'Brégenne?'

Through the paralysing fear, she forced herself to move. *It's over. They're gone.* But then why had they risen so suddenly from their graves, where they had lain for decades?

The graves you put them in.

'Brégenne, are you all right?' Irilin crouched over her, still slumped against the boulder where she'd cried herself out.

'I'm fine.' She sat up stiffly. 'I must have fallen asleep.'

The moonlight illumined Irilin's uncertain face. 'You were moaning,' she said. 'I heard you.'

'Bad dream.' Brégenne strived to sound nonchalant, but her voice was too thin and her hands shook too badly. She hid them under her cloak.

'I've had plenty of those,' Irilin murmured in sympathy. 'I dream of Shika's death. I dream of Kyndra when she was the star, standing among the burned soldiers, telling us that she wanted to destroy the world.' She paused. 'I dream of the battle at Khronosta, of feeling like a child, watching my friends fighting for their lives and being unable to help them.'

Brégenne didn't offer words of comfort. Irilin's distant face told her she didn't need or want any. 'Some times we're living through,' she said instead, a little ruefully, trying for a smile.

'Some times,' Irilin agreed, returning it. She held out a small, surprisingly strong hand and helped Brégenne to her feet. 'What were you doing back here anyway?'

'Thinking,' Brégenne lied. 'I feel like I'm abandoning Rairam and my responsibilities to Naris. But we need reinforcements. If we help those in Parakat, perhaps they will agree to join us.'

'And perhaps they'll be too damaged or scared,' Irilin said darkly. 'I heard Hagdon describe the place. It's monstrous. Aberrations are tortured, forced to work day and night on no rations.

When one dies, their body is simply flung into the chasm.'

'He told you that?'

'I asked him to tell me,' Irilin said, a touch defiantly.

Brégenne studied the young woman. 'You do realize that he looks out for you?'

'He looks out for everyone. We're all on the same side now.'

'Irilin, he looks out for *you*.'

She dropped her gaze. 'I didn't ask him to.'

'Nevertheless,' Brégenne replied, 'you should be careful around him.'

Irilin stiffened. She looked up, her eyes flashing. 'I don't need a lecture. I'm quite old enough to make my own decisions.'

There was nothing of the novice Brégenne remembered in her voice. Taken aback, she stared at her. Irilin's hair, almost as pale as her own, was bound up messily, as if she'd needed it away from her face in a hurry. Dirt smudged one of her cheeks and her chewed lips looked as if they'd borne the brunt of her fear and uncertainty over the last few weeks.

'Sorry,' Irilin said after a few moments. 'I didn't mean to snap.'

'I'm sorry too.' Brégenne shook her head. 'I haven't shared your troubles. I shouldn't have presumed.'

They made their way back to the now-silent camp. There was no sign of Nediah or Kait and Brégenne was grateful. She felt drained, hollowed out by the nightmare. 'I saved you some dinner,' Irilin said, handing her a bowl of something dark. 'It's a bit cool now. Hu made it. He may be one of Hagdon's adjutants, but he's also the best cook.' She paused. 'That's what I like about the Republic. Rank doesn't define people here as it does in an army. Everyone pitches in.'

Brégenne took the bowl and the bread inside it with a word

of thanks. A few minutes ago, stomach curdled with the dream, she couldn't have eaten a thing. Now she devoured the stew in a few mouthfuls, using the tough bread to soak up the last of the gravy.

'Well. Goodnight,' Irilin said a little awkwardly. Instead of going to her tent, she went to sit on a rock at the boundary of their camp where, after a moment, the silhouette of a man made room for her.

The next day began with farewells.

'The Kanaran border's watched,' Avery told Hagdon. Sent to scout ahead, the auburn-haired rebel had returned with the dawn. 'Iresonté must have guessed we'd come this way.'

Hagdon's forehead gained another few lines. 'She can't know our true target, or they'd have intercepted us before now. Plenty of good ambush spots along the Deadwood road.' With a glance at Kait and Nediah, he added, 'And she may be wary of our Wielders. She witnessed their abilities at Khronosta.'

'We can avoid the border,' Mercia said, coming up beside them. The lieutenant had swapped her plate armour for leather better suited to travel. 'But Kul'Gareth cannot accompany us further. North of here, the eastern mountain passes dry up. The only one open will be Sartyan-held Angyar. Unless you can turn yourself invisible –' she raised a dubious eyebrow – 'slipping past unnoticed will be difficult.'

'Then Kul'Das and I will leave you,' Gareth said and Brégenne felt a pang of worry. Despite his change, she couldn't forget the weeks they'd travelled together, watching his struggle with the gauntlet, his gradually shrinking frame, the dark circles that made wells of his eyes.

None of that showed now. He was healthy and strong, and

the colour had returned to his cheeks. That should have re-assured Brégenne; instead it unnerved her. Nevertheless, she moved towards him, grasped his arm, careful not to touch the gauntlets. 'Take care, Gareth. I'm sure I needn't tell you not to underestimate Ümvast.'

Gareth's smile was that of the novice of Naris and she was glad to see it. 'Don't worry about me, Brégenne. She might be Ümvast, but she's also my mother. I know her. I can deal with her.'

There it was; between one sentence and the next, Gareth's tone changed and Brégenne was suddenly more concerned for Ümvast.

'Gareth.' Irilin came forward, hesitating only once before embracing him. After a moment, he hugged her back. Irilin looked into his face. 'Remember Shika,' she said.

Brégenne was watching Gareth closely, but even she almost missed the flash in his eyes, so swiftly did it come and go. Perhaps Irilin caught it too because she stepped back, dropping her own gaze, as if she'd seen something there to frighten her.

Without saying anything further, Gareth swung into his saddle and Kul'Das copied him, far less gracefully. If she was honest with herself, Brégenne wouldn't be too sorry to see the woman go.

'Remember to send envois,' she called, as Gareth turned his horse east. 'I need to know what's going on in Rairam.' She tried to quash the trepidation she felt as Gareth and Kul'Das disappeared behind the curve of a hill. What had she unleashed on her homeland?

'Strike camp,' Hagdon called. 'And make sure the horses are not overburdened. We're taking the Yrsat ravine.'

Brégenne rode next to Irilin, trying not to dwell on last

night's confrontation. Nediah was a little ahead of her; she caught several stifled glances her way and cursed herself for saying so much. Kait rode beside Nediah and Brégenne didn't need to see her face to know she was in high spirits. How much of their argument had she overheard? Quite enough, Brégenne thought darkly. *Why* had she let her tongue run away with her like that? She sighed. Things had been simpler when she and Nediah had been apart.

That depressing thought plagued her all day, so she was glad when finally they called a halt. The afternoon had dragged through an unchanging landscape of granite-grey rock and strangled trees. 'These ravines once led to Yrsat,' Hagdon said, as they dismounted. 'A secret city interred in stone. Treachery did for it and Sartyans fired these passages. Many burned alive, caught in their own trap.' His dark eyes drifted overhead, to the carvings still visible beneath the weathered stone. 'We have much for which to answer,' he added softly. Brégenne noticed the nearest rebels watching him closely. Perhaps the fate of this ancient city drew attention to their differences. *Not a good thing*, she thought, *when we need to stand united*.

'Maybe we shouldn't stay here,' she called, ignoring her own reluctance to remount and ride on. Despite the years that separated them from this disaster, she made out a dark patina on the skin of the rock: the scars left by fire.

Hagdon shook his head. 'The ruins stretch for a league yet. This is considered the safest spot. The ledges are not so stable up ahead.'

'Aren't we sitting ducks here?' Kait said, gesturing at the narrow trail. 'What's to stop Iresonté's forces coming at us from both sides?'

'I doubt she knows where we are,' Mercia answered. 'And

our small numbers work to our advantage. The Republic's own forces are so few that she wouldn't expect us to divide them.'

'And that's supposed to reassure me,' Kait muttered. The lieutenant flashed her a sharp smile.

As she helped with the horses, Brégenne felt distinctly watched. She found herself peering upwards and over her shoulder, convinced she was the object of some nameless scrutiny. Perhaps it was merely the granite's sombre hue, the silence in a place that once buzzed with life, but the ruins of Yrsat raised the hairs on the back of her neck. How many other cities, great and small, had been crushed beneath the heel of Sartya? Were ruins like these and Kalast echoed elsewhere in Acre? Beside plains and seas, straddling lowlands – cities which fought and fell, now reclaimed by nature.

The Lunar was a grasp away. Brégenne didn't believe in ghosts, but she kept it close all the same.

'Subterfuge really is the only option,' Mercia said once they were camped. She started drawing in the deep char that carpeted the ravine. Brégenne tried not to think about what it might once have been. Instead she watched with growing alarm as Parakat began to take shape beneath Mercia's sketching finger. The prison was a fortress, protected by an inner and outer wall, buttressed along its length, with a single portcullis gate in the south. Towers stood sentinel at each corner; a chasm served as a moat, oddly reminiscent of Naris.

'The Parakat garrison isn't all that large,' Mercia said, sitting back on her heels and wiping her hand on her cloak. 'But they could hold that fortress against an army twice the size of the Fist. We do not even have an army.'

'Or men to waste in a fruitless siege,' Hagdon added. He

leaned forward, studying Mercia's sketch. 'Once that draw-bridge goes up, we're cut off. It'll be down to whoever we send in to lower it for the rest of us.' He looked at Mercia. 'You won't be able to take your whole unit inside. That would raise suspicion. So choose carefully.'

'Varlan's the most familiar with the layout of the fortress,' she answered, indicating a man in his middle years who sat oiling a sword nearby. He looked up at his name, nodded. 'He's been assigned to the wagons multiple times,' Mercia continued. 'As for myself, I've visited once.' Her expression darkened. 'Only once. I was fortunate.'

No one said anything in the wake of her words, until Irilin spoke up. 'If Mercia approaches Parakat without an aberration, it'll look suspicious. I'll go with her. Be her prisoner.'

'No,' Brégenne said at the same time as Hagdon. Irilin glared at them both. 'It's too dangerous,' Brégenne continued when Hagdon didn't speak further. 'We don't know what to expect.' She hesitated, knowing Irilin wouldn't appreciate being reminded. 'You're still a novice.'

Instead of retorting, Irilin said, 'That's why I won't raise suspicion. I look younger than I am – why not use that to our advantage for once?'

'If anyone's to go in, it should be—'

'Hear me out, Brégenne. No plan –' she glanced at Hagdon – 'survives first contact with the enemy. We can't place all our hopes in the ruse working first time. There are too many variables.'

Hagdon's mouth had twitched ever so briefly, but now his expression was serious as he regarded Irilin. 'Go on.'

'Mercia bluffing her way in is one thing. Escaping notice

long enough to lower the drawbridge is quite another.' Irilin jabbed her finger squarely in the middle of Mercia's sketch. 'What if she fails?'

When no one answered, she said, 'You'll need another way to get inside.'

'There isn't one,' Mercia said with a definitive shake of her head. 'Just the main gate. And the only method of reaching the gate is the drawbridge.'

Irilin's eyes glittered. 'In that case, we'll need to build our own.'

Amidst the others' confusion, Brégenne met Nediah's eyes and saw her own realization dawning in them. She looked away before she saw anything else. 'So *that*'s why you don't want me to go into the fortress,' she said to Irilin.

Mercia folded her arms. 'Could someone explain?'

'The Wielders' citadel is also surrounded by a chasm,' Brégenne said. 'When the bridge that spanned it collapsed, I helped build another.' She stood up, taking hold of the Lunar as she did so. It seemed her hours of practice had paid off; focusing moonlight into a solid platform no longer took all her concentration. A misty square appeared about three feet off the ground, pulsing slightly. She held out a hand. 'Stand on it.'

'You must be joking.' Mercia eyed the ephemeral, glowing square with distrust. 'I can see through it.'

With a small gesture, Brégenne turned the platform opaque, fog rather than mist. 'Better?'

'Not really,' the lieutenant complained. 'Can't you make it lower?'

Brégenne lowered it until it was barely a foot off the ground. Mercia swallowed, but everyone was watching now, Sartyan and rebel alike. She raised her boot, hesitated, then stepped onto the platform. She swayed a little, eyes very wide, and Brégenne expanded it just in case.

'It's . . . it's –' Mercia lifted alternate feet, leaned down to touch the glowing square with her palm – 'warm,' she finished. And then she began to laugh giddily. A few moments passed while her men stared at her in surprise before her laughter spread. Even Hagdon smiled, Brégenne noticed, but his eyes were thoughtful, already slotting this new playing piece into position.

With a short word of warning, she dissolved the square Mercia had just abandoned. The Sartyan lieutenant watched it wink out, wearing the same thoughtful expression as Hagdon. 'You can make it vanish instantly?' she asked Brégenne.

'At a moment's notice.'

Mercia smiled. 'I think I can find a use for such an ability,' she said with the look of someone fondly imagining her enemies tumbling into an abyss.

'Do you possess this particular power too?' Hagdon asked Nediah and Kait.

Brégenne inwardly winced, watching Kait's eyes harden into agates. 'No, Commander,' the tall woman said in an airy tone that belied her hostile expression.

'Kait is an excellent duellist,' Brégenne forced herself to say. It was worth it when the other woman's mouth dropped open in surprise. 'As I'm sure she's demonstrated. Nediah is the greatest healer you're ever likely to see. Out of us all, I'd consider his talents the most valuable. We're at war.'

Nediah looked at her, his expression unreadable. How had he become so adept at hiding his thoughts? *Years spent in my company*, she concluded bitterly.

'We do have a problem, however,' Hagdon said into the

prickly silence that followed Brégenne's words. He nodded at her. 'If we're forced to resort to your bridge-building, it will only work at night, when your companions are powerless.' He sighed, rubbed his chin. 'This will take some planning. We'll have to time the assault rather carefully.'

'How many will we be facing?' Nediah asked with a kind of weary apprehension. Brégenne could see it in his posture, in the way his hands were balled into fists; he dreaded the inevitable killing that was to come.

'I won't know exact numbers until I get in there,' Mercia said, 'but going by my last visit, about two hundred.'

'*Two hundred?*'

'Might be more.'

He sighed heavily. 'Will they consider surrender?'

'Only if we kill enough of them.' The lieutenant gave a casual shrug. 'Sartyans are *very* stubborn.'

Nediah's stare was direct. 'Including you?'

'Especially me. We're used to victory – no one's won a battle against the soldiers of the Fist in hundreds of years.' She tilted her head at Hagdon. 'Right, General?'

'Please don't call me that.'

Mercia grinned. 'Sorry.' She returned her gaze to Nediah. 'Don't worry. Between the Republic and my own unit, we might only have eighty, but surely you and your companions count for a hundred each?'

Nediah looked dubious. Kait, however, returned Mercia's grin with one of her own, fiercer and just a bit unstable. 'When the sun comes up in that fortress, you'll see for yourself,' she promised.

17

Kyndra

'On your feet,' the soldier barked at her. 'Hands where I can see them.' His accent was strange, a little like Hagdon's, but sharper.

Dazed, Kyndra complied. Through the slit in his helm, the soldier's eyes were sweeping her person, clearly searching for weapons. Her apparent lack of them seemed to throw him off balance. He took in her shivering, her clothes – which, though plain, probably looked terribly out of place here. She should have thought of that, Kyndra chastised herself, but she hadn't expected to land right in the middle of a military encampment. Or to be utterly defenceless. *Why* hadn't the stars warned her? *Why* had they let her go alone?

'Sartya?' she managed finally.

'If you mean are we allied to House Sartya, then yes,' the soldier replied. He removed his helm, revealing a face stiff with suspicion. 'How did you get here?'

Kyndra thought fast, took a chance. 'I mistranslocated,' she said. Translocation was one of the lost arts of Solinaris.

Immediately the soldier flinched, once more raising his sword between them. 'You're a Wielder?'

'A novice,' Kyndra said, hoping she looked suitably unsure. 'I was practising and I must have made a mistake.'

'A serious mistake to come out here.' The man's frown deepened. 'Solinaris is two hundred leagues away.'

Kyndra wished he'd lower the sword. The longer it pointed at her chest, the faster her heart beat. Fear prickled down her arms. They, too, were unmarked by the stars. What could *Era* have hoped to gain by hiding this vital fact from her? Had she known, she'd never have agreed to the plan.

That pulled her up short. Kyndra swallowed. *Era* had been evasive; perhaps it had known she wouldn't agree. The star wanted her to be here. But how could she defeat the eldest without her power? She put her head in her hands, striving not to voice her despair.

'Don't worry, novice,' the soldier said, evidently taking her silence for chagrin. 'You'll make a fine addition to Davaratch's household.' The next thing Kyndra knew, he'd clamped a pair of manacles on her wrists. They were more like bracelets, having no chain to connect them, and carried the familiar blue sheen of ambertrix. *They prevent a Wielder touching his or her power*, Kyndra guessed. Being neither a Solar nor a Lunar, they had no effect on her.

'What's wrong with your hand?'

The soldier was holding her wrist and gazing with some disgust at the bruised and mottled skin left by the eldest's curse. So it had travelled with her. Kyndra's heart sank even further. As she focused on it, she felt a spasm of weakness travel up her arm and bit her lip to keep from gasping. 'An infection,' she heard herself say.

The soldier dropped her hand as if it were a spitting snake, wiping his fingers furiously on his cloak. 'If it's contagious, it would be better to kill you now.'

'It's not,' Kyndra said quickly. 'Just the result of an experiment that went wrong.' She made sure to inject a tremor into her voice. It wasn't all subterfuge. What ill luck had landed her in this mess? Defenceless, she was at the mercy of the soldiers. And if she didn't manage to escape, what would happen when they asked her to draw on the Solar or Lunar? She could no more touch those powers now than she could during the tests in Naris. The memory was an unwelcome reminder of her helplessness.

I've come full circle. She hadn't thought she'd miss the stars and the chill that seeped into her veins, but she'd grown used to having people fear her; she'd begun to appreciate the comfort that came with power. The thought horrified her. What had she become? It was waiting for her in the future. As soon as she returned, *if* she returned, then *Kyndra* would revert to being no more than a name she wore for convenience.

She had to focus on the mission. Protect Davaratch. But how was she to do that without the stars?

The soldier was eyeing her, as if aware of her internal monologue. Kyndra drew a shaky breath. 'Where are we?' she asked.

'We're ten leagues to the north of New Sartya and on our way home for the winter festivities.' His eyes narrowed. 'You will be accompanying us.'

It sounded as if she was in the right place and time. Why not let the soldiers take her to the city? Kyndra thought. She glanced at the bands on her wrists. If they believed her power bound, they might not guard her so closely. She could escape – *and then what? How will I face the eldest without my power?*

I've coped without it most of my life, she told herself sternly. *I will cope without it now.* But the thought was a hollow one.

'You won't be taking me anywhere,' she said, knowing it might look strange if she didn't protest. 'I am a Wielder of Solinaris and under its protection.'

'You're a novice,' he retorted, 'and under no one's protection, least of all Solinaris.'

'They'll come for me,' Kyndra threatened. 'You don't want to make an enemy of the Wielders.'

The soldier's face darkened, but the suspicion had begun to fade from his eyes. 'They don't know where you are,' he said, 'and they're unlikely to try to find you.' His smile was nasty. 'What use has Solinaris for a novice as inept as you?'

Kyndra hung her head and the soldier laughed. 'Come,' he seized her roughly by the arm – her good arm, she noted – and steered her towards the distant campfire.

'What do you have there, Sergeant?' a young man said. He had dark hair and pale eyes – the same colouring as Iresonté, Kyndra noted.

'A stray pup from Solinaris,' the sergeant replied, still holding Kyndra's arm. 'She'll be coming with us. A present to celebrate the newest conquest, I think.'

'Pretty hair,' the younger man replied, getting to his feet. His gaze strayed to the ambertrix manacles around her wrists. 'Why don't you let us have a little fun with her first?'

Immediately Kyndra's heart began to pound. Other men had turned to look; some with the same expression as the young soldier. Quite suddenly, she realized that there were no women among them. She'd become so used to seeing women in the Sartyan Fist that their absence was jarring.

'We are not savages,' the sergeant said firmly, 'and she is not a whore. You'll keep away from her.'

'If you want her for yourself, just say so, Sergeant,' the young man replied insouciantly, earning himself a glare.

'I said you'll keep away from her.' The sergeant's voice carried a dangerous note. 'Any man I catch touching her loses his hands.'

There was angry muttering, but it went no further. Kyndra let out a breath, her heart still beating rapidly. She lowered her eyes.

'You stay close to me,' the sergeant said quietly. 'Not all of them can be trusted.'

'Would you really cut their hands off?'

'Probably not,' he replied, 'or they'd be no use as soldiers. But there are other things I can cut off.' His smile was grim.

She was thrust unceremoniously into a tent, the sergeant standing guard outside. The moment Kyndra found herself alone, she closed her eyes. *Era,* she thought, without much hope of an answer, *can you hear me?*

Nothing. Kyndra tried to feel out the edges of the void in her mind. *Era!*

Still nothing. She was about to give up when she touched . . . something. A surface, glassy and oddly familiar. Kyndra spread herself along it, searching for gaps, but there were none. It seemed impenetrable. And then, as if she really did press her hands against glass, she saw movement on the other side, as if a great eye had opened to stare back at her.

The realization came to Kyndra in a chill flash: the memory of pressure in her head, of a black wall, of the pain when she collided with it. The mind of a broken Starborn; the mind of Kierik.

The eye contracted. *Who are you?*

Kyndra pulled away with a terrified gasp, eyes flying open. Anohin had told her all those months ago: two Starborn cannot co-exist. This time, the Kierik who stood between her and the stars wasn't mad, but in his full power. If he sensed her, if he found her –

With difficulty, Kyndra reined in her riotous thoughts. *He can't find me,* she told herself, *as long as I stay away from the stars.* New despair dragged at her. She truly was alone. Even if she could contact the stars, they wouldn't help her, not when Kierik was still alive and in control. Another thing *Era* had failed to mention. She vowed she would have words with the star if, by some miracle, she managed to return to her time, history intact.

Instead of the stars, Kyndra reached out to Ma, closing her eyes and calling the woman's name over and over in the darkness of her mind.

Kyndra? Ma sounded surprised.

You have to bring me back. I can't use my power! She realized she sounded desperate, but couldn't stop herself. The sheer relief that Ma had answered threatened to spill out of her in a wild laugh.

Calm, came Ma's answer. *What has happened?*

Kierik. She almost cried the name. *Anohin told me, but I didn't think, didn't remember. Kierik's the Starborn of this time. I can't reach the stars while he's alive.*

She sensed Ma's dismay. But – *you can't come back,* the woman told her.

What? Why?

The eldest, she replied. *I felt the fabric of time stretch near to breaking, was able to pinpoint its source. He is there somewhere, in the same time as you. And he has the Yadin with him.*

Medavle? I thought anchors had to stay in the present?

They are supposed to, Ma said. She sounded angry. *But this jump back is so great, the eldest must have realized he could not achieve it without keeping the Yadin with him.* She paused. *It has its drawbacks. It might be something you can exploit. The Yadin will not be able to stray more than a mandala's width from the eldest, and there aren't enough of my people to create one larger than ten metres across. Separate them and the eldest's hold on that time will break. He will be forced to return home, the Yadin too.*

So I have to stay, Kyndra said, her stomach churning. She had to see this through. *Do you have any idea why the stars didn't warn me?* she asked Ma.

The other woman's answer took a while to come. *There is something deeper at work here, I feel it. An open loop that must be closed. If the stars are eternal, they may be able to see it. You, however, cannot and they must act through you. The smallest foreknowledge can cause the greatest harm.*

Kyndra frowned. *What are you saying?*

That their decision not to tell you was an act of self-preservation, an attempt to avoid being caught in a paradox.

Kyndra was about to reply when *Era*'s earlier words returned to her in a flash of insight. Was it self-preservation, she wondered, or were the stars simply obeying her own command to keep silent? She couldn't imagine herself ever giving such a command, not when she'd have known she'd be stripping her past self of defences.

Kyndra, Ma said, *you must stop the eldest. By whatever means necessary.*

If *Era* was right, this had happened before. She must somehow have stopped the assassination. Kyndra held fast to the thought. She'd found a way. She would find it again.

*

It took them two days to reach New Sartya. For Kyndra, the journey wasn't a pleasant one. Snowstorms bogged them down, forcing everyone into close proximity, and despite the sergeant's threat, she didn't like the looks some of the men gave her. *I could have burned them all.* The thought brought sickness rather than satisfaction. Removed from the stars, but with the memory of how it felt to wield them, she was trapped between her old life and her new. She tried to keep her mind on her task, but other images began to intrude, memories the stars had smothered under their chill influence. One lingered above all: her mother, Reena, her face smudged with tears, wondering whether her daughter was alive.

Kyndra's heart twisted. How could she have just stood there, hidden, and watched? It seemed monstrous to leave her parents in doubt. She strove to remember why she'd kept herself invisible, why she hadn't thought to reassure them, and realized that she just hadn't considered it important. Her mother's tears had meant nothing.

The afternoon had already begun to fail before Kyndra had her first view of New Sartya. She stood beside the sergeant on a small rise; from here, the earth sloped gently down, peppered with lights, which glimmered between the twilit folds of the land. A towering blaze dominated the southern horizon.

The sun hadn't quite slipped from the sky, but its light was nothing to the radiance of New Sartya. Kyndra stared, transfixed by the sight of so much ambertrix. If the Fist was the empire's muscle, ambertrix was its lifeblood. No wonder Sartya had crumbled when supply began to dwindle.

They started down the hill, making for the main road which led arrow-straight to the gates of the capital. The clustered lights belonged to manors, Kyndra saw – huge sprawling acres, hoarded behind high walls. There wasn't a hint of chimney smoke, or cooking food and no whiff of livestock. All the scents Kyndra associated with evening were absent. She felt very far from home.

Although traffic was heavy on the road, everyone melted away from the soldiers. Most people looked like merchants, or craftsmen, but there were clearly civilians amongst the crowd. A few walked; others travelled in strange carriages that appeared to move on their own. *They must be an invention of Thabarat,* Kyndra concluded, *the ambertrix college.* A horn blasted and the sergeant marched her swiftly to one side as an elegant carriage raced past, its speed that of a horse at full gallop. 'Nobles,' he muttered darkly. 'From House Lowmar. If they try anything . . .'

Several times they had to clear the road to let another noble carriage pass. Each time, the soldier's face soured further. 'Davaratch is taking a risk letting this vermin inside his walls.'

Kyndra's skin prickled. 'Why? What do you think they'll do?'

'The other Houses are vultures.' The sergeant nodded at yet another carriage. 'Always circling, looking for signs of weakness. The success of the Azakander conquest has shaken them. Davaratch is extending his reach.' His eyes grew distant. 'But it makes him vulnerable, stretches his forces thin. Many in the Houses would seek to take advantage.' The sergeant watched the gates of New Sartya draw closer. 'If Davaratch were to fall now . . .' He shook his head, seeming to recall himself.

If Davaratch were to fall now . . . Kyndra swallowed. It would mean the collapse of the empire.

She was thoroughly chilled by the time they reached the gates, shivering in her loaned cloak. 'Where are you taking me?' she asked the sergeant through numb lips.

'The manor garrison,' he replied shortly.

'And then?'

'You'll show the master-at-arms what you can do. He may well have a use for you.'

A chill colder than the freezing air stuck Kyndra. 'I'm a Solar,' she said, knowing it was merely postponing the inevitable. 'I can't do anything until the morning.'

'Then we will wait.'

Kyndra hefted her manacled wrists. 'How do you know I won't translocate myself as soon as you take these off?'

He looked faintly amused. 'Oh we're not going to take them off, at least not both. Just one will prevent you doing anything more complex than lighting a candle.'

'I've not done anything wrong,' she protested, knowing she had to maintain the charade of captured novice. 'You have no right to lock me up.'

'We have every right. Remember: it was you who trespassed on House Sartya's territory.'

'By accident!'

The sergeant gave her a long, hard look. 'There's something about you and your story that doesn't add up.' His eyes narrowed. 'You could easily be a spy for one of the other Houses. We *will* have the truth from you.'

Despite the freezing wind, Kyndra felt sweat break out on the back of her neck. Now more than ever she wished for *Fas*, to wrap herself in air, to vanish into the crowd. She should have foreseen this loss of her power; she'd experienced it back in Naris when Kierik stood between her and the stars.

'You are wise to be silent,' the sergeant told her. 'Once inside the garrison, you will not speak unless spoken to. Understand?'

'Yes.'

'Good. Do try to impress the master-at-arms. I'd hate to have wasted rations on someone bound for the gallows.'

He was trying to scare her, but she wouldn't be scared, Kyndra thought defiantly. In her own time, she was the most powerful person in the world. The thought didn't bring as much comfort as she'd hoped.

They passed through the gates. Most of the soldiers peeled off, leaving Kyndra alone with the sergeant and two others. Guards in red mail that would eventually be recognized throughout Acre as the infamous armour of the Fist lined the street beyond, which was lit by blueish orbs raised high on poles, bunting strung between them. Singing reached her from some unseen plaza.

Kyndra found herself staring. She wasn't the only one. Other visitors stopped to gape at the horseless carriages as they sped around seemingly at random. Some had open roofs; masked women, elegantly attired, held on to their coiffed hair as their male companions drove them laughing through the streets. So far, the only women Kyndra had seen were civilians, all of them accompanied by a man. It was equally as disorientating as it was disconcerting.

She caught the enticing whiff of roasting meat; at a nearby stall, a joint turned lazily over heated metal plates. They closely resembled the ones she'd seen in Rogan's house back in Cymenza. Her stomach rumbled, but the sergeant steered her in the opposite direction.

The city immersed her in a chaos of noise and light. Despite an ever more pressing need to get away from him, Kyndra was in a way grateful for the sergeant's presence – she'd never have found the Sartyan manor in this blazing labyrinth. Streets ran in circles, doubled back on themselves, snaked through alleyways and under roads raised up on great stone pillars. It was strange, but she found herself thinking of Medavle. *This* was the world to which the Yadin had awoken; a world of ambertrix, of unstoppable momentum, a world on the cusp of enormous change. Medavle had once told her that Kierik's actions deprived Rairam of Acrean invention – he'd supported this aspect of the empire at least.

Kyndra briefly closed her eyes. She really had trusted him – he'd helped her, even saved her life. Maybe Char was right and she should have realized how deeply he still loved Isla; how far he was prepared to go to bring her back. She should have paid more attention to his nightmares, to the way he'd begun to distance himself from her. Another failing of the stars, she thought bitterly. For all their power, they couldn't see inside the human heart.

When she blinked, refocusing on the colourful streets, she caught a flash of white.

Kyndra's breath froze. Desperately, she searched the crowds, stumbling forward, so that the sergeant had to yank her back. 'Don't even think about it,' he barked, but she barely heard him, trying to spot that familiar robe, the one he always wore. *Maybe I imagined it*, she thought. Perhaps it was just a trick of the streets. But if she really *had* seen Medavle, it meant that the eldest was here too, somewhere close by.

Ambertrix lamps marched like soldiers on duty down a series of curving roads. New Sartya was a huge spiral, tiered like a seashell, tightening and sloping up as it neared the centre. Kyndra's calves were aching now; her palms sweated with the thought of what would happen when they reached the Sartyan manor. She noticed the buildings becoming grander, lit by the natural blush of candles interspersed with ambertrix. Many carriages stood dark and still outside them; did every person in the city own one?

'Not everyone,' the sergeant said when she asked him. 'Only the very rich.' He nodded at the palisaded houses. 'There's a lot of wealth in New Sartya, a lot of influence.' His tone spoke volumes; Kyndra recalled his suspicions about the other noble Houses and narrowed her eyes at each grand mansion they passed. How easy would it be for a rival House to seize control of the city if Davaratch died? She shook her head, unused to politics and power plays. Another unwelcome reminder of how deeply she was out of her depth.

The more raucous cries of revelry faded as they drew nearer the manor, other sounds taking their place. Staccato bursts of applause from an open-air theatre, a fluting viola, a soprano's song soaring out of a glow-drenched garden. When they rounded the final corner, Kyndra didn't realize that she'd stopped moving until the sergeant's hand clamped down on her shoulder. 'A sight, is it not?' he said.

The gradual slope of the roads had raised them to a great height. Now the city lay below like a huge quilt with its neat patchwork of ambertrix lights. Ahead of them loomed a gateway, just wide enough to admit a carriage. Through it, the street dissolved into a structure that was more fortress than manor. From here, Kyndra couldn't see the top. What she could see was the statue in the process of being built at its base. Awe rooted her to the spot.

It was colossal, each booted foot half the size of Argat's airship. The figure wore a kind of armoured robe, carved of red marble. Pauldrons made small hills of the shoulders and both arms were outstretched, one not yet released from the mass of unshaped rock. The head, too, was uncut, awaiting a face.

Kyndra shivered. Whether that face would be Davaratch's might well be up to her.

Steeling herself, Kyndra started for the gate, only to feel the sergeant's hand tighten its grip on her shoulder. 'No further,' he said and gestured his two remaining soldiers into the fortress-like manor. 'We wait for the captain.' As he spoke, carriages drew up, elegant guests unfolding themselves from leather seats. Some drove straight through the gate, only to stop just inside. Men climbed out, tossed a small object to a waiting servant, who climbed in and drove the carriage on and out of sight. A major event must be taking place, Kyndra thought, watching closely. Other red-liveried servants stood amongst the guards, their gloved hands ready to seize and inspect invitations. If only she had one of their uniforms . . .

'Davaratch is holding his own festivities,' the sergeant said. He looked discomfited. 'None but the city's most prominent citizens are permitted inside the manor tonight.'

She had to get in there. Who knew how much time she had before the eldest reached Davaratch? Kyndra kept watch for him and Medavle, but saw neither. That didn't mean they weren't here, however.

I need a distraction.

It came a scant minute later in the form of a bright flash and a surge which Kyndra felt in her blood. A surge and a whisper: *Raad.* No, she thought, *no, it's impossible.* But there before her, coat still tossed by the wind of his passage, was Kierik the Starborn, a crisp invitation clutched in his fist.

18

Gareth

He couldn't remember, and it terrified him.

The further from the crypt he travelled, the mistier grew his memories of its dank stone passageways, its restless dead. Perhaps he'd only dreamed them and that journey in the dark. Sunlight sparked off the shining gauntlet he wore on his left arm and Gareth glanced at it. *How* exactly had he found Hond'Lif?

'Can we really afford to stop here?' Kul'Das asked as they rode towards the fortified walls of Paarth. 'We need to reach Rairam and your mother before Iresonté does.'

Gareth pulled himself back to the present with a shudder. 'We will,' he said. 'And anyway, the valley where we agreed to meet Argat is on the other side of the city.'

'The man is a rogue,' Kul'Das said distastefully. She hadn't enjoyed her last trip aboard the airship when they'd flown into Acre, he recalled. 'Argat does not care to follow anyone's orders except his own. And what you put in that envoi was definitely an order.'

'He owes me for fighting off those bandits.'

Kul'Das looked at him askance. 'You remember that?'

'Yes,' he said softly, flexing his fist inside Hond'Myrkr, the dark metal a shadow against the afternoon. At least, he recalled the ecstasy that had seized him as the gauntlet stripped the life from men's bodies. When he glanced back at Kul'Das, her gaze had turned wary, so he forced a smile. 'A debt is a debt, after all.'

She made a sound in her throat that wasn't quite agreement. It didn't matter. Gareth was confident Argat would do what he wanted. 'In the meantime,' he said, 'we go to the city. I cannot meet my mother dressed in rags.'

'Perhaps you're right. But armour takes a while to craft and I don't know how you plan to pay for it.'

The Sartyans were stopping every group at the city gates. Gareth and Kul'Das dismounted and waited in line. 'Looking for members of the Republic,' the merchant in front of them said and spat. 'As if a rebel would be stupid enough to walk around—' Shouts drowned the rest of his sentence. There was a short tussle and then two men were dragged out of view, both loudly proclaiming their innocence. The merchant spat again and glanced at the wintry sun. 'Waste of time.'

'What are you going to tell them?' Kul'Das asked in a low voice as they moved up the line.

'I'm working on it.' She left the decision to him, Gareth noted with some satisfaction. Once she'd outranked him – when he'd stumbled into Ümvast's hall half-dead, claiming guest-right. Now she held no power over him. None did, save Kyndra. Gareth tried to push the thought of the Starborn from his head. It would only remind him of Irilin and what she'd said about Shika.

He wouldn't have felt it, wouldn't have suffered. Gareth

swallowed. The deep ache of loss filled his chest. Shika had died months ago and no one had bothered to tell him.

Death is never the end, Hrafnasueltir.

That word froze the tears threatening to gather in his eyes. So derogatory, so familiar, as if he'd heard it somewhere before . . .

The guard at the gates interrupted his musing. 'What is your purpose here, traveller?'

'Stopping for supplies on the way to my homeland,' Gareth answered, trying to inject confidence into his voice. 'Nor'Voldt in the Territory.'

'You have the Yrmfast look,' the Sartyan said, his eyes flicking over Gareth's features. His gaze moved to the blond Kul'Das. 'Your companion, however, is no northerner.'

'My servant.' He hoped she wouldn't bristle too openly. 'I picked her up in Sarterion.'

'How long have you been away from home, traveller?'

'Months,' Gareth said crisply. 'I had business in the south.'

'Then you should know the Territory is a hotbed of Defiant scum. With the Fist preparing for war, it is the duty of all northerners to help root out these cells.'

'My family and holdings have always been loyal to the empire. If the Defiant seek to recruit for the Republic, they'll soon discover Yrmfast a far-from-fertile territory.' Gareth gave the guard a cold smile that seemed to assuage some of his suspicion. 'Speaking of home, my youngest brother comes of age this winter and I wish to gift him with a set of armour. Would you know of a suitably skilled smith in the city?'

The guard relaxed. 'This is Paarth. Our smiths are some of the best in the empire.' He rubbed his chin. 'Go to the ironworks and ask for Sim. Tell him Sergeant Laylan sent you.'

Gareth gave a brisk nod. 'My thanks.'

As they walked their horses unmolested through the gates, Kul'Das let out a breath. 'Where did you learn to talk like that?'

'Like what?'

'Like you're familiar with Acre. And that story you made up about a brother.'

Gareth blinked at her. 'I . . .' How *had* he come up with it? He couldn't remember now. 'Does it matter?' he said finally, quashing his own unease. 'It got us in, didn't it?'

Kul'Das narrowed her eyes, but she didn't press him further.

The buildings had a heavy, looming air. Paarth was a granite city, seemingly founded on the profits of its mines. The value of the guard's information soon became clear – Gareth had never seen so many smithies. Every corner held one, the forge's molten glow spilling out across the streets. 'Lucky we have a recommendation,' Kul'Das said, giving voice to his own thoughts.

After a few enquiries, they found the ironworks and tied their horses up outside. It was a fortress of a building, echoing with the rhythm of hammer on anvil. Steam from the quenching hung in the air like fog and sweat popped out on Kul'Das's brow. She stripped off her gloves, dragged a hand across her face and then looked at him accusingly. 'Why are you not hot?'

He shrugged. 'An after-effect of being dead, perhaps.' It was a mark of how far they'd come that she didn't wince.

Asking for Sim produced either eye rolls or terse grunts. 'Not a popular man,' Kul'Das said as they followed a woman's reluctant nod into the bowels of the ironworks.

'Except with customers,' Gareth said. 'They're jealous. I bet he gets all the lucrative commissions.'

'If that's the case, he'll have a waiting list.' She gestured at the other smiths hammering around them. 'We should try someone else.'

'I *want* the best,' Gareth said shortly. He wasn't entirely sure why it mattered. He had the nagging feeling that once, quite recently, in fact, he wouldn't even have entertained the idea of commissioning armour. The thought sent a stab through his head and he raised a hand to his temple.

'What is it?'

She never missed a thing, Kul'Das. He dropped his hand immediately. 'The noise is grating.'

'On you and me both,' she muttered. 'Let's find this Sim quickly.'

As if the steam had heard them, it parted to reveal a man clutching a length of white-hot metal. He barely glanced at them before saying, 'All transactions are handled by my assistant. Shop's in Silver Street.'

'Master Sim?' Gareth said smoothly. 'I do not wish to speak to your assistant. 'I am here for *you*.'

The smith put down his work. He raised his head and stared at them properly. A surprisingly slender man, he wore the traditional apron and heavy gloves of his trade. Gareth watched his eyes settle inevitably on the gauntlets. 'Fine work,' Sim said almost dreamily. He licked his lips, held out a hand. 'Would you mind?'

'I would.' Gareth said with quiet menace. 'The gauntlets stay with me.'

'Those sigils,' the smith said, as if he hadn't heard. 'Are they embossed or engraved?' He drew off his gloves and leaned forward, bare hand reaching out. 'I've never seen—'

Gareth seized his hand in Hond'Myrkr and the smith gasped. Eyes wide, he looked down and cried out as the tips of his fingers began to blacken. 'They stay with me,' Gareth repeated.

'What are you – let me go!'

Gareth released his grip and the smith staggered back, clutching his hand. 'What are you? What have you done? My fingers –'

'I want you to craft me a set of armour.'

The smith gaped at him, still cradling his hand.

'It must be worthy of me, of *these*.' Gareth held up Hond'Myrkr and Sim flinched back, horror burrowing its way into his face.

'Who *are* you?'

'I will not answer any question until you agree.'

Sim swallowed. 'I cannot work. My fingers . . .' He held them out. 'You've ruined me.' It wasn't just fear in his voice now, but anger and the creeping onset of tears.

'Give me your hand.'

The smith took a step back. 'Get away from me. Leave me alone.'

Gareth sighed impatiently. 'Why would I ask for armour and then cripple you? If you wish to work again, give me your hand.'

The smith swallowed. Hesitantly, he extended his blackened fingers and Gareth took them in Hond'Lif. The white gauntlet glowed in the gloom and the black receded from Sim's flesh, new skin growing in its place. 'You'll have to build up your calluses again,' Gareth said, 'but a small price to pay.'

The smith flexed his fingers, his wonder lasting only until he met Gareth's eyes. Then fear replaced it. 'What . . . what can I do for you, sir?'

'Do you have parchment?'

'Here.' Sim scrabbled around on a worktable, coming up

with a tatty sheet and a stick of charcoal. Gareth briefly closed his eyes and then began to sketch the schema in his head. The smith watched in silence until professional curiosity prompted him to say, 'Forgive me, sir, but the shape of the cuirass could be improved—' he cut off, flinching, as Gareth turned to look at him.

'No, continue.'

'If I may.' Sim took the charcoal, turned the paper towards him. 'This follows a sixth-century design. A strong design, but flawed.' He sketched deftly, a new shape beginning to emerge. 'I recommend riveting here and here – I take it you want full plate?'

'Yes,' Gareth said after a moment.

'You clearly don't need –' Sim's voice faltered as he glanced at the gauntlets. 'And a helm?'

'Just the cuirass, pauldrons, greaves and boots.'

'This emblem,' Sim said, tapping his charcoal against the parchment cuirass. 'It seems familiar. Is it your House heraldry?'

Gareth looked at his work, tracing the strokes that depicted crossed fists against a twisted mountain. He'd drawn it without thinking and, all of a sudden, he felt dizzy with a sense of dislocation. 'Not my House,' he said quietly. 'Let's just say it's mine.'

Sim put down the charcoal and rubbed his hands on the front of his apron. 'It will take three weeks.'

'You have three days.'

The smith shook his head. 'I have other commissions, commissions for which I've already received payment. I can't just—'

'Drop them,' Gareth said, taking a step closer. 'When I return in three days, the armour *will* be ready. Do you understand?'

'But –'

He raised Hond'Myrkr and the smith shrank back. 'This is not a request. Now take your measurements. And remember – I will be waiting.'

Sim swallowed, clearly steeling himself. 'There's the matter of payment, sir.'

Gareth reached into his pack, pulled out a set of golden goblets. The smith's face immediately darkened. 'I need ken, sir. Gold is worthless.'

'Look at them closely.'

Sim took one of the goblets, bringing it close to his face. He frowned once and then his eyes widened. 'You recognize it?' Gareth asked. 'It's Kalastian.'

The smith licked his lips, darting a glance at Gareth's face. 'How did you get these? Kalast is buried, cursed. Every attempt to excavate it has met with disaster.'

'I trust they will be sufficient?'

'Sufficient?' Sim returned his gaze to the shining goblets. 'I could live for a year on the ken the museum in New Sartya would pay for these.'

'Then we have an agreement.' Gareth turned away from the astonished smith. 'I will see you in three days.'

Kul'Das was very quiet as they left the ironworks, leading their horses through the streets. She kept her eyes fixed on a point somewhere in front of them. 'What's the matter?' Gareth asked. 'Is it the goblets? They really are Kalastian – I didn't cheat him.' Now that he thought about it, however, he couldn't actually remember picking them up.

She slowly shook her head. 'It's you.'

'Me?'

'You're different.'

Gareth frowned. 'In what way?'

Kul'Das stopped abruptly, whirling to face him. 'In every way! The way you speak, behave – look at how you treated that smith, hurting him, bullying him into doing what you wanted. You are not the person with whom I left Stjórna.' Her blue eyes darkened when they touched upon the gauntlets. 'I don't know what happened in Ben'haugr, what you might have suffered there, but it's changed you. And *not* for the better.'

The streets were quiet, squat industrial buildings muffling the sounds of the city. The silence grew as they stared at each other. Gareth considered her words. He hadn't really hurt the smith – he'd just wanted to ensure he had the armour on time. 'You're not afraid to say what you think,' he replied eventually. 'It's what I like about you, Kul'Das. But don't speak to me of that place again.'

If he were anyone else, Gareth suspected she'd have spat some effrontery. But Kul'Das held her tongue; he recognized the shadow of fear in her eyes and frowned. What was she afraid of? He wasn't going to harm her.

They began walking again, Gareth hardly noticing the city. Thoughts roiled inside him. *You're different.* Was he? He didn't feel different, except that his body was his own again. He summoned a small flame, concealed it in one cupped hand. The Solar felt the same, came as easily as it ever had. So what did Kul'Das mean? What *had* happened in Ben'haugr? He'd gone there to find Hond'Lif, had taken it from –

His temple began to throb. Gareth sucked in a pained breath and tried again. But the stabbing grew worse, forcing him to give up. What did it matter anyway? He'd gone to Ben'haugr, found the white gauntlet and lifted the curse

Hond'Myrkr had placed on his flesh. Now it was time to return home.

Except that something *was* different. There were . . . other memories inside him, memories that occasionally rose up to overwhelm him with the sights, sounds and smells of a past he had never lived. Except – he *had* lived it.

These thoughts made his head spin. Gareth abandoned them, returned his attention to their surroundings. 'We should find somewhere to stay.'

Kul'Das seemed relieved at the mundane change in subject. 'We passed a few inns.' She reached into a leather pouch at her waist, rolling a few of the strange stones between her fingers. 'I'm not sure what these will buy though.'

The ken had been a gift from the Republic – to help ease their passage, Hagdon had said. But neither of them knew their real value. Kul'Das looked at him askance. 'Will you let me do the talking this time? Diplomacy is clearly not one of your strengths.'

'Why bother with it?'

'Because I don't want my throat slit in the middle of the night because you offended some lowlife in the taproom.'

'They would not dare.' Gareth clenched Hond'Myrkr.

'I'd rather not take the chance,' she replied evenly. 'Who knows how many people witnessed that scene with the smith? Saw those goblets of yours? We can't afford to be arrested.'

Gareth sighed. 'Very well. We'll do it your way.'

Kul'Das let out an audible breath. 'Thank you.'

'For now.'

She was about to respond when he yanked on the reins of both horses and turned them sharply into a side street. 'Quick,' he snapped, the hairs on his neck prickling. 'Someone's following us.'

Kul'Das glanced over her shoulder before taking the reins of her horse from him. 'How do you know?'

'Walk faster. It's a man. I recognize him from before – he was watching us when we went into the ironworks.'

'Why would he follow us?'

'I don't know,' Gareth said softly. 'But he'll regret it.'

Kul'Das frowned. 'We don't want to attract more attention.'

'He's just one man. Let's see if we can't lose him in that market.'

'Market' wasn't exactly the right word, Gareth concluded upon seeing it. A market conjured up images of striped awnings, goods piled untidily beneath them, the cries of hawkers, clink of coin changing hands. The smells of frying meat from the inevitable carts wheeled in to sustain the crowd.

In Sartyan Paarth, there were no hawkers filling the square with their best prices and promises of quality. There weren't even many stalls, just tables with austere awnings, a few sample goods laid out for show. Customers stopped, considered the fare, moved on. Those intending to purchase signed a ledger; stones went on a set of scales, the vendor scribbled a note, tore it and handed one half to the customer. 'It doesn't look like they're buying anything,' Kul'Das murmured, as they watched one woman fold the note into her purse.

Despite its odd quiet, the market wasn't short of people. They did their best to blend in, but their haste and horses attracted a few looks. When they broke through to the other side, Kul'Gareth hurried them into an alleyway, where they stood in the shadows, waiting.

'There.' He pointed. A man emerged from the marketplace,

surreptitiously scanning the busy streets. The same one as before. 'Who is he?' Gareth breathed.

The stranger turned slowly on the spot. His gaze passed across the mouth of the alley before moving on. Then, appearing to reach a decision, he whirled and vanished back into the market. Kul'Das let out a long breath. 'What does he want with us?'

'Good question,' Gareth said darkly. 'Let's go and find this inn you saw.'

'Wait.' She pulled his ragged cloak more firmly about him. 'You should keep those gauntlets hidden. They draw too much attention.'

He shouldn't have to skulk in alleyways. He'd once walked proudly through cities like Paarth, men either falling back from him, or raising their fists in respectful acknowledgement. A moment later, Gareth blinked. No, that couldn't be right. He'd never been to Paarth, or any Acrean cities for that matter. He shook his head, but couldn't dislodge the thought that came right on the heels of the first.

One day, they will learn to respect me again.

19

Hagdon

The land grew harsher as they pressed north. Hagdon had been to this part of Acre before, but not for some years. Certainly not since he'd become general. After the fly-biting marsh which had made them all irritable, the terrain had hardened and begun to climb. Trees grew in clumps, thinning out as the gradient increased. Five days from Parakat, they passed the snowline. As the first flakes drifted down, he heard Brégenne give a pronounced sigh. 'I've seen enough snow to last me several years yet,' she said ruefully. 'Ümvast was full of it.'

'That must have been early for snow,' Irilin remarked.

'I was focused on Sartya being our chief concern.' Brégenne smiled wryly in Hagdon's direction. 'I overlooked the fact that reuniting the continents might have more global consequences.'

Irilin frowned. 'Like what?'

'Changes in the weather. And then there were the wyverns.'

'*Wyverns?*'

Brégenne nodded. 'Didn't I tell you this?'

'Not an unusual sight in the north,' Hagdon said, thinking

of the hulking white beasts. They were more nuisance than menace.

'Not an unusual sight in *Acre*,' Brégenne corrected. 'They've never been seen in Rairam before.'

'Ah. I can see why that might have been a problem.'

Her expression lost its humour. 'Ümvast's warriors didn't know how to fight the wyverns. Many were killed. When I left, the beasts pretty much had Stjórna besieged.' She turned her head to the east, towards Rairam. 'They planned to evacuate, but I couldn't stay to help. Gareth's life depended on finding the other gauntlet.'

'Perhaps he can help them now,' Irilin said. Wind had teased out a few strands of her hair, whipping it across her face. She brushed it back impatiently. It wasn't as pale as Brégenne's, whose hair was so blond as to be almost white; Irilin's was more golden. Hagdon realized he was watching her and looked hastily away.

He'd been trying to ignore it, hiding it beneath the monumental task ahead of him. But he couldn't stop his eyes drifting to her, lingering on her face as she spoke. He'd never met anyone like her. She seemed exotic to Hagdon and she was, he supposed, coming from Rairam. More than that – she was a Wielder, had lived in the ruins of Solinaris, that almost mythical citadel. When he raised his head, it was to find her watching him, as if she sensed his thoughts. She pulled her gaze away as swiftly as he had done.

It was safer to study the trail. They'd passed several signs of Sartyan patrols; clearly, Iresonté had issued orders to track him down. Hagdon's fists clenched involuntarily. When he caught up with her—

'There's someone out there,' Kait said. After they'd almost

lost a scout to an avalanche of scree, the Wielder had offered to do it 'the other way'. Hagdon shivered a little at the thought; magic still made him nervous. A faint nimbus surrounded Kait as she rode with those extra senses extended. Now it brightened. Clearly she was drawing more deeply on her power.

'How many?' he asked.

'Just over half our number.'

'Who are they?'

Kait briefly closed her eyes. 'Sartyans, I think.'

Hagdon cursed. 'We've got company,' he said to Mercia as she came cantering up to him.

'Sartyans?'

He nodded. 'Any idea who they could be?'

'Do they have a wagon with them?' Mercia asked Kait.

The tall Wielder shook her head and Mercia added her curse to Hagdon's. 'A patrol, then. Can we go around them?'

'They're already in the pass with us,' Kait told her. She looked anything but worried, seeming to tremble with nervous energy. Her horse picked up on it, prancing and snorting.

Hagdon had seen enough battle lust in men's eyes to recognize it. 'I'd like to *avoid* a fight if possible,' he said firmly. 'We might outnumber them, but these are Sartyan soldiers. We simply don't have the prowess to take them on without incurring casualties.' He glanced over his shoulder at his followers. Snow dusted their crow-feather cloaks, and he watched wariness spread as the news of a Sartyan patrol travelled back through their ranks. They knew as well as he that they hadn't the training to stand on equal footing with soldiers of the Fist.

He returned his gaze to Mercia. 'Are you up for some fast talking?'

'You know how I love to talk, Hagdon,' she said with a care-

214

free shrug. It was partly an act, Hagdon knew, an attempt to diffuse the fear he could sense in the Republic's forces. Mercia's Sartyans looked grim. If this went badly, they'd be crossing blades with comrades. Hagdon suddenly wondered how far their loyalty to Mercia, to himself, stretched. Today, he might find out.

'This is poor terrain for fighting,' he said, wheeling his horse around to face his forces, 'which is why we'll try it another way. Equally, the patrol will not want a fight in this weather.' The snow was falling faster now, drawing a white curtain over the scene. 'We're going to dismount,' Hagdon called, doing so himself. 'Mercia's group are the only ones who'll remain in the saddle. We'll masquerade as prisoners. If this is a regular patrol, they should let us pass.' He didn't voice his worry that it might not be a regular patrol, but one sent by Iresonté.

Hagdon pulled his hood close about his face, hoping the swirling snow would help conceal him. Then he dropped back among the Republic, hearing mutters as they dismounted. Several of Mercia's men rounded up the horses, corralling them in a group at the back.

'Commander,' Avery said in a low voice, 'are you sure this is wise? We're deliberately putting ourselves in a weak position.' Her eyes were bright beneath her hood.

'You don't trust our allies?'

'If you trust Mercia, that's good enough for me,' she replied, 'but how well does she know her men?'

Hagdon strove to suppress the self-same concern. If *he* didn't support the plan, the Republic wouldn't either. 'Mercia knows her unit,' he said, trying for a note of confidence. 'I do not believe she would have brought anyone she personally doubted.'

'I know they're loyal to her,' Avery said with a glance at the lieutenant, 'but are they loyal to *you*? That I'm not so sure of.'

'I don't need them to be loyal to me,' Hagdon said, knowing that they would eventually need to be if he was to stand against Iresonté, 'at least not here and now. I need them to follow Mercia's orders, which they will do.'

'I don't like it, Commander.' Avery had always been the more outspoken of his adjutants, unafraid to voice her opinion, even if it publicly contradicted his own. It was one of the qualities Hagdon valued in her. But right now –

'Just do it, Avery,' he said, keeping his tone quiet. 'This isn't the time or place for a battle.'

'Commander,' she said shortly, turning away. He watched her organize the Republic into a group, divesting them of their more obvious weapons. Hagdon hadn't ordered them to completely disarm – suspicion ran far too deep for that. And it was unnecessary, he thought. They just needed to fool the patrol long enough to get out of range.

Mercia's red-mailed Sartyans formed up around the Republic, penning them in the middle. 'Fall back,' Hagdon said to the Wielders. 'If this works, you won't be needed.' Kait, he noticed, looked rather put out.

'We'll be watching,' Nediah assured him. 'If it doesn't go to plan, I can shield the whole group for a limited time, but the afternoon wears on.' He gave the sky a meaningful glance.

'That's a lot of people, Nediah,' Brégenne said. 'Are you sure?'

'If he says he can do it, he can do it.' Kait folded her arms. 'No wonder it took him so long to gain the gold with you as his mentor.'

Brégenne flushed. 'I only asked if—'

'Do you both mind?' Nediah said with an unusual snap in his voice. 'We've bigger concerns.'

'Thank you for your offer,' Hagdon said, aware of the tension. 'I hope it won't come to that.'

'I do too,' the Wielder agreed, still sounding irritated. He swung down from his horse and handed the reins to a Sartyan. Then, without waiting for either woman, he moved back to join the corralled body of the Republic. Brégenne, Hagdon noticed, looked pained. Kait was smiling serenely.

'Come with me,' he said to Irilin, who'd already given up her horse. Without thinking, he took her hand. It was warm. He was immediately conscious of its softness and, a moment later, of his own calloused palm gripping hers. He let go quite suddenly, before they'd even gone a few steps. Irilin looked a little surprised. 'It's a while till evening,' Hagdon said. 'I don't want you near the fighting.'

'I thought there wasn't going to be any fighting?'

'In an ideal world. I've served with the army long enough to know we don't live in one.'

'For Sartya's sake, pull up your hood, Hagdon.' Mercia came cantering down from the front of the group. 'The last thing we need is someone recognizing you.'

The wind had blown it back. Hagdon rearranged the thick material about his face. With a sigh he unbuckled his greatsword and handed it to Mercia. 'Take care of it,' he said, his palms already itching to have it back.

Mercia raised an eyebrow. 'The sword of the Sartyan general,' she said, hefting it. 'You're running a risk, Hagdon. Even the rawest recruit would recognize this.'

'It's been with me too long,' he said with a casualness he didn't feel. 'I couldn't just leave it behind.'

'I'm sure Iresonté was very put out.' Mercia gave a wry smile. 'She probably combed the camp before realizing you'd taken it.'

'Yes. I imagine she plans to have it along with my head.'

'We'll see if we can't delay that a bit, then.' She turned her horse towards the front of the company, urging it back into a canter.

'Do you think we've any hope of fooling this patrol?' Irilin asked.

'As long as we keep our weapons under wraps.' Hagdon studied those around him and then beckoned his other adjutant, Hu, over. 'Does everyone know the plan?'

'They're not happy about it,' Hu said in a low voice, 'but they're less happy about the prospect of fighting Sartyans on unfamiliar ground. Nevertheless, Mercia needs to get us through quickly. For many, even the semblance of being Sartyan prisoners strikes too close to the bone.'

Hagdon nodded grimly, not needing to ask more. How many of these people had his tenure as general directly affected? He'd ordered countless raids on settlements from Causca to the Heartland and stayed to watch the after-effects of few. What was he doing here, trying to lead these people? Surely they deserved better.

It was a scant few minutes before they spotted the patrol. Hagdon squinted, doing a quick count. About fifty Sartyans, all mounted. At the sight of Mercia's group, they reined in, adopting defensive positions.

'Hail,' Mercia called out confidently. She guided her horse forward. A man rode out to meet her.

'Hail.' His eyes swept over their group. 'You address Captain Rikr. Who are you and where are you bound?'

218

Hagdon recognized the name, though the man who bore it looked much older than he remembered. He'd served as sergeant on one of the Hozenland raids. Hagdon tugged his hood further over his face.

'Lieutenant Mercia of Artiba,' Mercia said crisply. 'I've a group of rebels – none other than the Republic, in fact – bound for Parakat.'

Something flashed across the man's face. 'Parakat?' He grinned. Hagdon did not like it. 'Your force is small to escort so many, Lieutenant.' Their movements inconspicuous, his men had edged up, ready to surround Mercia. *He knows*, Hagdon thought with a chill. *Get out of there.*

Mercia gave a shrug. 'They're just a rabble, Captain. Untrained and unarmed. My men are quite capable of keeping them in check.' She tilted her head. 'Where did you say you'd come from?'

He held her gaze. 'I didn't.'

'He's just playing with her,' Hagdon hissed to Avery. 'Get ready. Pass the message on.' He looked at Irilin. 'Stay back.'

Mercia's hand slid towards her sword. 'Anyway, Captain, time is pressing and we need to reach Parakat before winter snows us in.' She began to turn her horse and that's when Rikr struck. His sword sprang from its sheath and he delivered a vicious slash that would have severed Mercia's arm at the elbow if she hadn't been expecting it.

Rikr gave a frustrated growl and disengaged. 'You didn't truly think that would work, Mercia? Giving your real name, riding so openly with crows in your midst? Sloppy, Lieutenant, very sloppy.'

'News travels fast,' Mercia said through clenched teeth.

'Word of your treachery has been circulated through the

Causcan garrisons.' Rikr smiled coldly. 'You thought Iresonté would let it lie? She might be busy with the Rairam campaign, but order needs to be upheld at home.'

The Causcan garrisons. Something tightened in Hagdon's belly. Did that mean Parakat was aware of Mercia's defection too? If so, their plan would go up in smoke.

'Were you truly heading for Parakat?' Rikr said. Hagdon didn't miss his use of the past tense; he meant to slaughter every last one of them. 'A suicide mission, if ever I heard of one, Mercia.'

'Only if they're expecting us.'

There – a flicker in the captain's face. Hagdon hoped that meant he *didn't* know whether the news had reached Parakat. He gripped the hilt of his handaxe, wishing for his sword. Battle was unavoidable now. He signalled Hu. Mercia would need cover under which to retreat. Varlan knew it too. Out of habit, perhaps, the Sartyan looked to Hagdon for orders.

Bowmen formed the rearmost line of the Republic. On Hagdon's signal, they dropped to one knee, nocking arrows. He watched them sail overhead, falling like deadly hail among Rikr's men, who raised shields against them. Mercia took the opportunity to retreat, wheeling her horse and cantering back to them while the arrow storm continued. But Sartyan plate was forged in layers of steel; the officers' strengthened by ambertrix. The arrow that struck Rikr did no more than rock him in his saddle and the captain snapped it scornfully in two.

His men fared worse, but few arrows found their mark. Hagdon glanced at his own forces, clad in ordinary mail. They didn't stand a chance against a return volley.

Rikr realized the same. He barked an order and the next

moment, the sky was filled with projectiles. Hagdon raised his shield, braced for their impact.

It took him a few moments to gather that it hadn't come. He chanced a look.

A golden shield shimmered overhead. Sartyan arrows struck sparks from it, bouncing off. Every one deepened the strain on Nediah's face as he held one arm out, fingers spread. Light surrounded him.

A yell, half cheer, half battle cry issued from the Republic. Mercia's Sartyans, of course, stayed silent, but their eyes glittered.

'Forward,' Hagdon called after exchanging a glance with Nediah. The Wielder nodded and Hagdon hoped that meant he could hold the shield while they closed the distance with Rikr. He swung out of formation to grab the reins of a horse. Mercia shouted and tossed him his sword. With reflexes born of a hundred campaigns, Hagdon caught it, comforted by the familiar grip. He spared a glance for Irilin. Brégenne was with her and he gestured for both women to stay at the rear, at least until they were able to use their abilities.

Kait kept to the very front of the shield, a penned cat stalking the bars of its cage, coiled to strike the moment it opened. She had a golden scimitar in each hand. Although Hagdon had seen them before, he couldn't help but stare at the unflinching way she gripped the hilts, flames dancing over her fingers. He half expected them to burn before realizing she *was* the fire; it encased her forearms in golden vambraces.

'I can't hold it for much longer,' Nediah gasped, sweat beading his face. His tanned skin was ashen, the glow about him fitful.

Hagdon nodded: *That's fine.*

The old thrill was in his veins, something he hadn't felt in months. He cantered his way to the front of the shield where Kait gave him a feral grin. Nediah's barrier failed the moment they met Rikr's forces. Hagdon just had time to see the Wielder slump in his saddle before he was forced to block a fierce swing. The soldier gripping the sword was old enough to have seen his own share of campaigns. Their eyes locked.

Hagdon took the man's head in the moment of recognition. It was unfair, an unforeseen advantage, he thought, as he met the blade of another Sartyan, swinging the greatsword in a scything arc to cut into the man's arm. An officer, by the marks on his shoulder, but not one Hagdon recognized. His sword bit into the red plate with ease and the soldier screamed, as much with surprise as with pain. Hagdon came in close, knocking the man out of his saddle. One of Mercia's men rode him down.

Only the emperor had a better blade than the Sartyan general. It had come with Hagdon's appointment: forged in a Lleu-yelin's breath, pure ambertrix from the belly of a dragon. Despite the fact that it no longer crackled with energy, it cut through Sartyan plate like butter. Blood slicked the bright metal.

Battle seethed around him. Steel on steel, blade on flesh, the shrieks of the maimed and dying. It sickened him, excited him. This was where he belonged, moment to moment balanced between life and death, at the mercy of chance. In an ugly melee such as this, luck was equal to skill.

He leapt from his saddle, straightened smoothly, and found himself back to back with Kait. Red stained her clothes and teeth, still fixed in that fierce rictus. Hagdon felt it mirrored on his own lips, his face sticky with blood. He heard a gurgle from behind him and glanced over his shoulder in time to see Kait pull one of her flaming swords free from a woman's chest. Clearly Sartyan plate was no match for the Solar blade either.

One of those strange silences that come so suddenly in the midst of fighting descended over them. Hagdon blinked. A moment later, he felt chagrined. A commander was supposed to hold himself outside the fray, taking stock of a battle's changing tides. Belatedly he surveyed the field.

It wasn't good. Blood had mixed with the dust of the pass, making a silted mire. Bodies sprawled indiscriminately, black feathers among red mail. A few horses were with them, their legs a limp tangle, proud necks twisted. Although he and Kait had carved a swathe through Rikr's unit, the rest of the Republic had not fared as well. Bunched, they were being forced back into the narrowest part of the trail. Ledges overhung each side and Hagdon spotted figures up there, bows in hand. An arrow storm in a bottleneck would decimate them.

Hagdon cursed. He shouldn't have let the archers out of his sight. He shared a look with Kait and watched his own dismay blossom across her face. Sartyans filled the space between him and his struggling forces. Mercia fought with bared teeth; almost singlehandedly keeping the Sartyan line at bay. As he watched, she slipped on the slick ground and fell to one knee. Avery chopped at the soldier about to take her head, thrusting him back just long enough for Mercia to regain her feet.

He'd been distracted too long. Hagdon clumsily parried a sword blow, feeling it shear through the old, patched mail he wore, and wished he still had his Sartyan plate. Pain spread with the blood welling from his slashed side, but he'd sustained enough injuries in battle to ignore it for the moment. He hamstrung his attacker, sword cutting through her armour with ease.

The scuffle had lasted seconds, but when he next looked up, Hagdon saw the Republic had lost ground. Automatically, his eyes sought out Irilin. She and Brégenne were near the back, still within easy range of the Sartyan archers. He felt his heart contract. They were defenceless until night.

'Ned!' Kait cried. She began to force her way through Rikr's men, lashing out with a ferocity that severed limbs, her fiery blades a whirl. She wouldn't make it, Hagdon thought, even as he turned to follow. There were too many between them and the Republic.

He laid about him with desperate fury, but Hagdon knew he couldn't last much longer – he was beginning to take as many hits as he parried; hits that would once have rebounded use-lessly off his armour. Now they left nicks and gashes, each one serving to weaken him further. When a shout came, he looked up, fearing the worst.

'Get back!' Nediah yelled. The Wielder was glowing gold, an easy target for the Sartyan archers to pick off. He met Hagdon's eyes, reinforcing his command with a gesture. Hagdon grabbed Kait.

He almost lost a hand, but she reversed her thrust at the last moment. 'What?' She countered another blow, her parry effective but lacklustre. She was covered in blood; Hagdon had no idea how much of it was her own.

'Nediah,' was all he had time to say. 'Stay back.'

A burst of light filled the ravine. Twin gouts of fire struck the ledges. When it cleared, Hagdon saw with dismay that only two of the archers were down. Before he could renew his advance, a series of terrible cracks echoed up the passage. Fault-lines spidered across the overhanging stone and it began to sheer away from the rockface.

Between the dust and din, Hagdon caught a glimpse of Nediah. A feathered shaft protruded from the Wielder's leg, but his face was set. A flickering shield sprang up over the Republic, leaving the Sartyans to take the brunt of the rockfall. There were screams as both ledges toppled into the trail, burying soldier and horse alike. Those Sartyans at the very rear managed to scramble away, though a stray boulder caught one man and sent him sprawling. He did not get up again.

Hagdon looked around. Perhaps ten of the fifty or so Sartyans remained. He had no idea how many the Republic had lost – the rockfall hid them from view. Kait panted behind him, catching her breath in the sudden respite.

And then a blade came tearing in from the right. Hagdon had only enough time to deflect it, not block it. The stroke cut deep into his sword arm; he felt blade meet bone.

Teeth gritted, eyes watering from the pain, he narrowly dodged a second swing. It was Rikr. The Sartyan captain was a mess. Blood seeped in a constant stream from a cut on his temple, and a smoking hole in his hauberk could only have been made by Kait. He limped, but it did nothing to dampen the smile on his lips.

'General Hagdon.' Rikr's smile widened. 'Or just James now, isn't it? For you to stray across my path . . . fate looks kindly upon me.'

Behind him, Hagdon could hear the sound of rock on rock, as the Republic attempted to shift the debris. 'I beg to disagree, Rikr,' he said, gesturing at the carnage. 'You are routed. Most of your men are dead.' He paused. 'You'd be wise to surrender.'

'Surrender to you? I'll not make that mistake. I know what you do to those who surrender.' He spat blood on the ground. 'I was there. In Hozenland, remember? I was one of those who took my blade to the throats of children. On your orders.'

A *boom* sounded and they both flinched. Rock tumbled and fell, revealing the path beyond the collapse and the dusty faces of Brégenne and Nediah. In the twilight, both Wielders shimmered with energy. They stepped carefully through, Mercia, Avery and Irilin on their heels. Hagdon felt a knot loosen in his chest. She was safe.

He turned back to Rikr. 'Those days are over,' he said coldly.

'A changed man, then?' Rikr laughed a laugh choked with blood. 'I've seen nothing to prove it. You fight like the rabid dog you've always been, Hagdon. You cut down men and women who, just weeks ago, called you friend and leader.' His gaze moved from his fallen soldiers to the Republic, now following Avery through the breach in the rockfall. 'How did you convince the black-cloaks to follow you? Out of fear? They know what you are as well as I.'

'That's right,' Avery said. 'We do.'

She held a spear at the ready. As Hagdon watched, frozen, she tilted her arm and threw. Someone screamed. Hagdon flinched.

The spear took Rikr in the chest, hurling him to the ground. Its haft glimmered with faint silver. Brégenne stood beside Avery, her skin still limned in light. 'I thought it needed a little something extra,' Hagdon heard her say. 'Or it might not have breached his armour.'

Hagdon let loose a pent-up breath. Had he truly believed Avery's spear was meant for him? *No*, he thought, but his knotted muscles told him otherwise. Everything Rikr had said was true and the Republic knew it. He couldn't look at any of them.

Fortunately, Mercia took charge. 'You,' she barked at the

remnants of Rikr's unit, 'have two choices. Surrender or swear allegiance.' She glanced at Hagdon. 'I don't recommend surrender.'

'What's the difference?' one woman asked in a low, bitter voice.

'The difference?' Mercia smiled at her. 'The difference is: you get to live.'

20

Kyndra

Shit, was all Kyndra's panicked mind could come up with. She crouched behind the sergeant and noticed others hiding too, all cowering back from the man who stood so calmly among them, proffering his invitation. She'd known Kierik had had dealings with Davaratch – they lay at the root of the Starborn's distrust of him – but no matter how much she wracked her brain, searching through the memories she'd inherited from Kierik, Kyndra couldn't find one of this moment.

The sergeant left her to join the other guards in barricading the way ahead. More carriages drew up and sounded their horns until the drivers realized what was going on. After that, a deadly hush took hold.

Another guard emerged from the gate, his decorated pauldrons proclaiming him some sort of officer. He took one look at Kierik and his face paled. 'You are not welcome here, Starborn.'

'I beg to differ,' Kierik said in a tone that was almost jovial. Beneath his star-cast skin, he seemed young, but it was impossible to guess his age. Dark hair fell to his collar, curling slightly at the ends. Kyndra felt an echo of the pull she had followed to the Deep all those months ago. With a sudden shiver, she remembered the black ravines that would one day score Kierik's face, those chill, dead eyes. And as she thought it, Kierik looked up, as if at a sudden sound. Kyndra edged backwards into the shadows and the moment passed.

'Davaratch himself invited me,' the Starborn said, giving the invitation a little shake.

'I highly doubt that. You have made your distaste of House Sartya perfectly clear.'

Kierik sighed. 'I have no desire to argue, Captain. Neither do I have a desire to ruin your party.' He swept out his other hand. 'You're holding up the guests. And I am one of them. See what it says –' he flicked the invitation – 'Kierik of Maeran.'

She could see the officer wavering and knew she wouldn't get another chance. Kyndra spotted her target: an open-topped carriage with a short canvas covering the rear. She continued her careful edging around the fringes of the scene; fortunately, all eyes were on Kierik and the officer. In the hubbub that followed the captain stepping aside and Kierik's polite thanks, Kyndra slipped under the canvas, flattening herself against the back of the seats.

There was a short cough, a crackle and the vehicle was in motion, trundling through the arch into the courtyard beyond. Kyndra could see a slice of night sky where the canvas didn't quite meet the seat tops. *Vestri* shone directly above her; though she knew they couldn't express human emotion, she imagined the star looking down with disdain on her cramped lodgings.

The vehicle halted. Doors opening and a low conversation told her it was changing hands. Kyndra hoped the servant wouldn't take them too far away from the manor – she needed to get inside quickly. *Kierik's in there*, she reminded herself, her heart knocking against her ribs. *Why don't I have his memory of this party?* Did he not recall it? Or perhaps the stars had suppressed it for their own reasons. They were the ones who presided over the inheritance of memories, after all.

The hum of the carriage sputtered and died. A door opened. Footsteps on stone. Kyndra tensed, waiting for the canvas to be drawn back, but the footsteps moved away. Throwing caution to the winds, she thrust the covering aside and leapt out. The red-liveried servant was heading for a small door set in the side of the building. He had his back to her, idly tossing a short, glowing baton from hand to hand.

Kyndra sprinted at him. The servant barely had time to turn before she tackled him to the ground and wrestled the glowing blue stick from his shocked hand. He was surely stronger, but she had surprise on her side and he couldn't stop her from slamming the end of the baton into his temple. It was a move Char had taught her, aimed to – hopefully – incapacitate rather than kill. The man went limp, eyes rolling up in his head, and Kyndra hoped she hadn't used too much force. She took a few deep breaths and then, with an apology the servant couldn't possibly hear, she pulled him behind the row of still dark carriages and stripped off his livery.

He was small for a man and the uniform fitted her fairly well. Tucking her hair under the red hat, Kyndra pulled it low over her eyes, hoping no one would look too closely. She tugged on his white gloves, having some difficulty forcing her weakened hand into the tight material. Then, leaving the semi-naked servant concealed in a bush, she took the blue baton, straightened her shoulders and marched up the steps to the side door. Servants had their own brand of magic – they were invisible. With luck she could work her way through the manor undisturbed.

Unfortunately, servants were not invisible to other servants. She'd gone no further than the corridor beyond the door when an older man seized her, plucking the baton from her hand. 'Most of the guests are here now and we need more waiters,' he snapped, steering her down another plain passageway. Kyndra tried to say something, but the man overrode her. 'I don't care if you haven't done it before. Stick to the outskirts of the hall and avoid any guests wearing red – they'll be relatives and more likely to find fault.' He thrust her through a pair of double doors.

A hundred suns blazed on the other side.

After half a dozen alarmed blinks, Kyndra realized they were just chandeliers, lit not with the soft light of candles, but with ambertrix. They chased all shadows from the great chamber, illuminating every niche which might shelter a lurking assassin. That was one thing at least. As long as Davaratch was somewhere in this vast lit space, he'd see the eldest coming. Or so she hoped.

'Get going,' the servant snapped, pushing a tray of drinks at her. Kyndra was forced to balance it on her good hand – the other couldn't take the weight of the tray, even with so delicate a cargo. In that moment, she'd never been more thankful for her innkeeper training, and almost laughed at the use she now put it to. Small bubbles blossomed in the golden wine, flowing perpetually upwards. *Calmaracian*, Kyndra thought, remembering her first taste of the vintage in Rogan's house.

The man glared at her until she started walking before letting the doors swing shut. There'd be no going back that way. Perhaps there was a servants' corridor on the other side. Kyndra began a slow circuit of the chamber, trying to see everything at once. She kept to the outskirts as the man suggested, pausing every so often by a group of nobles. All were gorgeously attired, the women dripping gems and peacock feathers. The men wore complementary outfits and were hardly less adorned; burnished medallions gleamed on their chests and their earlobes were studded with precious stones. Other than the guards standing at neat intervals around the hall, Kyndra spotted a few military men, dressed in armour quite similar to the set Hagdon had once worn. She avoided the red-clad nobles, many of whom shared the distinctive black eyes of House Sartya.

As the minutes passed, her palms began to sweat inside the gloves. Nothing looked out of the ordinary. Chatter echoed about the hall, filled with the clink of glasses and the tinkling laughs of women schooled to gentility. It was all so empty, so wrong, Kyndra thought, her mind full of burning cities and streets that reeked of death. Cocooned by the thick walls of wealth, where the smoke couldn't reach them, the nobles chittered endlessly like caged birds.

She supposed that was how Davaratch wanted it.

Her skin prickled. Just yards away, Kierik busily extricated himself from two women, both of whom wore flirtatious smiles. *Too stupid to fear him*, Kyndra thought, watching how Kierik's own smile did nothing to warm his eyes. She could almost see the thoughts racing behind them and she turned before he spotted her, offering her tray to a passing couple.

When she looked back, the Starborn was being escorted towards the rear of the hall. Guards pulled aside a red drape; Kyndra caught a glimpse of a man rising to greet him. Even at this distance, she made out the burning eyes of Davaratch. The curtain fell back.

'How rude,' she heard dimly as she breezed past a woman who'd stretched out her hand to seize a glass only to have it whipped away. Kyndra didn't spare her a glance. Instead she worked her way around the room towards the curtained alcove, stationing herself next to it, as if she'd been told to. The guards' eyes slid over her livery and on.

Working in an inn, she was used to isolating single conversations amidst a general hubbub. '. . . confess myself surprised,' she heard. Kyndra strained her ears, but didn't catch Kierik's reply. Whatever he'd said made Davaratch laugh, however. 'If you intend to kill me, Starborn, I suppose you'd better get it over and done with.'

Kyndra's insides clenched. She inched closer to the curtain.

'I don't intend to kill you,' she heard Kierik say quite clearly. 'At least not this night. I seek only to caution you.'

'I hear enough caution from my diplomats,' Davaratch replied, a bite in his tone. 'I do not require any more from you.'

'Perhaps you should . . .' Kyndra didn't catch the rest of the sentence, as Kierik lowered his voice. '. . . I cannot permit it.'

'Who are you to permit me anything?' Davaratch snapped. She heard the creak of a chair, as if he shifted restlessly within it. 'I mean to make House Sartya the foremost power in the Heartland.'

'And what then?' Kierik demanded. 'You and I both know you will not stop at the Heartland.'

Silence. After a moment, Davaratch said, 'Only men of little stature dream small.'

'I warn you, Davaratch. Sartya is a powerful House, but if it outgrows its status as such and seeks to dominate more lands than it already holds, I will not stand idly by.'

'With all the power you hold,' Davaratch said quietly, and Kyndra strained to hear him, 'do you not also desire dominion? It would be so simple for you to stretch out your hand and crush us lesser mortals.' He paused. 'What stops you, Kierik of Maeran?'

There was movement behind the curtain. Kyndra thought one of the men had risen to his feet. Then Kierik said, 'I've heard enough. This meeting is over.'

A woman screamed.

There was a disturbance in the middle of the hall, ripples spreading outward in the form of people scrambling to get away. Over the heads of panicked guests, Kyndra saw Medavle shrug off the last vestiges of his Lunar cloak, revealing the eldest at his side. The Khronostian was just as she remembered: stooped, wizened, leaning heavily on a staff.

Her blood turned cold. The tray slipped from her hand, the sound of its crash lost in the confusion. Davaratch burst through the drape in plain view of the eldest. It was all happening too fast. The ancient man smiled. He held a dagger, its blade glowing – Medavle must have imbued it with power drawn from his own veins like all Yadin. His face bore lines where none had been before. What had the eldest done to him?

She was too far away and powerless to act in any case. So Kyndra did the only thing she could think of: she threw back her head and screamed, 'Kierik!'

Her voice cut through the cries of the nobles, the patter of heels on marble, bringing with it a dreadful silence. Kierik stepped out from behind the drape, his skin silvered by *Tyr*. Their eyes locked.

'*You,*' Medavle said.

Kyndra tore her gaze away. The Yadin had gone rigid, fists balled and trembling at his sides. He took a step forward, his face twisted in a grimace of hatred.

'No further, Yadin,' the eldest croaked, stretching out a

gnarled hand to stop him. Medavle ignored it, his dark eyes never leaving Kierik.

'Murderer,' he spat. 'Your hands are stained with the blood of my people.'

Kierik's brow creased. 'You are Yadin,' he said after a moment and there was no mistaking the distaste in his voice. 'What are you doing here?'

'You will never harm her again,' Medavle cried and he broke into a run, straight towards Kierik.

'No!' The eldest hobbled after him. 'Yadin, I forbid it. Do not break the mandala!'

If Medavle heard him, he didn't pause, but flew at Kierik, energy encasing his fists. The eldest gave a strangled scream and hurled the dagger at Davaratch.

Time seemed to slow, as the blade flew end over end towards the future emperor. Guards ran for him, but it was plain they wouldn't make it. It was a good throw. Kyndra could see where it would strike the Sartyan, hitting squarely between his collar bones. Desperation seized her feet, hurtling her towards the doomed man.

Medavle brought back his arm as he ran, the glow brightening around his clenched fist. Kierik stayed perfectly still.

A thunderclap split the hall. Kyndra had a muddled glimpse of white bars before they snapped like brittle bones, filling the space with the mad pealing of a hundred bells. She covered her ears. Mid-leap, Medavle vanished. So did the blade, just inches from Davaratch's throat. But the Lunar that encased it threw him backwards with a roar. He tumbled across the slick marble, the skin on his neck blistering.

When Kyndra glanced round, the eldest too had gone.

Her heart hammered; her breath came in gasps. She could

hardly believe it was over. Muttering retook the hall and guards surrounded Davaratch. With their help, he was lifted into a sitting position – it looked as if he would live.

A hand closed on her wrist.

Kyndra stifled a yelp. She'd temporarily forgotten Kierik, so quiet a witness had he been. Now the Starborn stared down at her, his dark blue eyes – *her* eyes, she suddenly thought – stark on her face. Looking into his, she could see he wore the stars differently. While *Sigel* shone on her cheek, Kierik had *Tyr* there instead. *Thurn*, *Wynn* and *Lagus* glowed on his other cheek; dark hair half concealed the tails of *Noruri* and *Vestri* across his forehead. She shivered, struck by a thought. These were the stars he favoured most; the stars he would use to separate Rairam and Acre.

His brow furrowed. 'Who are you?'

She could hear *Veritan* in his voice, the star that sniffed out truth. As its claws dug into her mind, she gritted her teeth and resisted. 'No one,' she said.

He increased the pressure and Kyndra began to sweat with the effort of holding him back. *Veritan* clawed and scrabbled at her mind, as if it were an icy slope which offered little purchase. She wasn't sure how much longer she could hold it off. He *couldn't* discover the truth; if he knew what lay in his future . . .

The world blurred. Kyndra had a rushed impression of colour and light before she found herself on a windy bluff, high above the city. He'd used *Raad* to transport them both. *I didn't even know that was possible*. That she could use *Raad* to move another as well as herself. For a fleeting moment, Kyndra felt the ache of yearned-after knowledge. How much Kierik could teach her . . .

But his hand was still around her wrist. She jerked free with a gasp, stumbling back a step. 'What did you do?' she heard herself ask. 'Why did you take me?'

Kierik put his head on one side; she imagined a bird regarding a particularly fat worm. His dark, cold eyes – eyes that stared out at her every time she looked in a mirror – narrowed on her face. 'You seem familiar,' he said. 'How do you know my name?'

'Everyone knows your name,' she said cautiously. 'You're the Starborn.'

'Actually, very few know it,' Kierik replied, his eyes never leaving her face.

Kyndra forced herself to stay calm, to give nothing away, but it was difficult when the same thought ran constant circles around her mind: *We look so alike.* Surely Kierik must notice. Another thought chased the first. *This man is my father. My real father.*

She'd always found the truth terrifying, but that was when Kierik had been a madman, his cheeks star-scarred and blackened as if a fire had dragged a knife across his face. Now he stood before her, young and strong, the wind in his hair, his gaze alert and curious. The madman was a distant memory. She felt an unexpected pang for what he would lose, for what he would become.

'Not many can resist *Veritan*,' Kierik said abruptly. 'Are you from Solinaris?'

Kyndra almost laughed. 'A Wielder?' she said, unable to swallow her pride. 'You think a Wielder could resist the power of a Starborn?'

Kierik did not blink. 'I do not underestimate those in Solinaris. You look young, but that means little. Some dedicate their lives to perfecting illusions.'

'And a Starborn would be fooled by an illusion?'

Kierik sidestepped the question. 'Was that *your* Yadin?' he asked instead. 'What did you do to him?'

Like a wind suddenly changing direction, Kyndra's confidence deserted her. For a moment, she'd felt like the Starborn, powerful, unchallengeable. Now she was nothing but a young woman trying desperately to keep her secrets.

When she didn't answer, his expression darkened. 'You will tell me your name. Then you will explain to me what I just witnessed.'

'I can't,' she said, anger stirring at his tone. *Because I would doom myself and the world with me.* 'More than my life depends on it.'

She sensed his frustration. 'If you won't tell me, *Veritan* will.'

There was no regret in his voice, no threat even. Only resolve. She was a locked box without a key that he would break open if he had to. Kyndra braced herself, but it was still a shock when the star sank its talons into her mind. Weakened from the last assault, she staggered, one hand gripping a boulder that guarded the cliff edge.

Kierik stood watching her, impassive. She wanted to shout, to scream at him to stop lest the world be changed, but she poured all her concentration into resisting and had no voice to spare. He would win, unless she did something. But the stars weren't hers to command. Sweating, teeth clenched, Kyndra glanced over her shoulder. The edge was only a few strides away. If she threw herself off, Kierik might halt his assault to catch her.

Or she might die.

Kyndra's heart beat wildly in her ears. The world swam with

the effort of keeping the star out. She couldn't allow him to see the truth, even if it meant her death. There was far more at stake. *Ma!* she screamed, throwing her last strength into the call. *Help me!* Then, before her will failed, Kyndra took a running leap and hurled herself into the abyss.

21

Brégenne

They'd put the pass and the battle behind them, making camp in a sheltered cradle between two peaks. Rikr's surviving soldiers had for the moment been divested of weapons and now sat in a subdued group, dressing their wounds and cleaning their armour. Brégenne suspected they'd have shown the same silent discipline if they'd won the battle and were still part of the Fist.

'Is it bad?' she heard Kait ask. The tall woman knelt beside Nediah, one hand on his shoulder, as he eased the arrow out of his leg. The sun had all but left the sky; Brégenne knew the fitful flicker of Solar energy around Nediah's hands would do little to lessen his pain. She swallowed, resolutely continuing with her own healing. Hu's wound wasn't serious, but the black-cloaked man watched with a dewy gratitude in his eyes.

Brégenne snatched another glance in time to see the arrow come free. Nediah tossed it to the ground, gritting his teeth as the blood ran anew down his thigh. 'Could be worse,' he said. 'Sun's not high enough to heal it now.'

Kait ripped a long strip off her shirt. When she bent to tie it around the wound, Nediah plucked it out of her hands. 'I shouldn't have done it,' he said.

'Don't be ridiculous, Ned.'

His face darkened. 'Killing is hardly ridiculous, Kait.'

'You *saved* us. The Republic were barely holding their own.'

Nediah gave the ends of the rag a fierce tug; it soaked through in seconds. He said nothing.

'That rockfall was inspired.' Crouching, Kait placed a hand on his knee. Brégenne stiffened. 'And you managed to shield everyone again. If it weren't for you, they'd have slaughtered us.'

Nediah slowly unclenched his fists. 'That doesn't make it better.'

Hu gasped and Brégenne realized she held his injured arm in a death grip. 'Sorry,' she muttered, calming the last of the swelling.

'You've always been like this,' Kait said fondly. She stroked some hair out of Nediah's eyes. 'Even when you played along with me, you couldn't help but feel a little bit guilty.' She grinned. 'My conscience.'

Enough.

'It'll be fine now,' Brégenne growled at Hu before standing and crossing over to the pair of them. The strength of her anger shocked her. 'Nediah.'

He looked up at her warily. She'd said very little to him since the night of their argument – that night made her feel at turns embarrassed and newly outraged. Now there was a whole host of things Brégenne wanted to say, all bottled up inside and clamouring to be set free. 'You,' she snapped at Kait. 'Get out of my way.'

Kait's eyes widened and then swiftly narrowed. She did not move, but kept her hand firmly on Nediah's knee. 'Excuse me?'

'I won't ask again.' Brégenne still held the Lunar after healing Hu; power dripped from her fingers like quicksilver. She drew down a little more for emphasis.

'Why?' Kait asked suspiciously.

'Why do you think? Because I'm not about to let Nediah bleed to death.'

'Brégenne,' Nediah removed Kait's hand from his knee and straightened his leg, though it clearly caused him pain. 'I'm fine. The tourniquet will slow the bleeding enough to last until dawn.'

'That', she said crisply, 'is the most ridiculous thing I've ever heard.'

'Brégenne—'

'Be quiet. *You*,' Brégenne directed at Kait, 'go away and give me some room.'

Kait met her eyes. They stared defiantly at one another until Brégenne was sure the other woman would strike her, Solar or no Solar. Then Kait glanced at Nediah and the sodden bandage around his leg. 'Fine,' she muttered, standing. 'Don't take all night.'

She went to sit on a rock with a clear view of them both. Thankfully, Mercia wandered over to talk to her. Now that she was gone, Brégenne felt a bit chagrined and looked back at Nediah, scowling. 'Keep that leg elevated. Some healer you are.'

Nediah smiled, but it was wan. Brégenne could tell he was still thinking about the rockfall and the soldiers he'd killed. 'Kait's right,' she said, surprising herself.

'That's something I never thought to hear.'

'We were going to lose. You did what you had to do.'

'Yes, well.' Nediah lowered his eyes. 'It's nothing to be celebrated.'

'No, it isn't,' Brégenne agreed. She unwound the bandage and sent her awareness into the wound. 'This isn't too bad, actually.'

'I did tell you.'

She ignored this and began knitting the torn flesh. She couldn't heal as neatly as Nediah, but at least he wouldn't be in pain. 'You're good, you know,' he offered when new pink skin had replaced the ugly wound. 'You just need a bit more practice.'

'I need more than that,' Brégenne muttered. His thigh was hot beneath her hands; she felt an echoing heat in her face, a desire to slide her fingers further over his skin. She hastily pulled away.

Nediah made a grasping motion, as if he'd intended to catch hold of her. 'Brégenne,' he said, his gaze hesitant. 'About the other night—'

'You're done, I see.' Kait returned to stand over them, trailing an exasperated Mercia in her wake. The Sartyan woman rolled her eyes at Brégenne as if in apology. Brégenne felt her anger prickle anew. She rose smoothly and, without a backward glance, went to see to the other injured, trying not to wonder what Nediah had been about to say.

'Even with Rikr's men, we're too few to strike directly at Parakat,' Hagdon said a few days later. They were almost in spitting distance of the fortress, concealed by the snowy troughs and peaks of cliffs – a bleak backdrop, Brégenne thought. Their fire was small, but necessary; winter had firmly sunk its claws into the north.

'I can't believe you're even factoring them into our plans,' Kait said, tugging her gloves on more snugly. 'They were quite content to kill us a few days ago.'

'Sartyans don't work well without orders to follow,' Mercia said. The lieutenant was leaning back against a rock, looking quite at ease amidst the unforgiving landscape. She was a northerner herself and used to this cold. Brégenne shivered, reminded of her time in Ümvast. 'Rikr's men are without a commander,' Mercia continued, 'and they owe us their lives.'

'I still think we should have killed them,' Kait rejoined. 'At least let's not make them part of the assault.'

'We ought to be able to keep ten soldiers in check,' Hagdon said. 'Still, if you're concerned, I put them under your command. Feel free to dispose of them at the first whiff of treachery.'

Kait looked slightly mollified. 'Getting back to the matter at hand,' Hagdon added, 'I don't think we've much choice but to follow our original plan.'

'If they've received word of my joining you –' Mercia began.

'I was looking at Rikr's face when he answered. He, at least, believed they haven't.'

'Hagdon, they could turn on me the moment I cross that threshold.'

'They won't let you armed into Parakat,' Hagdon said firmly. 'If they believe you a traitor, that is.' He paused. 'Rumour, however, tends to travel faster than truth. Be prepared.'

'Have you decided on timing, Commander?' Brégenne asked him. 'If you want Kait to fight and Nediah on hand to heal, it'll need to be after dawn. If anything goes wrong, however, you'll need me to get your forces across the chasm.'

'I've given this some thought,' Hagdon said, scratching his cheek through the dark growth of beard. 'Mercia and Irilin can't act straightaway. They'll need to maintain the charade long enough to learn as much about the Parakat garrison as possible.

I need numbers.' He glanced at Mercia. 'All the information you can gather.'

'If they buy our story, we'll be separated,' Mercia said. 'Irilin will be put with the prisoners.'

'That means I'll be able to warn them of our assault.'

Brégenne thought Hagdon might have suppressed a shiver at her words. He looked away, that shadow once again in his face. 'I think you should approach at midnight,' he said.

'Bit suspicious,' Mercia replied with a grimace. 'Why would a patrol travel so late?'

'They'll have spent the last fortnight out in this.' Hagdon gestured at the snowy sky. 'If you knew a decent bed, fire and food awaited you nearby, would you stop or continue on?'

Mercia smiled slowly. 'Good point. All right.' She looked around at them all. We've a few hours before we move. Let's make the most of them.'

He was sitting alone as twilight fell, watching the western sky – a pose Brégenne herself adopted while she waited for the moon to return her to power. It was a rare moment; he wasn't often alone. Kait kept an irritatingly possessive eye on him most of the time, especially since the battle the other day. But tonight she was training with Mercia, sharing her knowledge of swordplay with the other woman. They seemed to get along well.

Nediah warmed his hands over a dying golden flame. It winked out as she approached and, without thinking, Brégenne replaced it with one of her own.

He started at the Lunar light and twisted around to look. They stared at each other. A few seconds passed before Brégenne went to sit beside him, stretching out her legs. For a while they said nothing at all. The sun sank and the sky cleared, revealing stars for the first time in days. 'You know,' Nediah murmured finally, with a nod to them, 'Hagdon said that before the ambertrix shortage, every Acrean city blazed with light. It hid the stars.'

The rising moon cast his profile in shades of silver and shadow. It was the way Brégenne had always seen him, achingly familiar. 'I can't imagine how that must have looked,' she said.

Gaze still turned upward, Nediah said, 'Sometimes I wonder what it's like for Kyndra. To us, the stars are . . . well, part of the night. But to her, they have names, abilities.' He shook his head. 'Starborn really aren't like Wielders at all.'

'I miss her,' Brégenne said honestly. 'So strange to think that without her, we wouldn't be sitting here –'

'– in Acre, about to storm a fortress,' Nediah added somewhat wryly. 'Everything is different.' He paused, looked at her, a little of his earlier hesitation in his eyes. '*You're* different.'

'Me?' *This is going to be about Kait*, she thought with a sinking feeling.

'Well,' Nediah said, 'the clothes, for starters.'

Brégenne blinked and, after a moment, she laughed. 'Why does that upset everyone so much? It's not as if I'm walking around in a ball dress. Alandred nearly choked when he saw me.'

She regretted the words as soon as they were out, knowing any mention of Alandred tended to raise Nediah's hackles. But he only gave a suggestive chuckle. 'I bet.'

Brégenne felt a blush on her cheeks and hoped the evening hid it. 'I'm not the only one who's different,' she said.

Nediah nodded. 'I suppose that's true. I feel like I've seen and done more in the last month than in my entire life.'

'You're not alone.' She leaned back on her hands. 'I didn't

think I'd ever have to escape a group of Wielders by catching hold of a rope ladder as it swung past my head, before being hauled onto the deck of an unchained airship.'

'What?' Nediah sounded delighted.

'Didn't I tell you that bit?' *No*, she realized hollowly. Their argument had put paid to any amicable reunion they might have had.

He grinned. 'I don't think so.'

Brégenne pushed regret aside. 'Argat saved the day,' she said, remembering how the *Eastern Set* had swept her away from harm. 'Without him, Gareth and I would never have escaped the Council's Wielders.'

He raised an eyebrow. 'Brégenne, you're a third of the Council.'

'Veeta and Gend probably replaced me the second I left.'

They sat in silence for a time. Brégenne sensed a strange tentativeness about their conversation, as if they were forging a new trail across one already blazed.

'I've missed this,' Nediah said then. 'I've missed you.'

Quite suddenly, Brégenne recalled the dream she'd woken from in Astra's house. With a pang, she remembered how it had felt to stand within the circle of his arms, to shiver at the brush of his fingertips across her bare shoulder. The flush returned to her cheeks, but she forced herself to say, 'What about Kait?'

They were sitting close, so close that her skin prickled. 'What about her?' Nediah said a bit too casually.

She couldn't look at him. 'All this time she's been here with you. I thought . . .'

'What?'

Despite her best efforts, the words found their way out. 'She's in love with you.'

Nediah was silent. 'I know,' he said finally, quietly.

Brégenne looked back at him, wanting to ask whether he felt the same, but, fearful of his answer, she couldn't bring herself to voice it. The chill wind wrapped them both, deepening with the onset of night.

'Brégenne.' Nediah seemed to be searching for something in her eyes. 'Why do you care about Kait? When we were in Naris, the night they broke our bond . . .' He swallowed. 'When you said you felt – did you mean it?'

It was back – her uncertainty, her hope and fear bound into a terrible knot. It was building a wall between them. Brégenne's throat dried. All those words inside her and she couldn't speak any of them.

But she didn't want him to go.

With a sigh, Nediah stood. Brégenne jumped up too, almost colliding with him. Her heart felt like it would push its way out of her chest; louder than the wind's whistle, he must be able to hear it.

As Nediah began to turn away, she caught his hand. Neither of them was wearing gloves and the effect of skin on skin sent a shock through her, like the sweet stab of drawing more power than she could hold. They locked eyes, locked hands.

'. . . Ready?' came a distant voice. 'We're moving into position.'

Brégenne wanted to stay there, wanted to move her hand to his face, to trace his lips with a finger, to have those lips on hers. There were so many things she wanted, as they stood there, touching, hearing the sounds of their comrades gathering for battle.

Perhaps Nediah saw it in her eyes, for his own widened, and he raised his other hand to her cheek, brushing back an escaped curl, just as he'd done that night on the spire in Naris. This time, she leaned in to his touch. He swept his thumb across her cheekbone and Brégenne barely breathed, frightened to move lest he stop.

She'd drawn close enough to feel the flush in his skin when the scrape of boots on rock intruded. Guiltily, they jumped apart. Brégenne somehow expected it to be Kait, but it was Irilin. The young woman wore a small smile. 'There you are,' she said. 'We're ready to go.'

'Right,' Brégenne muttered. Cold curled around the hand he'd been holding; almost regretfully, she pulled on her gloves. Nediah, she saw, still looked a little wide-eyed. 'Is everyone ready?'

'As much as they can be.' Irilin stuck her own hands under her armpits. 'I wish it wasn't so damn cold.'

'And you?' Nediah asked. 'Are you sure you want to do this?'

Irilin gave a hard nod. 'Who else is going to be Mercia's prisoner? Only Brégenne and I are Lunars and she has to remain here. The plan depends on me.'

'That doesn't mean you can't back out.'

'Actually, it does.' Irilin held his gaze, unflinching. 'I said I would do it. I *can* do it.' She paused, added softly, 'And if I die, well, it's in the name of a worthy cause.'

'I don't think Hagdon would like that,' Brégenne said. 'Or allow it.'

Irilin just shrugged.

They made their way back to camp to find it packed up. Hagdon led Irilin's horse over, silently offered his cupped hands to help boost her into the saddle. She accepted the offer with a murmured, 'Thank you.' The commander's eyes were haunted as he settled into his own saddle and he darted frequent glances her way.

They rode down a slope and up a shallow incline, Brégenne lighting the way for the horses, until Mercia reined in. 'Parakat lies beyond that summit,' she said, pointing towards the dark lip of the slope. 'We'll separate here. After we're in, don't carry a light to the top,' she added to Brégenne. 'It'll be a beacon to any sentries.'

'Torches,' Hagdon snapped, the command full of the Sartyan general. Mercia's men heard it and immediately set about lighting the torches that would announce their presence to the fortress garrison. Mercia raised an eyebrow, but didn't comment.

They were ready. There was no putting it off.

Hagdon seemed to be struggling with something. In the end he went to Irilin, who had dismounted, and took her arm. She looked up, clearly surprised. 'Aberrations are not as strong as you,' he said tightly. 'They rarely fight back – they don't know how.' His voice dropped lower. 'You will have to play your part.'

'I know my part,' she said, but her usual defiance was lacking. Perhaps, Brégenne thought, Irilin was remembering how Hagdon had described the conditions in Parakat, the horrors suffered by its inmates. She felt a flicker of worry.

'It won't be for long,' she said – to herself as much as to Irilin. 'As soon as things have died down, Mercia will lower the drawbridge for the rest of us.'

Hagdon still held the young woman's arm. 'If I see them hurt you,' he said quietly, 'I will come for you and damn the plan.'

Irilin stared at him a moment, a low flush in her cheeks and then she pulled her arm free. She went to Mercia, held out her crossed wrists and the lieutenant bound them, attaching a long piece of rope which she tied to her saddlebow. Hagdon watched stonily.

Brégenne followed the group until they vanished over the lip of the slope. Distant shouts came almost immediately, ringing from the fortress walls. A clanking preceded the drawbridge as it descended. She sat tight and tried to swallow the feeling that something was about to go horribly wrong.

22

Hagdon

He paced back and forth, boots dusted with the snow that had begun falling shortly after midnight. 'Where are they?' He'd asked the question aloud half a dozen times already. 'I need to know what's going on in there.' He couldn't bear the thought of Irilin in Parakat, remembering the bruised, famished bodies of its inmates.

Just then Brégenne signalled from the top of the slope, a flash of moonlight. 'Something's happening,' Hagdon heard himself say. He looked around. 'Nediah, Kait, come with me. Hu, follow us at a distance. Leave the horses picketed here. No lights.' Without waiting for a response, he started up the ridge.

Brégenne was crouched on the top. She'd bound her hair into a long plait that hung over her shoulder and her eyes glowed softly in the dark. 'The lights have left the walls,' she said. 'Either a shift change, or Mercia's taken them out. This is our best chance.'

Hagdon adjusted the sword on his back, pulled up his hood. 'Let's go, then.'

They made it to the bottom of the slope just as the drawbridge creaked into action. Hagdon waited. He could hear the bulk of the Republic behind him, but the clanking of the bridge covered the sound of boots on rock.

When the bridge was fully down and the portcullis lifted, he could see a figure standing in the entrance, framed by weak torchlight. It was Mercia, who beckoned him forward. Thinking of Irilin, Hagdon was halfway across the drawbridge when his instincts screamed at him. Mercia stood stiffly, her beckoning hand twisted palm out instead of in – the only way she was able to warn him.

Hagdon skidded to a halt. He was close enough to see her face now – eye already purpling, lip split open. Blood painted her chin. When he didn't move further, a soldier stepped out, grabbed Mercia and held a dagger to her throat.

'General,' a woman's voice called. 'Do come in.'

The drawbridge began to close, forcing Hagdon into a run. He jumped and rolled, hearing the bridge clang shut behind him. He landed badly and his shoulder, still tender after the crossbow injury, admonished him with a stab of pain. Gritting his teeth, he straightened.

'Have you come to inspect the troops?' the woman asked mockingly, stepping into the torchlight.

'Maeve,' he said. It was years ago and he had been young. Her blond hair was longer than he remembered; she'd bound it into a soldier's knot.

She flashed a cold smile. 'Nice to know you remember, but it's Captain Tserfel now.'

'I wasn't aware the stealth force garrisoned Parakat,' he replied mildly, despite the cold unfurling in his stomach.

'Such recklessness, Hagdon.' She took a slow walk around

Mercia. 'To send a known traitor into our midst . . .' Maeve stopped, facing him. 'Not a mistake you'd have made before.'

'Times change.'

'I'm aware.' She rolled her shoulders; the greathawks glinted on her pauldrons. 'Why are you here?'

The air rippled. Hagdon saw it; Maeve didn't. A moment later, Irilin stepped out of the shadows, hooked an arm around the captain's neck and slashed a dagger across her throat.

Before the bubble of shock burst, Irilin thrust the dying woman at her comrades and reached for Hagdon. He saw the dull shimmer of metal clamped about her wrist – an ambertrix manacle. 'Get it off,' she cried. 'Now, or we're dead.'

Hagdon grabbed the catch and wrenched it open. The ambertrix flickered a protest, but he wasn't an aberration and it couldn't stop him. As soon as the manacle left her wrist, Irilin smiled. It was wide and unpleasant. She swept a hand out; a silver shield appeared just in time to deflect the dozen or so bolts that flew at them.

Another volley came; Hagdon saw the telltale blue shimmer just before the crossbow fired. He leapt at Irilin, knocking her off her feet and sending them both rolling across the stone. The ambertrix bolt tore through the shield and it vanished.

'Not that again.' Irilin crawled out from under him, hand already glowing defensively, but before she could act, Mercia threw herself at the soldier with the crossbow. Busy reloading it, he didn't see her leap.

'I'm sorry,' Irilin said. 'As soon as that manacle was on, I couldn't help Mercia. I barely had enough power for a shadow-cloak.'

It was a detail he should have remembered. 'You were lucky

they didn't use two – what with the shortage, there aren't enough to go around.'

Irilin cocked her head, as if she'd heard something he hadn't. Then shouts erupted close by, echoing off the stones of the fortress. The sky, dark with falling snow, was suddenly bright. Crisp, clear, like the moon on a cloudless night. Hagdon looked up.

She could have been the moon, so radiantly did she shine. Brégenne stood on nothing but the air, frowning as she held the bridge over which the Republic and Mercia's remaining soldiers rushed. It stretched from the far side of the cliff to the court-yard, bypassing the portcullis entirely.

He heard the creak of a crossbow being wound and looked up in time to see the bolt fly at Brégenne. She lifted a hand and, almost negligently, brushed the projectile out of the air. Hagdon narrowed his eyes, looking for the blue glow of ambertrix – Bré-genne wouldn't be able to withstand a bolt from one of those bows – but Mercia had the guard pinned. She ripped the cross-bow out of his grip and, ignoring his cry of dismay, lobbed it over the parapet.

'Commander,' Avery said, landing lightly beside him. The Republic followed her, throwing themselves fiercely into the fray. Hagdon saw a kind of unholy fervour in many eyes; how many of these men and women had lost loved ones to Parakat?

'This is only the beginning, Hagdon,' Mercia called. Blood ran from her opponent's nostrils; he lay unconscious or dead. 'They've got a full three hundred stationed here.'

Hagdon cursed. Three hundred Sartyans . . . he only hoped Brégenne and Irilin could tip the balance. Kait leapt down beside him, naked steel in her hands. She was a force of nature and he added her to his scales. It still didn't look good.

'We need to get the aberrations fighting,' Irilin said, reading the thoughts from his face.

Hagdon shook his head. 'They won't do it, not when they see the odds stacked against us. They'll be too frightened.'

'Not all,' she replied. 'I met some of them. They haven't given up hope. I told them to be ready.' She turned. 'I'll get them. I need someone with me who's not a Wielder to remove the manacles.'

'I'll go,' Mercia said before Hagdon could answer. 'You're needed up here, Commander.'

'Too dangerous. I'll—'

Their moment of calm shattered. Hagdon parried the Sartyan blade that came for him and in the time it took to force the soldier back, disarm him and sever his hamstring, Irilin and Mercia had disappeared. The battle gave Hagdon a second to swear before closing over his head.

He fought his way through a sea of red. Blood, mail, it was all the same. Mercia's unit had painted feathers on their armour and shields; if not for that, Hagdon would have scythed them down as he did the rest. They came at him and he fell into the old trance, letting his body move in the way he'd trained it to. He hadn't earned his bloody reputation by remaining outside the fray. For that, the Fist had held him in high regard . . . at least before the Starborn arrived and everything changed.

More faces, more faceless. There was fear in their eyes when they saw him coming. Once, he would have smiled. Now he fought impassively, took wounds, gave wounds in return. His muscles burned, his breath, so carefully controlled, grew ragged. He was aware of Kait fighting nearby, her twin swords a blur as she leapt and slashed, a dervish of limbs and blades.

His handaxe was slick with blood. His blood? He didn't

know, but it was hard to grip. He'd lost a gauntlet somewhere in the melee and the hilt slipped in his bare hand. Hagdon glanced down to see a deep gash in the meat of his palm. He dimly recalled reaching out, catching a blade. Foolish move. His current opponent knocked the axe aside; it left his hand, skidding down the snow-slick stones, well out of reach. Hagdon drew his greatsword, but it was a poor choice for a tired man. Even lifting it was an effort.

And in that moment, aching, spattered with the mingled blood of men and women whose names he'd never know, that weariness spread through him. Was this how it would happen? Would his life end here on this miserable battlement, slick with blood and sleet? It seemed he'd spent every day of it fighting. His arm fell to his side, hand opening convulsively; as if in a dream, Hagdon watched the greatsword clang against stone.

He looked at his Sartyan opponent; something had changed in the man's eyes. A spark. A recognition. He raised his sword and Hagdon railed at his body to move.

'James!'

Light exploded around him, hurled him halfway across the wide battlement. He hit the wall and slid down it. The impact hurt, but dispelled whatever strange dream had frozen him. He'd already risen to hands and knees by the time she hurried over.

'I'm sorry,' Irilin said, dropping down beside him. 'I couldn't avoid hitting you too.'

Hagdon was going to say, 'No harm done', but it seemed rather ludicrous in the face of all his injuries. He felt her eyes travel over him. 'Nediah can heal you,' she said. 'It's only a few hours till dawn.'

'We have a battle to win first,' he replied, planting his sword, using it to drag himself up. Irilin rose with him. One of her hands twitched as if she wanted to support him, but it remained at her side.

'What happened?'

He followed her gaze to the dead soldier. The man's neck was twisted and snow settled on his open eyes. Irilin shivered. 'What happened?' she asked again.

'Nothing,' Hagdon lied, unwilling to think about that terrible weariness. Where had it come from? Would it seize him again when he least expected it? 'I was careless. Thanks for the help.'

Irilin looked as if she wanted to say more, but a muffled explosion came from below. They gazed at each other, wide-eyed. 'Let's go.' Hagdon experienced a fervent desire to lie down, but he forced himself to move. His wounds screamed at him; myriad new scars to add to his collection, he thought grimly. He seized Irilin's hand and pulled her into a run. It was warm, reassuring, the only real thing in this world of blood and snow.

The battlement was littered with the dead and dying. His own fight had taken him away from the larger battle, which had moved below, inside the keep itself. Hagdon felt a fierce pride in the Republic for holding their own, but then he remembered Brégenne. He saw her a moment later, more blaze than woman, fighting, surprisingly, beside Kait.

She might be using ordinary swords, but in the tall woman's hands, they were anything but ordinary. As he watched, Kait parried a blow from the left, dodged one from the right, spun and thrust her blade into a third Sartyan coming up behind her. She was as bloody as Hagdon himself; much of it, he guessed, belonged to her enemies.

'Where have you been?' she snapped at him between parries. 'Hu's going wild.'

'I'm here now,' Hagdon said shortly, automatically looking for his adjutant. He spotted the rebel at the very moment Hu took a blade in the back.

With a cry of fury, Hagdon launched himself forward, knowing it was already too late. Gaze fixed on Hu's killer, he cut down two Sartyans who threw themselves unwisely into his path, until he faced the woman. With some difficulty, she tugged her sword from Hu's body, turned to meet his attack. Her eyes grew round when she recognized him. 'General—'

It was her last word. Hagdon took her head.

The remaining Sartyans had identified Brégenne as the most serious threat and had closed around her. Hagdon glimpsed her face. She was tired. He wasn't sure how much time had passed; between the darkness and the blood, it could have been minutes, hours. Brégenne threw out splinters of moonlight, sharp darts that pierced armour and should have pierced flesh, but for those ambertrix-forged breastplates. The handful of Sartyans wearing them – officers, some of whom Hagdon recognized – pressed closer to the Wielder, so that she was forced to give ground. Brégenne summoned a spear. It glowed brighter and brighter in her grip until she threw it at her nearest opponent. The bolt tore through the dragon-plate, hurling the Sartyan into his comrades. The advance faltered.

But Brégenne stumbled, her strength sapped. Irilin gave a cry and sent rune upon rune into the backs of the men circling Brégenne. She took some down, but more were pouring out of the barracks to bolster ranks. Although several dozen rebels still stood, they were outnumbered and exhausted. Their plan had depended on a surprise assault, not a lengthy battle against superior forces. Even Kait was beginning to slow. As Hagdon watched, she took a slash across the cheek, which only just missed her eye. Teeth bared, she darted frequent, accusatory glances at the ceiling, as if chastising the dawn for its slow coming.

The promise of victory was a potent thing. Hagdon watched it ripple through the Sartyans, through men he might once have led to battle against the very rebellion he now fought for. They redoubled their attack. Brégenne's eyes met his then, a silent plea, and Hagdon knew what he had to do.

'Stop!' he thundered.

His shout made the closest soldiers jump, but the din of sword on sword filled the keep with echoes. Irilin looked around. 'They need to hear me!' he called to her.

Irilin fended off an attack; a blade scraped uselessly against her Lunar shield. Turning towards him, she pointed a finger and Hagdon found himself limned in silver. He almost cried out; the moonlight was alive, wreathing his limbs. It felt icy and hot at the same time.

His next shout truly was thunder.

The *boom* shook mortar from the stones. Weapons clattered; men and women covered their ears, looking for the source of the sound. Like some avenging spirit, Hagdon leapt onto a half-dismantled catapult, his shining figure stark in the smoky, torchlit space. All eyes turned to him, Sartyan, rebel and Wielder alike. In the quiet that followed, the only sounds that could be heard were heavy breathing, moans of agony from the prone and a distant pattering like feet on stone.

'Hagdon,' one of the officers said. His sword had serrated teeth – it was how Hagdon recognized him.

'Lieutenant Jauler,' he acknowledged. Speaking, his voice was still loud, but not overwhelming.

'You remembered my name,' Jauler said, rasping a little with exertion. 'A dubious honour, but an honour nonetheless.'

'I'm glad you think so.' Hagdon wasn't sure what he planned to say. All he knew was that he couldn't let the fighting recommence. 'To be frank, Lieutenant, you are the last person I would have suspected of supporting Iresonté.'

Jauler spat bloody saliva. 'True, I wouldn't cry if someone planted a blade between the bitch's eyes, but she's got the balls to do what you won't.'

'And what is that?'

'Avenge our men. Avenge the men the Starborn killed and march on Rairam.'

'Those men were *soldiers*.' He'd said the same to a different lieutenant, merely weeks before Iresonté's insurrection. 'Soldiers in the service of the emperor. They died doing their duty.'

'The emperor is dead.'

'I know,' Hagdon said, 'I killed him.'

A whisper through the ranks. Hagdon felt the weight of their gazes. 'Iresonté,' he added, 'stood by and watched.'

'Lies,' Jauler said immediately. 'It was she who tried to stop you.'

Hagdon laughed. Perhaps it was the hours he'd spent shedding blood, detached from reality, but the image of Iresonté throwing herself protectively in front of the emperor was ludicrous. Some of Jauler's men looked as if they wanted to back away, but the lieutenant's face darkened. 'Laugh while you can, Hagdon. You'll find little to amuse you in Iresonté's custody.'

'So I'm to be taken alive.' Hagdon swept his gaze over them all. 'I'd like to see you try.'

'If at all possible,' Jauler said. 'But Iresonté will settle for your head. Look around you. You're beaten, Hagdon.'

Hagdon did not look around. He knew it for the truth. Of those rebels he'd brought into Parakat, he guessed over half were dead. The fledgling Republic couldn't afford to lose even one and still he'd brought them to this forsaken place to die. 'There are always casualties in war,' he said.

'War?' It was Jauler's turn to laugh. 'This isn't war, Hagdon. It's civil unrest. You, of all people, should know the difference. You spent your life putting it down.' He sobered. 'Now the tables are turned. I suppose there's justice in that.'

This temporary truce was unravelling; Hagdon could feel it, see it in the contracting of hands on hilts, in eyes that flicked restlessly from side to side as each Sartyan took in the measure of their comrades. Brégenne and Irilin exchanged one charged glance.

And then the noise Hagdon had almost ceased to hear rose up: the slapping of bare feet on stone. With a chorus of cries, a gate burst open, spilling dozens of half-naked people into the space. Mercia was carried in on the shrieking tide, her expression halfway between unnerved and triumphant. The aberrations were armed with swords, axes – weapons apparently liberated from the barracks. But more poignantly, Hagdon saw familiar silver light sparking between hands, limning wasted flesh.

Prisoners fell upon jailers, some invariably onto the points of swords. The air crackled with the discharge of power. 'Uncontrolled!' Hagdon heard Brégenne yell to Irilin. Those Sartyans surrounding her had been forced to deal with the aberrations. Hagdon essayed a guess at numbers. A hundred? When they saw their fellows swarming over the Sartyans, more pushed their way through the gate and into the fray.

'To me!' Hagdon called, catching Avery's eye. She gave a shout of her own; the remaining Republic formed into a wedge and began to fight their way across. He did his best to cut them a path. Just before he reached them, a ragged man threw himself into the sweep of Hagdon's sword. Bellowing in surprise, Hagdon tried to pull back, but the steel scythed right through the prisoner, cutting him almost in half. Hot blood spattered across Hagdon's cheek and he found himself retching.

The aberration fell at Avery's feet. She looked at him and then up at Hagdon. 'I didn't mean to –' Hagdon spluttered, wiping the blood from his face. 'He fell –'

'I saw,' Avery said shortly. Sweat and blood stuck her auburn hair to her forehead. 'I know we were cornered, but was this a good idea? I'm not sure they understand which side we're on.'

Hagdon watched the prisoners, as they hurled themselves recklessly into the Sartyan ranks. 'Mercia must have been persuasive to get them to fight at all. They're half-dead – look at them.' Despite his words, he didn't want to look, not when he'd put so many of these people here himself. No doubt Avery was thinking the same.

The inmates at least gave Brégenne some breathing space. Hagdon saw her, aglow with Lunar energy – failing now with the imminent dawn – lashing out with whip-like light. Where it touched, skin turned blue as if burned by ice rather than heat. Irilin backed her up with runes that, upon exploding, tangled around legs, bringing their victims crashing to the floor. A group of inmates who seemed more cognizant than their comrades were noting where each rune struck, moving to the downed Sartyan and stabbing them repeatedly. So much for the possibility of prisoners, Hagdon thought. How many of these would throw down their weapons without Jauler to lead them?

Quite suddenly he became aware of a man watching him – an aberration leaning on a pikestaff. He surveyed the carnage beneath heavy brows, dark skin wan with months – years? – spent in Parakat's cellars. He didn't join the fighting, though Hagdon could tell from his stance that he knew how to hold a weapon.

Across the hall, Kait suddenly gave a cry of triumph. 'This is how it's done, old woman,' she tossed at Brégenne. To her opponents' consternation, she threw down her swords and extended her hands. Blades of light appeared in each. She ducked a swing from a Sartyan, straightened, lunged, and ran him through, sun-sword hissing as it met flesh. Brégenne was watching through narrowed eyes. Only a faint silver glow remained around her; Irilin's had already winked out.

Before Hagdon could move to cover them, Nediah strode through the keep's open doors, aflame with light. He'd promised – reluctantly – to stay clear of the fighting until dawn. He searched the chamber until he spotted Brégenne and something in his face eased. With one hand, he shielded the Lunar Wielders. Then he crooked the fingers of his other hand, dragging it through the air. A flaming wall roared up from the stone, penning a group of Sartyans behind it. Hagdon nodded his thanks.

Renewed by the Solar, Kait was relentless. Even the aberrations paused to watch as she continued her bloody dance. Hagdon took care of the few who escaped, all the while keeping an eye on Jauler. The lieutenant was now backed up against the fortress wall, flanked by a dozen officers.

'Terms!' Hagdon yelled.

Jauler glared at him. 'No terms. I'd sooner die than join a traitor.'

'Oh you'll die,' Hagdon assured him coldly. 'I meant for your men.'

The lieutenant's glare wavered a little. 'They will do as I order them.'

'Join you in death? When they have a chance to live?'

When Jauler didn't reply, Hagdon addressed the rest of the Sartyans. 'Your captain is dead. Your lieutenant's fate is sealed. To you, however, I offer a choice. Join the Republic, as Mercia has done, or join the corpses in the chasm.' He swept them with his gaze. 'Those you helped put there.'

One of the Sartyans, a woman, spat. 'Your hands are no cleaner than ours, *General*.'

Hagdon could see hate in the prisoners' faces, in the sunken eyes of their leader, leaning on his pikestaff. It didn't matter. They didn't have to follow him, only the banner he carried.

To his surprise, Irilin stepped forward. 'My companions and I are like you,' she called to the aberrations, 'Wielders from what was once Solinaris.' Hagdon heard whispers at the name; the fortress of the sun still carried the power of myth. 'Rairam has returned,' Irilin continued, her voice strengthening, 'and we are one world again. This is our chance for a new Acre governed by all.' She held out a hand, palm up. 'We are here to offer training to all aberrations – today you'll leave that name behind – if you'll agree to join us in the fight against Iresonté. United, we can break the power of the Fist. We can start again.'

In another time and place, such a speech might have roused *something*, but not here in a chill fortress at the top of the world. Not from dying people who hadn't seen the sun. The woman who'd spat at Hagdon began to laugh. '"Break the Fist"? Little girl, the Fist is unbreakable. There is no force to match us.'

265

'Match this,' Kait snarled. Before Hagdon could stop her, she hurled one of her swords, end over end, towards the woman. It shrank as it flew; when it pierced the Sartyan's forehead, it had the wicked blade of a small stiletto. Everyone heard the *thunk* as it struck, watched the woman's eyes roll up to the whites. She toppled into her companions, blood weaving down the bridge of her nose.

Kait splayed a hand. More golden knives appeared between her fingers. 'Anyone else?'

With last looks at Jauler, the Sartyans, as one, threw down their weapons. Kait smiled. 'Never fails to get results,' she remarked to no one in particular. The golden stiletto had vanished from the dead woman's skull, leaving nothing but a neatly cauterized hole.

'Assistance appreciated,' Hagdon said to her. He nodded at Jauler. 'Would you mind securing him?'

Kait looked faintly disappointed, but waved a hand. Chains yanked Jauler's arms to his sides, locked his ankles together. He fell back against the wall with a curse. 'Put him in a cell for now,' Hagdon said to Avery. She muttered a few quick words and a couple of the Republic dragged Jauler away.

With the lieutenant's exit came exhaustion, as if his presence had been the only thing keeping Hagdon awake. He leaned on his greatsword, hoping it looked casual. *Too old for this*. Carn would have chided him for the thought. What would his bondsman have made of this mess?

Hagdon realized his mind was flitting and pulled it back to the present in time to watch the man with the pikestaff impose himself between a group of aberrations and the corralled Sartyans recently released from Nediah's fire-wall. The prisoners' eyes were narrow, hungry; Hagdon had seen that look in men before. 'No,' he said at the same time as the man with the staff. They looked at each other, the prisoners looked at them. For a moment, there was silence.

'No more killing,' the dark-skinned man said huskily. His voice was dry, cracked, as if he'd not had occasion to use it much – Hagdon supposed he hadn't. His accent belonged among the people of the far west, Katakan or even Eranian. He was a long way from home.

'They would kill us,' a ragged woman said. Her hands opened and closed convulsively, as if she imagined curling them around a Sartyan throat. 'They *have* killed us.'

'Killing them in turn will not make it better,' the man told her.

'I don't want it to be better, Reuven. They took my children, slit their throats in front of me.' Tears stood in her eyes, but her voice remained hard and cold. 'I want them to end, as I ended.'

There were murmurs of what sounded unhappily to Hagdon like agreement. He tightened his grip on the hilt of his sword.

But Reuven – if that was indeed his name – placed a heavy hand on the woman's shoulder. 'Cowie,' he called and a man came forward. Curls of dirty blond framed a face that would have been young were it not for the lines Parakat had scored upon him. 'Take Narissa away from here.'

Cowie nodded, gripped the woman by the arm and steered her, a little forcibly, through the reinforced doors of the keep. The woman didn't struggle, but went empty-eyed. As soon as she was gone, some of the tension left the other prisoners. Hagdon breathed out, relaxed his grip on his sword.

'The rest of you—'

'I will look after them,' Nediah said.

Irilin came forward. 'This is Nediah, one of the Wielders I

told you about,' she said to Reuven. 'He's a healer. Please let him look at your people.'

Reuven studied Nediah in silence before finally nodding. When he turned his gaze on Irilin, however, it was frosty. 'You failed to mention the identity of your so-called "commander".'

Irilin held her ground. 'I thought you'd have refused to help us.'

Reuven shook his head. 'Or refused to believe you?'

'That too.'

'I do find it hard to believe that a man who so industriously upheld the banner of Sartya would turn freedom fighter.' His eyes flickered from Hagdon to Avery. 'Or that said freedom fighters would accept him as commander.'

'Desperate times,' Avery said noncommittedly. Every so often there came a moment like this where Hagdon wondered if she'd prefer to see him tossed into a shallow grave.

No more than you deserve. 'We have all done things we regret,' he heard himself say.

Reuven's face darkened. 'You say that to me, to these you condemned to a slow death—'

'I had little to do with Parakat.'

'But you had the ear of the emperor. You had power.' Reuven advanced on him. 'You were in a position to stop the persecution of innocent people simply because they – we – are different.'

'It may have looked that way,' Hagdon said quietly, 'but my prison was as real as yours, even if you couldn't see it.'

Reuven lifted the pikestaff. 'Don't you dare compare your life to ours, Sartyan.'

'People are dying while you stand and argue.' Nediah's eyes were steely. 'We need to move the injured somewhere warm.

Bring me hot water, linen – whatever supplies you can find. It will take me a while to tend to everybody and these wounds need to be cleaned as soon as possible.'

'I'll help,' Kait offered at once.

'Me too,' Mercia added, but she stumbled as she came over, hand clasped to her side. There was an ugly rent in her chainmail and blood dampened the padded shirt she wore beneath it. When Nediah made to touch her, she held up a hand. 'I can wait. Others will not.'

'We'll need litters,' Reuven said, reluctantly breaking their standoff. Hagdon guessed it was not the last he'd hear on the matter.

'Bring me some canvas and poles,' Kait said, wiping some of the blood off her face. 'I'll make litters to carry them.' She glanced at those aberrations still standing. 'Perhaps some of you can help me?'

They looked at her blankly. 'Or perhaps not,' Kait muttered.

'We aren't experienced in using our gifts,' Reuven said with a glance at his fellows. 'Many are scared to try.'

'That's something we can help with.' Brégenne came forward. 'It's why we're here.'

Reuven's eyes narrowed. 'I thought you came looking to recruit for your war.'

'I would be lying if I said that hadn't played a part.'

'An honest answer.' Reuven knelt beside an injured man. He draped the prisoner's arm around his own neck and lifted him as if he weighed nothing at all. He was clearly stronger than his years suggested. 'What about them?' Reuven nodded at the Sartyans.

'They'll cooperate,' Kait said. 'Won't you?' The menace in her voice was very real.

'They're part of the Republic now,' Hagdon said, 'whether they like it or not. No unit would take them in for fear they'd been compromised.' From the bitter looks on the soldiers' faces, they knew he spoke the truth.

Irilin found Hagdon an hour later in the armoury, after he'd shed his mail and washed the bloodstains from his skin. Now he was making an inventory, pleased with the number of weapons stored here. Hagdon took a practice swing, tested the sword's edge with a thumb. One thing you could say about Sartyans: they knew how to care for equipment.

'I thought you might be hiding here,' Irilin said, closing the heavy oak door behind her.

'I'm not hiding. My presence upsets the prisoners, especially Reuven. And Nediah's right – healing the injured needs to be our first priority.'

'Do you think they'll ever accept you?'

She had a habit of asking uncomfortable questions. Hagdon stared at the blade, at his own distorted reflection. He didn't answer. He didn't *know* the answer. When he looked up, Irilin was watching him. She saw everything, saw through him.

'Why did Kait call Brégenne "old woman" earlier?' It was a rather obvious change of subject and he winced.

'Oh, she was being petty,' Irilin said. She'd changed clothes too, Hagdon saw – just a simple tunic and trousers, but they suited her. Blond hair coiled freshly washed on her shoulders; whenever she moved, he caught a faint scent of soap. It made him unreasonably nervous. 'Brégenne's a bit older than Nediah and Kait.' Irilin paused to consider. 'At least sixty, I think.'

Hagdon fumbled his handling of the sword. It slid through his fingers and clattered unpleasantly on the flagstones. 'What?'

'You didn't know Wielders age a lot more slowly?'

'I thought it was only Shune,' he said with a frown, bending to retrieve the blade. 'Is it true for aberrations too?'

'I suppose so. We live longer as a result of our power. The archivist in Naris – Master Hebrin – it's rumoured he's approaching two hundred and fifty.'

'Does that mean you—' He broke off.

Irilin fiddled with her hands. 'Yes.'

Hagdon wished he hadn't changed the subject after all. The thought that Irilin would remain young while he grew old and died was oddly painful. He resettled the sword in its rack.

'Do you remember how we met?' she asked suddenly.

Taken aback, Hagdon blinked. 'You ambushed my unit.'

'*Ambushed?* We were your captives. We were just trying to escape.'

When he turned, she was leaning against a weapon rack, in an empty space between two shields. 'Really.' Hagdon came over. 'You could've used that shadow cloak of yours to slip away unseen into the night. But instead you set fire to my supplies, panicked my horses and caused all-out chaos.'

Irilin opened her mouth and closed it again. 'You grabbed my hair,' she said.

'And you scratched me, as I recall.' Hagdon smiled. 'Like a cat.'

Instead of laughing, Irilin stilled. She raised a hand. 'It was here,' she murmured, tracing his left cheek. Hagdon shivered under her touch. Before he knew it, he'd reached up and covered her hand with his. She flushed. He was all too aware of how close they stood – he could feel the heat of her body, the pulse that fluttered in her wrist.

'Irilin,' he whispered.

Her lips parted and she leaned in, her eyes large on his face. In them he saw himself, scarred and creased with the cares he carried, the burdens of a life lived with a sword in his fist. The sight was like cold water and he pulled away. 'I can't.' He took her hand from his cheek, returned it to her. 'I'm sorry.'

Irilin's brow creased. He immediately wanted to smooth it away. 'Why?'

'Because –' There were so many reasons – his past, his responsibilities, the war that bound them both. But what he said was, 'I don't want to hurt you.'

Irilin stared at him. 'Hurt me?'

'I can't be trusted.'

So tender a moment ago, her expression hardened. 'Shouldn't I be the judge of that?'

'You don't understand. Nothing is right with me, Irilin.' Hagdon did not look away. 'You deserve better.'

'And what about what I want?' she flared. 'Does that count for nothing?'

'You're young. You have your life ahead of you – a life I could never share.' The words pained him, but he forced himself to continue. 'You're a Wielder. We come from different worlds.'

Irilin shook her head. 'It's all the same world now.'

Why was she making this so difficult? Hagdon felt the heat in his face, the way his heart still raced. It would be so simple to reach out, to draw her to him. They were quite alone here.

He shuddered and thrust the dangerous thought aside. 'I can't,' he said again, and the hand Irilin had half lifted fell to her side. It was better this way, Hagdon told himself, fighting the regret that dragged at him; she just needed to realize it. As he all but fled the armoury, he thought he heard a sob. He brushed a hand across his eyes and kept on walking.

23

Gareth

'Now that is a *lot* of army.' Yara lowered the brass eyeglass, handed it to Argat. 'Take a look, Cap.'

Argat screwed up his mouth, as if he'd been forced to chew on a bunch of lemons. 'I've seen quite enough of them. They snake all the way back to that plain we flew over an hour ago.'

It had been a week since Gareth and Kul'Das had left Paarth and their mysterious pursuer behind. He glanced at the gauntlets, wondering if they were the reason he'd been followed. Who knew how many people would recognize them on sight? *I ought to be more careful.* The thought of losing them, of their being stolen, caused him physical pain.

'May I?' Gareth asked. He held out a hand for the eyeglass and, though they stood within an arm's reach of each other, Argat tossed it to him. The captain went out of his way to avoid touching the gauntlets. Ironic, Gareth thought, for a man who'd bargained so hard for them. He raised the eyeglass and it dutifully showed him just how much trouble they were in.

Iresonté had made good on her threat. The Fist moved fast, faster than an army its size should be able to move. They had almost reached the red valley where, according to Irilin, Shika had lost his life.

Life and death were now intimate friends. He knew how mutable they were, how fragile. So it was hard to believe that Shika was out of his reach. No living, no dead thing, should be out of his reach. Grief rose like a bubble, popped on the sharp surface of his thoughts.

He swallowed, returning the eyeglass to Yara. 'Thank you.'

'For showing you our end?' the first mate asked bitterly. 'We can't fight them.'

'We have to try.' He thought of the promise he'd made to his mother, a promise he could not now keep. Without the gauntlets, he was nothing. The mere thought of someone else wielding them made his blood boil. 'How swiftly can we reach Ümvast?'

Yara pursed her lips as she thought. 'Eight days. Depends on whether your people have already begun moving south.'

Eight days. If the Fist went through the valley, they would be in Rairam by then. But the men would surely revolt if Iresonté tried to force them through the hoarlands. No, they'd take to ship, landing on safer, if unknown, shores, relying on speed and the belief that Rairam had no formal defences. If he were Iresonté, he'd cut a path straight to the capital, to Market Primus. Astra Marahan and the other traders would fall flat on their faces when confronted with a force the size of the Fist. If Iresonté held the capital, the rest of Rairam would quickly fall into line.

'What are you thinking?' Yara asked, jolting him from his dark contemplation.

'I'm thinking that Iresonté will sail around and then strike inland for the capital. While I was with him, Hagdon received a report of war galleys being brought up from the south.'

Argat grunted. He made some incomprehensible gesture at a sailor, and a minute or so later the ship's speed increased. 'If she reaches Market Primus, it's over,' he said. 'The Assembly won't think twice before opening the gates. This Iresonté sounds like someone who shores up her influence by making examples.' He massaged his chin with a calloused hand. 'Killing a few thousand citizens would serve as a potent example to the rest of us.'

'Then we'd better make sure she doesn't reach the city,' Gareth said.

'With only five thousand warriors?' Yara shook her head. 'They don't stand a chance.'

'You're right,' Gareth said evenly, causing her to suck in a surprised breath. 'They don't stand a chance. Without *me*.' As soon as the words were out of his mouth, Gareth wanted to call them back. He wasn't sure why he'd say such a thing.

She raised an eyebrow. 'A foolish boast if ever I heard one.'

'Yara –' Argat began. Disquiet reigned in his eyes.

'Thirty thousand, Argat. Perhaps more. How can one man make even the slightest difference?'

'You doubt him?' Kul'Das's voice was very quiet. Throughout their conversation, she'd stood silent at the rail, staring fixedly at the horizon, sweat spotting her brow. Now, carefully, as if she were made of some breakable substance, she turned to face the first mate. 'I was there when he walked out of the barrows. I saw the dead rise at his command.' She didn't look at him. 'If any one person can make a difference, it's Kul'Gareth.'

Some of Yara's confidence drained away, but she still wore a stubborn frown. 'What about Kyndra?'

'The Starborn has her own trials,' Gareth said shortly. 'We will have to fight this battle alone.'

'Hagdon intends to fight alongside us,' Kul'Das added before turning swiftly towards the rail again. 'He and the Wielders planned to capture that prison and recruit its inmates.' She paused to swallow, her hands contracting on the wood. 'We should find out whether they were successful, how much aid they can send us.'

Gareth nodded. 'I will make an envoi.'

'And Naris?' Argat asked, his gaze passing briefly over the engraved mountain on Gareth's armour. Sim's work was flawless, fitting him perfectly. Gareth remembered the smith watching as he'd first donned it, a troubled mix of fear and satisfaction in his eyes. 'Do Rairam's best defence know nothing of the danger?' Argat finished.

'We've seen how ambertrix can limit a Wielder's power,' Gareth replied with a glance at Kul'Das. 'If they don't fight, Iresonté will have them all collared. The Wielders would kill many in the struggle, but numbers would prevail.' He paused. 'If they don't fight, Naris is finished.'

'Who speaks for the Wielders?'

'The Council,' Gareth said. 'Without Brégenne, there are only two of them and they might be hard to persuade. They wouldn't believe Brégenne when she warned them of the danger before.'

'Then they must be shown it,' Argat said.

'Our job is to reach Ümvast.' Gareth let his gaze stray to the north. 'My people *can* make a difference in this war.'

Yara fingered the cutlass in her belt. 'I hope so, for all our sakes.'

It was disconcerting to take the ship north-east, leaving Iresonté and the Fist behind. They'd waited long enough to witness the army turning for the coast, but Gareth didn't like the idea of letting them out of his sight. Where was Kyndra when they needed her? The Starborn had resources the rest of them did not. But stopping the Khronostians tearing history out from under them was more important. The battle for Rairam would have to be waged without her.

On the fifth morning, something dark appeared on the horizon.

Argat called Gareth up from below. Kul'Das was already on deck – air-sickness forced her to spend most of her time up here. The captain handed the eyeglass to Gareth. 'What do you make of that?'

It was a low smudge. He couldn't make it out. 'Take us closer,' Gareth said.

With a narrow look at him, Argat gave the order.

'Bastards,' Yara hissed after another twenty minutes' flight revealed the truth. She lowered the eyeglass. 'How many does she have?'

It was as if a great cold weight had replaced his stomach. Gareth shook his head. 'Ten thousand?' Even the thickening mist couldn't conceal the vastness of Iresonté's second army. They were camped on the edge of the ice fields. *Waiting for the thaw?* he wondered.

'Thirty thousand in the south, ten thousand in the north. *How* is Mariar going to stand up to that?' Yara tossed the eyeglass into a basket attached to the mast. 'We might as well surrender now and have done with it.'

'No,' Gareth said sharply, but the word hid his own doubt. There was an army at his mother's door and she knew nothing about it. 'We need to pick up speed, Argat,' he snapped. 'Ümvast has to be warned.'

The captain didn't argue, but his expression said it all – he agreed with Yara. As they turned east, the mists closed over the bloody sight of the Sartyan army. It was a sleeping beast, Gareth thought, on the cusp of waking. The thaw was just weeks away. Was this Iresonté's master plan? To strike into Rairam from the north and south simultaneously? To overwhelm them with numbers? He feared to wonder just how much she knew about Rairam's defences – or lack thereof.

After that, the mood on the ship changed. Argat paced the deck constantly, turning the eyeglass round and round in his hands. Yara kept mostly below, ensuring the boiler was fed efficiently. Gareth had always known time was of the essence, but now he realized they were running out of it.

The airship crossed the wasteland of rubble that marked the boundary between Rairam and Acre, sailing high above, and Gareth felt a tiny shift inside him. This was home, in a way Acre could never be. Even the faceless mass of evergreens beneath them looked familiar; the colours in the sunset oddly *real*, as if all the sunsets he'd seen in Acre were mere simulacra. *This is Acre*, he reminded himself, *it always was*. But Kierik's actions carried a legacy. He'd made Rairam *Mariar*, a world in its own right, and in some way it would always be apart.

The weather was milder here, though snow still freckled the high places. A bite in the air one morning reminded Gareth of his childhood in the forests, puffing out dragon's breath as he practised swordplay. These days memories sat uneasily inside him – they had a tendency to conflict with other memories equally vivid. It was the conflict that brought on the headaches, and Gareth hastily turned his attention outward once more.

Two days' flight north of Hrosst, they found Ümvast.

Argat whistled at the helm. Gareth and Kul'Das came to

join him while Yara remained at her usual post. The northerners were an impressive sight. They might lack the military precision of the Fist, Gareth thought, but their main camp was organized into quarters, each a small camp in its own right.

'Five thousand, you say.' Argat ran his eyes over the human sprawl below them. 'I'd say that's more like six or seven.'

Kul'Das blinked at the camp. 'Not all of them are warriors. I can see children down there.'

Fingers had begun to point up. Even from here, they could discern multiple shouts of surprise and warning. 'If they start shooting flaming arrows—' Argat began. A volley was sent up, but fell short of the hull.

'That's it,' the captain growled, and he spun the wheel. The airship veered off eastward.

'Stop,' Gareth said. 'Take us lower.'

'Lower?' Argat was purple. '*Lower?* So they can pepper us with arrows?'

'I want them to see me,' Gareth said calmly.

'If you damage my ship—'

'Just do it.' He and Argat locked gazes. 'Your ship will be safe, I promise.'

Argat cursed. 'If you're wrong, then gauntlets or not, I will hang you from the bowsprit.'

Gareth's only reply was a cold smile. With another string of curses, Argat ordered the ship to descend.

He made his way to the prow, where he was sure he could be seen. The chill wind blew the hair back from his face, flung his cloak out behind him. They lost height, and now Gareth could make out individual faces, all upturned. He raised his arms so that the gauntlets caught the light, and cries at the sight of them travelled back through the ranks of men and women. No more arrows came.

A tent much larger than those around it stood in the very centre of the camp. Gareth looked down at the woman who emerged from it. This low, he could hear the hollow *clack* as the wind rattled the bones in her mantle. Her gaze was chill and yet – before the airship banked towards the grassland beyond the edge of the camp – he thought she might have smiled.

'Ready her to land!' Argat called, the crew already scurrying to obey. They were much better at it now, Gareth noticed. Clearly they'd grounded the airship more than once during the past weeks.

They landed in a great spray of dirt, furrowing the earth behind them. When all was still, steam billowing from the extinguished braziers, Yara came up from below, her grinning face smeared with grease. 'Piece of cake,' she said, wiping her hands on her trousers.

Kul'Das shuddered, but she looked happier now that they were down. 'Never again,' Gareth heard her mutter. He watched as she threw back her head and straightened her shoulders. Although she wasn't one of them, she'd earned respect amongst Ümvast's people. Indeed there were cries of recognition from the deputation of warriors who met them at the camp's boundary.

'Kul'Das,' one man said with deference. 'We are pleased to have you amongst us again.' It was Egil – one of those who'd escorted Gareth and Brégenne to Stjórna. They'd shed blood together outside the great iron gates, fighting the wyverns. The wound he'd sustained there seemed to have healed.

The blond woman inclined her head graciously. 'Our quest has been successful, as you see. I return with Kul'Gareth Ilda-Son restored to health.'

Egil regarded him without expression. 'He is not a Kul until Ümvast acknowledges him as such.'

Kul'Das shot him a nervous look as if she expected him to bridle at the insult. Instead Gareth smiled, not unpleasantly. 'I understand. Take me to her.'

Egil didn't reply, staring transfixed at Gareth's wrists. 'Kingswold's gauntlets,' he murmured. 'They are as remarkable as the legends promised.'

'Indeed they are.'

'With such a weapon on our side, all shall fall before us.' Egil held out his hand. 'I will take charge of them for now.'

Gareth was aware of Kul'Das's gaze, of Argat and Yara behind him. It grew very still. When he didn't move, the warrior frowned, hand still extended before him. 'Only Ümvast is worthy to possess these,' he said, his tone hardening. 'You will relinquish them to me.'

'I am sorry, Egil,' Gareth said, barely keeping a rein on his anger. 'But that is not possible.'

The warrior blinked at him, as if he'd never expected to be refused. His expression darkened. 'You will go no further until you comply.'

'I lack both the time and inclination to argue with you.' Gareth kept his tone calm. It seemed to unnerve Kul'Das; she shifted from foot to foot beside him. 'Don't make me hurt you, Egil,' he added.

Immediately, they were surrounded by a dozen others, all with hands clamped about weapon hilts. 'Don't make me take the gauntlets by force,' Egil countered.

Gareth advanced on him. Weapons left sheaths, lifted to point at his chest. He ignored them, his eyes fixed on Egil's. 'Do you know what I went through to win these?' he asked softly, holding them up before the warrior's face. Without waiting for an answer, he said, 'Earth and darkness, bone and tomb. I passed through death. Passed and awoke on the other side, reborn.' He slowly curled his hands into fists. 'By trial of blood and battle, I have earned the right to them.'

He would never know what it was that convinced Egil to step aside – his evocation of Ben-haugr, or his use of the old words. But step aside Egil did, and his warriors with him. 'Follow me,' he said curtly.

Kul'Das let out an audible breath. 'You too, skyfarers,' a woman snapped at Argat and Yara. The first mate didn't look happy, but Argat's eyes were shining. The captain had once told a story about encountering two northmen in a tavern, Gareth recalled – the only time he'd met anyone from Ümvast. Surely Argat could never have dreamed of meeting the lord of the north herself.

They were escorted through the camp, attracting curious gazes from every side. Not only curiosity, Gareth noticed, but suspicion. Many faces were pinched with hunger or cold or just uncertainty – those who'd lived generations in the forest must find these plains disturbingly open and unprotected.

When they reached the large tent in the middle of the encampment, Ümvast was there to greet them. She looked as he remembered: tall, fur mantled, hair braided with some severity. Her still, cold face had always been hard to read; today was no exception.

'Blood of my blood,' she said formally, as he came to stand before her. 'I admit: I am surprised to see you again.'

As he looked at her, Gareth felt a sudden lurch; for a brief instant, his mother went from being someone he knew to a stranger. He seemed to regard her with interest, or something in him did, an interest aroused during a conversation he'd had in a dark place under the earth.

Pain stabbed his temples and the feeling faded. She was once again his mother. Gareth gritted his teeth, determined not to show weakness, especially not in front of her, or Egil and his warriors. As if she sensed the thought, Ümvast extended a hand. 'We shall talk inside.'

He followed her through the tent flap – a pavilion: it was too large to be called a tent – and Argat and Yara came nervously behind him. Ümvast settled herself on a campaign throne comprised mostly of weapon crates. Kul'Das resumed her customary place at her side.

'You have done well, Kul'Das,' Ümvast said to her. Then she frowned. 'Where is your staff?'

'It was broken,' Kul'Das said – with remarkable equanimity, Gareth thought, recalling her grief over the thing. 'We encountered some resistance in the Deadwood. A group of women intent on capturing –' she stuttered to a halt, looking abruptly scared.

'I know what you are, Kul'Das,' Ümvast said, ignoring the woman's gasp. 'Why do you think I tolerated your presence at my side? I wanted to know more about the power that took my son from me.'

Before Kul'Das could ask the question that was clearly balanced on her tongue, Ümvast turned away. 'Well, Kul'Gareth?' she said and he didn't miss her use of the title. 'Where are my gauntlets?'

He held out his fists, opened them slowly. Hond'Lif shone with its own inner light, glowing softly in the dim tent. By contrast, Hond'Myrkr was almost invisible, a glove-shaped hole cut out of the world.

'Glorious,' Ümvast breathed. Her hands twitched. With difficulty, it seemed, she moved her gaze to his face. 'And they healed you, I see.'

'I am once again among the living,' Gareth said a little drily. But the rest of him stood tensed, waiting for the moment when she would ask for the gauntlets.

But all she said was, 'Who are your companions?'

'Captain Argat at your service,' Argat said somewhat flamboyantly. 'And my first mate, Yara. I command the airship, the *Eastern Set*. I am a friend of Kul'Gareth and of Brégenne of Naris.'

He tripped slightly over the word *friend*, but Ümvast didn't seem to notice. 'An airship,' she mused, staring into the middle distance. 'I confess I had never seen one before today.'

'Infernal vessel,' Kul'Das muttered.

'And what news of Acre?'

'Not good,' Gareth said. 'Iresonté, the Sartyan general, marches her army here as we speak. Thirty thousand will land on the southern coast. My guess is they'll then make for the capital.'

'I would not mind seeing the Assembly taken down a notch,' Ümvast said, though her face had paled at the number. 'But we cannot let it happen. This Iresonté will learn soon enough that Mariar won't fall without a fight.'

'It's worse,' Gareth said, watching her carefully. 'There's another army. We passed them on our way here, camped on the edge of the ice fields. They'll avoid the fallen mountains, cutting across and then down through—'

'No.' Ümvast rose from her makeshift throne. Just then, standing tall, iron-countenanced, she was every inch the leader northern children had been taught to fear. 'They will *not* set foot in my homeland.'

'You can't stop them.' Wind found its way through cracks in the knotted canvas, stirred the cloak about his boots. 'They'll be here in weeks, maybe less.'

'But the wyverns —'

'The wyverns came from Acre. I doubt the Sartyans consider them an obstacle.' He added more quietly, 'They look to be ten thousand strong.'

His mother's face paled further. 'They outnumber us two to one.'

'And they are Sartyans,' Gareth said, 'experienced in battle. Their weapons are much more advanced than any you've encountered.'

Ümvast narrowed her eyes. 'But they must cross the forest and the forest is *ours*. We know the ground; they do not.'

'Our only advantage.'

'No,' Kul'Das said suddenly. 'We have you, Kul'Gareth.'

He was silent, his mind turning over the possibilities. Whichever way he looked at it, many would die. His people had never been tested against a force like Sartya.

'And you have me,' Ümvast said harshly. Her fist curled around the axe in her belt. 'If I die in the struggle, so be it. But I will take more than my share with me.'

'This needs planning.' Gareth began to stride up and down the mats that covered the pavilion floor. 'If we fail to stop them, we must at least buy time for those who cannot fight to escape.'

'Why not let us scout from the air?' Argat offered. 'I am aware of the danger, but I know how to fly my ship. I won't give them a chance to use their weapons.'

Gareth stopped, considering. 'I can't pretend an aerial view wouldn't give us an advantage. But we will need ground scouts too, those who know the forest best. See if we can slow them down.'

'I have the women for it.' Ümvast clapped and a man poked his head through the tent flap. 'Send for Freya, Sig and Derida. Tell them to bring whoever they consider their best trackers.'

The man backed out with a silent nod.

'There is a time for facing the enemy head-on and there is a time for subterfuge.' Gareth smiled, struck with the glimmers of a plan. 'The Sartyans won't expect an attack by their own troops.'

Ümvast frowned. 'I do not understand.'

'Help me isolate a unit and I will show you.' As he spoke, Gareth felt a flicker of unease. The plan in his head was like unformed clay. It would need moulding before it was ready to show his mother. Even as he frowned at the metaphor, he found himself speaking again. 'But first we must find them, weaken them. Ten thousand men and women need to eat. As you say, we know the forest, they do not. They'll find the widest path and stick to it. We can easily slip around them.' Ümvast watched him intently. 'We ambush their supply train at the rear, cut off their food and retreat. They'll send a unit to investigate. That unit is *mine*.'

Ümvast stared at him. 'Your journey has changed you,' she said. Her eyes flicked to the gauntlets. 'You were a boy when you left here.'

Gareth, too, looked at Hond'Myrkr and Hond'Lif. Their siren song was always on the edge of his mind. If he concentrated, he could hear them, light and dark, life and death, a melody to drive men mad. He smiled at his mother. It was time she and the world heard them too.

24

Kyndra

'Medavle,' she says. 'You can't do this. You mustn't.'

The Yadin stands on the glass peak, his newly lined face set in resolve. Behind him is a woman with hair like sunshine. One protective arm holds her back. 'If you had the means to save your people,' the Yadin says, 'wouldn't you use it?'

She has just the one answer. 'Better the death of five hundred Yadin than the death of the world.'

Medavle's eyes darken. 'You cannot believe that.'

'I must believe it. The stars cannot see beyond this point.'

He wavers. 'Meda,' the woman behind him says, 'if it is indeed a choice between us or the world, how can you hesitate? Even if you saved us, what would be the point if everything else was doomed?'

'No!' The word is a cry. He gathers her into his arms, holding her fiercely. 'I will not let you die again.'

'I never lived to begin with,' Isla whispers.

Kyndra jerked awake, the black dream leaving tendrils of image in her head, wisps of understanding. They mingled with memories of Kierik, of sparkling lights, of plummeting from a great height, of the eldest's thwarted shriek as Medavle broke his hold on the past. She blinked, flailing after some semblance of reality.

'You're awake.'

The voice was deep, more rumble than words. Char lay near her, curled like a cat, chin resting on his folded front legs. *That's right*, Kyndra thought, *I'm in Magtharda*. And by some miracle she was alive. She sat up and felt a stab of pain in her left arm. The curse had progressed, climbing up to her shoulder. Her arm more closely resembled a skin-covered bone.

'Ma said it might be worse.' Char stretched a wing. 'By travelling through time, you're exposing yourself to the river – or something like that.' He paused. 'Does it hurt?'

'It feels weak . . . and not mine. As if someone took my arm and replaced it with a false one.' Kyndra plucked at a fold of skin over her wrist. 'Funny – for some reason it makes me think of a hunter called Fin back in Brenwym who lost his leg to one of his own traps. He walked with a limb made of wood and metal.' She and Jhren had been terrified of him as children. 'He became a baker after that. Much safer.'

Char cocked his head. 'You sound different,' he said. 'What happened in the past?'

'I need to talk to Ma.' Kyndra climbed unsteadily to her feet. 'Where is she?'

'Resting,' Char rumbled, and she thought she detected reproof. 'Ma said she had to snatch you out of mid-air. What did you think you were doing?'

'I suspect we would all like to know the answer,' came a voice. They both turned to find Ma standing in the entryway. Arvaka hovered at her side, ready to steady her if she fell, but the woman's steps were sure, if a little heavy, as she crossed the dragon-sized chamber.

'Ma,' Kyndra said, going towards her, 'are you well?'

'I am fine, girl. Save your concern for yourself.' Hands on hips, she nodded at Kyndra's cursed arm. 'The more you travel the river, the worse it will become.'

'The eldest failed, Ma.'

'So he will try again. And you must stop him again.'

Kyndra shook her head. 'I don't know if I can. I managed to separate Medavle and the eldest – it worked as you thought.' She swallowed back the memory of *Veritan* trying to prise open her mind. 'But Kierik caught me. A few more moments and he'd have torn the truth from me. I can't risk meeting him again. I don't have any power in the past. The stars serve Kierik.'

Char rose from his crouch. 'What do you mean?'

'Two Starborn cannot co-exist. I was stupid not to remember what it was like before, when Kierik was alive. I can't speak to them – even my tattoos don't show up. In the past, I'm just the girl from Brenwym.' She blinked at the words as they emerged. *Why* had she said that?

Char seemed equally surprised. 'You mean you're . . . you,' he said, 'in the past, I mean. You're not a Starborn?'

'I am and I'm not.' Kyndra remembered that first awful moment crouched in the snow, unable to sense the stars. 'I can feel again. Fear, horror . . . it's dangerous. Emotions are a prison.'

'You sound like Kierik.' Realdon Shune sat in a dim corner, where Kyndra hadn't noticed him. The old Wielder rose, one hand pressed to the small of his back. Hobbling into the light, he added, 'I recall him saying much the same.'

Ma was frowning. 'Have you asked the stars why they did not warn you?'

'I mean to.' Kyndra sent her senses into the void. For one unreasoning moment, she thought to find the barrier there again, and was unable to suppress a sigh of relief when it wasn't. *Era*, she called.

Starborn, it replied immediately, sounding almost guilty.

I followed your advice. Trusted you. Revisited the past. Why did you not warn me about Kierik?

Would you have agreed to go? Era said, confirming her first unpleasant suspicion that the star had done it for reasons of its own. *As you are now – would you have agreed to give up the power you wield even temporarily?*

No. Kyndra ignored the little voice in the back of her mind. *You are obligated to serve me*, she told Era. *That includes being honest. I could have died.*

We do serve you, Era replied. *Which is why we hide certain truths until the time comes for you to hear them.*

Not this again. *More claiming to act on my command? The command I've given but haven't given yet?*

You begin to understand. Era sounded satisfied, as far as it could exhibit satisfaction.

Oh no. I'm not going back again.

You must. Other stars added their voices to Era's hollow whisper, making the two words resonate unpleasantly in Kyndra's head. She rubbed her temple. They'd never done that before. *You must because you already have. You must because you have not yet.*

Before, she'd have screamed with frustration. Now she stood silently, turning over the words like a damp stone, searching for meaning hidden underneath.

'Kyndra,' Ma said, breaking her trance. 'What do they say?'

She'd been staring into the middle distance, eyes unfocused. Now Kyndra blinked and looked at Ma. 'They say I must go back again.' Her voice sounded as hollow as *Era's*. 'They can't tell me more until the time is right. They claim *I* gave this command.'

Ma studied one of the ouroboros on her palms. 'It could be that you did,' she said slowly. 'And now we rush towards the moment you will give it.'

'You're as bad as they are,' Kyndra muttered. 'What if I refuse to go again?'

The stars cannot see beyond this point. It wasn't *Era* who spoke, but Kyndra's own voice, echoing out to her from the heart of the black dream. She felt her eyes widen. 'If even the stars are blind,' she said aloud, 'could it be that there is nothing left for them to see?'

Listen to your dreams, Era whispered. *They are there to guide you.*

'I don't understand any of this.' Char rose to his feet with a rustle and scrape of spines. 'You're saying that the stars believe the world itself could cease to exist?'

Kyndra nodded, her mind racing.

'What change could this eldest make that has the power to threaten the very world?' Arvaka asked.

Listen to your dreams. She'd had three of them now. Three visions she'd dismissed as the jumbled result of her worry over Medavle and the eldest. But what if they weren't dreams? What if they were *memories*?

She'd reached this conclusion before – back when she'd believed Kierik's memories were no more than dreams. Kyndra felt a seismic shift in her blood. *It's all linked*, she thought, *everything from the moment the Relic broke in Brenwym to finding Kierik, to accepting my heritage.* A vast tapestry of cause and effect had led her to this moment and would continue to lead her on to the very first thread . . . and the last.

Now you see it, Era whispered.

What change would threaten the world? The answer was there in the black dreams, in the memories – *her* memories, Kyndra realized. 'Solinaris,' she murmured. Then, glancing at Arvaka, she said, 'What if the eldest stops Kierik from separating Rairam and Acre? Kierik will never be defeated. He'll be alive to continue his fight against the empire. All of this –' she swept out a hand as if it could encompass the very earth they stood on – 'would be changed.'

'Not just changed,' Ma said. 'To stop an event responsible for so many other events would cause unimaginable chaos. I've said it before: the threads of time unpicked. *That* is what the stars cannot see beyond.'

Kyndra stilled. 'That means I *do* have to go back again.'

'Would the eldest really attempt something so dangerous?' Char asked. 'Can't he simply return to the same time Kyndra already travelled to and try again?'

Ma shook her head. 'That loop is closed now. It would be impossible for him, anchor or no, to maintain a grip on it.' She looked at Kyndra. 'Do the stars say when this next attempt is going to happen?'

You will know, Starborn. You cannot mistake the signs.

Why won't you just tell me? Kyndra didn't expect an answer and she didn't receive one. 'They say I'll know,' she said darkly, vowing to have words with her future self – the one that had ordered the stars to be silent. 'That there'll be signs.'

Char huffed out smoky blue. 'That's a big help.'

Ma, however, looked thoughtful. 'All Khronostian children are taught to read the signs in the world's pattern. If there are signs, I can read them as well as the eldest.'

Kyndra didn't like this uncertainty, this guesswork. And she worried about finding herself once again defenceless in the past, no matter how much *Era* insisted it was necessary. 'If this is so important, I can't go alone.' She felt her eyes drawn to the white serpents flashing through Ma's skin. 'Are you able to send someone with me?'

'I can,' Ma said, 'though it will tire me much faster.'

That's something. Her Starborn self didn't care for the idea of taking someone else along, but the memory of finding herself powerless was still too fresh.

The beat of wings filled the room. Arvaka ducked as another silver-gold bird skimmed his horns and swooped down towards Kyndra. She held out her good wrist, where the bird promptly dissolved into a puddle of words.

Kyndra raised her eyebrows. 'Brégenne says they've taken Parakat, the aberration fortress.'

'What?'

'They suffered casualties, but not enough to cripple them.' Kyndra glanced up as the words faded. 'It seems the Republic has a new base of operations, at least temporarily.'

'*Parakat*? The stones of that place are mortared with blood.' Shune shook his grey head. 'The emperor's treatment of aberrations was one of the reasons I turned against him. For all my status in court, I could do nothing to stop the slaughter without revealing myself as a Wielder. Had I done so, I'd have joined them.'

'She says many aberrations died in the conflict,' Kyndra told him. 'Of those that remain, some may not recover from their imprisonment.'

'Was it worth it, then?' Shune asked bitterly.

'It's a poignant rallying point.'

'And perhaps a chance to erase the crimes committed there,' Char added. Kyndra didn't understand the reproachful glance he sent her way.

The Wielder scrubbed a hand across his face. 'I'm too old for all of this,' he grumbled.

Kyndra studied him. 'You played your part in the emperor's death. I thought you wanted to see the end of Sartya.'

Realdon Shune returned her stare with one of his own. 'You, of all people, should understand: nothing lasts forever, but the certainty of change.'

25

Char

Char's desire to stretch his wings took him outside. The atmosphere had become stifling with the threat hanging over them all. And Kyndra . . . asleep she had looked so fragile, so vulnerable, the pulse in her throat a pale fluttering. Watching her, Char had thought she'd never seemed so *human*.

And then her eyes had opened and he'd realized he was wrong. In those eyes, the deep navy of night sky, Char had seen a chill power, a power beyond his comprehension. *Starborn.* How callously she now referred to emotions, he thought, when she'd once been so terrified of losing them. That person was gone. So why could he not stop thinking of her?

He launched himself into the air with a running leap, which he considered his most graceful yet until a voice called, 'If a human strapped on wings and threw themselves from a mountaintop, they would look much as you do.'

Char stopped clawing at the sky and let a gust turn him. Ekaar hovered nearby, her great dark wings keeping her effortlessly aloft. 'Don't be unkind,' he said, attempting to hover as she was and utterly failing. 'I've never had wings before.'

'It shows,' his mother said.

'You don't pull your punches, do you?'

The other dragon bunched the ridges on her brow in an unmistakable frown. 'Pull my . . . punches?'

'Human phrase, I guess,' he answered, trying out another hover. He thought he might be getting it when Ekaar suddenly called, 'Catch me if you can,' and swooped into a dive.

Mountain wind in his ears, Char followed her, feeling the air rush across the surface of his scales. He drew his legs in closer, flattened the spines around his neck and angled himself like a ship tacking against the wind. He gasped at the increase in speed. Ekaar's tail was just metres in front of him; he snapped at it playfully and she growled something over her shoulder.

Magtharda was an animal beneath them, ambertrix running like veins through grey-skinned stone. Char laughed with sheer exhilaration at his speed. They circled and climbed, dived and sprinted. Ekaar led him on a wild dance which, no matter how he tried, he couldn't quite match. She was laughing too.

Eventually, she folded her wings and plummeted. Char copied her, slightly alarmed at their speed. The ground was coming up much faster than it had a right to; he almost closed his eyes and braced for impact before remembering what his mother had taught him. At the last moment, he snapped his wings open and turned his flight into a stumbling run.

It wasn't graceful, but on the upside, he wasn't dead. Char considered it a definite victory.

'We will make a Lleu-yelin of you yet,' Ekaar said when he joined her. The wind caught in her ash-grey mane and it struck Char just how similar they were. Growing up the oddity among humans, mocked for his skin and his cat's eyes, he felt suddenly warm. It was a different warmth to the heat of blood and raw ambertrix that flowed beneath his scales; it was a warmth of belonging, something he'd never really felt before.

His mother's next words doused it. 'We must find you a suitable mate.'

'*What?*'

She sniffed. 'You are of an age, older even than is proper.' She paused, tilted her head as she seemed to do when thinking. 'Iliven perhaps, or Samastara. Though Iliven would be better. Any offspring of mine needs a strong hand.'

His jaw hung open; Char closed it with a snap. 'I don't think it's the time for . . . that. We've a war to win.'

'The *humans* have a war to win.'

'No,' Char said firmly. 'It involves everyone, every race that calls Acre home. We've been through this.'

Ekaar regarded him closely. 'Does this protest have something to do with the Starborn?' He caught a distinct whiff of disapproval.

Char looked away across the peaks. The first stars were appearing between spider-web clouds and Kyndra's name stuck in his throat. They had chosen their paths – which might for a while run parallel, but would never meet. 'I need time,' he heard himself say.

'Time is something we have had all too much of,' his mother said. 'But it is a reasonable request, Orkaan. Remember, however, that the longer you hold yourself apart from us, the harder it will be to adjust. We are your home now, your people.'

'I understand,' he replied and this time, instead of the warmth of belonging, her words woke a strange melancholy. The cloud webbing thickened overhead, slowly obscuring the stars. A patch of clear sky remained in the north and a star burned alone there, cold and distant.

Char was still staring at it long after Ekaar had gone. He was still staring when the moon rose somewhere behind the clouds and a presence came to stand beside him. He knew who it was by her scent.

Kyndra smelt like the cracking of ice, the slow shift of winter. She smelt like rock and the fires that ran deep underground. She smelt like the wind when it blew from the east, the Rairam wind, carrying forests and plains and distant cities forever sundered. Char shivered. Only one word could encompass so much: Starborn.

She laid a hand on his leg and they remained there silent for a time until he said, 'That star in the north – what is it?'

'*Noruri*,' she answered at once. 'One of the compass stars.' She paused. 'It's the star closest to humans. We've used it as a guide for thousands of years.'

He noticed she included herself among the humans, but that term could no longer be used to describe either of them. 'What was it like?' he asked softly. 'In the past, without your power.'

She drew a breath, but didn't speak.

'That bad?'

'It was a shock. I had forgotten so much. My parents . . . I needed to see them, to talk to them. Though it seems foolish now.'

'Why is that foolish? They're your parents. Don't you care about them?'

'They're just two people. We have bigger concerns.'

Char regarded her. Outwardly, she was the Kyndra he'd first met; inwardly, she was not. 'You didn't think that in the past.'

'I think it now,' she said with a little heat and then seemed surprised at her own reaction. 'What matters is that I stopped the eldest.'

'You're frightened,' he said abruptly, watching her eyes narrow. 'You're frightened of going back, of losing your power, of being Kyndra again.'

'I'm still Kyndra.'

'No, you're not.'

She was silent. 'All right,' she said finally. 'I'm not. Does it bother you?'

'You know it does.'

'Why?'

Char swallowed, turned his head away. It was easier to gaze at the darkness. 'It doesn't matter. It's done. These are choices we can't reverse.'

'Do you regret becoming Lleu-yelin?'

'I was always Lleu-yelin, even if I didn't know it. But this?' He held out a clawed leg, flexed his talons. 'I can't pretend it's easy. Or that it wasn't devastating.'

Kyndra took her hand away. 'What do you mean?'

'We –' He couldn't say it, not to her, not without the warmth in her face, in eyes which now reflected nothing but the stars. And it wasn't only her – he couldn't say it to himself. This body, this form . . . he suddenly felt like a human trapped in a dragon's skin.

'Oh,' she said softly. Once a blush might have touched her cheeks; now she was marble-faced and distant. 'That was just momentary, a distraction.'

Char felt cold. 'Not to me.'

'I see.'

She didn't, though, that much was obvious. 'Ekaar wants me to choose a mate,' he said flatly.

'I suppose she does,' Kyndra replied.

'That doesn't trouble you?'

She raised her eyebrows. 'Should it?'

Suddenly Char hated himself for starting this ludicrous conversation. What had he hoped to gain by it? Sympathy? Understanding? She wasn't capable of either, not any more. And clearly, he meant nothing at all to her.

His throat burned with ambertrix or tears – he wasn't sure if his dragon's body could cry. He wasn't sure of anything except that Kyndra was lost to him. But she'd been lost since that day in Samaya, when the emperor's sword had pierced his chest and awoken his heritage. It was time he accepted it.

Without warning, Char took a few steps away and threw himself upwards. The sky called to him, cleansing and cool, but it could not soothe the turmoil in his chest. He let it out with a great roar that struck the surrounding peaks; like sonorous bells, they echoed his voice back to him, a stone song worthy of a dragon's grief.

26

Brégenne

'Do you really think the Sartyans will hold to the oaths they swore?'

Hagdon looked up at Nediah's question, one scarred hand resting on a map of north-eastern Acre. Brégenne could see the place where it bordered Rairam, the only world she'd known. Now she found her gaze roaming, following the contours of other lands, the inked coasts of seas that had once existed only in history books. She felt dwarfed by these shreds of paper; each one proclaimed how small she was, how vast the world. Their goal of taking Parakat, which had once seemed so important, shrank before the might of Acre.

'They'll hold,' Mercia said, slamming the door behind her. She shed her gloves, shook the snow off her shoulders and threw her feathered cloak over a chair back.

Nediah turned to her. 'How can you be sure?'

'Because Hagdon's right,' Mercia said. 'Iresonté will see them as damaged goods. They've nowhere to go except to become outlaws at the mercy of both the Fist and the Republic.'

'I'm more worried about them stabbing us in the back,' Nediah replied.

Mercia's smile was chilly. 'We outnumber them now, even without the aberrations.' She eyed him squarely. 'And we have you and your friends. Would *you* try to stab a Wielder in the back?'

Nediah did not look wholly convinced, but he dropped the subject. His eyes met Brégenne's and she felt herself flush. They hadn't had another chance to speak. Their days had been taken up with caring for the injured, cleaning the fortress of battle and blood, laying the fallen to rest. She herself had helped to dig the graves, using the Lunar to soften the frozen earth. Hagdon had stood over Hu's, Avery at his side, and listened as she spoke a rite of parting. Only his eyes betrayed his feeling; his scarred soldier's face remained as hard as ever.

The rest of her time had been taken up by Reuven and Cowie, who seemed to be the aberrations' unofficial leaders. Reuven she could work with, but Brégenne didn't like Cowie at all. The sandy-haired young man seemed strange to her, in a way she couldn't put her finger on. There was just something odd about him, she thought, something tightly coiled that set her teeth on edge. But he was ever polite, ever helpful. He'd aided Nediah in his makeshift infirmary, taken bucket and brush to the floors, inventoried Parakat's storerooms and supplied Hagdon with detailed lists. Brégenne shook her head, pushing her doubts aside. Both Reuven and Cowie would be valuable ambassadors when she was ready to introduce the aberrations to Naris.

Nediah was still looking at her, a look that was not going unnoticed by Kait. The tall woman sat in a corner, one foot propped on a stool. She held a goblet of wine loosely on her knee. When Brégenne met her eyes, Kait hid her expression in another sip.

'Has there been any word from Kyndra?'

Hagdon's question jolted her out of her reverie. 'No,' Brégenne said, 'but we only sent the envoi yesterday.'

The Republic's commander flattened his hands across the map. 'We could do with reconvening. It feels as if we're fighting two separate battles, one of which I know nothing about.'

'Since we're all still here, I think it's safe to assume the Khronostians haven't succeeded in altering history.'

'Yet,' Kait added pointedly from her corner.

'I'd like that confirmed.' Hagdon glanced up, dark eyes sweeping the room. If he was searching for Irilin, he wouldn't find her; Brégenne knew she was down in the lower bailey with a couple of the Republic, doing her best to avoid him. Something had clearly happened between them, but Brégenne hadn't found a chance to ask Irilin about it.

Hagdon's gaze finally settled on Avery. 'And Taske?'

'He's gathered the cells from western Causca,' the auburn-haired woman reported. She wore a new scar like a battle trophy, a sword slash across the meat of her cheek. Nediah had offered to heal it, but Avery refused, murmuring that she would keep it in memory of Hu. 'Amon should be here any day,' she added, 'but the snows are deepening in the passes. He might be delayed.'

Hagdon nodded, returning his gaze to the map. 'According to Jauler's sergeant, Iresonté has split the Fist. She'll lead the greater southern arm, while the northern arm is under the command of Captain Mattias. They're currently camped at the source of the Orba River around *here*.' He jabbed the map and then looked up at Brégenne. 'Does that tally with the envoi you received from Gareth?'

She nodded. 'They flew over them on their way to Ümvast. He estimates their number at about ten thousand.'

Hagdon grimaced. 'I've heard of Mattias. He might be loyal to Iresonté, but he's no fool. He won't attempt the crossing until the thaw. The ice fields are too dangerous. Unfortunately for us, Iresonté has full access to the Cargarac ports.' He moved his finger down the map until it rested along the southern coast. 'The season's against her, but we must assume she'll land in Rairam before the spring. And she'll land in force. Sartyan galleys can hold up to five hundred men.'

'The Wielders are the south's only defence,' Brégenne said. She moved to the map, tapped a place with her fingertip. 'Naris is here. We've the Badlands between us and the coast. Iresonté could wreak havoc before we reach her. *If* we reach her,' she added, thinking of Veeta and Gend. Perhaps they'd only believe her warnings when they saw the Fist with their own eyes. And by then it would be too late.

'What about the north?'

'Gareth's people,' she said. 'But they're weakened by the early winter and the wyvern attacks. I doubt they could stand up to an army as well equipped as the Fist. But if Gareth can reach them . . .'

Hagdon frowned. 'You think one man will make a difference?'

'The difference he might make frightens me,' Brégenne said, remembering the eldritch light in Gareth's eyes.

Hagdon didn't look entirely convinced. She couldn't blame him. He hadn't travelled with Gareth, hadn't watched the gauntlet strip the novice of life. He hadn't seen Gareth die and return, or enter the haunted barrows of Ben-haugr. Hagdon had only seen him emerge, bearing the twin gauntlets: a force to reckon with, but a human force nonetheless.

Nediah moved closer to the map. 'Why this focus on Rairam, Hagdon? Is Iresonté so confident of her hold here in Acre?'

'Understand,' Hagdon said heavily, 'that Sartya bled the Heartland dry. Not only the Heartland, but a greater part of Causca and Baior too. You saw Baior for yourselves – a dusty wasteland where people barely have the strength to plough the land. Invading Rairam serves two purposes.' He held up corresponding fingers. 'First –' he curled one down – 'Rairam is a rich country with resources the Heartland desperately needs. And without a military presence, it's a sitting duck. Even if the Republic mustered the manpower to seize New Sartya, we wouldn't be able to hold it. Iresonté can easily establish a new capital in Rairam and march on us whenever she desires. Second –' he curled another finger down to make a fist – 'such a campaign cements Iresonté's control of the army. You heard Jauler. Many are angry at the Starborn and seek vengeance. What better way to channel it than to march on her homeland – our ancient enemy?'

As if to punctuate his words, the tower door banged open. Brégenne jumped. She wasn't the only one. Kait's wine slopped over the rim of her goblet; Avery spun to face the entrance; Hagdon's hand went immediately to his sword.

Clutching his chest, Varlan looked at Mercia. 'Lieutenant, there's a force approaching. And I've done quite enough dashing around,' he added in a mutter.

'This Taske of yours?' Mercia asked Hagdon.

'Let's hope so,' he answered tensely. Brégenne noticed his

hand was still curled around the hilt of his sword. 'Numbers, Varlan. Are they carrying a standard?'

'No standard,' the old soldier croaked, still panting from his run. 'And perhaps as many as a thousand.'

Hagdon swore. 'Are the gates closed?'

'Of course.'

'Come with me,' Hagdon barked. He led them out of the circular tower room, along a corridor newly adorned with the firebird heraldry of the Republic, through a reinforced door and onto the battlements above the curtain wall. From here they could clearly see a force, marching with military precision. Hagdon squinted into the early morning sun. 'Sartyans, I think but . . .'

There was a shout and a lone horseman broke away from the group, cantering across the bridge and well into arrow range. A moment later, a ragged standard was raised among the bulk of the force, a great plumed bird rippling against a midnight field. 'The Republic . . .' Brégenne heard Hagdon murmur, 'but that means—'

'Are you going to let us in, Hagdon?' the rider shouted, although the wind did its howling best to whip his words away.

'Taske!' Hagdon looked the happiest he had in days. 'What have you brought me?'

Amon Taske tipped back his hood; the grey-haired commandant stared up at them.

'Get me a pint of ale and I'll tell you.'

'Open the gates!' Hagdon called.

'We could have used your help a few days ago,' Avery said somewhat ruefully when Taske had joined them in the tower room, promised ale in hand. 'Parakat was better garrisoned than we anticipated.'

'You seem to have managed.' With a content sigh, Taske shifted his chair closer to the fire. 'I can't tell you how good it is to feel warm.'

'Twelve hundred Sartyans,' Hagdon said for the third time. He was still smiling. It transformed his face, Brégenne thought. She'd become used to the surly, serious commander, who seemed to approach each day as his last.

'And another five thousand pledged,' Taske said with a touch of smugness. 'Didn't I say there were still soldiers loyal to you?'

'You did, but I never thought—'

'They would follow you against Iresonté?' Taske rubbed a hand over his unshaven face. 'Many wouldn't. I had to do some fast talking on occasion, but I was careful. We put feelers out before approaching a garrison. And it didn't help that Iresonté has stripped the east bare. Most of these soldiers were stationed in the Heartland.'

Brégenne glanced up as the door opened. Irilin stood there, Reuven at her shoulder. She looked a little weary. 'Hello, Amon,' she said. 'What are you doing here?'

Hagdon was across the room in an instant. He seized Irilin's hands in his, looking, for a moment, as if he wanted to whirl her around. 'Taske's brought us reinforcements. Sartyans, no less.'

Irilin gazed at him in astonishment – clearly this new jubilant Hagdon surprised her too – before her eyes narrowed and she pulled deliberately away. 'That's . . . excellent news.'

'Isn't it?' Hagdon glanced down at their unlinked hands, as if wondering how they'd got that way. Then he looked swiftly back at Taske. 'I think I owe you some ken?'

Taske waved their bet aside. 'I'll take this fortress over ken.'

'Amon, this is Reuven,' Irilin said. 'He speaks for those formerly imprisoned here. Reuven, this is Amon Taske of the Republic.'

Brégenne watched the two men size each other up. 'Another erstwhile Sartyan?' Reuven asked coolly.

'Most of us are.' Taske matched him stare for stare.

'Change comes from the top?'

'Be grateful it does.' Taske grimaced. 'We are not the Defiant with their hit-and-run code, their slogans and their propaganda. We are an invisible network stretching from Cymenza to Kilkerain, people united in a desire to see the end of Sartyan rule. Acre was once a free world. It will take time, ken and dedication, but we will restore independence to all territories.' He paused. 'And it will take sacrifice. We do not pretend otherwise. If you wish to join us, that is the price.'

'We have paid the price already,' Reuven said, clenching one cracked fist. 'Whether we wanted to or not. We and all those before us, whose bodies now lie in the black below our feet.' He looked at Hagdon. 'Why should we give more?'

'No one is forcing you to,' Brégenne heard herself say. 'You have a choice. If you wish to return home, you are free to do so. But if you wish to stay and learn, to take your places among the descendants of Solinaris, you will have to stand with us.'

'We have no homes,' Reuven said harshly. 'They were burned or taken from us. We are not *free* to do any such thing.'

'You are free to fight for the right to rebuild them.' Taske stepped back. 'It may not sound like a choice, but it is the only one we can offer. It is more than Sartya has given you.'

Silence reigned among them. Hagdon was once again sober. Taske waited grim-faced. Avery and Mercia both stood with arms folded. Kait idly wound a stray bootlace about her finger, but Brégenne could tell she was listening. Nediah stared at Reuven, a small frown between his brows.

'It is not my choice alone,' the man said finally. 'Those still capable of it are grateful for the service you have done us, but we are tired. An ideal may not be enough.'

'How about vengeance, then?' Kait said. She threw down the lace.

It was one of her usual ill-timed and inflammatory statements, but Reuven laughed. And though it was an ugly laugh, devoid of humour, it crinkled the lines about his eyes. 'Vengeance,' he said, staring at Kait. 'Yes. That we *might* fight for.'

The fortress was large, but so was the task of quartering twelve hundred soldiers. Brégenne left it to Hagdon and Mercia and accompanied Reuven back to the chambers given over to Parakat's former inmates. They couldn't keep referring to them as aberrations, she thought, and they weren't yet Wielders. She wasn't sure if they were ready to learn. One woman watched her from the floor, where she sat huddled, arms locked about her knees. No longer dirty and rag-clad, she was still thin, stony-faced. *She must wish herself anywhere but here*, Brégenne thought. Even if their homes were gone, being forced to remain in Parakat must be a torment. *I will take them to Naris*, she vowed, *as soon as I know they're ready. And as soon as I think of a good enough argument to present to Veeta and Gend.*

'It's just a question of practice,' Nediah was saying to Cowie. The fair-haired young man had his head tipped on one side, as if listening attentively, but his eyes were distant. 'Once you've learned how to touch the Solar or Lunar, you can make the connection far more easily.'

'And is it the same feeling?' a woman asked. 'Touching the

Solar and Lunar?' Her name was Margery, Brégenne remembered. Of all the aberrations, including Reuven and Cowie, she seemed the strongest, the least cowed. It made sense; she'd only been in Parakat for a month.

Nediah frowned and looked at Brégenne. 'You know, I don't think I've ever compared notes. *Is* there a difference between touching the Solar and Lunar?'

'I can only describe what it's like to touch the Lunar,' Brégenne told Margery with a shrug. 'I struggled with it at first. I kept lunging at it, mentally scrabbling. My mentor taught me to be silent, to wait. Touching the Lunar is like –' she paused, searching for a suitable comparison – 'coaxing a bird into your hand. You need to be patient, inviting.' She could feel Nediah's gaze on her cheek. 'Inviting is difficult for me.'

'What good is a power you have to wait for?' Margery asked with mild disgust.

'Once you've mastered the technique, everything I described happens in a heartbeat,' Brégenne said.

'The Solar isn't like that at all.'

They looked at Nediah. It wasn't just Margery listening now, Brégenne noticed. Others had raised their heads too.

'How would you describe touching the Solar?' Nediah asked Kait. The tall woman was leaning against a wall, arms folded, her expression of boredom quite convincing.

'You're better with words,' she said shortly.

Nediah sighed. 'Well, it's not inviting. It's more like seizing the mane of a wild horse and holding on for dear life.'

'Seriously?' Brégenne couldn't believe they'd never had this discussion. 'A wild horse?'

'If we're sticking with animal metaphors, then yes.' Nediah shook a golden flame to life in his hand. Some of the prisoners drew back, others leaned in closer to see. Cowie was one. He moved to peer over the Wielder's shoulder, the fire dancing in his eyes. 'If you waited for the Solar, you'd be waiting forever.' Nediah closed his hand. 'You have to take it.' The flames licked around his fist.

When the silver point emerged from his chest, Brégenne took it to be a trick of the light. But the silver was red and the red spread in a widening circle, which grew when Cowie slid the dagger out as gently as he'd slid it in. The weapon fell from his hands to clatter on the stone floor, and the sound of its fall shattered the spell that had held them all frozen.

Brégenne heard a scream. It was high and terrible and she clapped her hands over her ears until she realized the sound came from her own throat. Nediah looked faintly bemused as his knees buckled. 'Take it,' Cowie said. He was gazing at his bloodstained hands, as if he somehow expected them to burst into flames.

Kait flashed across the room in three strides. She was howling wordlessly, bright swords unsheathed.

'No!'

Reuven's shout went unheeded. Kait plunged one of her blades into Cowie's chest and tore down. The burning sword sliced through flesh and bone; with the other, she took the man's head from his shoulders. Cowie's body fell in pieces and Kait kicked it away. Her face was starkly bloodless against the red splashed across her front.

Nediah touched his chest; fingers dipped in his own blood. Brégenne caught him as he toppled sideways, lowered him to the floor. She was aware of words pouring out of her, but she couldn't make sense of them. Her hands were on his chest, trying vainly to keep the blood inside.

Kait collapsed next to her. 'Heal yourself,' she shouted into Nediah's face. 'Come on, Ned. You've healed worse.'

Nediah's breath was coming in gasps, his green eyes clouding. 'Please,' Brégenne said, not knowing to whom she spoke. This couldn't be happening, couldn't happen. She seized Kait, shook her. 'Do something!'

'I can't.' It emerged as a sob. 'I can't heal, Brégenne. I can't.'

'You must be able to –' her hand was still around Kait's arm – 'to keep him alive until nightfall. Then I can heal him. Just until nightfall, Kait.'

'I can't,' Kait said again and to Brégenne's horror, she ripped her arm free and stood up, backing away. 'I don't know how. I don't know.'

'Someone.' When Brégenne looked back at Nediah, his eyes were closed. 'No, no.' Brégenne tore off her shirt, pressed it to his chest. The blood came seeping up, drenching the cloth in seconds. She couldn't seem to get her breath. She reached for the Lunar, fruitlessly, knowing hours stood between her and the night. Nediah had minutes. She couldn't wait that long.

'Kyndra,' she murmured suddenly, 'Kyndra can help us.'

'There's no time to send an envoi,' Kait snarled. She had her back flattened against the wall, almost as far from Nediah as she could get. Brégenne was aware of the prisoners and of Reuven backing away; she ignored them, instead shutting her eyes, trying to clear a space where she didn't see Nediah's pale face. He lay half in her lap, heavy, slipping away. One hand still pressing the material to his chest, she held him closer and she called. She didn't use the Lunar; she couldn't. It didn't occur to her that she was yelling into the silence of her own mind. She called Kyndra. Again and again, she called for the Starborn.

Brégenne?

The relief was so overpowering, Brégenne almost lost her concentration. But she held on to the sense of Kyndra with everything she had. *Come,* she thought wildly, *please come.*

Calm down, Brégenne. Where are you?

Parakat, she thought back. *It's Nediah. You have to help him. He's . . . he's dying.*

She thought she detected a faint sense of resignation before Kyndra said, *Very well.*

Hurry!

But there was no response. Brégenne opened her eyes. She could see a pulse in Nediah's neck, but it was slow, barely moving the skin above it. 'Kyndra,' she heard herself moan. 'Please hurry.'

'She can't hear you,' Kait said in a choked voice. Brégenne didn't spare her a look; she couldn't take her eyes from Nediah's face.

'Hold on,' she told him. 'Just a little longer. Please, Nediah.'

It was impossible to tell how much time passed. Brégenne could only measure it by the slowing of Nediah's pulse, by the increasing pallor of his face. She held him and she wept, occasionally clawing at the Lunar, trying to break through the dazzling cage that kept her power from her.

And then a hand touched her shoulder.

Brégenne tore her eyes from Nediah to look. Amazingly, unbelievably, Kyndra stood there. She was solid and real and Brégenne found herself gasping in relief. She'd thought about this moment for weeks, meeting Kyndra again after so much had changed between them. She'd thought about what she would say, how Kyndra would reply, even about what she'd look like. Now her appearance barely registered. Brégenne looked beyond her tattoos to the person beneath. Kyndra had saved

Nediah's life once before, catching him as the bridge to Naris collapsed. 'You have to heal him,' she said.

'I can't heal, Brégenne.'

Her ears registered the words, but her mind refused to process them. She lifted her arms slightly, Nediah still cradled in them. 'Kyndra. Heal him.'

Kyndra shook her head. She looked at Nediah with vague regret. 'It's a shame,' she said. 'How did this happen?'

Brégenne just stared at her. For the first time she focused on the tattoos engraved in Kyndra's skin, on her still face, her dark and distant eyes. 'You . . .' she breathed. 'How can you say that? He's your *friend*, Kyndra.'

'Yes, I know,' she replied with infuriating calm. 'But I've told you, I can't heal. The stars don't possess an understanding of mortal bodies. And even if they did, I'm not sure I could comprehend it without practice. Remember, Nediah studied his craft for years.'

Brégenne shook her head, a dam inside her threatening to burst. 'No. I can't believe this. You're Starborn. You can do anything.'

Kyndra pursed her lips. She regarded Nediah steadily, though her gaze seemed introspective. '*Isa* says there might be a way,' she said after a moment. 'But it's dangerous. I don't think it's a good idea.'

'What way?' Brégenne shouted. Every second they wasted talking –

'Can *you* heal him?'

'You know I—'

'If your power was available to you, could you heal him?'

'Enough to save his life,' Brégenne said, 'but he won't survive until nightfall.'

Kyndra put her head on one side, dark eyes surveying her. Even amidst the turmoil within, Brégenne felt that it was not a look you gave a person. 'I can strip away the barrier between you and your power.'

Brégenne frowned. 'You'd make it night?'

'I'm not a Khronostian,' Kyndra said with a definitive shake of her head. 'I can't fast-forward time. But Lunar is merely reflected Solar and you already wield it.'

'I don't understand.'

'It's quite simple. I can open you up to the Solar. You will be able to wield both – it's the same energy, after all.' Kyndra folded her arms. 'But it will probably kill you.'

Brégenne's heart raced. 'Kill me –?'

'The shock,' Kyndra explained. 'They might be the same energy, but the Solar form is very different. You have never encountered the energy in its primary state. If you don't harness it immediately, it will burn you up.'

'Do it,' Brégenne said.

Kyndra bit her lip; for the first time she looked perturbed. 'Brégenne, it's a waste. You're a talented Wielder. We need you. Why throw your life away?'

'Because it's mine. *Do* it, Kyndra.'

Kyndra looked away from her, her gaze travelling around the chamber, noting, it seemed for the first time, Reuven and the aberrations. They cowered from her, fearful eyes fixed on her face, on the tattoos burned into her skin. Kyndra didn't seem to notice their discomfort.

'Kyndra,' Brégenne cried. '*Please.*'

The Starborn sighed. 'If it's what you want.' Brégenne couldn't tell whether her air of sadness was genuine. In the next moment, it was gone and Kyndra's tone became business-like.

'Opening you up to the Solar will be stripping away a layer of protection you've had your entire life, one you probably didn't notice was there.' She clenched a fist and Brégenne noticed there was something wrong with her other hand – the whole arm hung strangely. But there was no room in her to ask the question. Her thoughts ran as swiftly as the blood in her veins. She looked back at Nediah's pallid face.

'I can do it,' she heard herself say, but inside she was far from sure. She thought about the dazzling cage, how it blinded and burned her when she tried to break out of it. If that was the Solar, how could anyone harness it? But Nediah could turn that inferno to gentler purposes. And everyone knew the Solar was naturally suited to healing, more so than the Lunar.

'Brégenne,' Kyndra said seriously, snapping her out of her thoughts, 'once I strip that barrier away, you're on your own. I can't help you master the Solar. And I won't be able to stop it from tearing you apart.' She knelt on the other side of Nediah's body so that they stared across him into each other's eyes. 'Do you understand?'

'Yes,' Brégenne whispered.

Kyndra reached over. She placed her star-scarred hand on Brégenne's forehead and the world burst into flame.

27

Brégenne

Light.

Heat.

But what she felt most was the agony. Searing, flesh-melting pain; she wished for death to end it. She was only dimly aware of the flames. Her clothes were gone, burned up in an instant. Her skin blistered before her eyes. Her hands held her head, bare now of hair. She screamed and with each scream, she inhaled more of the fire so that the breath boiled in her lungs.

Shapes loomed around her, indistinct through the flames. Everything was golden, a terrible *hungry* golden desperate to consume her and escape. It would burn the world to ash.

'Master it, Brégenne. *Now*.'

The words meant nothing. She wished for darkness; she wished for silver and silence. They had carried her for as long as she could remember. They were her life.

But they were gone and the fire was everything.

'Brégenne,' said the voice and it was her name. 'Seize it. Or it will destroy you.'

She gasped and cried, hugged herself more tightly, knowing

317

it was futile. The fire was already inside her. Seize it? Seizing it would be throwing herself into an inferno. Seizing it meant death.

Wasn't that what she wanted?

Although the voice spoke again, the words could not reach her through the fire. It crackled and jumped inside her body, a searing violation. *Help me*, she cried silently, *help me please*. Her plea fed the fire; it roared up, obscuring everything, leaving her alone in a prison of agony.

No, not alone. Somebody else was there – not the cold voice that issued its impossible commands, but someone closer, warmer, someone who knelt behind her, whose arms reached around her burning body. Brégenne looked down. The arms did not burn, clothes untouched by the fire.

'Like this,' Kait's voice said and the flames calmed a little. She took Brégenne's hands in hers. 'You have to accept it. Recognize it.'

She did, Brégenne thought. She had seen this fire before, fought it, been healed by it. 'The heart of the sun, Brégenne,' Kait whispered, still holding on to her. 'You just know it by another name.'

With her mouth blistered and baked, she had no moisture left to shape the word, so Brégenne said it silently, in the furnace that was her head. *Solar*.

The fire had been inside her – now she was inside the fire. Her body shrieked at her, raw and red, but no longer burning. Lithe forms were all around her; they took on shapes when she looked at them. A horse ran before a Solar wind, eagles flew in its slipstream. Grass grew around her shins, a forest with golden leaves and golden fruit, hanging ripe and heavy from golden boughs. She blinked. A river splashed through the trees, molten gold. It was almost overwhelming . . . almost.

Brégenne's burned feet walked her through it. Her fingers stroked the backs of nameless creatures. She let them guide her among the trees, following their whoops and calls, treading in their prints, until the forest ended and she stood upon the edge of a vast plain. The sun beat down overhead and, despite its brightness, she found herself staring into it, letting it wipe out every other sight.

'. . . Brégenne.'

There was no forest, no plain. Her eyes had been closed. When she opened them, after-images of the great sun stained the scene. She was somewhere dark, knees against a stone floor. A body lay at her feet.

Nediah.

She realized she was in agony. Her heart beat fretfully, fighting the shock of her burns. She might not have long. Kait let go of her hands and Brégenne placed them on Nediah's chest. They glowed brightly, almost brightly enough to obscure how the Solar had stripped off most of her skin. When she sank her awareness into Nediah's body, she found the barest flicker of life. He'd lost so much blood.

Brégenne had healed a chest wound before. Kyndra's step-father. It had been night; she had knelt on a wooden floor, a floor that had soon after succumbed to fire. A strange echo. The Solar was finally pliant in her hands. It pulsed as if it too possessed a heart. She followed the path of the knife through Nediah's body and, just as she'd done with Jarand, encouraged the flesh to knit. The sense of her own body faded as she worked, taking her sense of time with it. All that mattered was linking vessel to vessel, patching torn cartilage, retrieving fragments of bone which the blade had sheared off in its violent passage. Her skill was clumsy, but it was all she had. She wept while she worked, and the Solar sang to her, a little like the Lunar, but wilder, windier; several times, it almost escaped her grasp. Brégenne gripped it firmly, knowing she didn't have the strength to reach out again.

When she was satisfied she'd healed most of the damage, she pulled her awareness back and opened her eyes. Nediah's face was still pale and she placed her burned palm against his cheek. She felt a presence behind her. Kait had stayed; the back of Brégenne's neck was damp with her tears.

Numbness began to seep through her, taking away the pain, but everything else too. Brégenne leaned forward until their foreheads touched. 'I've done all I can,' she whispered, or maybe she didn't – maybe the words were only in her mind. 'Now it's your turn.' The numbness grew to cover her mouth; she couldn't draw breath. Her head spun and her hand slipped from Nediah's cheek. When the floor rose to meet her, she welcomed it.

Brégenne woke. She wished she hadn't. She couldn't open her eyes, but tears seeped from them, tears that stung scorched cheeks. Each breath was a gasp. Someone had written on her flesh in fiery ink; she could feel the letters' downward strokes, their diminutive flicks and tails. Who would do this? Who had dared? She struggled, but pain was her only answer. She tried to speak, but her lips wouldn't part except in a mewl she didn't recognize as her own.

Hold on, Brégenne.

A male voice, a young man's. It wasn't in her ears, but echoing alone in the hollow of her head. She thought she knew it, but no name reached her. *Who?* she thought, *Who?*

Hush. You held on to me, so I will hold on to you.

'Hold on, Brégenne.' Now it was a woman's voice. She felt someone take her hand and the spike of pain that followed forced more tears down her cheeks, more stinging. 'It's Irilin,' the voice said, 'You're going to be all right.'

It couldn't be anything but a lie. Brégenne held on to it as the only thing she had.

The world had fallen away.

That was what she remembered. First in light, then in darkness. There had been pain and there had been power. Perhaps they were one and the same. Voices. She remembered voices, one in her head; another outside it. *Hello?* she thought. *Where are you?*

Brégenne? It was the young man's voice and it carried surprise, pleasure. *You're awake.*

I don't know . . .

It's me. Janus. I'm . . . better.

He spoke across the bond. Memory crystallized along with disappointment. *I thought you were someone else.*

Nediah, came the voice. *That's who you thought I was. You cried out many times.*

More memory, more pieces falling so terribly into place. *What happened?* Janus asked, but she ignored him, snatching at the pieces, slamming them into the frame. Nediah, blood, the Solar, fire –

Her eyes flashed open.

The first thing she saw was her own hand, pale with fading

scars, closed on the coverlet. The second thing she saw was him.

Sunlight filled the circular room. She was in a tower. Nediah sat in a chair beside her bed, shadows making pools of his closed eyes. Fear shot through her, but a moment later, she realized his chest rose and fell with the normal rhythm of sleep. She drank in his face, drawn as it was, chin dark with stubble. He'd been clean-shaven when she'd seen him last. How many days had she lain here?

She must have made a sound because he twitched and woke. The sun caught on the gold in his eyes. He blinked and then he smiled. Widely, warmly. Brégenne found herself smiling too, though the action sent a twinge of pain through her jaw. 'You're alive,' she whispered.

'So are you.'

They looked at each other and began to laugh. Brégenne winced, but couldn't seem to stop. She let the sound pour out: relief, joy, something else light and ineffable. When he touched her cheek, she realized she was crying. 'Alive thanks to you,' Nediah said, as he wiped away her tear. He seemed hesitant; she could almost hear the question that hung in the air between them. When she didn't answer it, he sat back, picked up her hand instead, smoothing a finger over the white scars there. 'I've healed Solar burns before,' he said, 'but never so many at once. Even Kyndra—' Nediah broke off. 'What happened?' he asked softly.

'Kyndra must have told you.'

Nediah let go of her hand, leaning back in his chair as if suddenly weary. 'She's been busy with Hagdon. But what she said is impossible.' He touched his chest with a grimace.

'I'm sorry,' Brégenne said. 'It was clumsy healing. I hope you've been able to sort it out.'

'You saved my life, Brégenne.'

She smiled. 'Then all of this was worth it.'

Nediah shook his head, perhaps to refute her words, perhaps in disbelief. 'Kyndra claimed she made it possible for you to wield the Solar,' he said.

She knew what he wanted to see, but she couldn't bring herself to reach out to the force that had almost killed her.

Nediah noticed her hesitation. 'It's too soon, I understand.'

'No, it's just . . .' Brégenne looked away. 'I'm frightened.'

He touched her chin, turned her head to face him again. 'There's nothing to be frightened of. Kyndra said you're fine.' Nediah gave a short laugh. 'What am I saying? You're a Solar *and* a Lunar Wielder. That would frighten anyone.'

'How can you stand it?' Brégenne heard herself ask. 'The heat, that roar?'

Nediah summoned a flame, gazed into it. 'It's the only power I've known. I've nothing to compare it to. And walking the forest is always beautiful.'

Brégenne felt the breath catch in her throat. 'A golden forest? Golden trees, creatures?'

'So you saw it.' Nediah breathed out slowly. 'The forest is a novice's first experience of the Solar. It's where I found myself during the test.'

'And then the plain,' Brégenne said, remembering the power of that burning sun, being overwhelmed in its light.

Nediah bit his lip. 'You saw the plain as well? I didn't reach the plain until the Inferiate.' He sat back. 'She really threw you in at the deep end.'

'I don't think she had a choice. Kyndra said that once she

stripped away the barrier, I would be alone. I'd have to master the Solar by myself.' Brégenne eased into a new position, wincing as her muscles protested. She felt as if someone had beaten her all over.

A pillow slipped from the bed and Nediah bent to retrieve it. 'The pain will pass,' he said, resettling it behind her head. 'I did what I could for your burns. Your body will do the rest.'

'I want to get up.'

'In a day or two,' Nediah said firmly.

A piece of hair caught in her mouth. Brégenne took it out impatiently, but stopped, still holding it. She had a memory of her clothes burning, of her hair crisped to nothing. She raised her other hand, ran it over her head. Her hair stopped just below her jawline.

'I couldn't make it the same length as before,' Nediah said quietly. 'It grew when I healed the burns across your scalp.' His mouth quirked. 'It suits you.'

Brégenne dropped her hands, awkward and wishing for a mirror. *It's hair,* she told herself, *stop fretting over it.* 'Did you know Janus has woken up?' she said, changing the subject.

'What?'

'He was talking to me across the bond. He knew something was wrong.'

For the first time, Nediah looked worried. 'Did you tell him what had happened?'

'No.'

'I think it's best if we keep this in Acre for now. I don't know how the Council are going to react.'

'Collective apoplexy, I suspect.' They grinned at each other, though the action made Brégenne's face ache.

'Brégenne,' Nediah said when silence returned. 'Why did you do it?'

'Do what?'

'You know what I mean.'

Brégenne swallowed. His gaze was hot on her cheeks and she felt them flush. 'I couldn't . . . you were dying.'

'But *you* almost died.'

Her eyes prickled and Brégenne railed at them. She would not cry again. 'I couldn't lose you.'

'Why?' he asked fiercely.

The quiet in the room grew to encompass the world. They gazed at each other. The prickle in Brégenne's eyes travelled to her throat. The words were on her lips, but she couldn't speak them. What if he didn't say them back? What if he had another answer for her, one she dreaded, one he'd denied, one she still hadn't been able to dismiss? And the secret she hadn't told him coiled inside her; how could she say the words when that secret still stood between them? She'd never told anyone about the day she'd lost her sight . . . the day she'd returned to take her vengeance.

'I'm tired,' she said and these words were the bitterest she'd ever tasted. Brégenne turned her face away. *Coward.*

'I will let you rest.' She heard resignation in his voice. And sadness. She stared fixedly at the white woollen blanket until the door opened and closed and his footsteps receded.

But Brégenne didn't rest. She raised her eyes and looked at the door that separated them. It was heavy oak, banded with metal; a door worthy of a fortress. In the safety and silence of her mind, she let the words escape.

Because I love you.

28

Hagdon

'So all in all, our alliance with the aberrations is off to a *great* start.'

Mercia's sarcasm was justified, Hagdon thought. He'd been a fool to expect anything else from Parakat's inmates.

'But it has to be said,' the lieutenant leaned back, one booted foot lodged on the edge of the table, 'old Reuven's far politer now.'

Reuven could have been involved in Nediah's attempted murder, but Hagdon didn't think so. Cowie had shocked them all, even his fellow inmates, who'd gathered outside Nediah's door, waiting for him to wake. The Wielder had healed most of them personally, including Cowie himself, which made the attack all the more irrational. Reuven was clearly horrified, even as he mourned a man who'd been his friend.

Still, how could they now put such an unstable group in any position of power or trust? Hagdon rubbed his temples. 'What a mess.' From what he'd been told, they'd nearly lost Brégenne too. 'How are the Wielders?'

'Doing well, I hear.' Mercia unsheathed her sword and

began to polish the nicks out of the blade. 'As soon as he was conscious, Nediah healed Brégenne. You should have seen her. Bald as a plucked bird and blistered head to toe.' She shook her head. 'If that's what a Wielder's power does to you, I'm glad I'm not one of them.'

Hagdon agreed. As long as he and the aberrations shared the same ceiling, he couldn't relax. Wielders set his teeth on edge. Except Irilin. He'd barely seen her these past few days and when he had, she'd glared at him before turning her back and stalking off. He supposed he deserved it, Hagdon thought, remembering how he'd run from her before. He dragged a hand across his face and wondered, not for the first time, whether he might be losing his mind.

The door of the tower room was closed, but Kyndra walked through it as if it were smoke. Mercia jumped; her sword slid off her lap, clattered loudly to the floor. She cursed as she bent to retrieve it. 'Most people *knock*.'

Kyndra seemed unperturbed. 'I need to return, Hagdon. Ma and I have to be ready to act on a moment's notice.'

'Can you not lend us your aid?' he asked. 'If we had your support, we wouldn't have to wait on more men.'

'I can't,' the Starborn said, though she looked momentarily conflicted, as if she'd much rather help *him*, Hagdon thought. 'I can't afford to miss the signs. More than the fate of Rairam hangs in the balance.' She paused. 'If I succeed in stopping the eldest, you'll have my support.'

Hagdon felt strangely dislocated. If he'd walked a different path, *he* might be the one leading the invasion of Rairam. Now his mind was filled with wondering how to defend a land he'd never seen.

'You must call on the Wielders,' Kyndra said. 'Though I suspect they'll need to be coaxed out to fight.'

'That will be *my* job.'

Brégenne stood in the doorway. Her hair was a good deal shorter, Hagdon saw, and the tails of white scars crept from beneath her sleeves. She held on to the frame, seemingly casual, but Hagdon noticed the strain in her wrist.

Nediah appeared behind her. 'You're up,' he said flatly.

'Honestly, Nediah, you don't have to sound so injured about it.' Brégenne turned back to Kyndra. 'I'll take Nediah, Kait, Irilin and the inmates.' A little tension entered her voice. 'They need to get out of this place and soon. We'll head to Naris.' She let go of the doorframe, came further into the tower room. 'The Wielders *will* see reason.'

'I'm staying,' Irilin said, now also pushing her way into the room. She didn't look at Hagdon at all. 'I've pledged to the Republic. They need a Wielder with them.'

He didn't know whether he was relieved or disappointed. Remembering the armoury, Hagdon thought it might be a bit of both.

After a moment in which the two women seemed to engage in some sort of silent tussle, Brégenne sighed. 'We'll need to communicate. It makes sense for one of us to stay.'

'How are you feeling, Brégenne?'

It was the kind of question a concerned friend might ask. But from Kyndra, it sounded clinical, as if she enquired after the result of an interesting experiment. And Brégenne clearly knew it. Her eyes glittered as she regarded the Starborn. 'I'm well,' she said. 'Thanks to Nediah.' The tall Wielder put a hand on her shoulder.

'And he's well thanks to you,' Kyndra said with some satisfaction. '*Isa* is impressed, Brégenne. So am I.' She seemed to be the only one in the room unaware of the discomfort her words were causing.

Nediah's hand visibly tightened. 'You could have *killed* her, Kyndra.'

'Let it go, Nediah,' Brégenne murmured. 'She did it because I asked her to.'

'Why are you defending her?'

Kyndra was watching their argument with a small crease between her brows.

'You would have died,' Brégenne said.

'And you *could* have.'

'But we didn't,' she concluded firmly. 'So let it lie.' Brégenne turned back to Kyndra. 'Will you tell me of your encounter with the eldest before you go?'

Hearing about the House of Sartya – not yet the Sartyan Empire – both disturbed and fascinated Hagdon. Having grown up under imperial rule, he struggled to imagine Acre without an emperor. The swift picture Kyndra painted of the Heartland as a place of infighting and intrigue was difficult to imagine. And to think she'd seen Davaratch himself – the man who had given his name to every subsequent Sartyan ruler . . .

'Wait.' Brégenne held up a hand. 'You *lost* your power?'

'Essentially,' the Starborn said, rare emotion dimming her face. 'That era belongs to Kierik. The stars serve *him*. And I'm vulnerable in other ways.' She glanced down, as if she found the thought embarrassing.

They sat in chairs around the fire. The stack of wood had long been exhausted, so Nediah kept it alight with occasional gestures. Brégenne leaned in closer. 'What other ways?'

'I remember things,' Kyndra said shortly. When no one

spoke, she added, seemingly reluctant, 'about Brenwym, about my parents. About you and Nediah and my time in Naris.' She hesitated. 'About Char.'

In the ensuing silence, the fire popped, startling Hagdon. Kyndra looked up. 'It's dangerous for me,' she said in a flat voice. 'Feelings block my way to the stars. They're a handicap I could do without. I can't think clearly.'

Brégenne evidently wanted to say something; Hagdon could almost see the words on her tongue. Instead she swallowed them, gesturing to Kyndra's hand. 'What happened?'

'The eldest.' Kyndra pulled back her sleeve and Brégenne visibly recoiled. Even Hagdon found himself eyeing her arm with horror. The skin hung slack from the bone, mottled and translucent. 'Ma says it's a curse, a tiny time trap,' Kyndra told them dispassionately, turning her arm to the firelight. 'She's slowed its spread, but can't stop it. And travelling backwards and forwards in time makes it worse.' She pressed her lips together and, despite her tone, Hagdon thought he saw a hint of fear in the cold, starred face.

'Perhaps I can help –' Nediah began, but Kyndra pulled her sleeve down decisively.

'No,' she said. 'It can't be healed away. It's part of my pattern. Only the eldest's death will end it. Just one more reason to stop him.'

Though Hagdon did his best to be open-minded, it was a struggle. He accepted that the Khronostians could exert some control over time, but this . . . And talk of Kierik, the Starborn of legend, raised hairs all over his body. 'What does this eldest want?' he asked.

'Initially, Sartya's end,' Kyndra said. 'To undo the empire

before it grew to power. But I've seen the eldest. He's more creature than human.'

Coming from a Starborn, Hagdon thought with a chill, that was saying something.

'Ma believes this obsession has driven him to madness. None of his actions make sense any more. And he's dragging the rest of Khronosta down with him, recklessly sacrificing his own people.'

'And what of the Yadin? He still goes along with this?'

Kyndra's sigh sounded regretful. 'It seems so. But he's the weak link. Without Medavle, I wouldn't have succeeded in stopping the eldest. He can't see past his hatred for Kierik.' She shook her head. 'But the eldest won't discard him. He's the only anchor they have.'

'How is *our* anchor?'

'Shune? Bad-tempered but otherwise well.'

'Nothing's changed, then,' Hagdon muttered. Despite himself, he found he missed the irascible old Relator . . . the man with whom he'd shared the emperor's death. The memory bound them together; likely they'd each take it to their graves.

'But this is my job,' Kyndra said, breaking into his dark reverie. 'The Republic has its own battles to fight.'

'Although we're growing in size,' Mercia said, 'it's not fast enough. We need numbers to take on Iresonté.'

'Have you heard from Gareth?' Kyndra asked.

'Yes.' Brégenne shrugged deeper into her cloak. The fire could not completely kill the chill in the tower room. 'He and Ümvast are the only ones standing between Iresonté and control of the north.'

'I don't know what he can do with those gauntlets,' Kyndra

said, a touch uncertainly. 'Their power is bound to the earth, not the sky.' She folded her arms. 'I hate not knowing things.'

'Join the club,' Mercia said. 'We're too isolated up here,' she added to Hagdon. 'It's all very well to have a fortress, but not if those sympathetic to our cause won't be able to travel here until spring.'

'We could get a message to Rogan,' Hagdon mused. 'Taske says he's taken control of Cymenza. That presents a few opportunities.'

'I will leave you now,' Kyndra said, rising. 'Who knows what mischief the Lleu-yelin have cooked up in my absence?'

'Are they wonderful?' Irilin asked in a soft voice.

'Moderately,' Kyndra said and she actually smiled.

The Starborn had been gone only an hour when the call came echoing up the stairwell. 'Force approaching, Commander.'

Hagdon cursed. He could have done with the intimidating presence of a Starborn. Still, he thought, hurrying towards the battlements, with all the Sartyans garrisoned here, a few hundred intruders wouldn't present a problem.

'They look like Alchemists,' Mercia called down and Hagdon revised his opinion. He felt a frown growing between his brows. It couldn't be . . .

Standing on the battlements above Parakat's great gates, Hagdon narrowed his eyes. A lone horseman rode in the vanguard. A man, he thought, but he couldn't be sure – the usual silver Alchemist mask obscured his face. He wore a deep cowl and armour constructed of linked leather plates. Crossed straps over his chest held several small vials and a curved scimitar hung at his waist. Something in Hagdon's stomach began to clench.

'Definitely Alchemist armour,' Mercia said.

Kait stood at Mercia's shoulder, hands on hips, her gaze lingering on the newcomer's weapon. As he rode up to and across the drawbridge, seeming utterly at ease, she asked, 'Who are the Alchemists?'

'A specialist force,' Mercia told her, 'presumably under Sartyan control, but everyone knows they have a tendency to go their own way.' She shook her head, darted a swift look at Hagdon. 'But they're based exclusively in the south, a thousand leagues away.'

Hagdon felt his bare fists tighten on the parapet. The rider reined in almost directly beneath him and looked up. 'What do you do here?' Hagdon called, the high wind nearly whipping his words away. 'Parakat is no longer in Sartyan hands.'

'I was rather counting on it,' the figure answered in a man's amused tones. Hagdon's breath caught.

'Has it been so long you don't recognize me, James?' The rider reached up and, with a nonchalant twist, removed his mask and hood. Dark hair blew around an unshaven face, a face Hagdon hadn't seen in five years. He gripped the parapet harder, leaned out further. '*Mikael?*'

'Try not to fall on me, James. Being crushed by my own brother is not the way I'd pictured going.'

He sounded just the same, Hagdon thought, unable to believe it. 'What are you *doing* here?'

'For sands' sake, if you don't open this gate right now, I'll blow it up.' Mikael tapped a little red bottle in its leather holster. 'And,' he added with a backward glance at his fellow Alchemists, 'you'd better bloody have a keg or two on the side. Talking's thirsty work and we've a lot of ground to cover.'

*

Mikael threw down his fourth stripped chicken leg and leaned back in his chair. 'Not a bad spread for a recently captured fortress,' he said, carelessly licking the grease from his fingers. 'How many days have you held it? Ten?'

'Fifteen,' Hagdon said. He'd barely touched his food. 'How did you hear about it?'

'Your banners were sighted by a unit on relief duty,' Mikael answered between swigs of his ale. 'We happened upon them a couple of days ago.'

Hagdon grimaced. 'I think I know the end of this story.'

'What? You wanted them alive to carry the news to Iresonté?'

'Iresonté will find out anyway. I'm not in the business of wasting good soldiers. The Republic's ranks are in need of bolstering.'

Mikael let out a short bark of laughter – so familiar that a memory came to Hagdon of a tall man, arms around each of his sons' shoulders. The memory was old; his father had had to kneel.

'With Sartyans?' Mikael said, snapping him back to the present. 'All right, who are you and what have you done to my brother?'

Hagdon just looked at him. 'I'm not sure I know any more.'

'Sands' sake, it was a joke, James.' Mikael pushed away his plate. 'I don't think I like you like this. What would Paasa say?'

'Nothing, since she's dead,' Hagdon answered shortly.

Mikael's smile withered. 'What?'

'She and Tristan.'

The air around the table seemed to freeze. Everyone except Kait stared at their plates. When Hagdon glanced at her, she was all unashamed curiosity.

'How did I not hear of this?' Mikael's voice had lost all trace of humour. 'Why did you not send a message?'

'And what would I have put in it?' Hagdon was suddenly shouting. 'That his imperial majesty raped and murdered Tristan, that Paasa hanged herself from the grief – you know how much she loved him, how proud she was when he won a place at court.' His voice broke. 'When *I* won him a place at court.'

The silence was deafening. Hagdon couldn't look at any of them, but he forced himself to meet Mikael's eyes. 'How could I write any of it,' he whispered, 'when it was my fault?'

Mikael returned his gaze steadily. 'Come with me.'

His brother took him outside, where the sky had begun to darken, the snow to whirl in little white tornadoes. 'When I think of Paasa, I see a girl,' Mikael confessed as they walked across the upper bailey. 'That's how long ago I left. I know I returned when Tristan was born, but my duties called me away again so swiftly that I never really accepted she'd grown up.' He looked away, into the rising storm. 'I never knew Tristan.'

'He was a good boy,' Hagdon heard himself say. 'Bright, out-going, always helpful. Too good for the Sartyan court. He took after her rather than his father.'

'When did Paasa's husband die?'

'Tristan was five. I think he was the only thing that kept her going. She brought him up alone after that.'

'Sounds like she did a fine job.'

Hagdon said nothing.

'James.' Mikael gripped his arm, halted their walk. 'You can't blame yourself for their deaths.'

'If I hadn't put in a good word with the Relator –'

'Paasa would have refused to speak to you.' Mikael shrugged.

'That's one thing I remember – her stubbornness. She wanted the best for Tristan. Studying under Relator Shune *was* the best.'

'But it put him in the emperor's path.' Hagdon found himself gripping Mikael's arm in turn. 'I thought he'd be safe, I thought his majesty wouldn't dare touch Tristan. Not a Hagdon – not after our family's service.' He let go, looked away. 'How short-sighted I was. I'd built my life in the Fist, put loyalty to the emperor above all else. Even family.' Some part of him was shocked at the words pouring out, but he couldn't stop. 'And the worst of it,' he murmured, looking away into the whirling white, 'was that I continued to serve him, the man who'd murdered my kin. I'd pledged to protect him.'

'You weren't very good at it, then,' Mikael said drily. 'A sword through the heart is generally fatal.'

'You heard about that,' Hagdon said after a moment.

'*Everyone*'s heard about it. Well, they've heard the rumour at least.' He paused. 'I have to say I'm rather proud of you.'

Hagdon stared. 'You're proud to have a brother who committed regicide?'

'I'm proud to have a brother who avenged my family's *murder*.' Mikael's expression was deadly serious. 'I should have been there.'

'When I killed the emperor?' Hagdon asked with a frown.

Mikael shook his head. 'No. For Paasa – I should have been there for her. For you.'

'Well. You're here now.' He smiled weakly. 'Gods help me.'

29

Kyndra

'They did *what*?'

'I couldn't stop them,' Char said, his spiked tail curled defensively. 'I don't have any authority here.'

They stood in one of Magtharda's plazas. Snow fell thickly, hissing on contact with the ambertrix-heated stone. 'I leave for two days –' she felt a rare surge of anger – '*two days*. When did this meeting take place?'

'A day after you left,' Char said miserably.

Kyndra clenched her fist. 'This could jeopardize everything. We were supposed to wait for a sign.'

'That's what Arvaka told Sesh. But she said she'd had enough of waiting. She said it was high time we took the fight to the eldest.'

The idea appealed to *Sigel*. Kyndra could sense its desire to raze the Khronostian temple to the ground, and the eldest along with it.

'Is it such a bad thing?' Char asked.

'Yes,' Ma said, walking out of the white, 'when there are children's lives at stake.'

Char shifted uneasily. 'Surely Sesh wouldn't harm innocents.'

'My people were not so generous,' Ma said, eyes dark on his face. 'You are proof of that.' She grimaced, tugging her hood more closely about her head. 'Can we get out of this?'

They returned to the chamber the Lleu-yelin had set aside for them. The city was eerily silent, muffled in snow and absence. 'How many went?' Kyndra asked once the huge dragon-sized doors stood closed between them and the weather.

'All,' Char said, shaking the snow off his wings. 'Save a couple of the younger ones.' Droplets hit Realdon Shune and the Wielder cursed loudly, leaping, unusually spry, to his feet.

'Dratted creature.' He shook the book he'd been reading. 'Be more careful.'

Char rumbled something that sounded less than apologetic. 'The old man's—'

'– been wondering where you spirited yourself off to,' Shune snapped at Kyndra. 'You were the only thing keeping some measure of control here. And now the whole city's flown off in search of vengeance.'

'Brégenne called me,' Kyndra said with a shrug. 'Nediah was dying.'

Char swung his head to look at her. 'What?'

'One of the inmates stabbed him.'

'Shit,' Char said, sounding unexpectedly like his old self. 'What happened?'

'Brégenne couldn't heal him because it was day.'

'So *you* did?'

She shook her head. 'Weren't you listening before? I told you I can't heal.'

'But Nediah –'

'He's alive,' she said impatiently. 'I made it so that Brégenne could use the Solar. She healed him. Almost killed herself in the process. I did *warn* her.'

'What's this?' Shune looked up, a glitter in his deep-set eyes. 'You made a Lunar Wielder a Solar?'

'It's a simple process of stripping away the barrier between the energies.'

'Simple for you, perhaps, but –' Shune ran a wrinkled hand over his face – 'it's horrifying. To be ripped open like that.'

'She asked me to do it, so I did,' Kyndra said shortly. 'And she survived. Now can we get back to Khronosta? How long ago did the Lleu-yelin leave?'

Realdon Shune was still staring at her with his mouth open. Char had drawn away slightly, regarding her with some inexpressible emotion. She sighed. 'Someone answer.'

'A few hours ago,' Ma said. She turned her palms up, studied the pale ouroboros that dived in and out of her flesh. 'I don't understand why the eldest would move the temple so close to Magtharda.'

Unease prickled over Kyndra's skin. 'What?'

'Sesh's mate spotted it on his return from a hunting trip. He couldn't believe it. *I* couldn't believe it,' she added.

'Unfortunately,' Char said, 'the news that the temple was only hours away sent the Lleu-yelin into a frenzy. They called a meeting. Arvaka and I tried to dissuade them, but Ekaar and the others said they wouldn't get a better opportunity to exact revenge.'

Kyndra began to pace. 'I don't like this,' she muttered. 'Didn't any of them stop to think it might be a trap? Or worse – a distraction?'

'They wouldn't allow Ma into the meeting,' Char said with

a defensive glance at her. 'She tried to tell them it was too easy.'

'I can't believe Sesh would be so hotheaded,' Kyndra said and then immediately doubted her own words. She'd heard the Lleu-yelin swear blood-vengeance, her golden eyes shining with resolve.

'We have to stop them,' she decided. 'The Lleu-yelin have a head start, but I can travel faster. I might be able to get there before they attack.' She paused, looked at Char. 'But I've no real authority over the dragons. I don't want to fight them.'

'You could try talking them down,' Char said, plainly doubtful. 'Explain that the situation's delicate.' He snorted; blue briefly misted the air. 'They want to stop the eldest, after all, same as us.'

'But their way is like cracking open an egg with a hammer,' Kyndra said, her withered arm beginning to throb again. It had done so ever since her sojourn in the past. Although she gritted her teeth and ignored it, a chill voice seemed to whisper that time was running out.

'I wish to come with you,' Ma said. 'They are my people.'

Kyndra was about to shake her head when she recalled how Kierik had used *Raad* to spirit her away from the Sartyan manor. 'I might be able to take one of you,' she said slowly. 'But definitely not all three, and especially not a dragon.'

'I suppose we'll follow along, then,' Realdon Shune said, with a pained glance at Char's scaly hide. Char didn't look particularly pleased at the prospect of being left with the old Wielder either. Shune nodded at Kyndra. 'But I fear you will have to deal with the Lleu-yelin on your own.'

'I've dealt with worse,' Kyndra said grimly, remembering

Naris and the Nerian. Remembering Kierik's mad and distant eyes.

Who are you?

If you won't tell me, Veritan *will.*

A sudden dizziness took her. If Char hadn't steadied her in the crook of his leg, Kyndra might have fallen. 'Are you all right?' he asked, his breath hot on her cheek.

She blinked. 'I'm . . . fine.' For a fleeting moment, she'd felt a terrible weakness sweep through her. Kyndra glanced at her cursed arm. Time truly was running out.

Kyndra and Ma travelled by *Raad* and the compass stars, weightless, less than light. Kyndra swiftly discovered that extending the stars' power to include someone else was much harder. And carrying Ma presented its own challenges. She had to concentrate on holding the woman's pattern together and Ma's pattern was unlike any human's Kyndra had seen. It was mutable and multi-stranded, like one of the Khronostian mandalas. Concentrating too hard on it made her seasick.

As they neared the temple, her cursed arm began to throb with the regularity of a pendulum, another distraction. The valley Ma described wasn't far – about half a day's flight for a dragon. Kyndra reached it in minutes. Immediately, she saw she was too late; the Lleu-yelin besieged the temple, assaulting its carved walls with their crackling blue breath. The Lleu-yelin riders dug their talons into the carvings, ripping the delicate spirals and numerals to illegibility.

A deep frown split Ma's forehead. 'Something's wrong,' she breathed. 'They are not even trying to escape.' She peered at the building. 'I can't sense anything. No dancing, no mandalas. It's as if they've abandoned it.'

'If that's the case,' Kyndra replied, 'it doesn't look as though the Lleu-yelin have realized it.' She took a deep breath. 'Stop!' she thundered, *Ansu* magnifying her voice.

It got their attention. For a moment, everyone froze. And then, to Kyndra's disbelief, the attack resumed.

Kyndra growled a curse. She and Ma made for Sesh, whose tawny scales were webbed by a fine, glowing mesh of ambertrix armour. 'Sesh,' she snapped, donning *Tyr* like her own set of armour, 'this is madness.'

'No,' the Lleu-yelin replied, fangs bare and topaz-tipped. 'This is *vengeance*.'

'Think a moment. Where is the resistance?' Kyndra gestured at the too-silent temple. 'Whenever Khronosta comes under attack, it sheds its purchase on time and place to materialize somewhere else. Why is that not happening?'

Sesh dragged her talons through a carved wheel. 'If they do not wish to defend themselves, they will simply perish all the faster.'

'No,' Ma said. Boldly, she stood in front of Sesh, forcing the Lleu-yelin to retract her claws at the last moment. 'You are not thinking. If the eldest was here, he would defend the temple.'

'It's too late,' Sesh snarled. 'The blood price has been decided. It must be taken.'

'I could stop you,' Kyndra said.

Sesh looked at her. 'I do not doubt it, Starborn. But earn the enmity of my people? See Orkaan cast into exile? You do not want these things.'

'Why bring him into it?'

'He is your friend, even if you cannot see it. He will choose you over us. Ekaar says he has worn the human skin too long.'

'Call off the attack, Sesh.'

'No.'

Kyndra was at a loss. *Burn them, Sigel* sang, *and this temple they besiege.*

What would that accomplish? she asked, nettled.

None would then remain to defy you.

It was an attractive idea. She was tired of dealing with people who let emotion govern their actions instead of logic. But she didn't want to earn the dragons' enmity. 'Just let Ma and I pass,' she said. 'We don't even know if the eldest is here.'

'If he is not, then his people will pay the blood price instead.'

'The children too?'

Sesh hesitated. 'What do Starborn care for such things?'

Realdon Shune had once asked Kierik the same question as he stood in the hall of the Sentheon. Kyndra swallowed. And, like Kierik had, she ignored it. 'Haven't you considered this could be a distraction? To distract Ma, to distract me? While you're busy attacking an empty temple, the eldest could be preparing to act and we'll miss our chance to stop him.'

The temple gates gave way with a splintering crash. Just as Kyndra braced herself for the dragons' charge, Sesh called a halt. 'Very well, Starborn,' the tawny Lleu-yelin growled. 'Go. Discover the truth. But if there's even one Khronostian left inside, we will claim our debt.'

Ma didn't hesitate. She clambered over the remains of the gate and Kyndra followed her, looking about with interest – she'd never actually been inside Khronosta. An orange-stoned court-yard greeted her, sprinkled here and there with grains of white sand. Columns marched around it, encasing a corridor. Directly ahead of them rose the inner sanctum. Its doors stood open.

'This is not right,' Ma muttered. 'They haven't even acti-vated the basic wards.'

Inside the sanctum, the sense of emptiness was worse. Kyndra's boots disturbed sand already disturbed – it looked as if it had once been raked into lines, which branched off into chambers flanking the main passage. The concern on Ma's face deepened with every step they took. 'Something terrible has happened here,' she whispered.

The corridor turned and they found the first body.

'No.' Ma bent down, running her fingers over the woman's twisted skin. She looked like the *du-alakat*, Kyndra saw, but this was clearly no warrior. She wore white robes and her feet were bare, one a tiny baby's, the other large and veined.

'What's happened here?'

'The mandala,' Ma said, straightening. She quickened her pace; they left the dead woman behind. 'These are the untrained, the uninitiated. The eldest must have fed them to the mandala, stripped them of life energy.' Her voice shook. 'I can't believe he would do such a thing.'

They found more bodies. Some were those of young people, barely out of childhood. Ma's expression grew harder with every one they passed. The corpses all had two things in common, Kyndra saw – they wore the white robes of the uninitiated and carried the characteristic disfigurements of the *du-alakat*.

They emerged into a large chamber where the sand formed a chaos of whorls and spirals. It was littered with dead – at least thirty, Kyndra counted. 'Riel,' Ma said, a sob in her throat. 'And Keelu.' She knelt beside two corpses, their hands joined. Two young men, though it was hard to be sure; one had an old man's body, the other an old man's face. 'I looked after them,' Ma said, dashing her tears away. 'They were only six when I left.' She stood up very quickly, fire in her wet eyes. 'The eldest will pay for this.'

The Lleu-yelin need not worry about their blood debt, Kyndra thought. The eldest had claimed it for them.

A small sound. They both looked up. Kyndra took hold of *Tyr* and Ma drew her kali sticks. Her face said it all – she yearned for someone to punish. They advanced across the chamber, taking care not to disturb the dead. A small scraping came from behind a closed, locked door.

Ma placed her hand upon the door; the lock rusted to nothing. She exchanged a charged glance with Kyndra, who nodded, ready to reach for *Sigel*.

Ma pulled the door open.

Five children gazed up at her, their eyes wide and terrified. The room they'd been locked in was small – a storeroom perhaps, unlit. Even Kyndra grimaced at that. How long had they been shut in the darkness listening to the sounds of death beyond the door?

'Gods,' Ma breathed. 'He left them here. He left them to die in their own home.'

The children said nothing. All had shaven heads, Kyndra saw, and wore white robes like the other Khronostians. She wondered whether their parents were among the dead.

Once Ma had coaxed them out with soft words, they clung to her. She carried the two smallest, while the others held on to her cloak. 'Don't look,' she said as she led them through the ravaged temple. But the children looked anyway, silent gazes passing across people who were, almost certainly, their families.

No one spoke. But when they reached the courtyard and the watching Lleu-yelin, the older children gave little gasps of fright and hid behind Ma. She held out the two she carried towards Sesh. 'Do you still wish to claim your debt, dragon?'

Sesh studied Ma's tear-streaked face. 'What happened?'

'Khronosta is finished,' Ma said harshly. 'My people are dead.' She raised her chin. 'Do you understand now? Do you understand why this is greater than your vengeance? If the eldest is prepared to destroy his own people to achieve his ends, what do you think he will do to the world? Those he killed were not even *du-alakat*.'

Sesh blinked. 'Not *du-alakat*? Then where are *they*? And the eldest himself?'

Kyndra looked at Ma, saw her own realization dawning in the other woman's eyes. 'The signs,' Ma said, looking back at the temple. 'A ravaged citadel. A murdered people.' She glanced down at the children. 'The survivors as powerless as children.'

The words seemed to carry the eerie rhythm of rote. Kyndra felt them resonate somewhere deep inside her and at the same time *outside* her, in the white heart of the star, *Era*. 'Solinaris, the high Wielders, the novices,' she heard herself say. 'A pattern, an echo of the past.' She turned to gaze into the distant east. 'The eldest has gone to Naris.'

PART THREE

PART THREE

30

Gareth

He stalked through a frozen world.

Ice encased the evergreens in a crystalline skin, bent their branches earthward. Leafless trees were stalagmites rising from the forest floor. His breath steamed in the chill; each footfall broke a glittering crust. Gareth erased his passage with the Solar, taking care not to melt the snow beneath.

Such a useful power, came a thought. His thought, he supposed; who else's could it be? A strange thought for someone who had wielded the Solar most of his life, but Gareth shrugged it off. He couldn't afford to be distracted – he needed to keep his mind on his task.

The Solar *was* a useful power, but his plan depended on the gauntlets.

Between Argat's and Freya's reports, they had a fairly good idea of Sartyan numbers. It was a huge force, mostly infantry, and such a force moved slowly, its supply train stretching back into the north-eastern reaches of Acre. Guarded, the scouts informed Ümvast, but not as well as it should be. Either the

349

Sartyans were lazy – unlikely, he thought – or they believed that danger lay ahead, not behind.

Gareth smiled grimly. For trespassers in Ümvast's land, danger lay everywhere.

His mother led a comparatively small force, giving the bulk of the Sartyan army a wide berth. Paths through the forest were rare and narrow, restricting the Sartyans to the one major road. It would take them far too long to cut an alternative trail through the icy branches. Now they were far to the south of him, unaware of the danger closing in on their distant supply train.

A golden glitter struggled to reach him through the trees. He'd tried to teach Kul'Das how to send envois, but the delicate task was too difficult for someone without any knowledge or training. She had, however, managed to create the skeleton of one and they'd agreed it could serve as a signal.

The formless glow told him that Ümvast's force was in place.

Gareth breathed out slowly, readying himself. Once the attack began on the supply train, the path where he waited would be flooded with soldiers. He only hoped he'd be strong enough.

All was silent. He strained his ears for any sound, heart speeding with nerves. Inside the gauntlets, his palms sweated. It was his first test. What if the power didn't work as it should? What if there were too many of them? He was just one man . . .

Shouts muffled by snow and distance. He caught a blur of red through the white forest – a scout rushing to alert the men in the rearguard. Gareth let him pass unmolested; that, too, was part of the plan.

He tasted smoke on the wind, caught a glimpse of a sooty

streak winding up into the sky. His mother should be getting out of there now, her task accomplished. *His* was just beginning. When, finally, he heard the multiple pounding of boots on frozen earth, Gareth braced himself and stepped out into the open.

His sudden appearance brought them up short; he wondered what they saw when they looked at him. A broad-shouldered man, cloaked, armoured in dark steel, hair forever streaked with the frosty touch of Hond'Myrkr. And on his hands two gauntlets, one that magnified the dim afternoon light, one that absorbed it.

The Sartyans did not hesitate long. Two dozen confronted him; he could see more coming up behind. 'Who are you?' the foremost said.

Gareth didn't reply. Instead he crouched and pushed his right hand into solid ground. It was nearly over before it began – an arrow flew at him and he lunged for the Solar, bending the energy into a golden shield around him. But the effort forced a growl from his lips. He couldn't hold both powers in his head at once, not for long. He refocused on Hond'Myrkr and a black, writhing mass boiled out of the earth around the gauntlet, dark tendrils flowing away from him towards the Sartyans.

More arrows came, and though the golden shield repelled them, each impact sapped his strength, his concentration. He had to hold Hond'Lif back until the right time; the white gauntlet deafened him with its plea for release. He gritted his teeth, felt the first tendril touch the soldier who'd spoken.

Immediately the man began to scream. Black crawled up his boots, seeping between the gaps in his armour. When it reached his neck, the skin mottled, lips curling back from the teeth. The soldier's flesh sagged, caved in, bone started to show. And all the while he screamed, watching as his own red gauntlet slipped from a fleshless hand.

Enough. Gareth pulled Hond'Myrkr back, let the man, silent now, topple to earth. As he sent the black tendrils after other soldiers, he let go of Hond'Lif, feeling its energy flow into the corpse, light flaring in the shrivelled eye sockets. Instantly he was aware of the man – his name, his age, his last terrified thoughts. It was almost too much, too soon. Gareth let go of the Solar, rose to his feet, forcing the twin powers to continue their assault. Such a pleasure to watch them.

The Sartyans held their ground until the moment their weapons corroded in their hands. Then, discipline abandoned, they finally succumbed to terror. Thrusting comrades aside, they fled into the icy forest.

Gareth felt sweat on his brow, his breath came in gasps. He held two dozen Sartyans in his head; their thoughts tangling around his. This was nothing like the time he'd raised the dead of Ben'haugr, who had lain in sleep for centuries, whose minds had grown still and silent. These men and women had lived only moments ago, and their clamour and confusion filled his head. They fought him, but Hond'Lif was too strong, its mad song coursing white-blue through their veins. Faces turned to him, all in various stages of rot. Some were little more than skeletons – on these Hond'Myrkr had done its work too well. He'd have to be more careful in future. For his plan to work, they needed to look like soldiers rather than corpses.

He felt the thread linking them to him as a tugging behind his eyes, a feeling both familiar and strange. A few living Sartyans remained trapped among their erstwhile comrades, horror rooting them to the spot. 'Faren?' one man asked of a woman with a face almost intact. He stretched out his hand to her.

They'd been lovers in life, Gareth knew. He clenched Hond'Lif.

The woman smiled, a stiffening rictus. Then she drew her sword and ran the soldier through. Blue-white curled from her eyes and nostrils as she watched him slip off her blade.

In a frenzy of fear, the others shouldered aside the dead and ran. Gareth cursed. They mustn't be allowed to report back. He gave his servants a silent command and they spread out, thrusting their way through the frozen foliage, uncaring of the branches that tore the skin on their faces.

They were effective hunters, implacable, untiring. He did not recall them until every last Sartyan had fallen. Then, exhausted, he leaned against a tree and waited for the dead to return. They came out of the forest, creatures of horror and sinew, their walk already stiffening into a stumbling lurch. Satisfied no more Sartyans were coming, he withdrew Hond'Lif's power and the corpses were again corpses. They slumped to earth in a twisted pile of limbs and there they would stay until he called for them to rise.

Gareth closed his eyes. When he opened them, a dreadful sight greeted him. He stood in a ring of corpses – *his* corpses. His heart began to thump. Beneath his armour, a cold sweat covered him. Gareth turned and vomited, gripping a frozen tree against the sudden wave of weakness. He could smell them; their sweet rot filled his head. There was nothing left in his stomach, but still he heaved.

Gasping, the only living thing in a circle of dead, Gareth stumbled back, away from the corpses. What had he done? He remembered plunging his hand into the earth, the black tendrils of Hond'Myrkr spreading death. He remembered releasing Hond'Lif, taking pleasure in the way the gauntlet gave each soldier the semblance of life. He remembered coming up with the plan.

But now, confronted with its success, all Gareth could think about was the people he'd killed. *They're Sartyans*, he thought, wiping the freezing sweat from his forehead. *They'd have killed you.*

It didn't make it better. *What's happening to me?*

Weak, Hrafnasueltir.

No, he wouldn't think of that word. The time of darkness was past. Only the future mattered now, the upcoming battle, defending his homeland against those who wished to take it away. Gareth forced himself to look at the corpses of the soldiers he'd killed. With his help, they would win.

But what will you do then? he asked silently. *When the war is won, when battle is done, when there is no more need to fight? What will you do then?*

Gareth found, to his disquiet, that he did not know.

It took the head of the Sartyan army two days to realize that something was very wrong.

Standing under the shadowy moon, on the fringes of Ümvast's camp, Gareth pictured himself in the Sartyan leader's shoes. First, no new supplies had arrived from the distant train. Second, a whole unit had disappeared. There'd been a disturbance, they knew. But they'd seen no definitive sign of resistance from the natives.

And you won't, he thought to himself, *until it's too late.*

After all, what kind of resistance could stand against the Sartyan elite? Still, they'd sent out riders and then – when they did not return – another unit. When that unit failed to report in, the march finally halted. Now the army was camped on the southern fringes of the forest, admittedly a little too close to Ümvast's own camp for comfort.

Gareth found his mother in her tent, fists planted on a large table where a crude map lay unfurled. 'I am no general,' she said when he entered, pushing herself away with a huff of disgust. 'All this planning and posturing ill suits me.' She tapped the haft of her axe. 'This is the only thing I know, the only thing I can be sure of.'

'You can be sure of me,' he said.

She returned his gaze coolly. For the moment they were alone. 'I do not think so.'

'You doubt me?'

'No.' Ümvast jerked her head at the gauntlets. 'But I do not *know* you. So I cannot trust you.'

Her answer hurt, but it didn't surprise him. Seconds passed. 'Who are you?' his mother asked finally. 'What happened to my son?'

Gareth felt cold. 'I'm here, Mother.'

She shook her head, a slow, deliberate movement from right to left and back again. 'I think my son never left those tombs.' Her voice was nearly a whisper. 'I think he died there in the darkness and the dust.'

Her eyes were quite dry.

Gareth shivered; he couldn't help it, reminded so suddenly of the place he'd almost forgotten. Images flashed through his head, stabbed it with the pain of memory. Unrelieved stone, silent feasts, the dead trailing their tattered shrouds.

Corpses on muddied snow.

With difficulty, he pulled himself together, thrust the memories aside. 'You're free to believe what you want,' he said, more harshly than he intended. 'But I *am* here to help. If you believe nothing else, believe that.'

Her gaze slid from him to the map. 'I do.'

'Well.' Gareth crossed to it, tapped a scrawl on the ragged paper. 'Here is roughly where they're camped. We'll need to drive them away from the plains and up into the forest. If we allow them space to manoeuvre, we won't stand a chance.'

'And you think your . . . unit can manage this?'

Her hesitation hung in the air between them. 'I am hopeful,' Gareth said.

'*Hopeful* does not fill me with confidence.'

'Just do your part,' he answered tersely, knowing he hid a well of doubts. 'The Sartyans are hungry, cold and tired from a long march. Morale will be low – they're in unfamiliar territory and two hundred of their comrades are missing. I will drive them into the forest. It's your job to pick them off. They must be divided.'

'What of their commander?' she asked, planting hands on her hips. 'That's who we need to find.'

'Leave it to me. One of their officers will know.'

'And I suppose they'll just tell you.'

Gareth smiled. 'That's right. They will.'

'I want you to stay out of the battle,' Gareth said later to Argat and Yara as the winter afternoon drew to a close. 'Your skills are too valuable to lose.'

He half expected them to argue, but the two sailors just looked at each other. 'Fine by me,' Yara said with a shrug. Although she wore her usual serrated sword, she instead patted a spanner stuck through her belt. 'I'm more engineer than warrior anyway.'

'You too, Argat,' Gareth said.

'I don't need convincing.' Argat darted a look behind them, to where a heap of tumbled boulders lay on the plain. All three knew what they concealed. 'Though I suspect such a battle will become the stuff of stories, I'm happy to hear of it second hand.'

The wind had begun to turn, bringing with it a reek that wrinkled Yara's nose. As he'd walked through the assembled warriors, Gareth heard their muttered oaths of protection, their swiftly silenced talk. He felt their combined gaze on his back, fearful, unfriendly. *You are not one of us*, that gaze seemed to say. *You carry evil into our midst.*

They did not understand.

'Go back to your ship,' Gareth said. It was a mark of their unease that neither Argat nor Yara protested at the order. It was time. He took a deep breath and closed his eyes, feeling himself slide inexorably into a chill, nameless place where his own horror would not cripple him. Where there *was* no horror. When he opened his eyes, everything seemed a little different, sharper, as if a veil had lifted. He walked around the boulders.

And stood beside a hill of corpses.

Their red armour made them appear blood-drenched, but blood no longer flowed in any of them. Their veins were dust, or spidered through rotted flesh. Flies had found them even in the cold; they crawled and buzzed in an ecstasy of feeding. Here, the sound was louder than the wind that scoured the plain, which swept up the carrion stench and carried it to camp. No wonder the warriors had whispered.

It had taken him hours to march them here, tethered to them by Hond'Lif. Their minds had grown quieter as they left life further behind, but still it was an effort to hold so many. He'd rested often, allowing the bodies to tumble to the forest floor while he wiped the sweat from his brow. Then he'd called upon Hond'Lif and the power of the gauntlet raised them once again, marched them onward in a shambling line. They were a little over two hundred.

Gareth licked his lips as he observed them. Ordering them to fight, he sensed, would be harder than forcing them merely to walk. The afternoon grew darker; light faded to evening. Darkness would fool the Sartyans, but not for long. Some of the dead had helms to hide their ravaged faces. He'd march those in front, he thought, leaving the more damaged ones at the rear. Even the famed Sartyan discipline would crumble when they clashed blades with fellow soldiers, soldiers who did not bleed and die like men.

He breathed out slowly, emptying his mind to receive them. *'Vakti. Ek kalla-darr.'*

The words rose on his tongue, as if he'd spoken them a hundred times. They seemed imbued with greater power, with a dignity his native language could not match. So he let them come, ignoring the stabbing in his head. He had no room for doubt.

Hond'Lif began to glow, its song to soar in the vaults of his mind. Blue-white, pure, it plucked at his heart as if it were an instrument to be played. But Hond'Myrkr was there too, an iron melody, tugging the song down from its heights, imbuing it with the deep chords of ending.

'Ek heim-darr af svefn.'

He kept it tightly controlled, letting Hond'Lif raise them one at a time, then five then ten. Bound to his will, the dead soldiers did not acknowledge their surroundings. They clambered over their motionless comrades, treading on limbs and faces, lining up before him. It was easier now that they had lain for some days in death.

Gareth clenched his white fist. The soldiers dropped to one knee. 'Follow me,' he said once they rose.

Although he gave the camp a wide berth, he felt them there, the warriors of Ümvast, watching at the edge of the sparse torchlight. In the gathering dark, they would only make out stilted movements and, when a corpse turned its head, the bluish glow of Hond'Lif welling from eye sockets. If they were lucky, that's all they would see.

The forest extended out onto the plain, a many-limbed creature dragging itself southwards. The Sartyan army camped between two such limbs. Their torches lit up the sky, flames marking a wide perimeter. They were quiet for a large force; the hum of conversation not much louder than the wind.

Ümvast would be leading her warriors north and east, circling the army, counting on the night and the forest to hide her. All Gareth had to do was drive the Sartyans back into the trees. It sounded easy, but it wouldn't be. Given a choice, they'd head for open land where numbers counted for more.

He pulled up his hood and marched on, flanked by the dead.

A voice rang out, oddly magnified by the dark. 'Who comes?'

Gareth had made no secret of his advance. They were supposed to be seen. Shouts sprang up in the camp, as the news travelled from sentry to soldier to officer. 'One of the missing units,' he heard and smiled to himself.

They reached the perimeter under the watchful eyes of sentries. 'Are we glad to see you,' one called out; a young man unusually fresh-faced for the Fist. 'Captain Hendyn was worried we'd underestimated the natives.' He laughed. 'He'll be pleased to see otherwise. What unit are you from?'

No one replied. Gareth steeled himself and kept on walking. As he passed the sentry, his hand shot out and clamped about the young man's neck, rotting his throat before he could scream. Gareth let him go without breaking stride; the body slumped to earth and was trampled under the marching feet of the dead.

A white-faced soldier stood in their path, hand holding a trembling sword. 'Who are you?' he croaked before Gareth killed him with a touch. The third managed to shout a warning before he fell, but it was too late. They were already inside the palisade. *Spread out*, Gareth said to his soldiers. *Kill them, drive them back into the trees.*

They obeyed unquestioningly. Of course they did, he thought. They had no will now but Hond'Lif's, no freedom except what he chose to give them.

Cries filled the night, the usual Sartyan discipline seemed to be lacking. Perhaps it was the shock of facing their comrades, who fought with the stiff rigor of the dead. They weren't as agile as they had been in life, but they retained their skills. Forcing them to use those skills soon drenched Gareth in sweat. He was rusty, he found himself thinking. Once, such a simple act wouldn't have wearied him like this.

He could be anywhere – his mind was able to jump from soldier to soldier. Through the eyes of the foremost, he saw, at last, resistance. 'What are you doing?' an officer screamed as he clashed swords. It was all he could do to keep the corpse at bay – he seemed unwilling to harm one of his own.

But then the corpse's helm slipped, tumbling from its bent head and, through its eyes, Gareth watched the officer's face contort around a scream. He thrust his sword right through the corpse, which barely glanced at it before raising its own blade and taking the stunned officer's head.

There was pandemonium. Gareth pulled back; he couldn't afford to be distracted – it wouldn't take the Sartyans long to realize he wasn't as invulnerable as his soldiers. He stalked through the melee, his mother's blade clutched in one hand. Using the gauntlet to defend himself was challenging when Hond'Lif raged in his ears. And the Sartyans had begun to take heads – although it didn't stop the corpses, it meant he could no longer see out of their eyes. Despite the dismembered bodies he stepped over, the Sartyans were losing as many as they felled. He smiled grimly – a field of fresh dead meant that he could just raise more.

And then, glancing down, he saw the dead face of Serald.

Serald? He meant Shika. But of course, it was just a coincidence: a young Sartyan with the same bronzed skin, the same eyes. Dizziness struck him; the forest with its carpet of dead lurched to one side and he found himself on his knees.

No. The voice was in his head. *I will not falter.* What voice was that? Where was he?

Gareth blinked. His grip on Hond'Lif weakened. He felt the dead connected to the gauntlet, felt the way they stumbled over their own feet, how the Sartyans fighting them seized the upper hand.

No! This time the voice was a scream.

His heart hammered. Sweat dripped from his forehead. He held his temples, fighting the headache that threatened to engulf him. *Who – are – you?* Each word tore a shriek of pain from his throat. It joined the chorus of the dead and dying.

Suddenly, the pain was gone. There was a horrible taste in

his mouth – blood. Gareth spat; he'd bitten the inside of his cheek. It was like waking from a dream except that no dream could be as terrible as the reality in which he found himself.

It would have been easier, the voice said, *if you had not fought.*

It was in his head. Gareth froze. 'Who are you?' he whispered.

'You know who I am.' This time, it used his tongue.

Gareth retched. 'Get out. Get out of my body.'

I tried to make it painless, the voice told him, reverting to a mocking whisper in his head. *I tried to make it silent. If you hadn't fought me, you wouldn't* know, *wouldn't suffer as you do now. As you will for all the years of your life.* The voice paused. *Such long years. Truly, you are a gift.*

'No,' Gareth murmured. 'No!' The second word was an agonized scream, torn from deep inside him.

Kingswold laughed. The laughter bubbled out of his own throat. *I told you once before, Hrafnasueltir. The gauntlets are mine.*

31

Brégenne

She could not sleep.

Brégenne walked the chilly corridors of Parakat, arms wrapped around herself, vainly trying to keep the heat in. *This is foolish.* She had to rest. They were due to leave early. An unexpected break in the weather had come and they couldn't afford to miss the opportunity it offered. The journey south would be long; Naris was many leagues away.

Brégenne was conflicted as well as cold. Since the night she lay between life and death, Janus had gone silent. That didn't bode well. She'd reached out to him several times, asking for news. Either he was deliberately ignoring her or he'd been forbidden to speak. If he'd been forbidden to speak, that could only mean that the Council had something to hide.

'What's going on there?' she muttered. They'd probably try to arrest her as soon as she returned. Brégenne sighed. *Nothing has changed.*

But it would. When Iresonté landed the Fist on Rairam's shores, everything would change. She, Nediah and Kait had a lot of work to do. Brégenne pictured the other woman, unable to forget the feel of Kait's arms around her burning chest. She might have died if not for her, but whenever she tried to discuss it, Kait found somewhere else to be. Did she regret helping? Brégenne wondered. Even if she did, it seemed like a turning point. They could never return to how it used to be, those snipes and glares and cutting remarks. Nediah had been a focus for their enmity, but it went further, Brégenne realized, right back to the Nerian and Kait's disregard for the citadel that gave them sanctuary.

She rubbed a hand over her face. *Maybe it's time to put it all aside.*

Her boots scuffed the stone flags. She ought to go back to bed, try to salvage some sleep. But as she passed the door to another room, she noticed a fitful lick of firelight beneath it. So she wasn't the only one still awake. Realizing it was Nediah's door, she found herself trying the handle.

He jumped at the sudden *creak*. 'Sorry,' she hissed, closing the door behind her. 'I saw your light.'

'Brégenne.' Nediah rose as she came into the warm glow of the fireplace. 'You're awake?'

'Couldn't sleep,' she said and then she blinked. 'Nediah, what's that?'

'Oh.' Nediah glanced down at the nest of blankets and bolsters he'd clearly stolen from the bed. 'I got tired of being cold, so I brought the clothes over.'

'Can't be very comfortable,' Brégenne replied, tapping the flagstones with a foot.

'It's not so bad, actually. There are two rugs under here. And it's worth it to be near the fire.'

She shrugged. 'I won't argue with that. It'll be nice to go

south.' She sat down, pulled a blanket around herself and sighed. 'Better.'

Nediah regarded her with a small frown before resettling himself too. 'Wine? I've had it warming.'

'All right. Might help me sleep.' Brégenne accepted a cup. The red wine looked appealing against the beaten silver. 'Where did you get these?'

Nediah gestured to a polished bureau. 'Over there. I think this might have been an officer's room.'

She sipped. The wine tasted how it looked, spiced and dark, coating her throat in pleasant heat.

Nediah poured himself a cup and they sat and drank in companionable silence. It reminded Brégenne of the times they'd travelled across Rairam – then just Mariar – tracking the Breaking, sending the odd report back to the Council, enjoying each other's company. 'We've come a long way, haven't we?' she heard herself say.

'We have.' Nediah smiled.

Brégenne. Why did you do it?

She gazed into the flames, thinking of his question, the question she hadn't yet answered. 'I need to tell you something,' she said.

'Brégenne –'

'Me first.' She carefully placed her wine on the hearthstone before looking back at him. 'You've never asked me how I lost my sight.'

He stiffened. It clearly wasn't what he expected. 'I didn't want to pry,' he said after a moment.

'No.' She paused. 'And I wouldn't have answered if you had.'

'Then, forgive me, Brégenne, but why raise it now?'

Why *was* she raising it? If she told him what she hadn't told anyone, she'd lose him, lose the friendship that meant so much to her. But he wasn't just anyone. That was why he had to know. She swallowed the lump in her throat and steeled herself for the memories to come.

'I started to show signs of being a Wielder when I was ten.' Brégenne shook her head. 'I didn't know what it was then, of course. Just that, whenever the moon rose, I could do things other people could not. I kept them hidden.' She was aware of Nediah's attention, of his gaze on her face as she studied her palms. It was easier to stare at the whorls and lines in her flesh than into that gaze. 'I managed to hide it for two years. But one night, my mother caught me making a flame. She was scared.' Brégenne heard her voice drop. 'I told her it was fine, that it was nothing to worry about. I thought she believed me. We'd always been close.'

'What did she do?' Nediah asked, an edge in his voice, as if he knew what she might say and dreaded it.

'Told her sister. My aunt.' Brégenne picked up her wine, took an unwisely large gulp. 'She trusted her sister, wanted her advice. My aunt said it was nothing to worry about.' Brégenne felt her hand tighten on the cup. 'But then she told my uncle.'

Nediah said nothing. Even the fire's crackle had dimmed, so that Brégenne felt as if she sat in a gloom of quiet. It was harder to force words into it. 'My uncle believed it was witchcraft. Our village was a bit like Kyndra's, sheltered, superstitious. With kind words, he persuaded me to show him what I could do.' Behind her eyes, the images played out, a merry-go-round of faces and silver flames. She drew a breath. 'When he learned I could only use my powers at night, he claimed they were evil.'

'It makes me angry,' Nediah said, 'that so many children

suffer at the hands of the ignorant.' He put down his cup. 'No wonder you were so determined to rescue Kyndra.'

'She reminded me of me,' Brégenne admitted, thinking back to that night in Brenwym, hearing the accusations of witchcraft hurled at Kyndra. 'Brenwym was too close to the bone. I wanted to be out of there. And when the Breaking came, destroying that town, I was . . . glad.' She rubbed a hand over her face. 'That's terrible, isn't it? And Kyndra knew.'

'She didn't know *why*, though.'

'No.' Brégenne put down her wine too. A restlessness was in her; she got to her feet, walked a short distance away. Nediah stayed where he was, watching her. 'We arrived in time to save Kyndra. But Guiliel didn't come in time for me. They took me out into the woods,' she said very quickly, as if she could outrun her memories. 'It was summer, a beautiful day. My mother didn't know.'

'Brégenne,' Nediah said, 'you don't have to—'

'My aunt and uncle were there, my cousins too.' The temptation to stop was overwhelming, but she gritted her teeth. The words were a bitter medicine. 'It began calmly enough. My uncle explained that the moon gave me my powers, that every time I looked up at it, I was filled with evil, with a will to harm.' Her throat tightened and she turned her back to Nediah. 'I tried to say I'd never caused harm,' she told the dark wall, 'that I never would, but he'd made up his mind. He wouldn't listen.'

She heard Nediah rise, heard his footfalls on the carpet, and she held up a hand to stop him, still without turning. 'He ordered my cousins to hold me down. They were bigger, stronger. I was barely thirteen.' She drew a ragged breath. It was in her nose, the scent of crushed grass, flattened by her struggles. 'My aunt held my head. She stroked my hair, pretended compassion. I don't know,' she added in a whisper, 'maybe it was real. Maybe she thought – they all thought – they were doing me a kindness.

'There was pain and . . . between blinks, the sky was gone, the forest was gone. Everything but my own sobs and my cousins' sobs was gone.'

A tear rolled down her cheek. Brégenne let it fall to the carpet before scrubbing the rest away. That bitter medicine churned in her stomach. 'My mother was heartbroken. Beyond heartbroken. She was furious. My father had died years before, so she took matters into her own hands, threatened to kill her sister. My uncle stopped her, of course. They went before the village elders, but were cleared of wrongdoing. Neither my uncle nor aunt were punished.'

Nediah's hand touched her shoulder. Full of remembered horror, Brégenne only just stopped herself from flinching. 'I hid from the moon, from myself. My only comfort seemed to be in believing my uncle. That the moon was evil, that he had saved me.' Once so hard to say, the words were pouring out now, purging. They left a sour taste in her mouth. 'But I couldn't believe it, couldn't accept it. I stopped speaking to everyone, even my mother, who had to help me with everything. I wanted it to end.' She paused. 'And then Guiliel found me.'

'He told you about Wielders,' Nediah murmured, his touch light on her shoulder. 'Took you to Naris.'

Still facing the wall, Brégenne nodded. 'He became my mentor, suggested I find a way to use the Lunar power to see.'

'Brégenne.' Nediah's voice was hushed. 'I'm sorry.'

'That's not all.'

She turned to face him so that his hand slipped from her shoulder. 'I went back.'

A small frown appeared between Nediah's brows. 'To your village?'

'Yes. When I was twenty-five.'

'How did you get out of the citadel?'

'Bribed the Murtans,' Brégenne said.

Nediah half smiled. 'After all those lectures –'

'Yes, well.' She folded her arms. 'It was wrong, foolish. I shouldn't have done it. But it got me out of Naris. I was only thinking of one thing.' She looked up at him. 'Revenge.'

The smile died on Nediah's lips. Brégenne watched it disappear, a cold fist closing about her heart. 'I wasn't that good at Lunar seeing then,' she said, knowing that if she stopped, she wouldn't be able to start again. 'But I was good enough. Twelve years had passed and they were still there, right where I left them. My aunt and uncle. Their children were married by that time and I thought they lived alone. I was wrong.

'I should have taken their sight, forced them to live as I did. But I couldn't. I couldn't inflict that on anyone.' Brégenne's voice hardened. 'So I killed them.'

Nediah went very still.

'I killed them with the Lunar, with the very power they had claimed as evil. They were right, that night. And then my mother walked in.' Brégenne looked at her hands. They were clean and pale, the blood long since washed from them. But sometimes she thought she could still feel it, sticky and worthless. A waste. 'She walked in to see me covered in blood. I still remember her face as she began to scream. Every detail.'

Nediah turned away. She'd expected it, but still that little movement tore at Brégenne's heart. 'Their deaths brought me nothing, no relief, no joy. All I felt was emptiness.' Her voice wavered. 'Until you.'

She thought he trembled a little, but he did not look at her.

'I dedicated myself to Naris, upheld its laws, found potentials, rose high in the Council's favour. I suppose I was searching for a means to wash away my crime. And then you were brought to me,' Brégenne said, smiling, despite everything, at the memory. 'What I thought would be merely another report to write became a pupil, a friend – someone who, in many ways, was like me. In the beginning, it was another chance for absolution. In the end,' she murmured, 'it became something else. Without me ever realizing.'

Nediah let out a long breath. She wished he would turn around. 'No more secrets,' she whispered to his back. 'Now you know who I am.'

Tears threatened; she made to go, but before she could take a step, Nediah turned and seized her arm. 'Brégenne,' he said seriously, looking into her eyes. 'This changes nothing. I have always known who you are.'

She hadn't realized the tears had come despite herself until he kissed them away. His lips were warm on her cheek, teasing out other memories. The way the fire flickered over his skin made her think of all those times they'd camped in the wilderness, the comfort of shared adventure. The day she'd become his mentor and looked into his face for the first time. Their Attunement: more than anything, an acknowledgement of the deeper bond that linked them. There was no one she would rather stand beside. No one in the world she trusted more.

Nediah lowered his forehead to hers. 'Brégenne –' he whispered, but she covered the rest of his sentence with a kiss. Heat raced through her, a shiver on its heels. She tasted the spice on his breath, feeling the firmness of his lips against hers. He drew back slightly, brushed a stray lock of hair away from her eyes, and kissed her again.

Her face was hot; her heart pounded. Leaning against Nediah, she could feel his too, beating in time with her own. Her hands found the ties of his shirt; she undid them, pushing the material aside, sliding her hands up his back from waist to shoulders. He groaned softly and she remembered with a thrill that night in her rooms in Naris, the first sweet shock of touch.

His hands crept beneath her tunic; she let him drag it over her head, dropping it to the floor. Then he swept her up and carried her back to the blankets before the hearth. They fell into them. He trailed fingertips over her breasts, following them with his mouth. Her breath came faster, heat spread to the space between her thighs. Brégenne hooked one leg over his, relishing the feel of his body against hers. Exploring the newness of his bare chest, she traced the narrow strip of hair from the smooth scar beside his heart, to his belly to the waist of his trousers. An ache burned inside her, tingled in the tips of her fingers.

Nediah caught her hand, took his lips from her neck to look at her. 'We don't have to,' he said, voice slightly hoarse, and she knew he was thinking of last time, of the way she'd ended it between them.

Brégenne met his eyes; saw her own desire reflected there. 'I know,' she said. She took his hand, guided it to her own buttons. 'I want to.'

When they lay skin to skin, however, her breath caught, as the old fear threatened to engulf her. She could feel her muscles tightening, the memories of being held down, of being helpless, waiting to seize her again. It was so very difficult to trust. But Nediah stroked her hair, kissed her lips, moving slowly over every part of her, his hands deft and gentle, his mouth hot, until they were both trembling and all the fear was gone.

Later they lay, their faces to the embers, while Nediah traced the pattern on her back with a firm, intent finger. Brégenne shivered. 'Have you seen it?' he asked softly, flattening his palm against her skin. 'The tattoo that came with the Solar?'

'No,' she replied, acutely aware of his body against hers. 'What does it look like?'

'Moonrise,' Nediah said, 'sunrise. A sky.'

Brégenne smiled. 'How poetic.' She stared into the flames and her smile slowly faded. 'Kait won't like this,' she murmured.

'I doubt it will come as a surprise,' Nediah said. Gently, he pulled her over so that they lay front to front. The blankets held their heat, and the fading orange of the fire.

Brégenne looked up at him. 'Why do you say that?'

'Kait knows how I feel. Why do you think she's given you such a hard time?'

'What did you tell her?'

'That things could never be the same between us,' Nediah said, seeming to take her doubt in his stride. 'That I was sorry if I'd led her to believe otherwise.' He sighed. 'It's taking her a long time to accept that neither of us are the same people we were fifteen years ago.' He smoothed a lock of hair away from her ear. 'That maybe I'd come to love someone else, someone very different.'

Her eyes prickled. Brégenne reached up and touched his cheek, the stubble there slightly rough beneath her fingers. 'Nediah. I love you too.'

He lowered his head and kissed her slowly. Desire swept

through her in a wave she wished would last forever. 'Was that so hard?' he asked teasingly, drawing back.

'Yes.' She smiled. 'And no.'

They lay in silence for a time until Brégenne said, 'She helped me. Kait, I mean. She helped me master the Solar.'

Nediah raised his eyebrows. 'She did?'

'When I needed someone, suddenly she was there.' Brégenne met his eyes. 'I know she was probably doing it for you, but I think she saved my life.'

'I'm proud of her,' Nediah said after a moment.

'She won't talk to me now, though. She won't even look at me.'

'Perhaps she's in shock,' Nediah said and Brégenne punched him lightly on the arm.

'I was being serious.'

'So was I.' Nediah's smile faded. 'She just needs time.'

Brégenne listened to the murmuring of the hearth. 'How long until dawn?' she asked.

'Can't you tell?'

She concentrated. Sure enough, she felt a golden thread, much like the Lunar, leading off into the dark. 'Two hours.'

'We've a long journey.' Nediah's green eyes were more amber in the dying firelight. 'We haven't slept.'

She gave him a look. 'Do you *want* to sleep?'

He laughed and caught her up, holding her above him. 'Well it's not like we have anything else to do . . .'

32

Hagdon

He left Parakat in Avery's care.

'Change its name,' he suggested, pulling on gauntlets. 'If we're to turn it into our base of operations, it shouldn't have a name that inspires fear.'

'It will take people a long time to forget,' she replied stonily, eyes flicking from him to the raised portcullis. 'And it's still a fortress, a bastion of Sartya. We should tear it down.'

'One day,' he said. 'For now, it serves a purpose.'

'To you, everything serves a purpose.'

Hagdon didn't deny it. 'We are not in a position to choose, Avery. Parakat is a useful base, if isolated. Until we're in control of Acre –'

'You make us sound as dictatorial as the empire,' she said darkly.

'One thing's for certain – we'll have to be as ruthless.'

She shook her head slowly. 'No. I won't let the Republic stoop to the level of the Fist. We will not take by force.'

He rubbed flecks of rain from his face, watching the two-thousand-strong column winding its way out of the fortress and across the bridge. 'This is no time for idealism.'

'I disagree,' the rebel said, her eyes hard. 'This is the perfect time for idealism. We will begin again with dreamers as well as soldiers.'

Hagdon swallowed his natural retort. Perhaps she was right and he was too cynical by half. He'd been taught to consider an enterprise from every angle, to weigh the odds of success against the consequences of failure. Building a new world was just another battle. A battle vaster than any of them could comprehend, but a battle nonetheless. Avery would realize it eventually.

'Do as you will,' he said to her. 'You're in command here.'

She gave neither thank-you nor acknowledgement, instead saying, 'You cannot let Iresonté win in Rairam. If that land falls to Sartya, the Republic will dissolve around us.'

Hagdon turned, so that his back was to her, his face to the distant east. Wind stirred the hem of his cloak, caught in his feathered mantle. 'If it means my life,' he said softly.

He dreamed.

'James', she whispers, her face silver under the moon. Her cheekbones are ridges of shadow, her eyes pale lakes. He cannot look into them. If he does, he is lost. But her voice implores him, calls him by name. And it has power.

He looks.

At once he wants her, is terrified at the violence of his own emotion. He holds up his hands, as if to ward her off. 'Don't, Irilin.' His voice is a bare whisper, not the command he intends.

She takes his outstretched hands and kisses them. His will crumbles. He pulls her to him. When he tips her face up, there are tears trailing red across her cheeks.

'No,' he gasps, wiping them away, but they come faster. 'You aren't hurt. I said I'd protect you.'

'I am not the one hurt,' she says sadly. 'You are.'

He looks down. There is a rent in his armour, a monstrous gash through which his lifeblood spills waterfall-fast. Light-headed, he dips his fingers, watches the blood spinning to the blackened grass beneath his feet. Pain hits; his knees fold.

Irilin touches the red tears – his blood – that stain her cheeks. 'I am not the one hurt,' she says again. 'James.'

'James.'

Hagdon opened his eyes. As if to prove it was still intact, his heart thudded, making the breath come short and fast in his throat. Irilin knelt beside his pallet, her hand hovering near his face. Without warning, he caught it, held it. She gave a little gasp at the sudden movement. Their faces were inches apart. The pulse fluttered in her throat, in her wrist beneath his fingers. He stared at the pale line of her lips, slightly parted, and at the V where collar framed collarbone. She smelt of the night, crisp and clear; her cheeks flushed from the cold.

Neither of them moved. Thoughts harried each other through his head, thoughts of his dreaming – the desire, the moonlight, the blood. Then Hagdon drew a shuddering breath and let her go. He turned his face to the tent wall, hoping she hadn't seen.

'I'm sorry,' she said, sounding shaken, 'I didn't mean to wake you.'

'I'm glad you did,' he muttered, sitting up. He met her eyes. 'Does this mean you've forgiven me?'

Irilin drew back, rose to her feet. 'I don't know what you mean.'

'Of course,' he said, relieved to hear a little lightness in her tone. 'Sorry.' Hagdon swung his legs off the pallet bed. They felt weak, quivered beneath him. Was it fear?

'You were dreaming,' Irilin said.

'Yes.'

'A nightmare.'

After a moment, Hagdon said, 'Yes.'

She fixed him with the stare he knew too well, the one that went right to his bones. 'Are you worried about the battle?'

'Aren't you?' he countered.

'Of course. But I thought you –'

'Oh no. Every battle is a new monster to be slain. And no matter how many monsters you've felled, the next is always different. And you find yourself thinking, "This time, will I be the one to fall?"'

Irilin folded her arms, seeming exasperated. 'Were you always this dramatic?'

The sound he made was somewhere between a grunt and a chuckle. 'So Carn used to say. Perhaps I should have been an actor.' He sighed. 'But we've a way to go before the battle.' He blinked out at the night. 'Are you sure it's a good idea to go through the hoarlands, especially in the dark?'

For a moment she looked haunted. Hagdon knew she'd lost a friend to the wraiths of the red valley. 'It's the only way we'll catch Iresonté before she reaches the capital,' Irilin said finally. 'We have to try.' There was a certain dark anticipation in her smile. 'Besides, we have Brégenne now. If the wraiths are still there, they won't stand a chance.'

Hagdon stooped, retrieved his belt from the floor. 'Would she really make all the difference? You told me these wraiths sapped a Wielder's power.'

'They do. But Brégenne –' Irilin shrugged. 'Well, she's Brégenne.'

'That argument doesn't fill me with confidence.'

She shook her head, sighed. 'You wouldn't understand.'

'Clearly not. Help me with this?'

He felt her small, deft hands on the buckles of his breastplate, cinching it tight to his body. For some reason, his heart was beating unusually fast. His palms tingled as he stepped away. 'Thank you. Carn usually did this.' He paused. 'It's still strange to me that he's not here.'

'It's still strange to me that Shika's not here,' Irilin said.

'Doesn't get easier, does it?'

Mutely, she shook her head. Looking at her still face, her downcast eyes, Hagdon chided himself. *Trust you to kill the conversation. She doesn't want to hear about death.* 'Come on.' He took her hand by way of apology. 'I've rested enough. I'm sure it's nearly time to leave.'

Her hand tightened on his. Hagdon thought of the dream again, but he didn't let go.

The others had gathered outside. 'The soldiers don't like it,' Mercia said, marching up to him. Like the other Sartyans, she'd painted her armour black to match the Republic's mantles. If they were going up against Iresonté, there needed to be no confusion as to who fought for whom.

'Neither do our forces,' Taske said. The old commandant towered over them both, feathered cloak giving him the look of a giant bird of prey. 'They've all heard the stories. Hundreds have vanished in the hoarlands.'

'But they didn't have Wielders with them,' Hagdon said. 'And besides, that was before the Starborn's intervention.'

'The shortcut would give us a huge advantage.' Taske

stroked his chin. 'How long will it take to cross?'

'With our numbers, about a day,' Irilin said. She glanced at the moon. 'Or a night, rather.'

'We need to risk it.' Hagdon looked around at them all. 'We don't have time to find a way over the mountains. And we don't have ships to carry us. It has to be the hoarlands.'

'I will go first,' Brégenne said, coming up to them. Hagdon studied her. Ever since they'd left Parakat, there'd been something different in her bearing, a new confidence. He was glad she was with them, at least for the crossing to Rairam. Then Brégenne would leave for Naris, while they'd head for the capital to intercept Iresonté. Hagdon fervently hoped she could persuade the other Wielders to fight. They'd been joined by others on the way south: seven Defiant cells, led by a man called Ségin; people Rogan had summoned in the name of the Republic from cities all over Causca and further west. Add in Taske's pledged Sartyans and Mikael's Alchemists, and they were still outnumbered. They needed the Wielders of Naris to tip the balance.

Hagdon frowned. 'Where *is* Mikael?'

'I thought I saw him heading to the lip of the valley,' Irilin said. 'Perhaps he's gone to scout.'

'Great. I had better go after him before he gets himself killed.'

'If the wraiths are still there, they'll only be interested in the Wielders,' Brégenne said. 'We'll go in the vanguard, ensure their attention stays on us.'

Hagdon and Mercia both nodded. All of a sudden, there was tension, as if something they'd only played at had become real. 'See you on the other side,' Hagdon said tensely.

'In Rairam,' Mercia murmured.

He understood. They were about to walk into legend. 'In Rairam,' he agreed.

Irilin looked between them and smiled. 'It's just home,' she said.

33

Brégenne

Her horse stepped onto the red soil.

Braced for assault, Brégenne waited, but nothing tried to claw at the Lunar, nothing coalesced into smoky being. She let out a breath. It didn't mean they were safe. There was a peculiar pressure in the valley. Even the moon had weight here, as if it would fall at any moment, crashing to earth like a great hailstone. No wonder the hoarlands were considered cursed.

Despite Hagdon's protestations, the Alchemist, Mikael, was at her side. He rode with a glass ball in either hand, red and green. 'What do they do?' she asked him, her voice hushed.

Mikael grinned. It seemed nothing much fazed him. 'This one –' he hefted the green – 'releases a toxin that attacks the nervous system. This one –' he hefted the red – 'explodes.' He leaned over conspiratorially, said in an audible whisper, 'The red one's my favourite.'

'Mikael,' Hagdon snapped from behind.

'She asked a question, brother.' The Alchemist stroked the red ball with a thumb before carefully placing it, with an air of disappointment, in a pouch at his waist. 'You're right, though,' he said. 'Firestorm won't do for this situation.'

'Neither will that toxin. We're up against wraiths, Mikael. *Bodiless* spectres. I doubt they possess nervous systems.'

'Holding it makes me feel better,' the Alchemist said and, not for the first time, Brégenne wondered if he wasn't a little bit mad.

They moved deeper into the valley and conversation died. The pressure in the air increased. Irilin rode with her shoulders hunched, Brégenne saw, memories clear on her face. 'It feels like last time,' the young woman whispered. 'Where are they?'

Brégenne felt watched. *Something* was out there. 'Just keep going,' she said in a low voice.

The only things that moved were the stars as they wheeled gracefully overhead. Even the wind ceased; silence reigned in the valley. 'Perhaps whatever Kyndra did destroyed them,' Irilin murmured, but she did not look convinced.

As night dragged towards dawn and they began to near the far side, Nediah spoke up from behind. 'They let us get this far before. Be ready.'

Before he'd finished the last word, Irilin gave a yelp and burst into silver flame.

'That's quite enough of that,' Brégenne said firmly. She leaned over and clamped a hand on Irilin's wrist. The Lunar died immediately.

'How are you doing that?' the young woman asked, her eyes wide. 'I can still feel them, but it's as if you've raised a wall against them.'

'You could do it too,' Brégenne replied, scanning the darkened landscape. It wouldn't be dark for much longer. Ahead of them, the sky was rapidly paling into morning. 'It's the same as imposing a block on another Wielder.' As she spoke, she had a vision of Alandred slamming back against her door, her Lunar block dowsing the silver on his skin. She grinned to herself.

Irilin stared at her. 'Why are you smiling?'

'No reason.' But there *was* a reason: she was trying to distract herself, trying not to look at the lightening sky, knowing what she'd have to do if the wraiths continued their assault. *Give it up*, she thought silently at them. *Don't make me use it.* But she felt the attack strengthen, as more of them scrabbled to tear control of the Lunar away from her and Irilin both.

It was strange to be fighting things she couldn't see. The wraiths' attack was a silent one, and Brégenne felt sweat on her brow. They grew increasingly frantic as the land began to slope upwards to the lip of the valley. The sensation was one of scrabbling, as of fingers desperately seeking purchase on rock. Brégenne steeled herself – they would not reach the far side before the Lunar failed.

She felt a hand on her shoulder. She hadn't realized how tense she'd become. 'I'm here,' Nediah said quietly. 'Remember, Brégenne. You have to seize it.'

The sun crested the ridge. She sensed the wraiths' attention fall away from her, turning to Nediah and Kait. Brégenne let go of Irilin, reached her awareness out to the other Wielders instead. It was easier if she could touch them, but they might have to gallop out of here.

It was as Nediah described. The Solar was like a horse of burning gold that flashed by her. Abandoning fear, Brégenne snatched at its mane.

Instantly, the Solar caught her up; she raced through a realm of fire. But it didn't burn her, not this time. She bent it to her will, just as she did the Lunar, and found it surprisingly pliable in her hands. Before the wraiths could tap power from Nediah and Kait, she blocked them both.

Consternation. Shock. They were base emotions, unsophisticated, but tangible all the same. 'Run,' Brégenne said. The effort of maintaining the blocks and keeping her own connection open turned the word into a growl. She saw Mikael and Hagdon out of the corner of her eye, both scanning the empty slope, unaware of the invisible battle she waged.

'I said run!' she shouted, kicking her horse into a gallop. And then it was a confusion of hooves and shouts, as the message passed back through the ranks. 'Get over the ridge,' she shouted at Nediah. 'Don't give them a chance to steal energy.' Nediah didn't look happy about it, but he and Kait galloped up and out of the valley where the wraiths couldn't follow.

As soon as they were out of range, Brégenne let the blocks on them fade. Holding fast to her own, she wheeled her horse around to guard the rest of the army.

Denied energy, the wraiths couldn't take form. Whatever Kyndra had done to them seemed to have worked – Brégenne spotted a wispy coalescence that struggled vainly to hold a shape before falling to tatters. Still, she held her post until every last soldier had left the valley. Sweat trickled down her neck from the strain of shielding herself. The wraiths' attack only let up once she had put the hoarlands behind her.

'Are you all right?' Nediah came running over, helped her down from the horse.

Brégenne sagged against him. 'Yes. Just tired. Did you ever find out what those things were?'

'Medavle believed they're all that's left of the Yadin,' Nediah said soberly. He looked towards the valley. 'If it's true, they didn't deserve such a fate.'

Brégenne followed him back to the camp they'd set up on the barren rock that marked what she'd once thought the end of the world. To the north-west sprawled the crumbled mountains, Rairam's new border. To the east were the Badlands with Murta the only town for leagues. And to the north . . .

Brégenne turned to look at Naris. The twisted peak she called home. It was as black as ever, its skirts swallowed by the chasm, its summit lost in heavy cloud. She felt a peculiar thrill – of nerves, of excitement, she didn't know. She found Nediah gazing at it too, a remoteness in his green eyes.

'It seems different somehow,' he murmured. 'Smaller than I remember.'

She knew what he meant. Naris had been the centre of her world; it had *filled* her world. But now she'd walked in Acre and had only the barest glimpse of its vastness. There was so much still to see. And this tiny corner of a continent, once so vital, now seemed tucked away, distant and removed.

Yet it was home.

'Janus still won't talk to me,' she said, wondering what the Wielders had planned for her. 'He must be under guard, or being watched.'

'We'll find out soon enough,' Nediah said. He took her hand, long fingers twining through hers. It was a small thing, but Brégenne shivered at his touch. It was still so new – this gentle openness, the absence of uncertainty. He raised a hand to her face, tilted her chin. 'Nediah,' she murmured, 'everyone is looking.'

'Then let them look,' he said and Brégenne just had time to smile before he kissed her. The slow, insistent way he eased his lips over hers still made her knees weak, her heart pound. Nediah did not hurry; by the time he pulled away, she felt a little giddy. 'Later,' he promised with an intensity that made her blush. He let her go and she watched as he went to sort through his pack.

Brégenne glanced around. Everyone suddenly seemed to have something vital to do. She caught Irilin staring at Hagdon, who met her eyes and swiftly looked away. Irilin watched him a moment more before she sighed and went to help Mercia.

'You must think you've won,' came a low voice from behind.

She knew who it was without turning. They were in a little circle of calm – Nediah was out of earshot, Hagdon was speaking to Taske, Mikael walked among his fellow Alchemists, distributing something small from a pouch in his hand.

'It's never been about winning or losing,' she said.

Kait strode into her line of sight. 'Taking the moral high ground, as usual.'

Brégenne felt her stomach clench. 'What do you want from me, Kait?'

'You know what I want, Brégenne. The only thing I've ever wanted for myself.' Her eyes burned; they had that ragged look Brégenne had come to recognize. 'When I joined the Nerian, I gave up my freedom,' Kait said. 'I was selfless. I dedicated myself to a cause that wasn't my own.'

'Selfless – is that what you call it? So it was selflessness that made you rebel against the Council? Selflessness that drove you to murder innocent people? Selflessness that made you abandon Nediah—'

'Don't you dare,' Kait hissed in a low, venomous voice. 'Don't you dare say to *me* –'

'What?' Brégenne advanced on her. 'Say what, Kait? The truth? That you left the man you loved? That the Nerian were more important to you?'

The high spots of colour in Kait's cheeks grew brighter. 'I won't—'

'You have no idea,' Brégenne heard herself say. '*No idea.*' There were tears in her voice, but tears of anger. 'For months, he barely spoke. And when he did, it was to say your name.'

'But you were quick enough to step in,' Kait snarled. 'I thought mentors were supposed to guide and protect their charges, not sleep with them.'

Brégenne flushed. 'I never—'

'No one else would have you. He was vulnerable. So you took your chance.'

Her heart was pounding. 'It wasn't like that. I didn't intend for this to happen.' With renewed anger, she added, 'And I don't see why I should defend myself when I've done nothing wrong.'

Kait stepped close to her, so close that the ends of her long hair brushed Brégenne's shoulder. 'I don't know why I ever helped you.'

'I do. For Nediah's sake. You could have let me die. But then, he'd have died too.' She looked into Kait's brown eyes. 'You could have let me die,' Brégenne repeated more softly, 'but you didn't. You held me when I was alone.'

Kait's step back was almost a stumble. Her eyes shone with tears or chagrin, or was it regret? 'And you knew what you were doing,' Brégenne said. 'What it would mean if Nediah and I both lived.' She'd thought she'd have to force the words out, but now they came freely, as if eager to escape. 'So, though you may not forgive me for it, though you may hate me, I'm thanking you.'

Kait's expression splintered. With a wrenching cry, some-where between rage and grief, she fled into the camp. Shaken, Brégenne watched her go. When she ran past Mercia, the woman abandoned her conversation with Irilin and started after her, calling her name.

Brégenne wasn't even aware of Nediah coming up beside her. 'What was that about?' he asked.

'Nothing.' She couldn't look at him. 'It was nothing.'

Before they left for Naris, she changed into the robes.

She'd found the material in Cymenza, where they'd briefly halted, the city now fully under the control of the Republic. 'Wielders respond to spectacle,' she'd explained, 'as much as they respond to reasoned argument. We have to impress them.'

'You're bringing fifty or so aberrations,' Hagdon had pointed out. 'Isn't that enough to convince them to listen to you?'

'Maybe, maybe not.' Brégenne thought of Alandred, of Veeta, Gend and Hebrin. She remembered the arguments that had forced her to take matters into her own hands. No, she would need something more than a ragged rabble of potentials, even if they were from Acre.

'I think you'll certainly get their attention,' Irilin told her now.

Brégenne ran a hand down the silk. One half of the robes was silver, the other gold. 'I hope so,' she said fervently. 'But I need more than attention. I need their agreement too.'

'Are you ready?' Nediah asked, leading her horse over.

Brégenne took a breath. 'Is Kait coming?'

'I can't find her.' Nediah's gaze strayed to the mountain. 'Somehow I doubt she wants to see Naris again.'

Brégenne felt strangely empty. 'We had better get going, then.' Slightly hampered by the robes, she climbed into her saddle.

'I'm counting on you,' Hagdon told her, standing at her

stirrup. 'If Rairam's to keep its freedom, the Wielders need to fight.'

'They will,' she vowed. 'I will see you in two weeks, where we agreed.'

The dark-eyed commander simply nodded. He glanced at Irilin. 'Are you sure you wish to stay?'

'I'm sure,' she said firmly, a hint of bite in her tone. Brégenne suspected Hagdon had asked the question more than once and received the same response.

She took a last look at their gathered forces. What did they make of this strange, mythical country Hagdon had led them to? Some eyes met hers and she wondered what they saw when they looked at her.

Nediah spoke to the erstwhile prisoners, Reuven at his shoulder. The inmates stared at them both, and for the first time, Brégenne saw true expression on their faces, the blankness washed like mud from their skin. Underneath, amongst the shadows of fear and uncertainty, were the first glimmers of hope.

'No one will try to keep you here against your will,' Nediah said. 'Naris is not a prison. But we ask that you stay to learn the rudiments of control, just as we've been teaching you on your journey here. You wield a power that poses a threat to others, to innocent people. Like every Wielder, you have a duty of care to them. That is the price and the true meaning of power.'

Brégenne smiled. She could not have put it better.

She led the way out of the camp while Nediah walked beside Reuven and the inmates, holding his horse by the bridle. They kept a good distance from the chasm, which the former prisoners eyed fearfully. It was too much like Parakat, Brégenne thought, with a worried glance at their faces. But Reuven didn't spare it a look and the others followed his lead. They arrived at the bridge in less than an hour. When she looked back, Hagdon and his army were hidden by the roll of the land.

Brégenne gazed up at the mountain she called home. Was it really? The many faces of Naris returned her scrutiny with their own implacable judgement. Her actions *would* be judged, of that she was certain, but it could wait. The world could not.

The new bridge wasn't as impressive as the one that had crumbled into the abyss, but it was solid; Brégenne had helped build it. She led the way across. At the great double doors, she paused and Nediah gave her a reassuring smile. She had a sudden wish to be alone with him, to shut out the world and its war, but she squared her shoulders, lifted a hand and the huge doors swung inward.

The hinges creaked, sending echoes down the long passageway beyond. Some of the inmates cried out, eyes fixed on the little fires floating in the air. 'They won't hurt you,' Nediah said, sweeping his hand through one to show them. They didn't seem particularly reassured.

The sound of the doors opening had drawn a gaggle of novices. Brégenne saw recognition in their faces, but they hung back, fearful, it seemed, of her ragged group. When they reached the arch of the atrium, the way ahead was barred by a dozen silken-robed figures.

'Let me through.' Elbowing accompanied the voice as a man pushed his way to the front of the group.

'Hello, Alandred,' Brégenne said with some resignation.

The Wielder stared at her, his gaze flicking from her silver-gold robes to her face, framed by her shorter hair. 'Brégenne. You came back.' Joy seemed at war with dread in his voice.

'Evidently.' She couldn't quite keep the sarcasm out of her reply. 'And I haven't come alone.'

Alandred blinked. He took in the large group that shifted nervously behind her. 'Who are—?'

'Master Brégenne is under arrest,' came a new voice and the crowded novices parted before a tall man. It was Magnus, one of the Wielders sent to capture her. The same one Gareth had struck with the gauntlet.

Perhaps he divined the memory in her face. 'Where is the novice?' Magnus asked darkly. His jaw wasn't quite as it had been, she noticed now. His skin was stretched tightly over the bone, pallid where it had once been olive.

'Gareth is with his people,' she said shortly.

Magnus narrowed his eyes. 'He will be retrieved.'

'I doubt it.'

'Flippancy does you no credit, Brégenne. Who are these people? What do you mean by bringing them here? Answer me.' The final words were an order.

'Don't speak to her like that.' Nediah stepped forward and she put a warning hand on his arm.

'Master Nediah,' Magnus said with a raise of his eyebrows. 'The Council long assumed you had met your end in Acre.'

'I hate to disappoint you, then.'

For the first time, Brégenne spotted the red slashes in Magnus's robes. 'As you see,' he said, noticing her look. 'I was elected to take your place.'

Great. Of all the possible choices . . . 'I want to speak to Veeta and Gend,' she said. 'And then to all of Naris, masters and novices alike.'

'You are in no position to issue demands, Brégenne. As of now, any status you had is revoked. You will be confined until the Council has met to discuss your fate.'

Brégenne sighed. 'I won't ask again, Magnus.'

The other Wielder's look turned ugly. 'You are also in no position to resist.' He raised a hand and a golden chain dangled from his fingers. With a flick of his wrist, it flew at her, binding her hands before her, snapping her ankles together. A collective gasp came from the assembled novices.

Brégenne regarded him calmly. 'Take these off, please. I have no wish to fight you in front of the novices.'

Magnus just stared at her. And then he began to laugh, the sound echoing hollowly in the vaulted passage. No one joined him. Brégenne felt the combined gaze of the inmates on her back, waiting for her response.

'You astonish me, Brégenne,' Magnus said, humour finally fading. 'Even when we had you cornered in Market Primus, utterly defenceless, you persisted in thinking the rules didn't apply to you. Nothing has changed, it seems.'

'The rules *don't* apply to me,' she said and snapped the chains.

For a startled moment, Magnus just stared at her. Then, as she raised a hand wreathed in Solar flame, his face drained of colour. 'Impossible.'

With a twitch of her fingers, Brégenne thrust him aside. Magnus skidded, collided with the wall. 'I did warn you,' she said. She began to walk, the crowd bending before her like meadow grass before the wind.

Behind her, Magnus growled, but she'd been waiting for it. A golden chain flew from her hand, wrapped around his wrist and returned to her. She heard his strangled curse as he tried to grasp the Solar and failed. It was the same trick she'd used on Alandred. A glance at him showed he knew it too; he was faintly smiling. Instead of leaving Magnus, Brégenne strengthened the chain and started walking again, forcing the Wielder to stumble along in her wake. The muttering became exclamations as she dragged the newest member of the Council into the bright atrium.

It didn't take them long to arrive. 'What is the meaning of this?' Veeta cried as she strode across the space, her red-slashed robes swirling in her wake. For a moment, Brégenne thought of her predecessor, Helira, of her chill eyes, her cheeks like plains of ice. But Veeta's were flushed, her anger hotter, less contained. It was difficult, sometimes, to remember that they used to be friends.

She dumped Magnus at the other woman's feet. He tried to claw at the Solar, but her block held. 'You can't do this,' he snarled, stumbling as far away as her tether allowed. 'I am a member of the Council.'

'So was I,' Brégenne said, 'so you see how little your title impresses me.'

'Brégenne.' Gend had arrived soundlessly. She'd forgotten how huge and still he was, rather like the mountain that enclosed them. 'So you've returned.'

'Skip the lecture,' she snapped, nettled now. 'My news can't wait.'

Veeta opened her mouth, furious, but then she seemed to register Brégenne's Solar glow and her words died.

'She's cutting me off,' Magnus snarled. 'It has to be a trick.'

'Trust you to touch on the issue of *least* importance,' Brégenne said. 'Yes, I wield the Solar too. Yes, I've brought you fifty untrained Wielders. But it's imperative I address everyone right now.'

She watched Veeta's eyes move beyond her to Nediah and Reuven, who stood guard over their ragged charges.

'I bring news of war,' Brégenne said. 'A Sartyan general has marched her army into Mariar – into Rairam. By all reports, she is making for the capital.'

'We know,' Veeta said crisply. 'A Murtan trader brought the tidings several days ago.'

Brégenne blinked at her. 'You know? Then *why* are you still trying to arrest me?'

'If you thought your news would somehow excuse your past actions, you are quite mistaken.'

Brégenne shook her head, stunned. She'd known it would be hard, but this . . .

'Look at you.'

Heads turned at the new voice, roughened by years in chains. It was a voice, Brégenne thought, which had seen and suffered and endured. Reuven scanned the atrium, his gaze taking in novice and master, lingering on sumptuous robes, the healthy glow in faces. 'Look at you,' he repeated disdainfully. 'None of you have felt even a splinter of the torment these people have borne.' He lifted a hand to the former inmates of Parakat. Haunted eyes looked back at him. 'As I approached this place, surrounded by an abyss, I thought for a brief moment that I would find the same. Instead, I see you well fed, content, safe. The abilities that doomed us to a life of imprisonment are here nurtured and rewarded.' He slowly shook his head. 'You have no inkling, no clue, how fortunate you are, how kind life has been to you.

'But we have come here to tell you, at Brégenne's behest, that if you disregard the Sartyan threat, our fate will be yours. We have come to show you our faces and the marks scored in our skin. Look your fill. This is the only warning you will get. It is more than we received.'

In another person, Brégenne would have called it a good

speech, but that would have belittled the truth. Reuven was the centre of a vast silence that rippled out into the hall. Before she could break it, Alandred said, 'Tell us what you know, Brégenne.'

She gave him a grateful nod. 'The Sartyan emperor is dead, killed by insurrection. Now the bulk of the army is led by a woman called Iresonté, who intends to capture Rairam, finishing what the first emperor, Davaratch, began. There is a resistance movement in Acre called the Republic, which Nediah and I have been helping, but alone it isn't strong enough to defeat the Fist. They are at the very least thirty thousand strong. And they have ambertrix, a force that can counter a Wielder's power.'

Murmurs of disbelief. 'It's true,' Nediah said, coming to stand at Brégenne's side. 'Brégenne has experienced it herself. One shot or strike with an ambertrix weapon can shatter a shield.'

'They can only be destroyed through conventional means,' Brégenne added, 'or by manipulation of conventional means.'

'How are we to fight them, then?'

Brégenne's sharp ears plucked the anonymous question out of the air. 'By marching out to meet them, by refusing to let history repeat itself. We will not suffer the siege that doomed Solinaris. We can sit out this battle, let Iresonté take the capital. But make no mistake: she *will* come for us. And when she does, Naris will fall.'

Mutters greeted her this time. She saw the beginnings of fear on some faces. Others, mostly masters, looked dubious, but none scoffed openly. Perhaps they felt the threat of Parakat which Reuven had conjured in the hall.

'What of the Starborn?' Alandred asked finally. 'What of Kyndra?'

Others picked up his words. 'Where is she? Will she fight?'

'Kyndra fights her own battle,' Brégenne said. 'There are people in Acre who have the power to alter the past. If they succeed, nothing we do here will have any meaning.'

As she knew it would, the declaration raised more questions than it answered. Brégenne used the Solar to magnify her voice and the shouts died, perhaps at her obvious exercise of a power she should not have been able to wield.

'I will be happy to share everything I know about Sartya and Acre. I will pledge to lead those who choose to defend Naris –' she glanced at the members of the Council – 'but I cannot do so from behind bars. Everything I have done has been in service to this citadel and to Rairam. If I took matters into my own hands, it was because no one else recognized the danger.' She paused to look into all the faces turned to her. 'The danger is *real*. And it's here.'

34

Char

The Khronostian children were fascinated by the Lleu-yelin, as well as scared. Char could feel them staring at his scales, at his folded wings that elicited gasps whenever he extended them. They wouldn't leave Ma's side, but clung to her legs, watching everything through huge haunted eyes. 'What are we going to do with them?' he asked.

Ma glanced down at her passengers. 'I don't know. They cannot stay here.' She had her back turned to the eerie silence of Khronosta, as if unwilling even to look at the temple she'd once called home. Char felt sick at the thought of what she'd found inside. How much had these children seen before they were locked away? It was plain the eldest never intended for them to be rescued, but to burn along with the temple in dragons' fire. 'And they cannot come with us,' Ma added. 'We've wasted enough time. The eldest and his *du-alakat* will be half-way to Naris by now.'

'I don't understand,' Kyndra said. She didn't look well, Char thought. The skin on her left side had a greyish tinge; he could see the marks of the eldest's curse as mottled fingers creeping towards her neck. 'Why would he go to Naris, to the Wielders' stronghold? When he travelled back before, he didn't have to be geographically near New Sartya.'

Ma pressed her lips together in thought. 'You say you stopped the eldest by separating him from Medavle?'

'He's trying to prevent me from doing it again?'

'It is the only reason I can think of to explain his going to Naris.' Ma studied her. 'The Yadin was involved in Kierik's downfall. He is intimately connected to the time and place it happened. On the ground from which Solinaris once rose, his link with the eldest will be stronger – strong enough, I fear, that merely separating them a mandala's length apart will not . . .' She trailed off, worry in the whites of her eyes. It made Char want to go to her, but what comfort could he offer?

'Ma?' Kyndra said.

One of Ma's hands rested on the tallest girl's shoulder. 'We must follow him and quickly. We've lost time coming out here. Can you warn the Wielders?' she added to Kyndra.

The Starborn nodded. 'I will send a message to Brégenne. She and Nediah should be in Naris by now.' Kyndra swept a hand through the air and a formless shadow appeared beneath her fingers, two shining points of light that Char couldn't help but imagine as eyes. Kyndra concentrated for a few moments before banishing the thing with another wave. The gesture was casual, but Char, watching closely, saw a spasm pass across her face.

'You're in pain,' he rumbled softly.

She looked at him, vulnerable for a moment. 'It's more a feeling of weakness. But I'm all right. Whatever Ma did is holding it off.'

'Not for long, girl.' Ma studied her, eyes lingering on Kyndra's greying neck. As if embarrassed by the gaze, Kyndra pulled her collar closed with a grimace, hiding the wasted flesh.

'And what do you intend for us, Starborn?'

Sesh had listened impassively to their conversation, but now she came to stand before Kyndra, golden eyes narrowed on her face. 'Do not seek to trick us. If we fly to this Naris in pursuit of vengeance, we will conveniently be in position to fight the Sartyan army which marches on your home. Isn't that what you intend to ask of us?'

Though Sesh towered over her, Kyndra had her own height, Char thought, in the tilt of her chin, in her stance that proclaimed she could burn the world if she so chose. A memory came, of standing shoulder to shoulder with her in Rogan's parlour, gazing at the beauty of the Lleu-yelin caught in the threads of a tapestry. So much had happened since that evening. Char flexed his taloned feet, felt the weight of the horns that curled from his head, the delicate membranes of his folded wings. Only the ambertrix remained the same – that roiling turmoil deep in his chest.

'I don't intend to ask anything of you,' Kyndra said, unflinching. 'Your help would be appreciated, but you are a free people.'

Sesh chuckled darkly. 'A free people except for our amberstrazatrix. If Sartya is defeated and everything you work for comes to pass, nothing will change. Men still crave power.'

'That is in your hands.' Kyndra's expression hardened. 'But remember the lesson of Sartya. An empire was founded on the power you traded away. That decision led to five hundred years of conquest and, ultimately, your imprisonment. The consequences cannot always be foreseen.'

'If I desired a lecture, I would ask for one,' Sesh retorted. She folded her arms, rattling the mesh armour against her scales. 'But very well, Starborn. We will see this through. As soon as it's done, we return to Magtharda. A new Chimer must be chosen.'

'I'm grateful for your help.' Kyndra turned to the others. 'We need to go.' Her eyes flickered to the children. 'Could we perhaps leave them with Rogan in Cymenza?'

Ma bent down. None of the children had spoken a word since being rescued. 'I must go away for a time,' she told them. 'And it is too dangerous to take you with me.' She cupped one girl's chin, her hand dark against the child's paler skin. 'But I will come back. I will come back as I came back before. And this time, I will not leave you.'

'Another cold ride,' Realdon Shuñe grumbled, eyeing the dragons and their rough hides. 'But,' he stroked his chin, 'I have to say, I'm curious to see Solinaris again.'

'It's not Solinaris any more,' Kyndra said. 'You won't recognize it.'

'My bones will.' In the lined face, Char thought he detected a pain as ancient as Shune himself. 'No matter how many years pass, or how many stones come loose from its walls, no man forgets his home.'

35

Gareth

For all their boasting, the northerners had no stomach for death. It disgusted them – the stench, the bodies, the flies that even the cold didn't dissuade. Death turned the forest into a brutal place, where the clash of steel frightened off the beasts Ümvast's people relied on for food, fouled the river where they filled their skins. Death was an invasion more terrible than the Sartyan horde.

The plan had worked too well. One failure of discipline in unknown territory had led to a sordid week-long pursuit through thick snows and biting chill. The Sartyans had scattered into the forest where they were easier to pick off. Still, they'd put up a fight and the northerners had lost their fair share of warriors too. They'd have lost more if not for him.

Gareth sat with his head in his hands. It was better to stare at the dark between his fingers than at the chill faces of his own people. They knew what he was – they'd known it even before *he* had. Kingswold hadn't spoken to him again. He didn't need to; Gareth could feel him there now like his own shadow. A shadow that grew stronger every time he called on the power of the gauntlets.

Now he cursed himself for his foolishness. Even the smallest use strengthened Kingswold. For the moment, Gareth was in control. But for how long? What would happen when Kingswold finally became strong enough? Would Gareth be reduced to a voice in *his* head? The northerners relied on him to lead them. They relied, however unwillingly, on the power of the gauntlets.

Would he save his people only to lose himself?

They'd taken about five hundred prisoners. Where pride had once injected defiance, the cold and the terror of the dead had drained the Sartyans of everything except defeat. Weaponless, they huddled under the lifeless gaze of their own commander. Gareth had installed him there as warden; a constant reminder of the fate that awaited any rebellion. When he walked among them, none would meet his eyes.

Neither would Ümvast's men.

Ümvast herself pretended composure whenever they spoke. But Gareth knew the truth: even his mother feared him. And now he knew she was right to do so.

I think my son never left those tombs. I think he died there in the darkness and the dust.

He did die there, Gareth thought at her. *He just didn't realize it.*

'What are we going to do with the prisoners? Force them to fight for us?'

Gareth raised his head to find Kul'Das standing beside him. She shivered and shrugged deeper into her fur cloak. Here on the plains, they did not have even the luxury of leafless trees to stem the wind.

'They can fight for us or die,' Ümvast said. She came to stand on his other side, keeping her distance.

'They may pledge to fight now, but what happens when they meet their comrades on the field?' Kul'Das's face was bleak. 'There is nothing to stop them switching allegiance.'

'Nothing except Kul'Gareth.'

His mother had always been a hard woman to read; looking at her now, Gareth could not guess her thoughts. She'd stopped referring to him as her son.

'You think their fear of him will stand even then? Would they really fight for their murderers?'

'You ascribe your own principles to them,' Gareth said suddenly. He rose to his feet. 'Sartyans are not like you. If they are defeated, they are defeated.'

Kul'Das frowned. 'Meaning what?'

'Meaning they have a certain honour. We won. They might not like it, but they'll accept it. They wouldn't be allowed to return to the Fist anyway, after such a defeat.'

Both women were silent and the authority with which he'd been speaking abruptly deserted him. Another vestige of Kingswold? Gareth shuddered. Were signs like these his only clues? That gradually, inexorably, *Gareth* would fade and Kingswold would take his place? A Kingswold that wore Gareth's face.

'Iresonté is burning villages along the coast,' Kul'Das said. 'Brégenne sent an envoi. They can see the smoke from Naris.' She gazed at their own army, a fiery blot on the plains. 'We need to pick up the pace.'

'I will take my ship and scout ahead,' Argat said, striding up to them. The captain wore a borrowed fur mantle about his shoulders and a hood hid his thinning hair. 'Yara is checking her over as we speak. I'll be ready to fly as soon as the sky lightens.'

'It's a good idea,' Gareth said before Ümvast could voice an objection. 'Argat has already had dealings with the Trade Assembly. By now they'll have seen the threat for themselves.' He glanced at the Sartyan captives. 'They didn't believe it the last time we were there.'

'More fool them,' Argat spat on the frozen ground. 'They'll believe it when they're knee-deep in the rubble of their hall.'

'Hagdon will have enough problems reaching the capital before Iresonté,' Gareth continued, 'let alone having to deal with the Assembly. Do whatever you can to help, Argat.'

'I don't need telling,' the captain snapped. 'How long will it take you to reach Market Primus?'

'Two weeks, if we march until after sundown each day,' Ümvast said. 'We leave at dawn.'

Argat gave a curt nod. It was the closest he ever came to a respectful gesture. 'Two weeks, then.' He turned and made his way through their forces. Beyond the torches that marked the boundary of their camp, the airship loomed as a blacker shadow against the dark.

'We ought to retire,' Kul'Das said. 'It will be a hard march.'

That same night, someone tried to kill him.

Hond'Myrkr warned him of the danger. He'd been dreaming of a tangled forest and a nameless pursuit. Whether he was hunter or hunted, he didn't know, but the liquid eyes of deer observed him from under leafy boughs and it was their silent scrutiny that he ran from. Without warning, Hond'Myrkr began to smoke, a choking stench that caught in his throat and eyes, blinding him so that he blinked and coughed himself awake.

The knife poised over his throat trembled once before plunging downwards.

Gareth rolled; the blade hit the pillow, snagged in its thick folds. Straw spilled out. Lunging to his feet, he swung at the cloaked figure and sent it sprawling over a chest full of maps. He snatched up the knife and advanced on his would-be assassin, who was desperately trying to regain their feet. In one swift motion, Gareth tore off the hood.

'I'm sorry,'

It was just a boy. He couldn't be older than fifteen, brown haired like the rest of his people. His eyes widened as they stared up at Gareth, his struggles to rise temporarily ceasing. 'What are you called?' Gareth asked him.

'Vareg.'

Gareth tossed the knife in his hand. 'And why were you trying to kill me, Vareg?'

'It was the straw,' the boy said, pulling a long piece of string from his belt. 'I drew it.' His gaze followed the tumbling passage of the knife. 'Please don't kill me.'

'I'm sure you can see, Vareg, why such a request elicits little sympathy.' Gareth raised an eyebrow. 'You were not about to show me the same courtesy.'

The boy stuck out his chin. 'I had to do it. I couldn't back down in front of the others. It would have been dishonourable.'

'You were about to slit a sleeping man's throat. I find it hard to see the honour in that.'

Vareg's lip trembled. After a moment's consideration, Gareth said, 'Tell me. Who put you up to this?'

The boy shot a covert look towards the tent entrance. 'I can't tell you. They'd kill me if I told.'

'And I will kill you if do not,' Gareth said with a suggestive flick of the knife. The lantern light shivered along its dull grey length.

The boy licked his lips. He glanced again at the canvas flap as if estimating whether he could reach it before the knife found him. 'I wouldn't try it, if I were you,' Gareth advised.

Vareg sagged. 'It was Egil,' he confessed with the look of someone standing on the scaffold. 'And six others.'

'Egil?' Gareth blinked. That *was* surprising. Despite their earlier confrontation, he'd considered the man an ally, at least, if not a friend. 'So you drew lots?' he asked.

The boy nodded mutely, eyes never leaving the knife.

'And you were unlucky.'

Vareg said nothing. His swallow was loud in the silence. 'You'll give me their names,' Gareth told him. 'It is not a request.'

Slowly, as if each word sapped a little of his strength, the boy said, 'Rolff and Ofina Gray-son, Hilde Shanter-son, Avul-staid Bern-son, Gudrun Sreth-son, Nilsene Anders-son.' The last name was a whisper and he wilted once it had left his mouth.

'Thank you.' Gareth stashed the knife. Vareg watched it disappear and glanced hopefully at the entrance once more. 'You may go.'

The boy jumped up with a relieved gasp, but had taken only a few steps before Hond'Myrkr's power pulled him up short. Gareth crooked a finger, wrenched Vareg's arms to his sides, rooted his feet to the floor. Little tendrils of black held them there, crisscrossing his boots like vines. 'You may go *when* I've given you my reply.'

'Reply?' The word emerged as a whisper over strained chords.

'To your murderous compatriots.'

'I'm sorry.' Vareg panted, throat bobbing nosily with each swallow. 'We won't try again.'

'I know, but I am glad to hear you say it.'

'Don't you – don't you want to know why?'

'I don't need to know why. It is simple enough.' Gareth stooped slightly to look him in the eyes. 'All men crave power and envy those who wield it. This is not the first time someone has tried to kill me. And it will not be the last.'

Vareg looked as if he wanted to shrink back, though he couldn't move. 'My reply,' Gareth said, straightening. 'Yes.'

With a silent command, he bade the tendrils weave slowly up the boy's legs. Vareg tried to scream; only a gasp emerged. His eyes were huge, straining as the tendrils encircled his heart.

'*You* are my reply,' Gareth murmured into the boy's ear. 'I will send you back to them, as a warning and a promise. When the next traitorous thought crosses their minds, they need only look at you to be reminded of the fate that awaits them.'

The boy shuddered. His hands clenched and unclenched, grasping vainly at the air. They were such little hands, barely large enough to hold a sword . . .

The thought was like a blade to the heart. Gareth blinked, gasped, staring at the tendrils spidering from Hond'Myrkr. With a cry of horror, he dampened them. The boy's body crumpled to the floor. Gareth knelt to shake him, mouthing the same word over and over. The boy couldn't be dead. If the boy was dead, it meant *he*, Gareth, had killed him – for who else would people see when they looked at him?

Why? he cried silently, holding the limp body. *Why would you do this?*

'You see how they fear you?' It was his own voice, issuing from his own throat. But it wasn't *Gareth*. 'They plot,' Kingswold said. 'They scheme and they snivel. You cannot allow it to stand.'

'He was just a boy,' Gareth snarled, wrenching his voice back. He hadn't even *felt* Kingswold take control. Was there already no barrier, no difference between them?

Boys grow into men, Hrafnasueltir. If not for me, you would never have woken.

His hands shook inside the gauntlets. No, Gareth realized, just one hand. The fist encased in Hond'Lif lay calm and still upon his left knee. Staring at it, he whispered, 'I wish I hadn't.'

36

Brégenne

She woke quite suddenly in Nediah's arms.

At first she had no idea where they were. Brégenne blinked the blurry image into clarity and her sleep-muddled mind recognized her old room in Naris. That's right – they'd given her Council apartment to Magnus. She preferred it here anyway.

Her skin prickled.

Goosebumps rose on her arms and the feeling that had woken her intensified. 'Nediah,' she hissed, wondering why she was keeping her voice low. 'Wake up. Something isn't—' She broke off as a formless shadow coalesced in the air. Two points of light burned like eyes.

Brégenne. It was Kyndra's voice. *The eldest comes for Naris. Warn the Wielders.* It faded, taking the Starborn's voice away.

Nediah opened his eyes blearily, his smile dying on his lips when he saw her face. 'What is it?'

'Khronostians,' she said, scrambling up, pulling on clothes. 'They're coming here.'

'What?' Nediah jumped up too and Brégenne wondered if he felt what she felt: a sense of invasion beating through the

409

stone heart of Naris. Both dressed, they stepped into the corridor and heard screaming. Brégenne looked at Nediah and they broke into a run.

Two hours past dawn. All the Lunars in the citadel would be defenceless, Brégenne thought as she dashed down the passageways, her feet carrying her automatically to the atrium. The screaming grew louder; she could feel Solar energy ripped from the sky in great bursts. They were fighting for their lives.

Panting, Brégenne burst into the huge echoing space. Bandaged figures wove and danced between its walls and Nediah seized her wrist. '*Du-alakat.*' He had seen them before, of course. But Brégenne only knew what they'd told her.

The Khronostians moved with a desperate intent, their weapons a blur. Brown-robed bodies littered the floor, but Master Kael was down and Barrar too, a Lunar, bleeding from a staved-in skull.

Brégenne clenched her fists, a terrible anger rising. How dare they come here? How dare they harm children? 'Brégenne –' she heard Nediah warn, but she was already moving.

'Shields!' she yelled, her magnified voice slicing through the screams. 'Novices – to me.' As she walked, she brought her hands together and swiftly apart; a huge golden net flew outwards: a *khetah*, the shield they'd used to protect Naris from the Breaking. It was supposed to be maintained by a dozen Wielders, but Brégenne knew she could hold it alone, at least as long as it took to get the novices to safety. She felt the far edges strengthen and looked back to see Nediah holding them together.

White-faced, the novices ran for her, ducking behind the shield. She felt some of the older ones bolster the *khetah* and she nodded gratefully. Blows rained off the bright Solar walls that guarded them, but in vain. Only ambertrix could have broken through.

Brégenne and her charges backed towards the largest passage and the *du-alakat* turned their attention to the lone masters left in the hall. She hoped they were smart enough to put up shields of their own. 'Warn others,' she told the novices as she let go of the *khetah*. 'Then get away from here. Use the tunnels beneath the kitchens and take the Murtans with you.'

'Master Brégenne?' It was Ranine, Janus's friend. There were tears in her eyes. 'I can't find Janus. Please tell him of the danger.'

Janus, Brégenne said across the bond, *where are you? The citadel's under attack.*

I know, came his reply. *I am going to fight.*

No – She cursed. 'Ranine, take the novices and go. I'll see if I can find him.'

The round-faced girl gave her a tremulous look, but she collected up the children and, with a last beseeching plea, led them away.

Nediah at her shoulder, Brégenne turned back towards the atrium. 'How did they get here?' he said, as they both summoned their own shields. 'What do they want?'

The moment she stepped back into the vast hall, Brégenne saw the eldest. Kyndra had described him – a bent figure, more creature than man, grasping a staff nearly half his height again. Medavle stood guard at his side.

The Yadin was changed. Lines scored his once-ageless face, which had a sunken look, as if some vital force had been drained from him. His white robes were stained, ripped at cuff and hem, and he was unshaven. Still, as his black eyes swept over her, they burned with resolve.

The eldest held up a shrunken hand. Time slowed . . . stopped.

A *boom* shook the atrium. Brégenne blinked. The eldest had vanished and reappeared towards the back of the hall and the *du-alakat* had fanned out through the Wielders, their sticks against now-unprotected throats. Time had passed – or hadn't – as she'd stood frozen. But something had happened to speed it up again. The eldest fixed his gaze on the archway that led outside.

Kyndra stepped into the atrium.

Power rippled off her, an aura that made Brégenne's ears ring. She saw her as if through a heat haze; each footfall rang on the polished floor. A tall woman walked at her side: Ma, Brégenne presumed, noticing the symbols that swirled across her palms. Beneath his hood, the eldest's lips twisted in annoyance, in distaste. But the *du-alakat* looked less sure. Some eyed Ma's upturned palms with a certain reverence. White serpents surfaced in her flesh, coiled their tails about her wrists, constantly moving.

'Stop.' Kyndra's command filled the space, rebounded from the distant ceiling. 'It ends here.'

'No,' the eldest hissed. 'It begins here.' He struck the floor with his staff. White sand rained from the bottom, as if the wood were hollow and filled with it. With a dexterity that belied his age, the eldest swung the staff in concentric circles, creating a crude mandala.

Ma frowned. 'Eldest, wait. How do you intend to travel without dancers? The *du-alakat* cannot dance *and* defend themselves from us.'

'They will not have to.'

Brégenne watched a slow horror dawn on Ma's face. 'You do not intend to return.'

The eldest continued his sand-drawing, the *du-alakat* falling back to guard him. 'I go to create a better future,' he gasped. 'What need have I to return to this broken time?'

Ma's hands tightened around her drawn kali sticks. 'You sacrificed my people for this power. Countless innocent lives.'

'Our people readily gave them,' the eldest spat, 'to see Khronosta renewed.'

'They are not *your* people.' Ma's voice promised violence. 'You are a murderer. And you do not speak for the dead.'

'Medavle,' Kyndra appealed to the Yadin. 'The eldest is wrong. He cannot build a better future. All he can do is destroy the only one we have.'

The Yadin frowned, glanced at the eldest. 'What do you mean?'

'Too many threads connect at Solinaris. If they are unpicked, the stars cannot see beyond the moment of change.' She took a step towards him. 'There won't be a past, present or future. There won't be a world.'

For the first time since Brégenne had seen him, the resolve in Medavle's face flickered. 'Is it so dangerous?' he asked the eldest.

'After the road we've travelled together, you would turn for home *now*?' The wizened man brought his staff to a halt. 'When we are nearly at our destination?' His eyes narrowed. 'When you are minutes from seeing Isla again?'

The Yadin looked back at her. 'I am sorry, Kyndra.'

'He's manipulating you,' she said, sounding almost sad. 'You would doom the world for a woman?'

'I know,' Medavle answered her, 'and yes. A thousand times.'

As the sand began to glow, its grains rising into the air to cocoon the eldest and his *du-alakat*, Medavle held out his hand to the ancient Khronostian, who took it. The hall distorted around the group and they disappeared.

Kyndra fell to one knee with a gasp, good hand braced against the floor. Brégenne hurried over. The Starborn's face had a bluish tinge, visible even under the points of light that pulsed in her skin. 'Kyndra,' Brégenne helped her to her feet, 'are you all right?'

Kyndra swallowed grimly. 'I don't think so, Brégenne. I don't have long unless I can catch the eldest.' She looked at Ma. 'Surely Medavle won't be so keen to help when he discovers the eldest intends to save Kierik. If I could just show him the truth –'

'I should begin charging for my services.' Realdon Shune limped into the atrium, sharp eyes ranging over the rugged walls, the pillars with their carven beasts, the polished floor. 'So this is what became of Solinaris.' Sadness hid beneath his scorn. 'The Wielders truly fell from grace.'

'What is going on here?'

Brégenne sighed. They did not have time for the Council. 'Who are these people, Brégenne?' Veeta said. She led the group, Magnus and Gend at either shoulder. Her eyes widened as she noticed the bodies on the floor. Rushing to one, she knelt and turned it over.

'Cail,' Kyndra said suddenly, from behind. The novice was clearly dead, blue eyes open, fixed on nothing. 'I knew him,' the Starborn added, 'from Rush's class.'

'Who has done this?' Veeta asked thickly, one hand on Cail's still chest. Nediah was moving from body to body, aglow with healing energy, but only a handful needed it. The rest were already beyond help.

'Khronostians,' Brégenne said, coming over to stand beside Cail's body. He looked so young, a bloody bruise marring the side of his head. She felt her anger surge up anew. 'They will answer for these deaths.'

'Vengeance will make no difference to him,' Veeta said. She stroked the boy's fair hair away from his eyes and rose unsteadily. 'Tell me everything.'

'Later,' Kyndra said harshly. 'Ma, send me back.'

'You are weakening,' she replied. 'You cannot go alone'

Kyndra's eyes narrowed. 'I can manage.'

'This is too important. Remember – you don't have control of your power in Kierik's time.'

The Starborn threw up her hands. 'Who, then? The Wielders have to stop Iresonté.'

Just then Brégenne became aware of a huffing, scrabbling sound from the mouth of the passage that led to Naris's entrance. It went on for a few seconds, growing louder all the time. The nearest masters began to edge away.

With a triumphant gasp, a dragon burst into the atrium.

Brégenne felt her eyes widen. Hearing about the Lleu-yelin and seeing one in the flesh were two very different things. The dragon was perhaps thirty feet long from nose to tail and dusky black. Claws left scratches on the stone; its neck was fringed with wicked spines, which bristled at the Solar spears aimed at it.

'Stop!' Kyndra yelled. 'Char is with us.'

Ma put her hands on her hips and turned to face the dragon. 'I told you to stay outside.'

'Sesh is getting impatient,' Char said, his mane only flattening once the threat of the spears passed. 'The last time she was impatient, the Lleu-yelin attacked Khronosta.'

'Well, then,' Ma said, 'I hope you are ready.'

'Wait.' Kyndra looked between the two of them. 'You're sending Char with me? *A dragon?* How am I going to explain a dragon?'

'He won't be a dragon in the past.'

Char stilled. 'What?'

'I suspect the river will force you back into your previous shape. It will only be temporary. Once you return here, your pattern will reassert itself.'

Char shook his scales, as if shivering at the possibility. 'But why?'

'Time is a form of disintegration. You are travelling to an era in which you never existed. Thus the river will force you to reconstruct yourself. You lived most of your life as a human.' Her gaze was shrewd. 'It is how you still see yourself, Boy.'

When Char seemed speechless, Kyndra said, 'But it's not the same for the eldest. He looked no different when I travelled back before.'

Ma shook her head. 'He wouldn't. The disfigurements of his body were caused by the river in the first place. I told you. The mandalas were never meant to be used in the way he used them. The river has warped his pattern forever.'

Kyndra was silent. She looked at Brégenne and Brégenne found herself mesmerized by her eyes. If she gazed into them long enough, the stars gazed back. 'Go, Kyndra,' she heard herself say. 'We have our own battle to fight here.'

'Will it not tax you to send us both?' Kyndra asked Ma.

'Yes. But we have our anchor.' She nodded at Shune. 'I can

maintain the connection with his help.' Ma gestured at the disturbed sand, scattered in the eldest's wake. 'I will copy the eldest's signature so I can send you to the same hour he travelled to. We have talked too long.'

'Wait.' Veeta held up a hand. 'I do not understand any of this. You speak of Solinaris, of going back in time. It is impossible.'

'I can't promise to explain it well to you,' Brégenne said. 'But I will try. Right now, Kyndra has to go.'

'You would leave us to face a threat as great as this Iresonté without our chief weapon?' Gend's deep voice was disbelieving. 'You say the army is thirty thousand strong. There are perhaps seventy of us who can fight and only during the hours our power is active. How are we supposed to succeed without a Starborn's help?'

'We have other allies to call upon.' Brégenne nodded at Char. 'Your people?'

He nodded. 'Sesh has already agreed to help.'

'And Iresonté will get no reinforcement from her northern army,' Brégenne continued. 'Gareth reports they were defeated. He and Ümvast are marching south as we speak.'

'I am not sure we want his "help",' Magnus said darkly, touching his scarred jaw.

'We are not in a position to refuse it.' Brégenne looked once more at Kyndra. 'Go.'

Since Ma deemed it safer to perform the ritual outside the confines of the citadel, Char had to squeeze himself back through the passage. The rest of the Lleu-yelin gathered outside. Beside her, Brégenne felt Veeta stiffen at the sight of them. Even Gend's stony face cracked into an expression of awe. They were wondrous, as if they'd stepped out of the pages of a storybook. Veeta let loose a sigh. 'I did not think to ever witness such a thing.'

'Brégenne,' Kyndra said, leading her forward. 'This is Sesh, who speaks for the Lleu-yelin.'

Brégenne had to crane her neck to look into the pointed face of the dragon rider. Sesh was tawny bronze, her scales shielded by fine mesh armour. When she opened her mouth to speak, Brégenne couldn't help but notice the alarming length of her canines. 'Well met, Wielder. The Starborn claims to trust you with her life.'

She was temporarily at a loss for words. 'I am honoured,' Brégenne said finally with a surprised glance at Kyndra. 'And I will be honoured to fight alongside you.'

An explosive rumble ended their exchange. 'I will not permit it,' snapped a female voice and Brégenne turned to look. A huge black dragon confronted Char, horned head lowered angrily.

'Mother,' Char said, 'I must. This world, this future, depends on stopping the eldest. Kyndra cannot shoulder that burden alone.'

'I have only just found you.' It was difficult to discern in the deep thunder of the dragon's voice, but Brégenne thought she heard tears. 'I will not lose you again.'

Char lowered his head to hers. 'I do not wish to cause you pain. But I must do this. It is important to me. There are things for which I must make amends however I might.' He added something, somewhat haltingly, in a sibilant language Brégenne couldn't understand.

'Ekaar.' One of the riders put a large hand on the dragon's leg. 'Let him go.'

She swung around. 'We might never see him again, Arvaka. Do you not care about our only offspring?'

'Of course I care. But Orkaan is a risling now. He is free to make his choices.'

Ekaar was silent. Then, slowly, she turned back to Char. 'If you do not return,' she said in a low hiss, 'I will never forgive you, Orkaan.'

Char took a step back. Brégenne didn't blame him. Ekaar was a trembling thing of fury and grief, as if she had already lost him. Char looked away from her. 'I'm ready.'

'I envy you,' Realdon Shune said, longing in his cracked voice. 'To walk the crystal halls again, to stand in the tower of the Sentheon and hear the night song of the Lunar birds as they wake.' Memory misted his eyes. 'Even on the eve of her fall, Solinaris kept her glory.'

Char crouched so that Kyndra could climb on. 'Don't let go of us, Ma,' she said and for the first time since she'd accepted the mantle of Starborn, Brégenne heard a sliver of fear in her voice. Ma nodded. She and Char looked at each other and something passed between them, something deeper, Brégenne thought, than any emotion that had passed between Char and Ekaar.

'Good luck,' Brégenne said, feeling Nediah come to stand beside her. Together they watched as Ma spread her hands and white light webbed Kyndra and Char. The strands of it joined all four of them – Ma and Shune too – and the old man's face twisted. Brégenne thought she heard bells and the rushing of water. The light became blinding, forcing her to close her eyes against it. When she opened them, Kyndra and Char were gone.

37

Kyndra

Flying. *She crosses the crystal floor, seeing facets of herself in its endless reflections. Her mind is made up. This can only end one way, the way it's supposed to – the way it already has. That it took her so long to realize . . .*

Falling. *Her footfalls echo on the glass. The tower beckons and her destiny. She cannot outrun it, for she has already faced it. And yet it abides, still incomplete, waiting for her to face it once again.*

The endless rushing; a terrible rolling river that tumbled her and Char like leaves in high wind. Char: she clung to his back, her fingers seizing up on the black scales. He roared his own protest, as they were thrown through the maelstrom of time. And then her fingers slipped, for there were no scales to grip, no broad back to support her. They both fell, clinging to each other for dear life.

The impact forced the breath from her lungs, shattering the black dream that had been so clear a moment ago. For a few wild seconds, all Kyndra could see was darkness. She blinked, gasped in air, and slowly her sight returned. She was lying on grass, the scent of it strong and green in her nose: stems broken under her weight. She groaned, trying to shuffle her thoughts into order.

Another groan came from nearby and she realized there were legs tangled in hers. Heart pounding, Kyndra rolled over. It was just Char though, shaking his grey head, raising himself up on grey-skinned hands.

Reality hit a moment later. 'Ma was right,' she gasped. 'You're not a dragon.'

Char blinked. He flexed his fists, ran fingers over his face and chest. 'This is so impossible.' He looked just as he had when she'd first met him, everything from headscarf to desert garb to kali sticks. Kyndra watched as he reached down and drew them reverently out of their scabbard.

'Can you still use ambertrix?'

Char frowned. 'I don't think so. I can feel something in my chest, but it's like it used to be. Uncontrolled.'

Kyndra grimaced. 'We'll have to rely on those sticks and our wits, then.'

Char grinned. 'Just like old times.'

She was about to reply when suddenly he took her arm. 'Kyndra, look.'

It rose like a mirage, a glittering edifice of glass and light. Pennants flew from its topmost spires, snapping in the wind. So high, they seemed to merge with the heavens. Kyndra felt a soaring in her heart. Solinaris: the fortress of the sun. The rush of emotion told her more plainly than the absent void that she was just Kyndra again. She felt a peculiar mix of dread and . . . relief.

'I can't believe it,' Char whispered. 'It can't be real.'

'I read stories,' Kyndra said, equally quiet. 'Glimpsed it in visions. But neither can compare.' She couldn't seem to tear her eyes away. 'We're really here.'

As they watched, mesmerized, the sun emerged from a cloud, igniting the citadel, setting the walls aflame. The sight abruptly doused Kyndra's wonder. She imagined the Sartyan cannons belching smoke, staining the glass black – that glass would melt, catching the Wielders in crystal death. 'Come on.' She heard sadness in her voice, knowing what awaited the citadel and unable to change its fate. 'Let's get closer.'

When she tried to stand up, using her one good arm, her legs shook beneath her. A wave of weakness rolled through Kyndra and she found herself panting. 'Kyndra.' Char steadied her. There was concern in his eyes when they studied her paling face. 'Is it the curse?'

She nodded. 'It's moving faster now. We need to hurry.'

They walked downhill – though Kyndra's walk was more of a limp – keeping low when they could, always on the lookout for watchers. The afternoon grew brighter, until Kyndra could hardly bear to look at Solinaris, so radiant it became. Facets trapped the light; a thousand suns blazing behind the glass. 'It's not just for show,' she murmured, studying the caged light through narrowed eyes, the way it moved like liquid inside its transparent prison. 'The whole citadel is an *akan* – an object Wielders use to store energy,' she added when Char raised a questioning eyebrow. 'Ingenious. I wonder what other knowledge was lost when Solinaris fell.'

Char was looking at her, slightly askance. 'I'm still me,' she said with a sigh. 'As inconvenient as it is.'

'It's not inconvenient to me,' he said with an intensity that made her blush. As they began walking again, Kyndra raised a surreptitious hand to her cheek, wondering at the heat beneath her fingers.

The glare off the citadel hid the workers until Kyndra and Char were nearly on top of them. Char grabbed her in warning and they hastily fell back. There were around fifty – ordinary people, by the looks of their rough shirts, fussing around wagons. Each face was a fog of fear and resentment and they glanced frequently to the west. Kyndra squinted; it looked as if a metal tide advanced across the land. Her heart began to race. 'Sartya,' she whispered. They were almost upon the citadel. Exclamations spread through the workers and the activity became frenzied. 'Stockpiling supplies.' Kyndra nodded at the rolling wagons, the crack of the whip that quickened the oxen's lumbering pace. 'For the siege.'

Char's yellow eyes widened. 'Are we in time?'

'Yes, but we need to get inside. Kierik's memories of this day are foggy. Medavle laid his trap in the archives; Kierik activated it when he stole the knowledge of how to destroy the Yadin. The attack began after he addressed the Sentheon.' She shook her head, a deep regret in her bones. 'Solinaris's final day.'

Kyndra let her gaze stray upward, though it hurt her eyes. 'Kierik will climb to the tallest tower.' A flash of image came to her, something she'd dreamed – her own feet climbing a glittering stair – and then it was gone.

'Kyndra?' Char touched her arm. 'Are you all right?'

She gave her head a shake, hoping to dislodge the memories threatening to envelop her – memories from a man who hadn't yet made them, *her* memories from a confrontation she hadn't yet had . . . 'I'm fine. All this – it really is confusing.'

'I'm glad you think so too,' Char said wryly.

They were silent for a time. Then Kyndra, studying the supply wagons, said, 'Are you thinking what I'm thinking?'

'What are you thinking?'

'That I've had some luck sneaking into and out of places in the back of wagons.'

'Gods, that's a terrible idea.' Char gestured at the people. 'There's no way we could explain our presence, especially if a Wielder saw us.'

Kyndra chewed her lip. 'Can you think of a better way to get inside?'

'Yes,' Char said. 'Let's just walk in.'

She stared at him. 'Are you mad?'

'You said it yourself: we can't afford to wait around. We don't look all that different from the people loading the wagons. Let's just pretend we're working with them.'

To Kyndra's immense surprise, Char was right. They waited until the foreman's back was turned and then simply took places either side of the rearmost wagon, which didn't yet have anyone assigned to it. Kyndra pulled her sleeve over her hand and raised her collar to hide as much of her neck as she could.

Crates filled the entryway. A passage led off to one side, down which the workers scurried. 'Hurry up,' a man barked at them and they were forced to carry their own share of supplies. Kyndra found the lightest sack she could, tucking it under her good arm, and they fell in behind the others. On the inside, Solinaris's glass walls were opaque, as if shadows massed behind them. Their boots echoed on the crystal floor.

The passage led to a series of storerooms. Depositing their sacks, Kyndra and Char moved casually past the other workers, deeper into the warren. 'How far do these stretch?' Char whispered as they flitted from room to room, seeking an exit. The further they went, the more scholarly the shelves became; reams upon reams of blank scrolls, ink, quill pens. Sets of robes were folded neatly according to size and Kyndra seized two of them, throwing one to Char.

He unfolded the brown material. 'What's this?'

'Novice robe,' Kyndra said. She plucked at her clothes. 'We won't be able to move around otherwise. I suspect servants aren't allowed in the citadel proper.' They hastily dragged the robes over their own clothes. Char had to help her; Kyndra could no longer lift her left arm; it was as if all the bones had been removed. She hated being like this, dependent on others for the simplest of tasks. And yet, when Char touched her, she didn't mind, feeling her heart beating harder when he brushed her skin.

'Do you know your way around the citadel?' he asked.

She made a face. 'Maybe. I think I can find the atrium, if we manage to escape these storerooms.'

Eventually, they did, though it took longer than Kyndra had hoped. 'Where is the eldest?' she wondered aloud as they emerged into a crystalline passageway.

'If it's any consolation, he'll have to keep out of sight,' Char said. 'I doubt he could pass for a novice.'

Despite everything, they looked at each other and grinned.

'I never thought I'd see you like this again,' Char said after a moment.

Kyndra shrugged, hoping to look casual. 'Don't get used to it.' But his words had birthed a staggering idea. *If I stayed here, I could live as me. I'd understand what it means to have friends again. I could* feel.

She shot a covert look at Char. He'd dropped his gaze to his fingers, flexing them as if marvelling at their dexterity, at how it felt to have hands again instead of talons. She knew he struggled with his new form, perhaps even regretted the change. If he had the choice, would he stay here, abandoning Ma and Ekaar, choosing instead to live as a human?

Would they live together?

Kyndra gave herself a mental shake. The future depended on her – she had responsibilities. Who would watch over Acre if she abandoned them? But the thought curled up at a crossroads in her mind where it refused to let her be.

'What's the plan, then?' Char asked.

'We need to find the eldest before he finds Kierik. Or he'll warn Kierik that separating Rairam from Acre will destroy him.' As she spoke, Kyndra remembered the terror of that final inherited memory, the feel of a world in her mind, in her hands. She shivered. Had Kierik really intended to rule Mariar as Shune accused? Now that she'd met him, she couldn't imagine it. Denying Sartya its prize had been his way of maintaining balance.

'Kyndra?'

She realized she'd stopped walking. 'Sorry,' she said faintly. It was everything she herself had worked towards since setting foot in Acre. Seeking balance. She'd denied her heritage, but couldn't deny her nature. Kyndra put it from her mind. They had to find the eldest. And Medavle. 'I hope he doesn't do anything stupid,' she muttered.

'Who?'

'Medavle.'

'Surely he's only here to search for this Isla of his,' Char said, glancing round, as if the Yadin woman might just happen across their path. 'Then he'll take her out of the citadel.'

426

Kyndra grimaced. 'If he realizes the eldest's planning to *save* Kierik—'

'Novices, what are you doing?'

Kyndra and Char pulled up short. *I should have been paying attention*, Kyndra thought angrily. The Wielder's robes were golden like those worn by masters in Naris, but these seemed constantly to move and reshape themselves around him like mist stirred by a lazy wind. As she stared at the man, she felt her mouth open. His face was unlined, but she recognized its arrogant cast. 'Shune,' she said automatically.

He scowled. 'Master Shune to you, novice.' He tilted his head on one side, gaze moving between her and Char. 'I don't believe I know either of you.'

Kyndra's throat dried. She darted a glance at Char, hoping Shune wouldn't find something to question in his appearance, but Char's eyes remained normal, albeit strikingly yellow.

'Well, there are so many novices these days,' Shune concluded dismissively. 'It's taxing to keep track of you all. Makes me glad I did not take up a teaching post.' He folded his arms. 'You should be studying.'

Kyndra felt some of the tension leave her. 'Yes, Master. We were only taking a short walk.'

'Off with you, then.'

For one wild moment, she found herself wanting to blurt out everything, to warn Shune of what was to come. Thankfully, the urge passed and they had no choice but to turn and retrace their steps. Kyndra wiped her palms on her brown robes. She could feel Shune's eyes on her back. 'We need to be more careful,' she whispered once they were out of sight.

'That was weird,' Char said. 'He hasn't changed much, has he?'

'Seriously?'

'Well, apart from looking a thousand years old. But turns out he was always bad-tempered.'

Char was in a remarkably good mood, considering their situation. Kyndra suspected it was something to do with being back in human form. On impulse, she gave him a smile and again was startled at how much his face brightened. He raised a hand to her cheek.

There was a flash of white over his shoulder. Recognizing the Yadin garments, Kyndra darted around Char, a shout building in her throat. But when the man turned and she saw his face beneath the hood, it wasn't Medavle's.

It was Anohin's.

38

Hagdon

They came with the *drrumm drrumm* of hilts on shields. A shattering warsong more promise than warning. The smoke from burning settlements rose in their wake.

That was how the scout told it.

Hagdon listened expressionlessly. One thought filled his mind: *Now I know how it feels to receive news of my own advance.* A storm on the horizon. Thunder before him, blood in his footprints, the rain that washed it away.

Instead, Iresonté was the storm. She'd cut a swathe through southern Rairam, firing villages, killing any who stood in her path. Kyndra had warned him, Hagdon thought; Rairam was powerless to stop Sartya. It made him smile bitterly. With what absurd ease would he have taken this land if he still served his emperor.

Now he was here to defend it.

It would be a close thing. *They* could move faster than Iresonté and her vast army; *she* had less distance to cover. And Hagdon didn't know what they'd find on reaching the capital. What was Rairam's capital like? Did it even have proper walls?

With a sinking feeling, Hagdon suspected it might not. This land had been at peace for five hundred years. As he'd done a dozen times already, he shook his head at the direction his life had taken.

And yet, unexpectedly, he was happier in himself than he'd been in a long time. Despite the inescapable battle that awaited them, despite the all-too-real likelihood of death, he felt this was where he was supposed to be.

He looked to his left. Irilin rode there, her horse keeping pace with his. Hagdon found himself smiling. 'Your Rairam is very beautiful,' he said. They'd left the rocky lands around Naris behind and were moving through a series of lush valleys.

Irilin's hands tightened on the reins. He thought her smile a little strained. 'It's nothing compared to Calmarac.'

'Calmarac is overrated because of the wine.' He lowered his voice mock-conspiratorially. 'To be honest, I never much cared for it.'

She laughed. 'Me neither. But Kyndra was very taken with it. Did you know she used to work in an inn serving drinks?'

'You must be joking.' With her cold face and serious eyes, Hagdon just couldn't imagine the Starborn squeezing between tables with a tray. 'That has to be the most surreal thing you've ever said.'

'I only met her when she came to Naris,' Irilin replied, her expression still a little distant. 'She was confused and scared. She missed her home. But she was defiant too, determined to escape her fate.' She slid him a look from under lowered lids. 'In the end, she decided to face it.'

When he didn't answer, Irilin touched his arm. 'What is it, James?'

If she knew the real him and even half of what he'd done,

Hagdon thought, she would not speak his name so gently. 'I never pictured myself defending Rairam,' he said.

'I never pictured myself riding in an army, but here I am.'

'Here we are,' he agreed. 'Have you been to this Market Primus?'

She shook her head. 'Kyndra has. Brégenne and Gareth too. They had a lot of trouble convincing the Trade Assembly that Acre had returned.'

'*Rairam* returned.'

'Matter of perspective.'

'How do you think they'll react on seeing us?'

'Shit their collective pants, I expect.' Mercia pulled her horse alongside theirs.

'What a colourful image,' Hagdon muttered. 'I was speaking seriously.'

'Right. Sorry.' Mercia grinned. 'I doubt I'm far wrong though.'

She wasn't far wrong.

It was hard to miss a force the size of theirs, considering the flat terrain that surrounded the city. Hagdon ordered a white flag flown when they came within sight of the walls. There *were* walls, but, true to his fears, they hadn't been built to keep out an army. As they rode closer, he saw cracks in the stone, forced open by climbing ivy. That meant the foundations were weak too. No siege, then. He couldn't say he wasn't relieved. He much preferred open battle to the drawn-out grind of a siege. But against an army the size of Iresonté's . . . he had to admit the odds were in her favour.

Unless Kul'Gareth and the Wielders joined them.

He rode up to the gates, accompanied by Kait and Mercia. 'I'll handle any arrows, should things go badly,' Kait said with equanimity. He'd noticed a change in the tall woman since the other Wielders had left. She'd stalked about the camp at first, simmering with a nameless emotion only Mercia seemed able to diffuse. The two of them had become fast friends.

'I'm hoping it doesn't come to that.' Hagdon squinted up at a distinctly ramshackle watchtower, which overlooked the crude gates. Faces peered from it, anxious faces that eyed their white flag with great suspicion. He could feel the arrows trained on him.

The gates opened to let a delegation through. The smell of sawdust still hung in the air and Hagdon guessed they'd been hastily made. The woman who led it was perhaps ten years older than he, with a proud, angular face and coiffed hair. She and the two men behind her wore some kind of state robes, the emblem of weighing scales sewn upon the breast.

'Declare yourselves,' she ordered and Hagdon gave her points for bravado, particularly in the face of their superior force.

'Commander James Hagdon.' He rode forward, hands held loosely away from his body, hoping none of the watchtower soldiers let their fingers slip. 'I don't know how much you were told about the threat to your city –' he faltered under her stony gaze – 'but we are here to aid you.'

It hadn't been an elegant or especially informative introduction, but the woman seemed unsurprised by his words. 'We are friends of Brégenne, the Wielder,' Irilin spoke up.

'Who left my home far too precipitously,' the woman said. 'I still have her horse in my stable.'

'She did what she had to.' Irilin paused. 'Are you Astra Marahan?'

'I am,' the woman said with a twitch of her eyebrows. 'And you are?'

'Irilin Straa. I'm a Wielder too.' Irilin glanced at Hagdon. 'What Commander Hagdon says is true. Brégenne warned you about the Sartyan Fist. They will be here in a day.'

'We've had reports,' Astra said crisply. Her eyes narrowed. 'A large force burning everything in its path, be it village or people.'

'Then you know the threat is real,' Irilin said. 'The army is led by a woman called Iresonté. She means to seize this land for her own, starting with Market Primus.' She turned in her saddle and said, with a gesture that encompassed their whole force, 'We mean to stop her.'

'I see,' Astra said. 'And are we to let our city be your battle-field? The streets are already full of homeless we cannot house.'

'We will not enter the city,' Hagdon said. 'It's indefensible. And it would be impossible to prevent civilian casualties.' He could not quash a flicker of dread as he added, 'We will fight Iresonté head to head.'

'Wait a minute, Astra.' One of the men behind her pushed forward. 'We don't know any of these people. Who is to say *they* are not the force that has pillaged and murdered its way to our city?'

Irilin's mouth opened in disbelief. 'How dare you? We've gone without sleep to get here before Iresonté and *that*'s your response? To accuse us of her crimes?'

'Gentlemen,' Astra said firmly, looking at Irilin's flushed face. 'This is not the time. Brégenne—'

'You trust the word of a woman who brought her own battle to your door?' the other man demanded. Despite his attitude, he looked pale beneath his thick beard. 'She and those magicians of hers set fire to your carriage.'

'I never liked it anyway,' Astra said. 'I've made up my mind, Talmanier. If they were here to kill us, do you think we'd be having this conversation?'

Talmanier opened his mouth, but was interrupted by a loud whirring. Hagdon realized he'd been hearing it for some time as a background noise that had grown steadily louder. As one, they looked up.

Hagdon's mouth fell open. It was a flying ship. An actual ship, complete with figurehead and angled sails, held aloft by two huge balloons. He gaped as it banked in a smooth circle of the city; the whirring came from two paddles that spun at its rear. It landed in a nearby field, spraying up a great shower of dirt.

'Argat.' It was more growl than name and Hagdon glanced at Astra. Her face was steely.

'He seems to possess a special ability to punctuate a conversation,' Talmanier said and then winced at the daggers Astra glared at him.

The paddles slowed, stopped. A small group disembarked. Astra's expression became even chillier as she watched them close the distance. A man led them, leather coat snapping in the breeze. Hagdon tried to focus on him, but he couldn't keep his eyes off the glorious ship. 'And it flies without ambertrix,' he murmured wonderingly.

'It beggars belief, Argat,' Astra said, 'that you *dare* to show your face here again.'

'Oh come now.' Argat was clearly enjoying himself. 'Isn't it time we put all this unpleasantness behind us?'

'You're a thief, Argat, and a liar. That ship –' she stabbed a finger at it – 'is the property of the Assembly.'

Argat's expression immediately cooled. 'No, Astra. She's

mine. And I will not be giving her back.' His gaze ranged over Hagdon and those gathered behind him. 'Where's Brégenne?'

'In Naris,' Irilin said, 'gathering the Wielders.'

'I wish her luck with that.' Argat nodded at the city. 'The Wielders didn't look at all happy to see her last time we were here.'

'Do you have news of Gareth?' Irilin asked him. 'Is he coming to help us?'

Argat nodded. 'I estimate they're two days to the north.'

'They'll have to march through the night to reach us in time,' Hagdon said with a frown. 'And tired men don't fight well.'

Irilin gave him a searching look before turning back to Argat. 'Have you seen Iresonté and the Fist?'

'Camped a day behind you.' Argat's grin was wolfish. 'Did their best to shoot me out of the sky.'

'They have artillery, then.' Hagdon shook his head. 'I feared as much.'

'We saw at least five,' Argat said, running a hand over his thinning hair. 'Huge things spitting blue.'

'Cannon, yes. They're difficult to take down. Unless you're a Starborn,' Hagdon added ruefully, remembering those reports of Kyndra melting them like ice in the sun.

'By the look on your face, I'm guessing we don't have one to spare.'

'Kyndra has her hands full with the Khronostians.' Hagdon gazed around at them all. 'This is our battle.'

A day wasn't long in which to formulate a strategy, especially a strategy that depended on forces they didn't have yet. 'As we are, we can't face Iresonté head-on,' Hagdon confessed to Irilin.

He'd set up his command tent on the summit of a small hill that offered a view of the terrain. They'd dug earthworks, aided by Kait and, tonight, Irilin. With their help, the defences had gone up more swiftly than Hagdon could have hoped. Mikael's Alchemists were camped off to the west, the Republic to the east, leaving his Sartyan forces in the middle. They were his strongest asset, as far as he was concerned. The Republic had received only basic training on their journey here and, despite numerous stories about the Alchemists, he had no real idea of their capabilities. Mikael was notoriously tight-lipped on the subject, only assuring him that they could hold their own. Hagdon ground his teeth. Trying to plan a defence without all the facts drove him mad.

'The Wielders are on their way.'

'What about Kul'Gareth?' Hagdon began to pace. 'Captain Argat claimed his forces number several thousand. They could well tip the balance.'

'They can only move so fast,' Irilin said. 'We will have to trust they'll be here.'

'Trust is not enough. There's no time. They *need* to be here.'

'James.' It was almost a snap. 'They will be.'

Hagdon stopped pacing. 'I want you to stay out of the battle.'

'No.'

'Irilin.' Her pale hair framed her face, gleaming in the lanterns that lit the tent. 'You cannot fight in daylight. And I cannot protect you,' he added in a low voice.

'I don't need protecting,' she retorted. 'I can look out for myself.'

'If Iresonté realizes how much I—' Hagdon broke off, suddenly unable to look at her. 'If she finds out how important you are to me,' he whispered to the tent wall, 'she will kill you.'

Irilin was silent. He heard her swallow. 'James,' she said after a few moments, 'will you do something for me?'

Immediately he turned back to her. 'Anything.'

'Will you – will you kiss me?'

Hagdon stared at her. The world seemed to slow so that it held just the two of them. His heart began a furious pounding in his chest.

Her eyes searched his face. 'If you don't want to –'

'I'm not very good at it,' he heard himself say.

There was a voice in his head, warning him not to, but Irilin filled his vision. He wasn't sure what to do with his hands. They felt too big for him; his fingers looked rough against her cheek. Her skin was unfairly soft, a little flushed from the evening chill. As her arms crept hesitantly around him, he bent his head and brushed his lips across her forehead.

Irilin made a sound in her throat. Her hands tightened. Before he could draw away, she tilted her chin up and found his lips with hers.

Thought dissolved. The kiss seemed to encompass every glance they'd exchanged, from first to last, from enemies to friends. One hand in her hair, tumbling it free from the knot she'd tied it in, the other at her back, so he could pull her harder against him. She gasped against his mouth, her fingers creeping to the skin beneath his collar, to the top of his chest.

'Commander.'

The voice was outside, its intrusion a cold gust through an open window. It froze them both.

'Commander. There's something you need to see.'

Hagdon raised his head, coming back to himself. 'A moment,' he called.

'It's urgent—'

'Gods, man, I said a moment.'

There was silence. Irilin reached for him, but he caught her hand, held it away, all the while fighting the urge to kiss her again. Her lips were slightly swollen; the sight sent a delightful heat through him, but he couldn't. All his misgivings, so unimportant just a moment ago, crowded him, and Hagdon felt ashamed at how easily he'd given in. He let her go and stepped back, dragging a hand over his face. 'I'm sorry.'

'Why?' she asked softly.

'Commander,' the voice came again, 'you really need to see—'

'*Yes.*' He snatched his gauntlets from a table, pulled them on. Irilin stepped closer again and he felt his breath catch, but she only straightened the collar she'd earlier pushed aside.

'I know what you said before,' she murmured, briefly touching his cheek. 'But can we at least talk about it?'

Hagdon couldn't bring himself to say no. He could still feel the pressure of her lips on his, as he held the tent flap aside for her. Irilin gave him a look from under her lashes as she passed, a look that caused him to tremble anew.

A black-cloaked soldier waited outside. Silently, he pointed.

Hagdon squinted at the sky. Something was racing the sunset – some*things*, he amended, attempting a count. Perhaps twenty. He could hear the leathery slap as wings struck air. A roar echoed through the hills and distant screams rose from the city, carried to him on the evening wind.

Of course, Rairam had never seen the Lleu-yelin. He found himself grinning.

'Are those dragons?' Irilin whispered, her eyes huge. She'd never seen one either, Hagdon realized. The Lleu-yelin were almost upon their camp. Fingers pointed and heads tilted upwards to watch as they came in to land.

Each dragon had a rider. A rider and several humans. Hagdon made his way over to the largest. Close up, it was even more impressive, with deep blue scales the size of his spread hand. Wicked talons tipped each foot, and a mane lay sleek against its neck.

Its rider's scales were topaz, pointed face distinctly feminine. 'Commander Hagdon?' she asked, dismounting and stalking over to him. Hagdon had to look up – she was at least seven feet tall, with horns and talons that appeared as lethal as her partner's. When he nodded, she said, 'I am Sesh. I speak for the Lleu-yelin.' The words were a little sibilant, as if they did not sit naturally on her tongue.

'Well met,' Hagdon answered politely. 'If you've come to lend us your aid, you are *very* welcome.'

'We owe the Starborn a debt.' Sesh shrugged as if the titanic battle awaiting them were a small thing. 'We will fight this once and then return to Magtharda.' Her cat-eyes narrowed. 'We have meddled too much in human affairs and paid the price.'

'I am grateful for your help,' Hagdon said sincerely. 'Iresonté has a number of weapons we cannot hope to match. Five ambertrix cannon and, I imagine, multiple munitions including ambertrix cloaks.' His look was speculative. 'Can you do anything to tip the balance?'

Sesh considered him. 'Perhaps. We are unfamiliar with the many shapes you humans have forced amberstrazatrix to assume. In many cases it is almost unrecognizable. Nevertheless, we should be able to counter it.'

'Take out those cannon and you will have repaid any debt tenfold,' Hagdon said, shuddering at the thought of the pot-bellied weapons he'd once stood behind. 'Just one could ruin us.'

Sesh nodded, unperturbed. 'Humans cannot be trusted with power. Always in the end it leads to death.'

'I think we can agree on that.'

'Give me your sword,' Sesh said suddenly.

Hagdon blinked. He reached over his shoulder and drew the greatsword from its sheath.

The Lleu-yelin turned it in her hands, tapping the blade with a claw. It looked like a child's toy in her grasp. 'This is one of ours. The metal carries our scent.' She held it out to her partner. 'Would you, my love?'

Hagdon heard a growling rumble and stepped back, pulling Irilin with him. But the force that emerged from the dragon's mouth was a carefully controlled stream of blue, which enveloped the sword. The weapon glowed brightly before the light sank into the metal, leaving just a trace of azure behind. When Hagdon tentatively took it back, it felt alive in his hand. 'It hasn't been charged for years,' he said wonderingly. 'My thanks.'

'May it serve well,' was all Sesh said.

'Where is Kyndra?' Irilin asked. Her eyes were still rather wide, Hagdon noticed, and they flickered between Sesh and the blue dragon as if unsure where to settle. 'And the others?'

'We're here,' came a voice and Hagdon saw Brégenne walking towards them, Nediah beside her. Other robed figures were dismounting: Wielders, perhaps fifty of them, he estimated. He felt a heady rush of relief and found himself grinning at Irilin. She slipped a hand into his.

'I am *very* glad to see you,' Hagdon said to Brégenne.

'Kul'Gareth isn't here yet and I must admit I was growing nervous.'

'I've brought as many Wielders as are able to fight,' she replied, her eyes alighting briefly on his and Irilin's linked hands.

'Where's Kyndra?' Irilin repeated.

'Doing what she can to save us,' said a new voice and Hagdon looked round to see a young man, golden-haired, with a strange scar across one half of his face. It was shaped like the pinions of a vast bird, feather-marks branded into his skin. He favoured the same side, as if the scar covered the whole half of his body too.

'Janus is right,' Brégenne said with a nod to him. 'The eldest attacked Naris and then he and Medavle escaped. Kyndra and Char followed, but I'm worried about her. The eldest's curse is taking its toll. She doesn't have long to find him.'

Irilin's shoulders slumped. 'Then, even if we win here, it could all be for nothing.'

'We must trust in her,' Hagdon said, giving Irilin's hand a squeeze. He was unwilling to think of the consequences of failure on the eve of battle. 'As she must trust in us to ensure she has a world to return to which is free of the Fist.'

39

Char

The straw-haired man gave Kyndra a strange look. He seemed on edge, as if his darting eyes expected someone to turn up at any moment. 'Do I know you?' he asked.

Char saw Kyndra swallow. 'No,' she said. 'But I know of you.' She hesitated. 'You're Anohin. The Yadin who serves Kierik.'

A series of emotions passed like wind-spurred clouds across Anohin's face. He straightened. 'That is correct. You appear well-informed, mistress.'

Kyndra gave a slight shake of her head. 'Why do you serve him?'

'Because he is worthy of service. More so than any Wielder.'

'He doesn't care about you.'

Anohin's expression hardened, a dangerous light coming into his eyes. 'You presume to know a Starborn's mind?'

Kyndra's answering smile was grim. 'I spend every day trying to.'

Anohin trembled; Char could sense the anger in him, boiling just below the surface. 'You speak of things you cannot possibly understand.'

Kyndra stared at Anohin closely; the Yadin stared back. It might have gone on interminably if she hadn't said, quite suddenly, 'You *love* him.'

Anohin blanched. Without a word, he turned and strode away, boots echoing hollowly on the glass floor.

Kyndra seemed sad. 'He's not worth it, you know,' she called after him. 'Staying with him will destroy you.'

Anohin's shoulders hunched briefly, but he kept on walking.

'That was the Yadin you spoke of,' Char said, 'the one who looked after Kierik?'

She nodded and bit her lip. 'I shouldn't have said any of that. It was stupid.'

'I don't think you made any difference. He seems blind when it comes to the Starborn.' Char found himself flinching under the weight of his own words. He looked away, finding it easier to stare at the glass walls than at Kyndra.

'Come on. If Anohin's here, Kierik won't be far behind. We should keep an eye on him.'

They started after him, careful to leave a safe distance. Anohin led them on a winding journey through the citadel. He stopped off at several places, collecting items. Kyndra and Char hid each time he came out of a door, or doubled back.

'What's he doing?' Char nodded at the pouches around the Yadin's waist that held the fruits of his journey.

'Perhaps gathering artefacts Kierik wants to save.' Kyndra frowned. 'But he can't know that Solinaris will be completely destroyed. It was the force of Kierik's mind breaking that tore the citadel apart.'

All at once she stumbled, clutching her head. 'Kyndra,' Char caught and steadied her as she wavered on her feet, 'what is it?'

She raised a hand to her temple. 'The black dreams. I – I saw something. Just a flash.'

'Black dreams?' Char let her go. They couldn't afford to lose Anohin.

'I should call them memories. Didn't I explain in Magtharda?'

Char smiled somewhat bitterly. 'No. You were a Starborn then. All you said was that the stars couldn't see beyond a certain point.'

Kyndra's face paled at the memory. 'They started on the way to Magtharda,' she said. 'They're important, but they only show me snatches of things.' She looked at him. 'I think they're memories from the time I was here before.'

'That makes no sense.'

'I know.' Her expression turned bitter. '*Era* wouldn't tell me the truth. It's scared of creating a paradox I can't escape.' She paused. 'It's scared that the stars won't have a Starborn to wield them.'

Char frowned. 'I thought the stars were emotionless.'

'Perhaps scared is the wrong word. Concerned?' She picked up her damaged arm, held it close to her. 'Without a Starborn, the stars are powerless. Without a world, there are no Starborn.'

After a moment, Char said, 'These dreams – memories. What do they show you?'

'Medavle,' Kyndra said immediately. 'The eldest. A tower top. A winding crystal stair.'

'Sounds like Solinaris.'

'It is,' she said shortly. 'Do you understand? I *was* here before. I must have had a hand in the way things turned out. But I'm working blind. I can't remember what I did last time.' She hissed in frustration. 'And *Era* claims *I* commanded the stars not to tell me. How can they be sure I'll make the same decisions?'

The passages were becoming wider, more crowded. The vaulted glass ceiling reflected the hurried steps of novices, the purposeful strides of masters, trailed more often than not by other Yadin. Char noticed the looks they gave Anohin as they passed him: bewilderment, pity, even barely concealed disgust. He was a pariah to his own people.

The growing flood of Wielders swept them through a final archway into a huge open space. It reminded Char of the hall in Naris, but to compare the two —

'The atrium,' Kyndra whispered.

Char drank in the sights of the great chamber. It didn't appear to match the outward dimensions of the citadel, its floor sloping gently into the distance. Their footfalls stirred a fine mist about their ankles, which settled as dew on the leaves of crystal trees.

He blinked. Trees. A river.

The water swirled within its glassy banks. Gleaming swans sailed upon it, their feathers white-gold. Songbirds nested in the branches of willows that caressed the surface of the river; he could see their tiny claws anchoring them while they slept. 'Lunar birds,' Kyndra said with a nod to them. 'They'll wake at twilight.'

Other creatures prowled or scampered among the shining groves. Char saw a lynx playfully stalking a squirrel, while its fellows chirruped down at it, safe in the topmost branches. Blushing roses twined about trunks, a drop of dew on each petal. There was even a gentle breeze; Char felt it tugging at his hair, heard it rustling through the leaves, setting them a-chime.

It was glass. It was *all* glass.

'Beautiful,' Kyndra murmured, 'and horrible.'

Char agreed. There *was* something horrible about the glade in its utter perfection, in its artificial, changeless nature. True nature was change. Seasons moved, leaves fell, animals killed and were killed in turn. This vision, so outwardly beautiful, was ugly in its falseness.

'It's wrong,' he said. 'How can they not see it?'

'Because they are slaves to it,' came a voice.

Kyndra and Char spun round. The speaker wore white robes. A flute hung at his waist. 'Medavle,' Kyndra exclaimed. 'You're here!'

He frowned. 'How do you know my name, novice?'

Kyndra plainly realized her mistake. Her eyes alighted on the flute, which Char knew she herself had destroyed during their confrontation in Samaya. 'I . . . must have overheard it,' she stammered.

Medavle regarded her, his dark gaze suspicious. 'We haven't spoken before. I am surprised a novice would take note of a Yadin's name.'

'Why wouldn't I?'

'One day you will see differently.' This past Medavle seemed on edge. His hands curled and uncurled at his sides, fingers straying, perhaps unconsciously, to the flute. 'You will be taught not to see us as people.'

'Like the Starborn?' Kyndra said quietly.

Char took a step back at the deep anger that rose in Medavle's face. He knew at once that Kyndra had gone too far. 'Who are you?' the Yadin demanded. 'None of your words sound like an ordinary novice's.'

Thunder spared Kyndra from answering. Char barely kept his feet. Shadow filled the hall and flame; when it lifted, he saw a scorchmark on the western wall. It was huge, easily the height of three men lying head to toe. The stink of smoke in his nose, he heard cries of alarm, cries of impossibility. People began to run, some deeper into the citadel, others to the crystal wall, where a crack busily spidered its way across the glass. Solar power shored it up, but another missile came, once more filling the hall with its thunder.

Medavle's face paled. 'Isla,' he whispered and the next minute he was lost in the maddening crowd.

'It's started.' Kyndra grabbed Char. 'Where is he? Where is the eldest?'

Char shook his head. 'We need to find Kierik.'

'If he sees me, he'll recognize me from last time,' Kyndra said, dread in her eyes at the thought. 'He won't let me escape again.'

'But that's where we'll find the eldest. You heard him – one word to Kierik and the Starborn will abandon his plan.'

'Kierik might be harder to dissuade than the eldest realizes,' Kyndra said. 'He prepared this for years. The eldest will have to reveal everything to him, explain everything – and that will take time.'

'He has *du-alakat* with him, remember? They'll stand out.' Char scanned the panicked hall. 'Perhaps they were waiting for this. Now the attack's begun, they can hide in the confusion.' He had a moment to see her eyes widen before Kyndra yanked them both behind the trunk of a great glass oak. It was too distorted to see through, so they peered around its sides.

Kierik had appeared: calm in the midst of chaos. Two things struck Char. First, the sheer presence of the Starborn, seeming to bend the world around him. Second, how much he looked like Kyndra.

She was staring at him too. He'd known that Kierik, implausible as it sounded, had fathered her. But it wasn't until this moment, glancing from one to the other, that he really accepted it as indisputable. Though Kyndra's hair was redder, it had the same curl; their faces shared the same slim shape, their hands long and slender-fingered. But most similar of all were their eyes: the chill blue of midnight.

'Gods,' he said, 'you look just like him.'

'Thanks for the reminder,' she replied drily.

'How could he not have seen it?'

'Because he wasn't looking for it.' Kyndra blushed. 'The whole idea of children, of *making* children –' she blushed harder – 'is alien to the stars. They don't understand affection, love.' She looked from him to Kierik. 'Even if I told him outright, he'd struggle to accept it.'

They ducked back behind the tree as Kierik turned on the spot, scanning the hall. 'He's looking for Anohin,' Kyndra muttered. 'He won't begin until he arrives. I can't believe we lost sight of him.' They watched the Starborn sigh and set off for a glittering archway. He cut a path through the citadel's frightened citizens, some of whom stopped to speak to him. Char couldn't be sure from this distance but it looked as though they were pleading. Kierik gave them all the same response: a sharp shake of his head.

Unnoticed amidst the screams and the roar of flame, the Lunar birds twitched and woke; began to pipe their sweet song to the distant ceiling.

Beside him, Kyndra stiffened. 'There he is.' She pointed. Flanked by five *du-alakat*, the eldest made no attempt to conceal himself. But few spared him a glance anyway, Char saw, too caught up in defending the citadel. There was no sign of Medavle – the Medavle of their time.

They watched the eldest hobble towards the archway Kierik had taken, leaning heavily on his staff. 'He's weakened,' Char said, noting how often the eldest paused to catch his breath. 'This last journey must have been too much.'

'For him and me both,' Kyndra murmured. Although perspiration beaded her forehead, when Char took her hand, she felt cold to the touch. She made to pull away, but he tightened his hold.

'Wait.' His heart had begun to thump painfully. 'Before we go . . .' Now that he needed to say them, the words stuck in his throat.

'We don't have time,' Kyndra said, frowning at her captured hand. 'Can't it wait?'

'No.'

She blinked at the fierce word. 'What's wrong, Char?'

'If we survive this –'

'We will.' But she didn't sound so certain.

'Let me finish.' Char drew a breath. 'If we survive this, we'll go back and everything will be like before. I'll lose this form. You –' He briefly closed his eyes at the pain the thought caused. 'You'll be the Starborn again. You won't care any more.'

Kyndra stopped trying to free her arm. Her face was very serious. 'I know,' she whispered. 'I wish I didn't have to be.'

'It sounds crazy, but –' he looked her straight in the eyes – 'the eldest isn't going back. *We* don't need to go back either. We can kill him, make sure history plays out as it should. But then we could stay.'

Kyndra just stared at him.

'I'm sorry, I know it's—'

'I've thought about it too,' she said, and Char stopped in surprise. 'Every time I find myself . . . *myself.*' Kyndra swallowed, but the catch was still in her voice. 'Every time I remember the things I said to you, to Brégenne, to the people I care for. Every harsh or unfeeling word – they all come back to me, to show me how much I have lost. How much I will lose.'

'Then don't.' He tightened his hold on her hand. 'Don't go back. Here, you have a chance to stay as you.'

'And what about you, Char?' she said with a glance at their linked hands. 'Why would *you* want to stay? Would you abandon your family when you've only just found them?'

He thought of Ekaar and Arvaka, remembering the warm promise of belonging. But Ma's face pushed them both aside and the pain at never seeing her again was a shard of ice in his chest.

'I'd miss them,' he said honestly. 'I'd miss Ma more than I can say. But –' he raised his other hand to her face – 'we'd be together.'

He heard her intake of breath. 'You would stay for me?' she whispered.

'I thought you knew that.'

They gazed at each other. Kyndra's lips trembled, but she didn't speak. Without her tattoos, without the chill reflection of the stars in her face, he could pretend she was who she seemed: a young woman with hair the colour of desert sand at sunset, someone he had come, despite everything that had happened, no matter how foolish, to love.

Kyndra closed her eyes. When she opened them, he knew she'd made her choice.

40

Hagdon

Dawn came all too soon. And with it, a dreadful blast Hagdon knew well. The horn of Sartya, too large for any man to carry, bellowed its challenge across the last intervening leagues. The dragons confirmed it: thirty thousand marched behind Iresonté. If they couldn't remove her quickly, the carnage would be unimaginable.

Still, Hagdon had that spark in his belly, heightening his senses, setting his nerves singing. The sword itched in his hand; he could feel the ambertrix crackling like a caged storm. It longed for release. The sun rose bloody, a herald of what was to come.

Irilin stood beside him. Hagdon could sense the tension in her. His hand lifted to find hers and she took it, holding it tightly. Her eyes were fixed, as were his, on their enemy.

The Fist glittered in the sunrise. An army had its own beauty, he thought, watching the light catch on sword and lance. Even knowing what kind of work those sharpened bits of steel were made for did not lessen their splendour. He swallowed, imagining the bloody marsh this valley would become.

'Are we ready?' The voice interrupted his trance and Hagdon turned to see Kait. She wore the armour of the Republic and had tied her hair up out of the way. At her side hung two ordinary scimitars. She saw him looking and said with a shrug, 'For when the sun goes down.'

The words chilled him. By the time the sun went down, this battle would all too likely be over.

'Hagdon.' Mercia nodded at him. 'Seems this is it.'

'Seems it is,' he replied, only half in the moment. The rest of him was already ahead, planning their route through the valley to the hill where a figure sat atop a horse, framed against the dawn. He tore his eyes away, looked back at the group surrounding him. 'The Fist's strength is also its weakness. It is trained to follow high command, unquestioningly. If Iresonté and her captains fall, the Fist will falter. She is the driving force. Our combined armies' job is to buy us time to reach her.' Hagdon looked at Mikael; the Alchemists' traditional silver mask hid his brother's face. He assumed it also protected Mikael from whatever was in those phials of his. 'Iresonté trusts the stealth force to guard her. It's your job to keep them distracted.'

'I think we can manage that,' Mikael said, the mask lending his voice a slight echo. He fingered one of the phials on his belt. 'But don't take too long, James. Our ammunition isn't limitless.'

Hagdon turned to Sesh. 'With a small enough group, we may be able to slip through the bulk of the Fist while it's distracted. You will need to keep the cannon off us and the Alchemists.'

Sesh cracked her knuckles. 'I understand. But you, Commander, have given yourself the most dangerous task. Is it not prudent for you to remain outside the battle?'

'So I told him,' Irilin muttered.

'This is the only way to avoid a slaughter,' Hagdon said firmly. 'If we wish to preserve lives on both sides, we must cut off the head of the serpent. Yes, it's dangerous. And that is why I cannot trust it to anyone else.'

To his relief, Sesh nodded.

'*So you made it, Hagdon.*'

The voice boomed across the landscape, words almost drowned by their own thunder. Several among their group jumped, but Hagdon knew the trick, had used it himself. A smaller version of the Sartyan horn that amplified speech.

'*We need not fight this day.*'

Beside him, Kait snorted. 'She must think you very stupid.'

'Her words aren't meant for me,' Hagdon said, 'but for our forces, the Sartyans who now fight for us, the Republic who know they cannot match the Fist in battle. She's seeking to break their confidence.'

'*It is not too late. Surrender and the city will be spared. Your soldiers will have their lives.*'

'At what price?' Mercia murmured.

'*I am even willing to spare your life, Hagdon, if you swear allegiance to me.*'

It was Hagdon's turn to snort. 'My head will roll the first chance she gets.' Amon Taske had come to stand at his side. 'Spread the word,' he told him, 'that Iresonté will show us no mercy, whether we surrender or not.'

The former commandant nodded. He put a hand on Hagdon's shoulder before silently moving away.

'We've unsettled her,' Hagdon told them all. 'That's what this talk is about. The Lleu-yelin showing up must have been a blow.'

Sesh gave him a sharp smile.

'*You have an hour. After that, no quarter will be given.*'

'Two can play at this game,' Kait said. 'Want me to reply?'

'No.' Hagdon narrowed his eyes at the distant figure on the hill. 'I'd prefer to give Iresonté the reply her words deserve: none.'

As the promised hour dragged on, however, Hagdon began to feel an increasing panic. Cannon weren't the only things they had to worry about, not with thirty thousand soldiers to their ten. Only Solar Wielders could fight at the moment, which meant leaving a good half outside the fray. They needed Kul'Gareth.

'It's taken us all night,' came Astra's voice as Hagdon paced outside his command tent, 'but we've scraped together five hundred militia.'

'It's not safe for you here,' he told her. 'The attack is imminent. Why didn't you evacuate with—'

'With the elderly and the children?' Astra said scathingly.

'Return to the city, at least. It offers some shelter.'

'Certainly not. This is my home. I will not hide behind walls while strangers defend it. The least I can do is bear witness. Many of my people may lose their lives today.'

Hagdon glanced at a group currently filtering in among the Republic, white surcoats emblazoned with the Assembly's heraldry. They looked like what they were: city guards more used to dealing with the drunk and disorderly than armed soldiers. But they couldn't afford to turn away aid, no matter what form it took.

'Thank you,' he said to Astra, hoping he hid his doubt.

Iresonté gave no warning. The cannon spat blue and the next instant a flaming ball fell among the hills to the west. Hagdon hoped Taske's forces weren't too tightly bunched. He'd given orders that they were to move in quickly once the attack began, close with Iresonté's soldiers – she wouldn't drop projectiles among her own men.

With a growl, Sesh leapt onto her partner's back, positioning herself just behind his horns. The other Lleu-yelin followed her lead and the battle-flight of the dragons was a wonder to behold. Hagdon clearly heard the Sartyan cries of dismay as the glittering phalanx raced overhead. Once the cannon were neutralized, Argat could begin an aerial bombardment of his own.

Another cannon fired, this shot aimed at the city. It fell short, but only just, leaving a smoking crater in the road. 'Come on,' Hagdon said under his breath, but the dragons were having a hard time reaching the artillery; he saw one dive and then swerve to avoid a hail of arrows. The Lleu-yelin weren't immune to conventional weapons, it seemed.

A *boom* sounded; the ground shook beneath Hagdon's feet as a column of azure fire rushed into the sky. Screams reached him and he smiled. *One cannon down.*

The victory cost them. Hagdon saw an emerald form spiral to earth, an ugly hole torn in its wing. The rider kept their feet as they landed in a shower of dirt, crushing Sartyans. But their greatest advantage was lost. Hagdon caught a last glimpse before they disappeared under a swarm of red figures.

A rage-filled roar echoed across the battlefield. Two more Lleu-yelin dived to their comrade's aid, ripping and tearing with talons, the raw ambertrix that crackled from their throats deadly as lightning.

'The cannon,' Hagdon said under his breath. 'Don't get distracted.'

A sixth sense honed through years of conflict made his skin

prickle. He looked to his left in time to see the cannon fire. 'Run,' he yelled, dragging Irilin with him. He flung them both off the low hill's summit, rolling over and over in the long grass while above them the ground exploded.

'Are you all right?' he gasped when his ears stopped ringing. Irilin had a graze on her cheek, but seemed otherwise unhurt. She nodded and the fear inside him eased.

Kait and Mercia were picking themselves up nearby. A golden shield popped out of existence and Kait dusted down her hands. 'Shields do have their uses, I'll admit.' She slipped an arm around Mercia's waist and pulled the soldier to her feet.

Mercia grinned. 'Don't go anywhere.'

'I wasn't planning to.'

There was no immediate sign of Astra, or Mikael. But only scant moments passed before his brother appeared, nursing a broken phial in his hands. When he pushed his mask back, he looked furious. 'That took me months to perfect.' He hurled the broken bottle to the grass. '*Months*. Iresonté will pay for this.'

'We can't wait longer,' Hagdon said, rubbing a bruised elbow. 'We need to get our forces out of the long-range cannon.'

Mercia drew a silver-chased horn from her belt and gave two short blasts. Soaring above, the Lleu-yelin echoed it.

Hagdon took hold of Irilin's shoulders. 'Make for the city. It's too dangerous for you to remain out here exposed.'

She shook her head. 'How can I hide when my friends are here fighting? When *you* are—'

'Irilin.' He almost shook her in his vehemence. 'You cannot come with me. How will I fight when I know you're in constant danger?'

She closed her mouth on her retort. It was, he thought, the only argument that might sway her.

'All right,' she said after a long moment. 'But James. Please be careful.'

Before he could think better of it, Hagdon pulled her to him, kissed her fiercely. 'I will,' he promised, his voice husky, 'if you are.'

They broke apart. With a last look at her, Hagdon joined his forces. They closed up around him, hiding Irilin from view. He hoped she would do as he asked.

They advanced in a black phalanx, the Sartyans on the outside, their first and strongest line of defence. Then the Republic, crows' feathers rippling; finally the Alchemists, sinister and silver. Wielders protected their flanks on either side, hidden by the low curl of the land, but the wind carried sounds of fierce fighting. Another voice called out, magnified by ambertrix, and though Hagdon couldn't discern the order, his forces soon came under a barrage of arrows.

The Wielders blocked the worst. Brégenne had positioned herself and Nediah at the front, Kait in the middle, and three others at the rear, including the young man called Janus. Hagdon watched her exchange one charged glance with Kait before they wove their shields together. Some arrows inevitably hit their marks and Hagdon found himself stepping over the corpses of those on the fringes of the shield. 'Pick up the pace!' he yelled.

They endured two more barrages before they reached the Sartyan shield wall. Hagdon's heart quailed when he saw it. He knew how effective a technique it was, especially against an inferior force. It seemed to loom over him, tower shields slotted neatly atop one another, an impenetrable barricade.

'Allow me, brother,' Mikael murmured. He gave a whistle and drew a red phial from the belt at his waist. It looked remarkably like the one he'd longed to use in the hoarlands. Mikael gave it a sharp tap and the blood-like liquid inside began to boil. Hagdon knew it wasn't magic, but it could have been for all he understood it.

'Keep back.' Mikael hurled the phial over the heads of their soldiers. Alchemists along the line copied him, some throwing blue or green bottles, all of which shattered against the shields, splattering their contents over the metal.

Which ignited. Hagdon wasn't the only one who drew in a breath at the sheer power of those flames. The Sartyans hidden by their shields dropped them, trying to stamp out the fire licking over armour and flesh. Whatever substances the Alchemists used did not behave like normal fire, eating into the metal like acid, leaping from soldier to solder.

The wall broke. With a ragged cheer, Hagdon's combined forces surged forward, taking advantage of the weakened line. The ambertrix greatsword felt lighter in his hands, as if the air no longer offered resistance. He swung it with deadly force and neither blade nor armour could withstand it. The battlefury was just beginning to build in his veins when he heard a series of screeches. 'Down!' Hagdon shouted and flung himself lengthwise just before a terrible whistling whipped overhead. He heard thuds as stone hit flesh and screams, the sounds of bodies thudding to earth.

Swearing, he looked up. They'd concealed the triple-headed cannon behind their lines until the right moment. Sartyans had peeled off to either side, leaving the soldiers who manned it a clear shot. Before he could stop her, Kait rose, shining stilettos in her hands. With a cold shock, Hagdon saw Mercia sprawled at her feet, blood running freely down her face. Kait gave a furious cry and flung her knives – not at the cannon but at the soldiers behind it. The golden blades took down five of them, but the next shot was already primed and Kait was still standing.

She raised a shield, but it shattered under the force of a dozen stone balls, roughly half of which struck, hurling her to the ground. Kait lay there, gasping and bloodied, blinking up at the sky. Mikael seized the chance to throw a phial at the remaining soldiers. Fire exploded, scattered them from their posts. On the heels of the explosion, a dragon swooped down and melted the cannon in a blast of pure ambertrix.

It was all happening too fast for Hagdon. He spared another look at Kait, unsure how bad her wounds were. Mercia had crawled over to her. 'Bloody stupid,' he heard her say. 'Why'd you do a thing like that?'

'I thought they'd killed you, that's why,' Kait retorted, the words costing her a wracking cough. Blood flecked her lips.

'Sorry, Hagdon,' Mercia said. 'I have to stay and look after my friend.'

'Don't be foolish, Mercia. The commander here needs you far more than I do.'

'I'd be less than useless. If you haven't noticed, I'm dying too.'

'You're not going to die,' Nediah said, appearing through the smoke. 'Either of you.'

He worked quickly, teeth gritted in concentration. 'It's temporary,' Hagdon heard the healer shout over the roar and clatter of fighting. 'Try not to overexert yourself.' His eyes flicked to Kait. 'You too. You've cracked a few ribs. We don't have the time for me to heal them up properly, so be careful.'

'Thanks for getting me on my feet,' Kait told him tersely. A golden scimitar shimmered to life in her hand. 'If I'm going to die, I want to do it standing.' Ignoring Nediah's grimace, she gave her other hand to Mercia. 'Let's go, Hagdon. Let's see this through.'

Hagdon nodded. Flanked by Mikael and the remnants of his forces, he pushed on towards the hill.

Did he imagine it, or were there fewer cannon blasts now? When a shadow passed over him, Hagdon looked up, expecting a dragon, but it was the airship, flying just out of arrow range. Dark shapes tumbled from its decks: barrels falling to earth with a crash, spilling tar and fire everywhere. It would be a miracle if they didn't hit some of their own forces. And still the Sartyans came: a red tide that could not be held off. Kait and Mercia fought back to back, guarding *his* back and Hagdon knew he'd have fallen without them. Brégenne and Nediah moved across the battlefield as a unit, Nediah healing where he could, Brégenne covering him. Hagdon carried his own share of wounds, all minor, but taken together they were slowly whittling him down. And he needed his strength to face Iresonté.

He was dimly aware that several Lleu-yelin riders had joined him on the ground, fighting with breath and talon, enveloped by a blue nimbus. But the carpet of dead was growing thicker now and some wore faces he recognized. Eyes stared blindly up, and though he knew they saw nothing, his fevered brain told him they gazed at *him*, at the blood that covered him like a second skin. With a roar dredged up from somewhere inside, Hagdon ploughed on, slipping on bodies and outflung limbs, the hill fixed in his vision. No more cannon blasts came; the Lleu-yelin had held up their end of the bargain.

They had almost reached the slopes when a hundred black figures stepped out of the air, throwing off blue-limned cloaks.

Hagdon stopped short, wrenched from his trance by the sight of so many stealth force. Behind him, Mercia swore.

At the summit of the hill, a figure dismounted. 'It ends here,' Iresonté called, her voice echoing oddly inside the general's helm – that twisted visage Hagdon knew so well. 'There's nowhere left to go.'

He turned, cursed. Sartyans flowed in to bar the way back. Even with the Lleu-yelin's help, even with the Wielders, it seemed they'd barely made a dent in the Fist. Or if they had, their numbers were so great that it did not matter.

'Been fun, Commander,' Mercia said through gritted teeth. She was bleeding again, as she looked from the stealth force to the Fist, her face pale, but set. 'We'll take a share of these bastards with us.'

The hilt of his sword had become hard to grip. Hagdon sheathed it, drew his handaxes instead. His fists tightened around them; so close – he could not bear to be so close and fail. Mikael had lost a fair portion of Alchemists. Perhaps fifty remained. Against the stealth force and their poisoned blades. Against the innumerable legions of the Fist.

'Your army is routed,' Iresonté called, 'such as it was.'

He was out of time. The Fist began to advance, forcing them back onto the points of stealth-force blades. Hagdon steeled himself, knowing he could not defend against so many at once. They were closing in on him, scything through his circles of protection until he could not bear to watch his people die.

With a furious cry, he pushed one of his soldiers aside, deflecting the blow meant for him, and shoving the Sartyan backwards. He turned to meet another strike, heard Mercia shout something and ducked in time to avoid a hurled stiletto.

The woman who'd thrown it staggered back, one of Kait's own glowing knives in her neck.

There were too many of them and too many gaps in his armour through which a poisoned blade could slip. Hagdon whirled and slashed, each swing draining more of his stamina.

The Sartyan attacking him faltered. Hagdon took the chance to slam the pommel of his axe into the man's temple and he dropped. He turned to meet his next opponent, but there wasn't one; everything had stopped.

A moment later, he heard it too: the ululating cry of a hunting horn. And more than one, tumbling over each other in a brash cacophony that raised the hairs on his neck. The nearest Sartyans turned to look.

Through the rain that had begun to sheet over them, he saw a host pouring down the sides of the valley. They were on foot and there was something odd about their gait. The sky was so dark as to be almost night, but a brief flash of lightning revealed their drawn weapons, already bloody. When the next arrived and he saw them clearly, Hagdon's hand slipped on his axe.

They wore Sartyan armour.

The new host crashed into the ranks of the Fist, who were utterly unprepared for them. Amidst cries of pain were cries of confusion and horror. Unable to comprehend what he was seeing, Hagdon realized another host followed in the wake of the first – a much larger host, all on foot and bellowing a chant that was faintly recognizable. A moment later, Hagdon remembered where he'd heard it: the warriors of the Yrmfast Territory. Relief coursed through him, bringing with it new energy. Kul'Gareth had arrived at last.

Hagdon saw him then: a broad-shouldered figure, glowing with eldritch light. If he looked closely, he saw the same light in the eyes of the first force and realized, with a thrill of dread, what they were. No wonder the Fist was in disarray: they faced their own slain comrades.

'Hagdon, what do you think you're doing?' Mercia yelled. 'Get up there.'

He didn't need telling twice. They broke through the Sartyan line, fighting shoulder to shoulder with dead men; the Republic, Wielders and Alchemists fell on the stealth force and Hagdon lost himself in the melee.

He fought his way up the shallow incline. His body seemed to move on its own, as if some master puppeteer had tied strings to each joint. Hagdon felt a growing sense of inevitability, rather like the fate he so scorned. There was no such thing, he'd told Irilin. Fate absolved men of responsibility, and that idea was more dangerous than any empire, than any magic.

The strange instinct left him as suddenly as it had come and Hagdon found himself at the summit of the slope. Three stealth-force agents – captains, by the look of them – guarded Iresonté. They fell on him without hesitation, their blades quick and sure and tipped with poison. But flesh had been pierced to get him here, blood spilled, lives taken. He wouldn't let any of it go to waste. So he fought with the rabid fury that had earned him his name, his reputation, and each agent fell before his axe blades.

Panting, he lowered them. Alone now, Iresonté reached up and removed the general's helm. Her pale eyes betrayed no fear. She tossed it on the ground and drew her sword. Ambertrix cascaded down the blade. It was a little like the emperor's, Hagdon saw, with a serrated edge, but lighter, made to fit Iresonté's hand.

'I told you that when we met again, it would be for the last time.'

'I remember,' he said. He threw his axes to the grass, drew instead the Sartyan general's greatsword. Hunger in the metal, it seemed appropriate. There was nothing in his mind now but the woman in front of him, her chill face and narrowed eyes.

'I admit your latest move is a good one.' They began to circle each other, blades between them. He noticed she held hers with both hands. 'I did not expect an attack from my own men.' Her tone was unfazed, as if she spoke of a mutiny rather than the undead. 'Who is he?'

Hagdon knew who she meant. 'He is a friend of Irilin's, calls himself Kul'Gareth. Those gauntlets he wears belonged to Kingswold.'

'Irilin,' she said, and Hagdon did not like the sound of it in her mouth. 'The girl you seem so fond of.'

Hagdon kept his face blank, but his heart had begun to pound.

'And, from what I hear, she seems so fond of you,' Iresonté continued. 'I don't suppose you've told her much about your past.' She smiled darkly. 'When I am done with you, maybe *I'll* tell her. I promise to keep you alive long enough to watch.'

She was trying to provoke him. It worked. With a growl, Hagdon swung, but Iresonté leapt neatly out of range, spinning and bringing her own blade around to strike his. Blue sparks flew. 'I see I've hit a nerve,' she said as they disengaged.

Hagdon tried again, but a slow, powerful weapon wasn't ideal against an opponent trained by the stealth force. Iresonté dodged rather than parried, using her momentum to counter-attack so swiftly that her blade severed the straps of his breast-plate. Hagdon cursed. Lest it unbalance him, he tore at the straps on the other side, letting the plate fall to the grass.

'Not as fast as you once were,' Iresonté commented, but her cheeks were rosy with exertion.

'And you're out of practice,' he said. 'Even a few months as general has made you lazy. A mistake I never made.'

'Only because you enjoy your *butchery*.' With a flick of her wrist, she sent a stiletto flying at him. Hagdon had expected it; she must have half a dozen knives hidden about her person. He dodged and the blade buried itself in the hilltop. 'You always have.'

'And I suppose you don't,' he retorted, coming at her with an overhand swing. She was definitely out of practice – the edge of his blade caught her shoulder, ambertrix slicing through her armour like butter. Iresonté gasped, clapping an automatic hand to her wound. Blood welled up between her fingers.

'Believe it or not,' she hissed at him, 'but I don't.' She plunged her other hand into a pouch at her waist. Before Hagdon could react, the air turned grey. He couldn't see – it was as if a dust storm had blown up, a smoky fog that caught in his throat, made him cough. A stealth-force trick. Hagdon turned on the spot, trying to keep silent, knowing Iresonté was listening for any movement. But heavy armour wasn't built for secrecy and the next instant, a blade came slicing out of the fog, spattering his cheek with his own blood.

Hagdon staggered. The wound burned with more than pain. It tingled; he could feel the poison mingling with his blood, seeping into his flesh.

'It will kill you slowly,' Iresonté said from out of the grey. 'Very slowly. I'm loath to give you a swift end.'

Hagdon bit his lip before he could ask whether there was an antidote. Instead he tightened his grip on his sword. If he was going to die, he'd take her with him.

The hilltop was exposed; the storm wind scattered the dust and Hagdon could again see. Iresonté smiled at him. She threw down a small bloody blade – his blood – and returned to circling him. Hagdon tried to ignore the slow prickle creeping through his face, down his neck. There was pain, pain that would only grow worse. He swallowed, ignoring it.

'Tell me one thing,' he said.

Iresonté cocked her head. 'What?'

'Why do you hate me so much?'

She laughed. 'I don't hate you, Hagdon. It's never been personal.'

Through gritted teeth he said, 'You expect me to believe that?'

'The world does not revolve around you, James. I saw a chance and I took it.' Her eyes narrowed. 'The emperor was a fat fool – it was *his* mistake that enabled this.' She jerked her head at the battlefield below them, a vast game board of red and black. 'He had a general whose loyalty was unquestionable. If he hadn't touched your family, I'd never have been able to drive a wedge between you.'

Hagdon's head was spinning. He staggered and the movement wasn't entirely feigned. He could feel the poison beginning to burn in his nerve endings. She'd said it would take him a long time to die. He leaned on his sword, bent over, spat blood onto the ground. Iresonté drew closer. Through narrowed lids, he watched her lips move, felt her breath against his face. 'When I am done with you, I will find your brother and the girl. And I will send them down to join you. And then I will do what no *emperor* ever managed. I will take Rairam.'

Hagdon moved. It was a small movement, barely a jerk of

his hand, she was so near. The blade slid home between her ribs. He'd used his stagger to hide it. Iresonté's eyes went wide. She looked down, disbelievingly.

He caught her as she fell. Their faces were very close; death conferred an odd intimacy. Blood trickled from her lips as she looked up at him, beyond him. 'No,' she whispered.

Hagdon turned to follow her gaze. From their vantage point, he could see the tide of battle beginning to turn. A huge golden blaze moved through the mud of the valley, as the Wielders reformed into one. He imagined Brégenne down there, her hands full of Solar fire, calling commands. The wind carried a roar and a smell like the metallic stink of a forge. Perhaps he could fight his way through before the poison took him.

When he looked back, Iresonté was dead. Hagdon laid her on the grass, staring at her until pain rushed in to fill the empty space inside him. His legs wouldn't obey, twitching uselessly against the earth. His spine felt as if huge hands slowly twisted it; Hagdon couldn't hold back a cry. He rolled onto his side, curled up, wracked with agony as the poison travelled through his body. The world lost meaning, his continual screams drowned in the din of battle that still raged below. Any thought of reaching the Wielders vanished.

After a time, his voice gave out. After a longer time, the rain ceased to fall upon his face. A bright bloody light burned somewhere to his left and a darkness grew on his right. Sunset, he realized, night.

He found himself in a strange place; a place where he was perhaps too damaged to feel pain. It wasn't death because there were stars and a sky, and a ground beneath him.

It wasn't death because she was there.

Like his dream, there was blood in her hair, on her face, as if she wept it. *You're hurt.* He couldn't move, couldn't speak the words aloud.

I am not the one hurt, James.

The blood wasn't hers. She'd laid her cheek against his, he realized, and now wore his blood like a veil. *He* was the one hurt and he felt relief, such relief as he'd never known.

41

Kyndra

She climbed the crystal stair. War raged outside. The Sartyan cannons fired, covering the men who, at this moment, were storming the gates of Solinaris.

War raged inside.

With each step, she felt herself changing. She'd had a choice. She'd made it. And now she lived with the consequences.

'Who will guard Acre?'

Those four short words sliced apart the dream in Char's face. She watched it die and felt an echoing pain in her heart. She relished it, knowing it would soon be gone. 'I thought you'd say that,' he whispered, still holding her tightly. 'I dreaded it. But I knew you would.'

'We can only ever be who we are.' She forced a smile. 'Someone wise told me that.'

'I wish I hadn't.'

'Char —'

'You don't have to say any more.' His yellow eyes burned. 'But if you don't mind, I'd like something to remember you by.'

He made it sound as if she were dying. She supposed she was, in a way.

His lips closed over hers. In the heat and heart of the moment, Kyndra had no room for regret.

She touched her lips. Feeling the ghost of his kiss. Already a spectre, it was fast fading into memory.

From somewhere below came a battle cry, which carried all the fury of a dragon.

'Go, Kyndra.' Char drew his kali sticks. 'I'll deal with these and then I'll follow.'

That's how she'd last seen him, facing two *du-alakat*, the fine scale pattern standing out around his eyes and nose.

She put one foot in front of the other and the black dreams massed in her head. *This* was the stair. She recognized the bones of its spiral. There was no sign of the eldest, but Kyndra did not hurry – the curse wouldn't allow her to. She'd climbed this stair before. It was one certain thing amidst the confusion.

I must stop the eldest, she told herself, but was that really why she was here?

Between one step and the next, the glass turned black. Onyx beneath her feet, onyx under her fingers, the hand she trailed for support along the winding wall. Before too long, a rectangular portal loomed ahead: a door, oulined in light. Kyndra pushed it open.

She found herself on top of a tower: the highest of Naris's many spires. Above her the sky was an indeterminate blue; it could have been any hour between dusk and dawn. How long had it taken her to climb the stair?

It wasn't important. She saw the eldest.

His very presence struck her as wrong. He should not be here. There was no space in this moment for him or the words he whispered into Kierik's ear. Though decades had passed since she'd last seen the Starborn, he had barely changed; his hair was still rich and dark, his face a young man's, his eyes the same cold navy as her own. Kierik stood in the very centre of the tower top, a great book lying open at his feet. The wind from its pages stirred Kyndra's hair, a darkish gust that whipped around her legs. At Kierik's side was Anohin, his eyes wide and terrified at feeling the brush of death.

'She is come as I said,' Kyndra heard the eldest declare.

Kierik turned. 'It's *you*.'

She tried to stand tall, but the eldest raised his hand and a moment later, her withered arm was agony. It spread to her shoulder, reaching up her neck, extending cold fingers into her chest. She gasped for breath. He would kill her, she realized. He would kill her in front of Kierik to bolster whatever lies he'd whispered into the Starborn's ear.

Pain found her heart and Kyndra couldn't stop herself from screaming. It felt as if dry fingers were crushing her to dust. Her knees buckled; she clawed uselessly at her chest. Darkness closed in from either side. *I can't fail.* But the stars could not aid her; Char was far below. And Kierik stood as if frozen, gaze moving between the two of them as if he couldn't decide who to help.

At first she thought it a mirage: the last fevered imagining of her dying brain.

A blade jutted from the eldest's throat.

Kyndra blinked, feeling the pain recede. The eldest's hood fell back; his face was so wizened as to barely earn the name; ancient and folded in on itself, twisted by his misuse of Khronos's power. As she watched, the blood on his throat dried to dust; dust poured from the wound in a grey cascade, dissolving the eldest's body like acid, revealing the man who crouched behind him, hand curled around the dagger's hilt.

Medavle straightened – the Medavle she knew, who'd travelled back with the eldest. His robes were torn and stained, but a fierce light shone in his eyes. He nodded at Kyndra. She pulled back her sleeve to find her skin unmarked; new energy flowed into her. She hadn't realized how weak she'd become.

Medavle extended his hand and another took it. The bulk of his body had hidden her, but now that she stood at his side, Kyndra saw she was Yadin too, white-robed with long blond hair, streaked here and there with soot. 'Give me the book,' Medavle said, raising the hand that held the dagger.

Kierik had observed the eldest's demise emotionlessly. But now his expression darkened. 'You dare to challenge me, Yadin?'

'I defeated you once before.' Medavle gestured with the blade. 'Give it to me.'

Kierik laughed. 'I need not remind you that I can release this –' he nodded at the book – 'whenever I choose. It will sweep you and all your kind away.'

For some reason, Medavle looked grieved. 'I cannot let you do that,' he said.

A moment later, Kyndra understood. 'Medavle, no,' she gasped. 'You have to let him release it, or he won't be –' She stuttered to a halt, unable to say *destroyed* in front of Kierik.

The Yadin shook his head. 'If that is the price of saving my people then, bitter though it is, I will pay it.'

'Why kill the eldest only to do what he planned to?'

'I killed the eldest for you. I care nothing for Khronosta,' Medavle said with a cold glance at the eldest's remains. 'I only helped him because he could lead me to Isla.' His hand visibly tightened on the other Yadin's. 'But now that I am here, now that I have the chance to change my people's fate, how can I walk away?'

'You mustn't,' Kyndra said desperately. 'Ma warned you.'

'If you had the means to save your people, wouldn't you use it?'

The words of the black dream were in her mouth. 'Better the death of five hundred Yadin than the death of the world.'

Medavle slowly shook his head. 'You cannot believe that.'

'I must believe it.' *The stars cannot see beyond this point.*

'Yes,' Kierik said suddenly. Kyndra could see the shadow of Mariar in his face; it must be costing him a great deal of effort to hold his weaving steady. 'If it consoles you, Yadin, know that your deaths will mean the deaths of these Sartyan vermin who crawl upon my land.'

Medavle's face contorted, but Isla spoke before he could. 'Meda.' Her voice carried a timbre as honeyed as her hair. 'If it is indeed a choice between us or the world, how can you hesitate? Even if you saved us, what would be the point, if everything else was doomed?'

'No! You don't understand. Our deaths will be meaningless.' Medavle gathered her into his arms, holding her fiercely. 'And I will not let you die again.'

'I never lived to begin with,' Isla whispered.

'No,' Kierik agreed, 'you didn't.'

Anohin screamed. Kyndra threw up her arms instinctively before she realized what had happened. A thin wail split the air as a shadow descended over them all, a black shadow that reeked of death. It broke around Anohin like the sea about a rock; the Yadin trembled, clutching at Kierik's hand that sat protectively upon his shoulder. Heart in her mouth, Kyndra whirled around.

Medavle and Isla died looking into each other's eyes.

'No!' She couldn't help the cry torn from her throat, as their empty robes crumpled to the tower top. She couldn't believe the dark-eyed Yadin was gone. He'd been with her from the start, watching as she broke the Relic; the act which began it all. Kyndra clenched her fists. 'I didn't want this,' she told the space where Medavle had stood. 'You should have left when you had the chance.' If only he and Isla had been further away –

'Why do you mourn them?'

It took Kierik's question to snap her into awareness. The Medavle she knew was gone, but the other – the one she'd met earlier – should still be alive, fruitlessly combing the citadel for Isla. He'd tied his lifeforce to Kierik's: that act had both saved him and doomed the Starborn.

A chill spread through Kyndra's veins. Kierik *should* be on his knees, his mind shattered by the black wind, which had failed to kill Medavle. The Medavle who believed he had defeated a Starborn, who would live to tell her so.

But he hadn't defeated him. Kierik stood before her, a small frown puckering his brow. *I don't understand*, she thought feverishly. This should have played out as it already had.

Anohin's eyes were wet as he gazed at the empty robes.

Kyndra's mind ran in hopeless circles. Kierik would remain whole. What would that do to the world? Ma had said too many events were tied to the fall of Solinaris. If Solinaris did not fall, if the Breaking did not strike Mariar, if Kierik survived to rule over them –

The events that led to her birth would never take place. And yet she was here.

Why? Why?

Listen to your dreams.

She hadn't, Kyndra realized. If she'd truly listened, she'd

have remembered that on her first night in Acre, resting upon the slopes of the red valley, she had woken burning from a dream of fire: the first black dream; the first *memory*. There had been a confusion of images – the Breaking, Rairam, Kierik – but amidst them a kernel of truth. She *had* fought Kierik atop a tower, the world splitting apart under their struggle.

Kyndra's eyes widened. She extended her hand, turned it palm up. '*Sigel*.'

She watched the command rip across Kierik's face. His grip on the stars that held Mariar faltered; she felt the tower tremble beneath her feet. The star filled her hand with flame; flame burned on her cheek.

'No,' Kierik whispered.

It is now, Era told her, its voice ringing in her head. *We will grant you power, but you must prove yourself the stronger.*

Although the touch of the star brought clarity, it didn't still the turmoil in her chest. She stood squarely between her two selves – *Kyndra*, the girl from Brenwym, and *the Starborn*, the being who lived forever apart. There would have to be a reckoning, just as there would have to be one between her and Kierik.

Just as there has been, Era murmured. *Just as there will be.*

But Kierik was her flesh and blood, someone who fought against the tyranny of Sartya as she did. They were more alike than she realized. Below them, the Sartyan cannon still fired, pounding the citadel that had stood for seven hundred years.

Kyndra raised her head. 'I'm sorry, Father.'

Kierik stilled. 'What did you call me?'

Anohin interposed himself between her and Kierik, but Kierik thrust him aside. 'Who are you?' the Starborn demanded.

'One day,' Kyndra answered, 'centuries from now, you will

ask and I will tell you my name.' She held out her other hand. 'Veritan.'

Sweat appeared on Kierik's forehead. He wasn't touching the star, but he'd be able to feel it used. Kyndra knew that the effort of holding Mariar steady in his mind was the only reason he hadn't yet challenged her.

She looked at Anohin. 'One day we will meet again too.'

I saved you because Anohin believed you would help Kierik. Instead you killed him and stole his power. Kait's words echoed back to her and Kyndra briefly closed her eyes. She had no choice. It was time to close the loop, to patch the hole the eldest had torn in history.

Before doubt set in, she directed the full force of *Veritan* against the Yadin. '*The only thing Anohin will truly remember from this day is my promise to help his master.*' The star turned her voice into a ringing chorus and Anohin stiffened. '*The rest he will believe as I once did: that Kierik destroyed the Yadin, that Medavle was responsible for his defeat. This is now Anohin's truth.*'

The Yadin swayed. She watched his eyes roll up, showing only the whites before he toppled to the floor.

'You forget', Kierik said through clenched teeth, 'that I am here. I will remember all of this.'

Kyndra let *Veritan* go. As soon as she did, she *felt* the pain of what she had done. The lie she had told; the lie that one day Anohin would tell to her. When she looked at Kierik, another image overlay the Starborn – the image of the scarred man huddled before the Nerian – and she shook her head, a lump in her throat. 'Just a madman's memories,' she said.

'You truly are Starborn.' Kierik raised a hand. 'The Starborn who will come after me.'

'After you and *from* you.'

He studied her, seeming to see her for the very first time. She felt his gaze on her face, on the hair that curled just as his did, on the eyes they both shared. 'It's impossible,' he breathed finally. 'I will father no children.'

'You will,' she said. 'Just me.'

She might as well have told him that the sun rose in the west – such was his look of disbelief. 'I could not come to care for any woman.'

Again Kyndra saw him as she'd first seen him: fists against his temples, crouched and crying; the Nerian keeping their distance in a twisted union of fear and reverence. 'Not as you are now,' she murmured.

Kierik heard her. 'You plan to fight me? You are a child. I have seen out a hundred winters, know the names of each and every star. I hold a score in my mind as we speak. You may be Starborn, but you're untested. And you realize it. I can see it in your face.'

Kyndra could feel it brewing, the confrontation that could not now be put off. But the horror of what she had to do, the price she would pay for her victory, almost dropped her to her knees. Breaking Kierik meant breaking Mariar too. The storm that would claim so many lives, that would drive her from her home as it burned – it would be her fault. All that death, destruction and grief would lie at her feet.

But if Kierik won, the dead could number legions. She seemed to hear Ma's voice ringing across the gulf that separated them. *Time is one of the stitches that holds together the fabric of existence.* If the world itself and its entire people would cease to be, how could Kyndra stand aside?

But she couldn't do it.

As *Kyndra*, she couldn't do it.

Forgetting Kierik, she crouched, hands curled against her chest. She stood at the crossroads in her mind and it was a desolate place where her actions were ghosts to haunt her. In that grey and featureless expanse, there was nowhere for the truth to hide. She had done terrible things and lived with the consequences. But Kyndra saw, clearly, that she wouldn't be able to live with this.

She rose to her feet in one swift movement. *Era*, she commanded and the star hearkened to her call. *You will not speak of what I do today. To anyone, including me.*

And I have not, Era replied in its hollow tones. *I obey, Starborn.*

Only one being could shoulder the burden that would crush a human. If she remained as herself, her actions would destroy her. The world was more important than a single woman's soul. Kyndra fed the last of her doubt, the last of herself into *Sigel*. The star consumed it hungrily, as it longed to consume everything. She raised her other hand and the demon star, *Hagal*, flowed over her fingers like dark oil.

Sigel, Kierik's command cracked through the void, *you are mine*.

If creating Mariar hadn't weakened him, he might have ripped *Sigel* from her grasp. But even Kierik could only hold so many stars at once and Kyndra was relying on *Sigel*'s own need to be wielded, to unleash its fire and ruin upon the world.

'Stop.' He sounded panicked, the most emotion he'd yet shown. 'You must let me finish. While I am linked to Mariar—'

'You are both vulnerable,' Kyndra said coldly. Anohin's bitterness echoed in the vaults of her memory. *The Breaking is Medavle's legacy, his curse upon a world whose creation he opposed.*

478

But it was *her* legacy. A small price to pay to keep the world in balance. She looked into Kierik's eyes. 'You understand,' she whispered.

He had just enough time to widen them before she struck. She felt him curl his mind over Mariar in an attempt to shield it from her assault. But it wasn't Mariar she intended to attack – it was Kierik himself. As she'd done with the wraiths in the hoarlands, she splayed a hand and *Hagal* enveloped the Star-born's body. For just a moment he disappeared entirely under its shadow, but with a roar of effort, re-emerged, his skin shining with the silver-grey of *Tyr*.

Kyndra had prepared for it. Casting her mind out across Mariar, she found the join between the two worlds – in the westernmost mountains – and began to pull at their roots. *Sigel* gloried in it, rending the stone as if it was unformed clay.

'No!' Kierik cried. He dropped *Tyr* and seized *Ur* and *Isa*, shoring up the damage *Sigel* had wrought. She was ready for that too. She used the wail of *Kene* as a distraction; even Kierik wasn't immune to the banshee star. Without *Tyr*'s protection, he cried out, clamping his hands over his ears in a fruitless attempt to block out the sound. Before Kyndra could bring *Sigel* to bear again, however, Kierik lowered his hands. He struck with a snarl and Kyndra felt *Kene* torn from her grasp. The backlash sent her sprawling.

'Stop,' Kierik said again. He was panting; the attack had clearly cost him. 'We do not have to fight.'

'I have no choice,' Kyndra replied, picking herself up. 'I cannot let you go. You will seek to rule Mariar just as you threatened in the Sentheon. Solinaris will oppose you. War will follow.'

Kierik shook his head. 'I would not rule as the empire rules. I created Mariar because I wanted peace. Why would I then start a war?'

He struck. Kyndra gasped at the suddenness of his assault; she'd let him distract her. She could feel him clawing at her control of *Sigel*, hear him promise the star fire and blood. *You heard him*, she thought at *Sigel*, infusing all her will into the words. *He wishes peace. In Mariar, he will have no need for you. But I offer this.* Kyndra imagined a tide of fire flowing over Solinaris. She imagined glass turning to black stone, raining ruin on the Sartyans below. She remembered that morning, which seemed so long ago now, when she first felt the presence of Acre. She remembered what it was like to tear down the last of Kierik's barriers, to reunite the two worlds.

Sigel grew brighter in her mind, in her hand. She called fire. A thunderous crack and then it streamed from the heavens, pulled from the void. A firestorm that, if left unchecked, would ravage the world.

Kierik blanched. 'You foolish—' The rest of his words were lost in a cry as Kyndra turned the full force of *Sigel* on him. He seized *Elat*, the lesser fire, but *Elat* was a spark amidst an inferno. He was already holding *Lagus*, and he drew water from the clouds to crush her beneath a foaming torrent. But Kyndra stood tall, her flesh become fire. She and *Sigel* had been as one and neither of them had forgotten that joining.

Kierik met her next attack with nothing but his will. He was strong, stronger than she could have imagined while holding so many stars. His flesh caught fire too as they locked wills, battling for control of *Sigel*. The earth threatened to split apart under their struggle. Kyndra felt it rumble beneath her feet, as flame called to flame. The tower shuddered.

And Kierik stumbled. Hidden under *Sigel*, *Hagal* had continued its quiet work, wearing at the borders of his mind. Now the Starborn's eyes flew wide and he began to scream. Kyndra felt it all, the creeping disintegration that sped up as Kierik's will failed him. She felt it almost as if it were her own mind being torn apart. But she kept the star on him, refusing to weaken. Kierik cried tears of shadow. He fell to his hands and knees and a great fracture opened in the skies above him, a sheet of lightning cracking across the roiling clouds.

Cries reached her from below. The Sartyan attack faltered, as soldiers cowered beneath the maelstrom. Kierik's screams tore at Kyndra. Her mind was full of that terrible memory she'd seen amongst the Nerian; of the agony she'd thought was the black wind – the spell that had killed the Yadin. But it was *Hagal*, and the star's steady annihilation of Kierik's mind brought her no satisfaction. The shadow oozing over his skin doused each glowing tattoo, turning them into the scars she remembered. She'd reduced a proud man to a broken creature.

Kyndra turned her head away, sought solace in the icy void.

Perhaps even *Hagal*, merciless *Hagal*, found her actions distasteful, for it abandoned her, leaving Kierik a ragged heap on the tower top. The sky bellowed above her – the fracture racing in all directions, carrying the first Breaking to each corner of Mariar.

'Kyndra!'

Char burst through the glass door, just as the frame shattered around him. The tower rocked beneath their feet, supports finally giving way.

'Get behind me,' she shouted. Dashing across the tower top, Char's gaze alighted on Kierik and Anohin, but his question was lost in a peal of thunder. Kyndra clenched her fists around *Sigel* and *Ur*. As the glass citadel began to crack, she called up fire in one hand, earth in the other. With the twin powers, she hardened the glass to stone. In the lava tunnels beneath the citadel, the tunnels she had once traversed with Kait, fire roared again, forcing up molten rock. Kyndra brought it out of the ground, carried in the white heart of *Sigel*, and, spreading her hands, drove it into the sky. Columns of fire rose around her like geysers. When she was satisfied, she cooled them with *Lagus*.

She could still see the swirls of flame in the rock – they were the faces that would one day peer at her as she rode across the newly formed chasm. The day she would see Naris for the first time.

When she looked out across the land, the devastation was total. A wasteland, the rock blackened by fire and the searing touch of *Sigel*. Lava had rolled over the Sartyan army, melting their siege weapons, removing any trace of them from Kierik's world.

A moan reached her: Anohin sat up, groggily shaking his head. Kyndra seized *Fas* and Char's wrist; they both faded from sight. She watched as the Yadin crawled to his master. Kierik had curled into a foetal ball on the stone, bloody grazes on his face and arms. Anohin reached out a hand to him and Kierik flinched. For a stunned moment, Anohin gazed at his master, his expression an agony of horror and disbelief. Then he began to weep.

Kyndra stood before the ruin of Kierik and Anohin. She stood before the ruin of Solinaris and its Wielders. On the stone at her feet was a wisp of tattered white, a robe once worn by a Yadin, whose long years had ended here. Deep inside her, through a door of dim light, a young woman fled the ruin she had wrought, and Kyndra closed the way behind her.

42

Brégenne

Later they would describe the march of the Wielders as a golden dawn that swept across the land. They would say a woman walked at their head, moonlight in one hand, sunlight in the other, her robes rippling in the wind of her power. *Moon-and-Sun*, they would call her, the greatest Wielder there ever was.

They would say many things, Brégenne thought, that weren't true.

'But they *are* true,' Nediah reproached her.

'First, it wasn't even dawn. Second, I'm not the greatest Wielder who ever was. Thirdly, *I'm still alive*.'

'A fact for which I'm daily grateful.' He slipped an arm about her waist. 'I have big plans for you.'

'Oh, really?' she said with an arch of her brow. 'Do I get a say in these plans?'

Nediah kissed her forehead. 'If I'm feeling generous.'

Brégenne grumbled something. 'Anyway,' she said, freeing herself. 'It's not just me. You realize you're now "Nediah, who can heal any injury short of death itself".'

'I know it's a let-down,' Nediah said, mock-distastefully. 'I'm working on it.'

Brégenne laughed. 'If there are stories to be told, they should be about Kyndra.'

'She has plenty of her own.' Nediah paused and she wondered if they were thinking the same thought, remembering the same scene: Kyndra plummeting from the sky, landing in the middle of the battlefield, straightening from her crouch. Cracks radiated from the earth as if a falling star had struck it. She looked up, said in a great voice that must have carried for leagues, '*STOP*.' And none resisted that command. Her gaze fell on those still standing and they dropped their weapons. She might wear the body of a young woman, but there was nothing young about her face or the aura of power that bent the world around her. She scanned the battlefield, dark with dead and she raised a hand. '*Etoh*.' A cleansing fire, so bright that none of them could look at it, scorched across the land. When Brégenne opened her eyes, the dead were gone, including the terrible army Gareth had raised.

Or Kul'Gareth, as he called himself. Brégenne did not think much of the novice remained alive behind those eyes. The necromancer had faced Kyndra. Wind caught in his cloak, whirled it around his armoured form. He was taller than she, a deep chill in his eyes, and for a moment Brégenne was worried for the Starborn. She'd witnessed the twisted power of the gauntlets first hand, watched the ease with which Kul'Gareth slew and then raised the dead as slaves.

'It's your fault,' Kul'Gareth said in low tones. 'You killed him.'

'Shika.'

She spoke the name impassively and Kul'Gareth's fists

clenched, his rage as palpable as a storm. 'You will pay for his death,' he said.

'I did not kill him, Gareth.'

'You let him die. With all the power you wield, *you let him die*.' The cold visage broke and Brégenne could see a dreadful pain, a loss that seemed to go beyond Shika, beyond a single death. It was a loss nursed for hundreds of years.

Kyndra's eyes narrowed. 'I see you, Aeralt Kingswold,' she said. 'No pattern is hidden from me.'

Kul'Gareth went very still. They locked gazes.

'I can destroy the gauntlets you wear as easily as I can destroy you.'

'Once,' the necromancer whispered, 'I fought side by side with a Starborn.' Wind rattled the grasses. Neither of them moved.

'I won't,' Kyndra said, breaking the stalemate. 'Not today. But I *will* be watching.'

As if to emphasize her warning, a great black dragon swooped in to land behind her. Char, Brégenne realized, with Ma upon his back.

Kul'Gareth turned away. Catching the reins of his horse, he swung into the saddle and pointed its proud head northward. He did not look back.

'If only we'd realized sooner,' Brégenne said now, feeling a hollowness in her heart. 'Do you think any part of Gareth still lives?'

'Maybe,' Nediah replied, clearly doubtful. 'Don't blame yourself, Brégenne.'

'I could have done something.' Exactly what, Brégenne didn't know. None of them understood the bond between Kingswold and the gauntlets. And now it was too late.

'Are you ready?' Mercia appeared in the entrance of their tent, one of hundreds erected outside Market Primus. With the city still under repair, everyone needed to be housed until some sense of order was established. There would be meetings, Brégenne thought with distaste, a great many meetings, in which she'd have to represent Naris and the interests of its Wielders. And she'd already lost her ally in the Assembly; Astra Marahan had been laid to rest yesterday in a private ceremony attended only by her family.

'It's time,' Mercia said, shaking Brégenne out of her reverie. The soldier's expression was as sombre as Brégenne had ever seen it. 'We have a way to go.'

Wordlessly, they followed the Sartyan woman out of the tent. Finally reunited with her horse, Myst, Brégenne stroked the mare's neck before climbing into the saddle. Once Nediah was mounted too, they joined the head of a small procession, which wound its way across what days ago had been a battle-field. Their destination was a small hill, rising above the sere valley. The season was still young, Brégenne thought, but come summer, green would carpet the land, and soften the new-cut stones of Hagdon's cairn.

They gathered around it: Amon Taske, Mercia and Kait, a Sartyan captain called Dyen, who'd arrived just yesterday. Argat and Yara, even Ma. Char circled above, each wingbeat rippling the grass of the hilltop. A distant roar came from the north and Brégenne raised her head to see other Lleu-yelin, each soaring as Char was, in wide, slow circles.

Mikael stood beside his brother's grave, one hand resting on the waist-high stones. He wore his grief plainly; fresh tears staining his cheeks. Brégenne looked for Irilin, but the young woman was absent.

There was no formality to it; those who wished to speak spoke, of Hagdon's dedication to duty, of his leadership, his sacrifice. The wind scoured the exposed hilltop. Brégenne hunched her shoulders against it, and against the strangely tense atmosphere. Scanning the faces around her, she saw resignation rather than grief and that vague aura of sadness shared when someone dies. The only two who openly wept were perhaps the two who'd known Hagdon best: Mikael and Mercia. Brégenne remembered the commander's haunted eyes, the doom that rode with him. The only person who'd seemed able to lessen it was Irilin, and she wasn't here.

A flash caught her eye. Kyndra was standing on the far side of the cairn. The Starborn rarely stayed in one place for long. She seemed to consider it her personal duty to put Acre back together. She nodded when she saw Brégenne watching, and Brégenne returned it. On second glance, Kyndra was gone.

After it was done, they turned their backs on the cairn, leaving Hagdon to rest beneath a lowering sky. It was a good spot, Brégenne thought. Perhaps the soldier could find peace here, in the land he'd helped to free from the shadow of the Fist.

The commander's tent still stood. Mikael had taken a few personal items to bury among the stones, but they weren't sure what to do with the rest. It was where, an hour later, Brégenne found Irilin.

'Why didn't you come?' she asked quietly, pulling the tent flap closed behind her.

Irilin said nothing. Her face was very pale. Brégenne realized she was holding something: a piece of paper torn, it seemed, from a journal. It slipped between Irilin's lax fingers and fluttered to the floor. When she did not move to retrieve it, Brégenne picked it up. The handwriting was familiar; she recognized it immediately as Hagdon's. With a glance at Irilin, Brégenne lowered her eyes to the page.

> *Tonight, I made a promise, Irilin. That if we survived the battle, I would be honest with you. I should have been honest from the start and can only say I am sorry. I never dreamed I'd find someone I could come to care for so deeply or, more astonishingly, someone who could come to care for me. I should be telling you these things in person.*
>
> *You frighten me, Irilin. You seem to see every part of me, even those parts of which I am ashamed, those parts I have tried to leave behind. It would be dishonest to pretend I do not have blood on my conscience, and I do not wish to hide it. I admit that in the beginning, I embraced the Republic's cause as a way to make amends for my crimes. But I've truly come to believe in it. The Republic is Acre's future, just as Sartya was Acre's past, and I'm proud to have a hand in shaping it.*
>
> *I'm sorry I ran from you that day in Parakat. I wasn't prepared to see myself in the way you saw me. But you were right – I should have trusted you, trusted you to know what you wanted, even if I did not understand why.*
>
> *I still don't understand, Irilin, but I hope you will agree to teach me.*

Brégenne looked up from the page to find Irilin watching her. 'How could he?' the young woman flared, knuckles white on her cloak. 'I hate him. I hate him.' And with a wrenching, broken cry, she fell into Brégenne's arms.

Two weeks later, Brégenne stood on the Murtan dock, the *Eastern Set* whirring gently in its berth. 'Thank you, Argat,' she said, shaking hands with him. 'For everything, I suppose.'

The airship captain smiled wolfishly. 'It's been a pleasure, Brégenne. Plenty of fodder for my book.' Behind him, Yara rolled her eyes.

Brégenne gestured at the scorched hull, the chunk of missing rail. 'I'm sorry about your ship.'

'She still flies,' Yara said, with a fond smile. 'And this is my chance to make some improvements. I think her design could be streamlined.' Brégenne watched her expression glaze over. 'If only I could get hold of this marvellous-sounding ambertrix.'

'I don't mean to dash your hopes, but I think the dragons will be less inclined to share it after everything that's happened.' Brégenne shook her head. 'I know good was done with it, but ambertrix also fuelled a bloody conquest. Eventually, it led to the Lleu-yelin's own imprisonment.' She sighed. 'Maybe they're right and humans can't be trusted with such a power.'

'Speak for yourself,' Yara retorted. Then she laughed and hugged Brégenne. 'I'll miss fleecing you at dice,' she whispered in her ear and Brégenne smiled. When Yara drew back, she nodded in Nediah's direction. 'I'm glad you're happy.'

'Take care of yourself, Yara.'

'Oi,' Yara shouted, 'Mercia, Kait, are you coming? Don't back out on me now. Grace and I are in desperate need of intelligent conversation.'

There came a faint affirmative cry from one of the sailors and Argat raised an eyebrow. 'What?' Yara shot at him.

'I didn't say anything.' With a last nod at Brégenne, Argat stalked back to his ship, muttering under his breath.

'Kait.' Nediah caught her arm as the tall woman turned to follow. 'You don't have to leave.'

Kait simply looked at him. 'Yes,' she said. 'I do.' She flicked her eyes towards Brégenne, who couldn't read the expression in them. 'I've said all I wanted to say to both of you. What would be the point of stringing it out?'

Nediah exhaled slowly and released his hold, his face faintly sad as Kait turned and walked away. Halfway down the dock, she paused to look over her shoulder. 'Goodbye, Nediah.'

'Where are you going?'

'Somewhere new.' Kait shrugged. 'I've had my fill of Wielders, Starborn and Sartyans.'

Mercia coughed pointedly. 'You don't count,' Kait told her with a fond smile.

'Charming,'

'Hurry up,' Yara called from the rail. 'My purse is on the thin side.'

Kait spared Brégenne a last glance, but said nothing. She took Mercia's hand and the two women climbed aboard the *Eastern Set*. Murtans gathered to watch the airship leave, many open-mouthed as it rose anchorless into the afternoon.

Brégenne felt Nediah come to stand at her shoulder. They watched the craft until it dwindled to a speck in the western sky. 'I wonder where they'll end up,' he murmured.

'Knowing Argat, somewhere dangerous.'

'I suppose we'd better go back,' Nediah said after a moment. 'I don't think this Sentheon idea of Shune's is going to take off. They'll be killing each other before long.'

'Not if I can help it.' She turned, holding out her hand to him. Across the bond newly forged between them, she said, *Coming?*

Nediah took it. *Always*. And together they walked through the town.

The Starborn

Kyndra stalked up and down the vast hall, boot heels echoing beneath the vaulted roof. She wore what Char had told her to wear – an ordinary tunic, trousers and coat. At least they were black. Her hair spilled over her shoulders in a splash of colour. *Why* had she given her promise again? She couldn't see the point in it, but Char had been insistent. He'd taken something she'd said in the past very seriously and, after telling her to remain here, had flown off.

She should be in New Sartya. There was a lot of ground to cover before she'd allow the merchants of the Trade Assembly to visit the court. The Republic at least seemed to have eastern Acre under control. They'd abandoned Parakat and were operating out of Cymenza instead. She gave silent thanks to Avery, Taske and Rogan. And, of course, Irilin, who'd been instrumental in establishing channels between the Republic and the remaining officers of the Fist.

Kyndra realized that she'd sped up. Surely she wasn't nervous. No, she was impatient – she just didn't have time for this. Char had been gone a week already. A week! Didn't he know how delicate the political situation in Acre was? Maybe Ma could talk some sense into him. She'd returned to the children of Khronosta and led them into the wild to start again. Where exactly, Kyndra didn't know.

Ansu picked up the sound of wingbeats and Kyndra strode to the window. Her home had many windows, hexagonal portals through which the starlight streamed. She'd pulled burning rock from the skies to build her stronghold, raising the castle stone by pitted stone. It was a good spot in the mountains of northern Acre, not too far from Magtharda. Isolated, perhaps, but that was how she liked it.

Char was a rapidly growing speck in the grey afternoon. Kyndra used *Dagha* to sharpen her eyesight and spotted two people on his back, a man and a woman. Both leaned forward, clinging to his black scales.

The dragon landed gracefully, claws dug into an outcropping she'd made for him. The man helped the woman down. Kyndra watched their awe temper their uncertainty as they gazed at the castle, its mighty turrets reaching into the heavens, and she felt a flash of pride in her handiwork.

With a gesture, Kyndra bade the great stone doors swing open and stepped outside. The wind immediately caught in her hair, tossing her long coat behind her. 'Welcome to the Reach, Mother.'

Reena turned. Eyes wide, she took a faltering step. Then she was running, slipping on the dew-slick rock, up the wide steps that led to the castle's door. She pulled up just short of it and stared at her. 'Kyndra.' The name emerged as a tentative whisper.

'Hello, Mother.'

Reena bit her lip. Her hands trembled and she wound them

into a knot before her. 'I . . . you look different.' She seemed on the verge of embracing Kyndra, but something held her back.

'Why don't you come in?' Kyndra looked over Reena's shoulder to Jarand, who had followed his wife up the stairs. 'All of you.'

In tense silence, they moved into the stronghold. Char fitted easily through the great portal; Kyndra had designed it with him in mind. She waved a hand and the stone doors crashed shut behind them. Reena jumped.

A long table dominated the main hall, capable of seating at least a hundred people – as if she'd ever actually hold a feast, Kyndra thought wryly. Half a dozen armchairs sat before a huge fireplace. Kyndra used *Elat* to light it and her mother jumped again, the firelight licking over her pale face as she glanced from Kyndra to the hearth and back again.

'You must be hungry,' Kyndra said when they were settled. 'It's a long flight from Brenwym.'

'Oh, Kyndra.' Reena threw her arms around her neck and Kyndra stiffened. 'It's really you,' her mother murmured. 'You're here. You're alive.'

Kyndra was about to extricate herself when, over Reena's shoulder, she caught Char shaking his head. With a silent sigh, she endured the embrace a little longer.

Finally, Reena drew back. 'You live here?' she asked, darting a glance at the shadowy corners beyond the fire's reach. 'Alone? How did you find it? It's surely too big for one person.'

'I built it,' Kyndra said.

'You . . .' Reena's eyes moved over her and Kyndra knew she was studying the tattoos emblazoned in her skin. 'You're like *him*.'

Jarand hadn't said anything since they'd entered. Unlike

Reena, he didn't move to embrace her – perhaps he sensed her discomfort. Now he looked askance at his wife, who carefully avoided his eyes.

'Kierik?' Kyndra said without preamble. 'Yes. He was the Starborn before me.'

Behind Reena, Char gave her a stare of Great Significance. *What?* she thought at him.

I told you to be tactful.

I am being tactful.

'Kierik,' her mother whispered. 'That was his name?'

Kyndra nodded. 'I met him.'

Reena's fidgeting stilled. 'You found him? Did he . . . did he mention me?'

She was aware of Char's gaze. Tactful. Right. She thought back to that morning in Naris, to the confrontation between Medavle and Anohin, to the moment the stars first marked her and Kierik regained his sanity. 'He called me "daughter of Reena",' Kyndra offered. 'Asked my name.'

'He remembered me, then,' her mother said with a sad smile.

'Yes. He told me he wished I'd never been born. And then he died.'

'Oh.' Reena looked down at her lap. 'I see.'

Char rolled his eyes. *Good work, Kyndra.*

This was your idea.

Gods, just change the subject.

Thankfully, Jarand beat Kyndra to it. 'I told Reena you were alive,' he said with a brave attempt at levity. 'She didn't believe me. Never trusted that white-eyed woman, you see.'

'Brégenne saved my life,' Kyndra told them. 'Nediah too, on several occasions.' She tilted her head. 'I have to admit, you both seem less shocked than I anticipated. You've just been flown to a lost world.'

'Not much beats the shock of a dragon landing in your garden,' Jarand said ruefully.

Kyndra felt herself smiling. When Reena saw it, something in her face eased. 'What happened, Kyndra?' her mother asked, almost plaintively. 'How can you do all these things? Where have you been?'

Kyndra summoned a goblet of wine from the table. It appeared in her hand and she took a sip, meeting Char's yellow eyes over the rim. 'Make yourselves comfortable,' she said, leaning back in her chair. 'It's a very, *very* long story.'

GLOSSARY OF PROMINENT STARS

Ansu – one that listens
Austri – the eastern compass star
Dagha – the far-seer
Elat – the lesser fire
Era – the star of cycles, of passage
Etoh – cleansing, ending
Fas – unseen, unheard, invisible
Hagal – the demon star, whose name means shadow
Isa and Yeras – the bridges over the void
Kene – the banshee star
Lagus – Sigel's sibling, it has power over all water
Mannas – the star of finding
Noruri – the northern compass star
Pyrth – the preserver of secrets
Raad – to move swiftly
Sigel – a ruinous star, its name roughly translates to fire
and force
Soruri – the southern compass star
Tyr – relentless, the warrior
Thurn – a binding star, it tangles, imprisons
Ur – the bastion star

Lucy Hounsom

Veritan – truth-seeker
Vestri – the western compass star
Wynn – the greater wind, another sibling of Sigel

Jointly compiled from notes kept by
Kierik of Maeran and Kyndra of Rairam